THE CROSS-EYED MUTT

A story written and drawn by

Étienne Davodeau

nbm GRAPHIC NOVELS

Nantier • Beall • Minoustchine
NEW YORK

Étienne Davodeau would like to thank particularly Yves Maisonneuve for his availability, as well as Pascal Rabaté, Joub, Francoise Roy and the Wise Guys.

ISBN: 978-1-68112-097-3
Library of Congress Control Number: 2017903341
© Futuropolis / musée du Louvre Éditions 2013
© NBM 2017 for the English translation
Translation by Joe Johnson
Lettering by Ortho
Printed in China
1st printing June 2017

This book is also available digitally wherever e-books are sold.

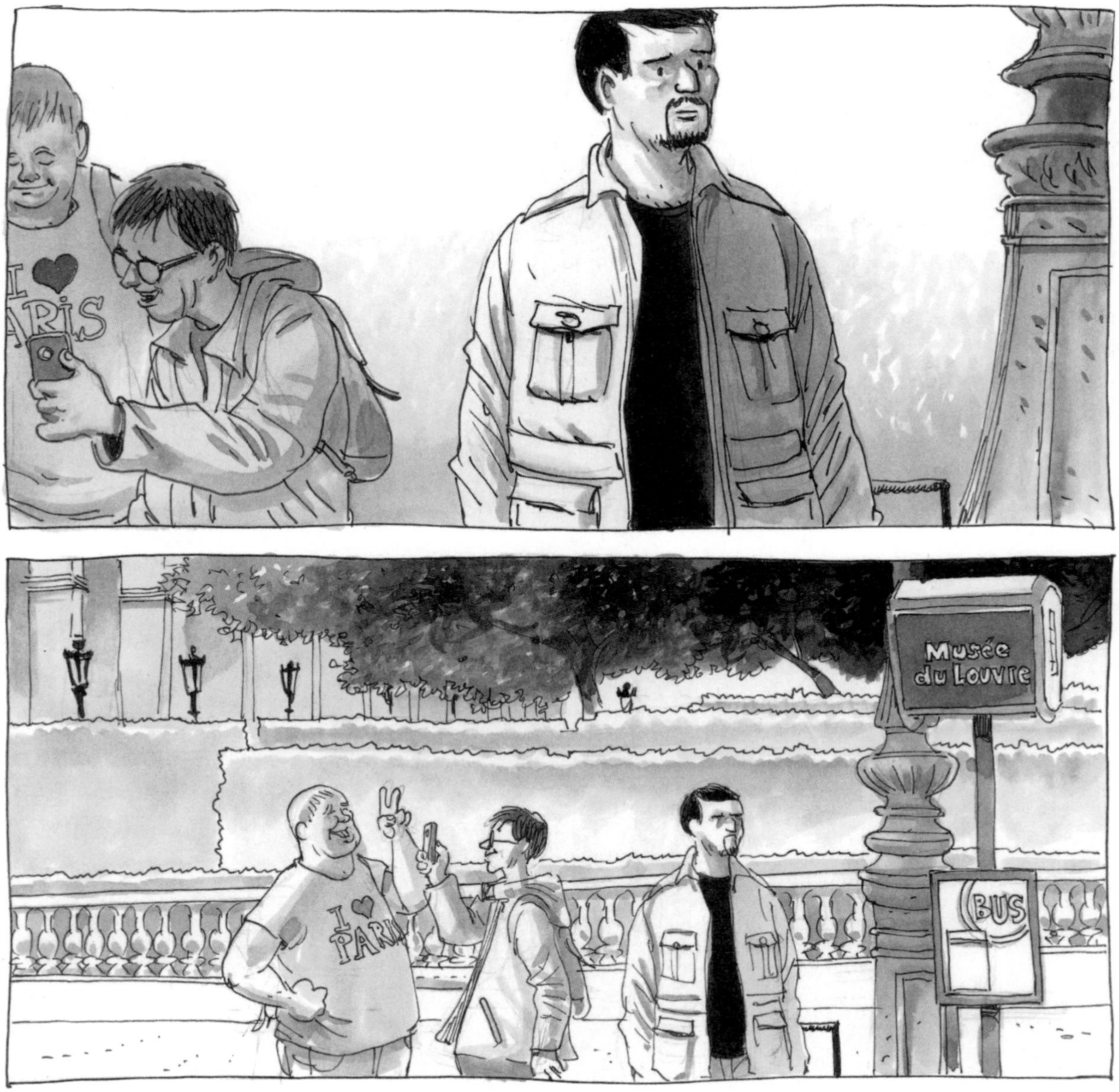
Musée du Louvre
BUS

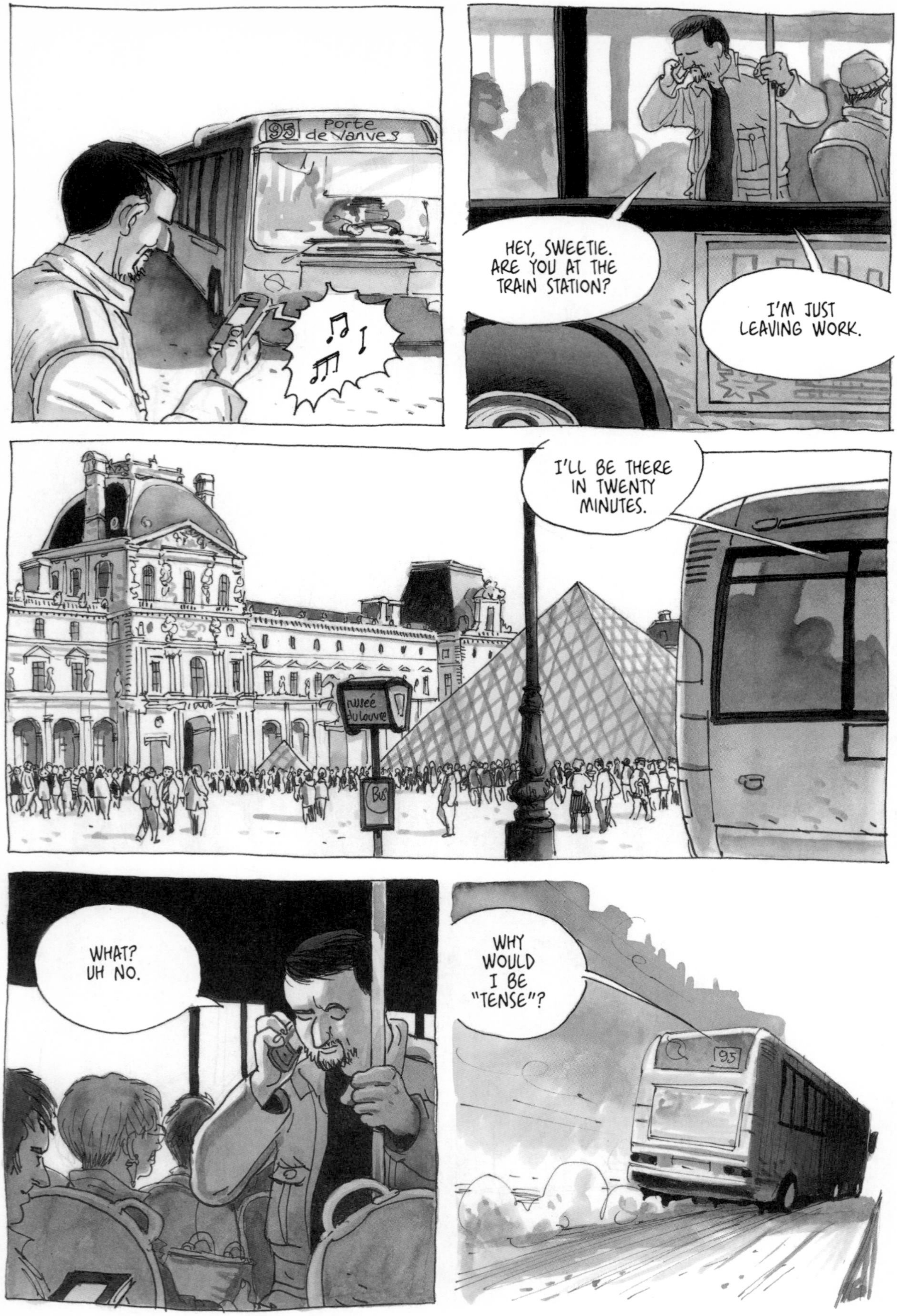

Porte de Vanves
HEY, SWEETIE. ARE YOU AT THE TRAIN STATION?
I'M JUST LEAVING WORK.
I'LL BE THERE IN TWENTY MINUTES.
WHAT? UH NO.
WHY WOULD I BE "TENSE"?

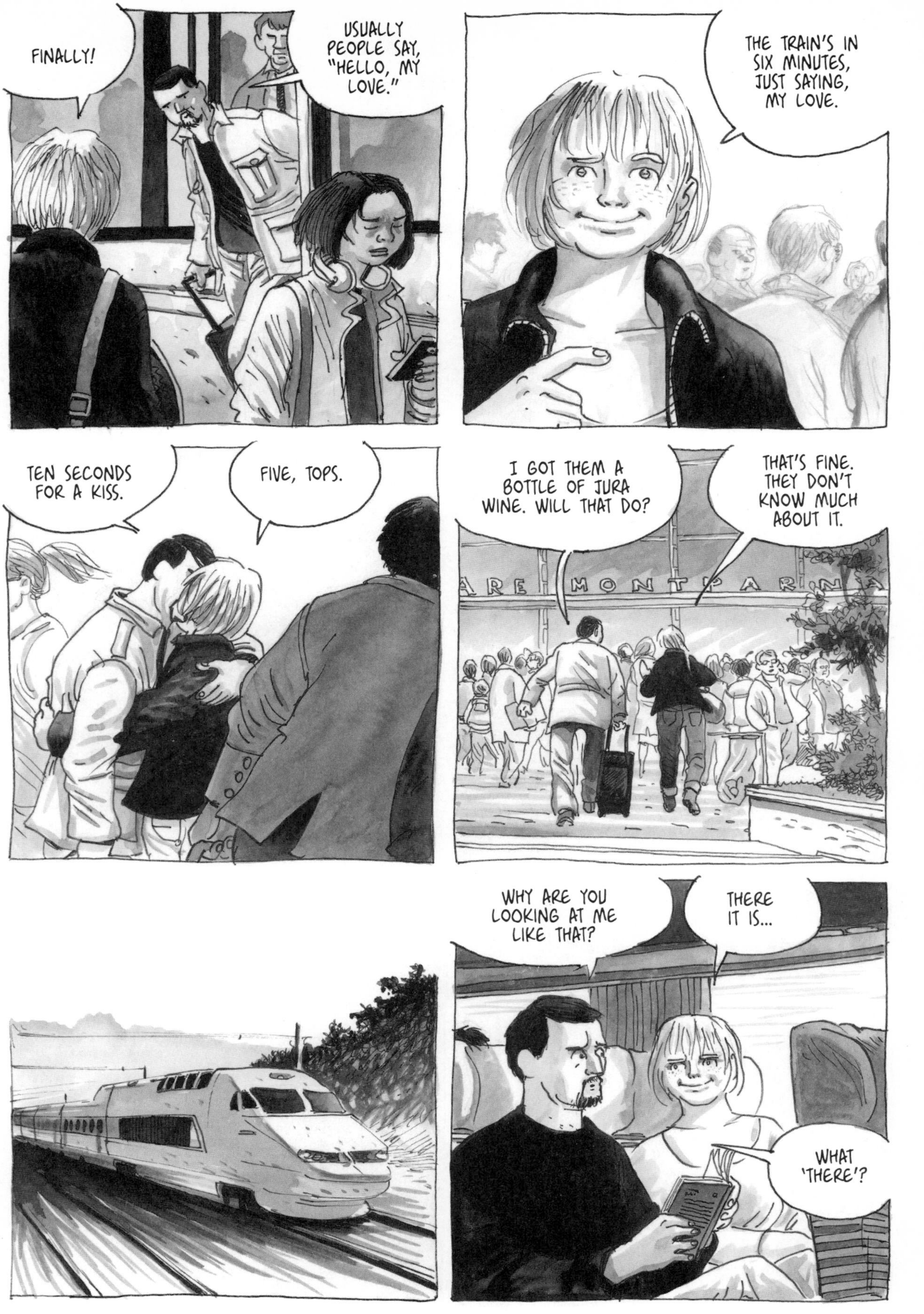
FINALLY!
USUALLY PEOPLE SAY, "HELLO, MY LOVE."
THE TRAIN'S IN SIX MINUTES, JUST SAYING, MY LOVE.
TEN SECONDS FOR A KISS.
FIVE, TOPS.
I GOT THEM A BOTTLE OF JURA WINE. WILL THAT DO?
THAT'S FINE. THEY DON'T KNOW MUCH ABOUT IT.
WHY ARE YOU LOOKING AT ME LIKE THAT?
THERE IT IS...
WHAT 'THERE'?

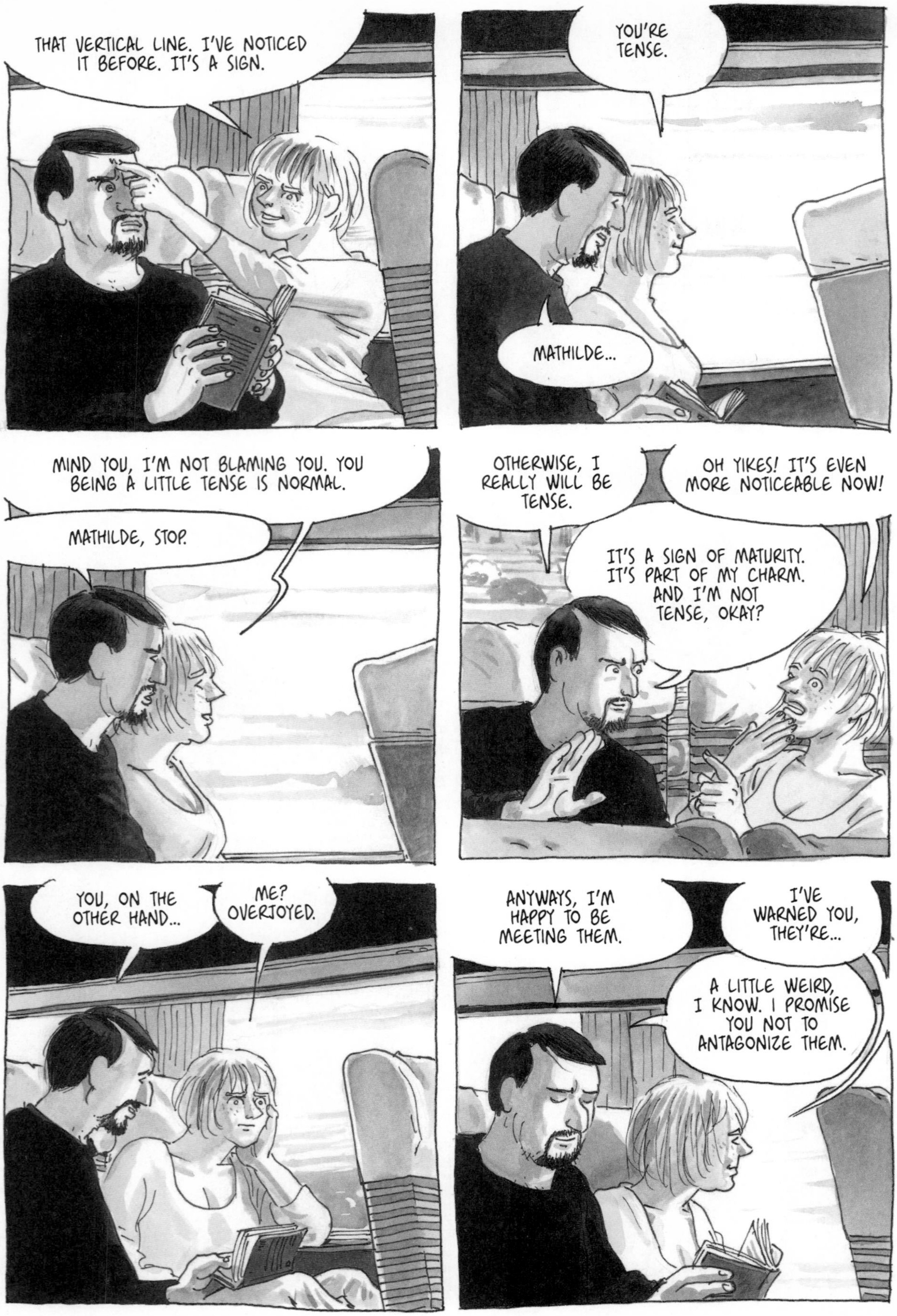
THAT VERTICAL LINE. I'VE NOTICED IT BEFORE. IT'S A SIGN.
YOU'RE TENSE.
MATHILDE...
MIND YOU, I'M NOT BLAMING YOU. YOU BEING A LITTLE TENSE IS NORMAL.
MATHILDE, STOP.
OTHERWISE, I REALLY WILL BE TENSE.
OH YIKES! IT'S EVEN MORE NOTICEABLE NOW!
IT'S A SIGN OF MATURITY. IT'S PART OF MY CHARM. AND I'M NOT TENSE, OKAY?
YOU, ON THE OTHER HAND...
ME? OVERJOYED.
ANYWAYS, I'M HAPPY TO BE MEETING THEM.
I'VE WARNED YOU, THEY'RE...
A LITTLE WEIRD, I KNOW. I PROMISE YOU NOT TO ANTAGONIZE THEM.

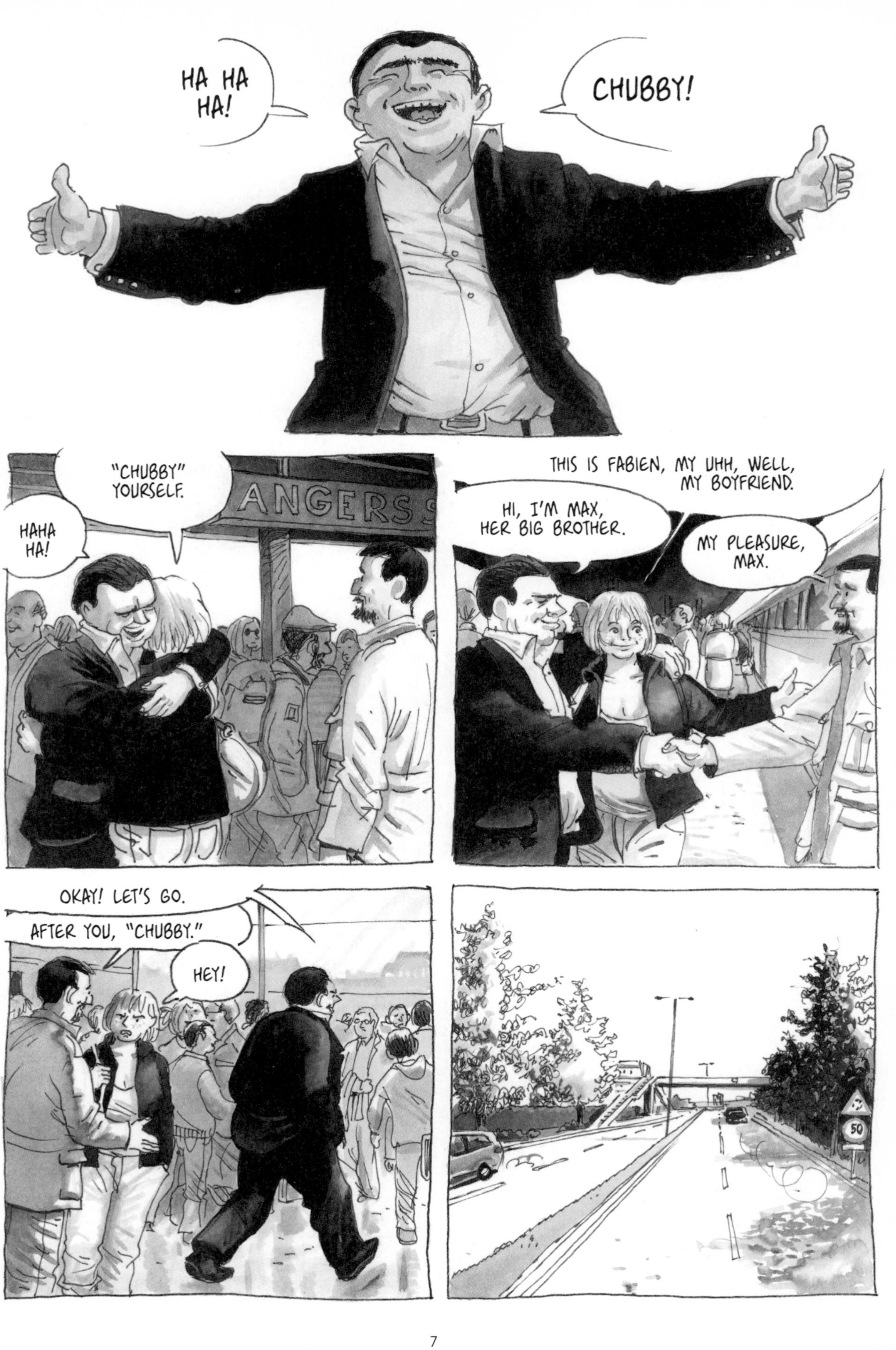
HA HA HA!
CHUBBY!
HAHA HA!
"CHUBBY" YOURSELF.
ANGERS
THIS IS FABIEN, MY UHH, WELL, MY BOYFRIEND.
HI, I'M MAX, HER BIG BROTHER.
MY PLEASURE, MAX.
OKAY! LET'S GO.
AFTER YOU, "CHUBBY."
HEY!
50

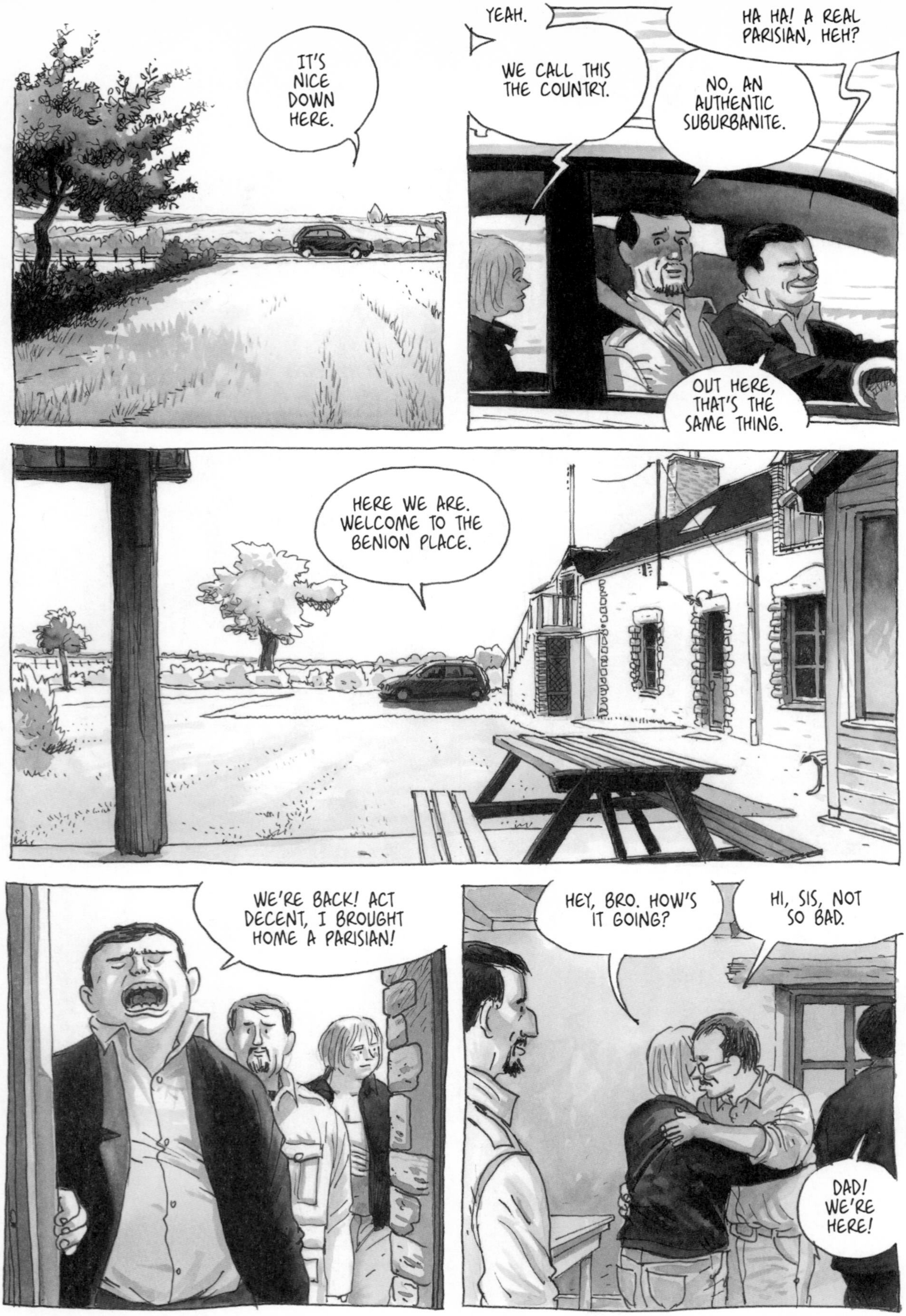

IT'S NICE DOWN HERE.
YEAH.
WE CALL THIS THE COUNTRY.
HA HA! A REAL PARISIAN, HEH?
NO, AN AUTHENTIC SUBURBANITE.
OUT HERE, THAT'S THE SAME THING.
HERE WE ARE. WELCOME TO THE BENION PLACE.
WE'RE BACK! ACT DECENT, I BROUGHT HOME A PARISIAN!
HEY, BRO. HOW'S IT GOING?
HI, SIS, NOT SO BAD.
DAD! WE'RE HERE!

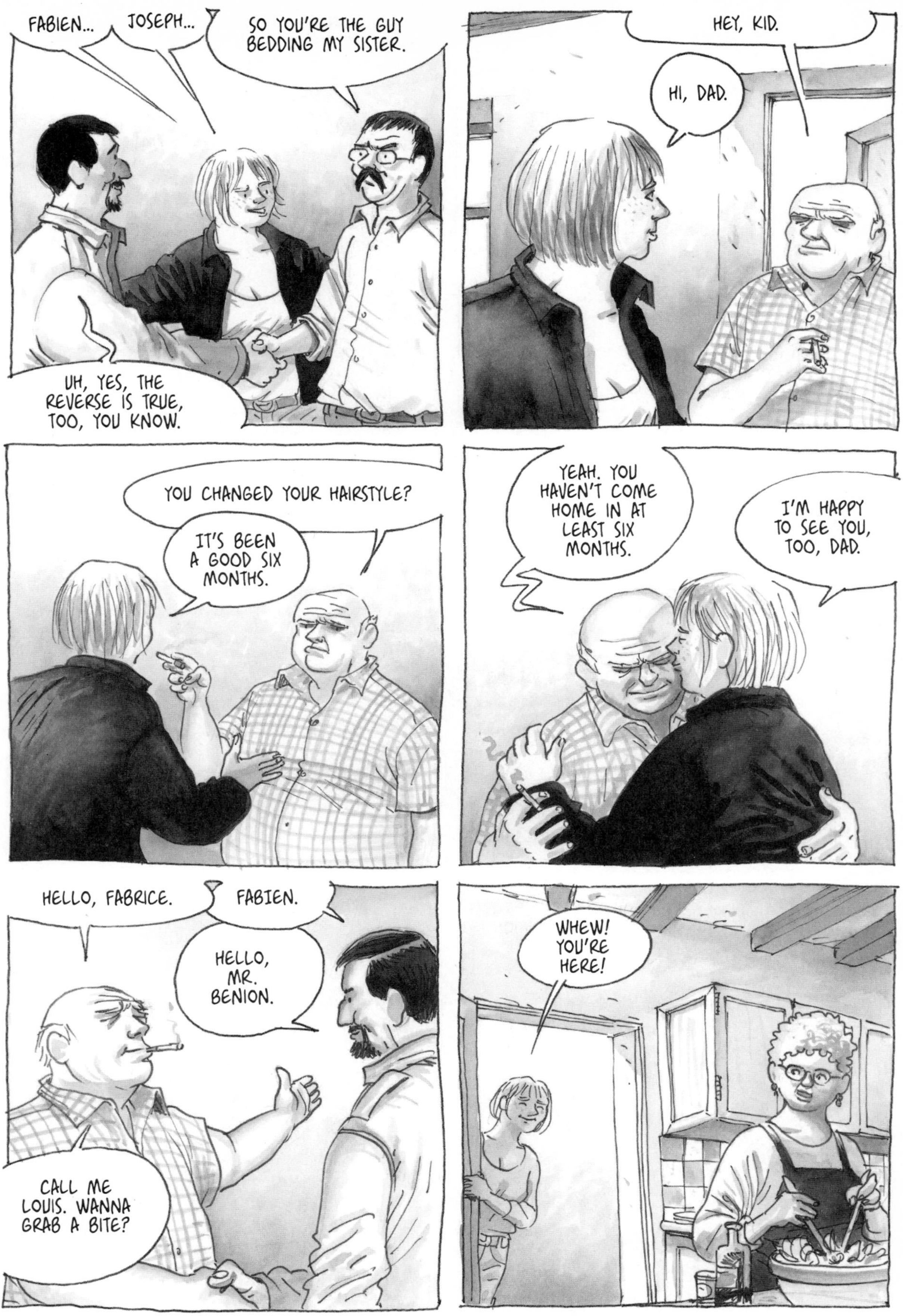
FABIEN...
JOSEPH...
SO YOU'RE THE GUY BEDDING MY SISTER.
UH, YES, THE REVERSE IS TRUE, TOO, YOU KNOW.
HEY, KID.
HI, DAD.
YOU CHANGED YOUR HAIRSTYLE?
IT'S BEEN A GOOD SIX MONTHS.
YEAH. YOU HAVEN'T COME HOME IN AT LEAST SIX MONTHS.
I'M HAPPY TO SEE YOU, TOO, DAD.
HELLO, FABRICE.
FABIEN.
HELLO, MR. BENION.
CALL ME LOUIS. WANNA GRAB A BITE?
WHEW! YOU'RE HERE!

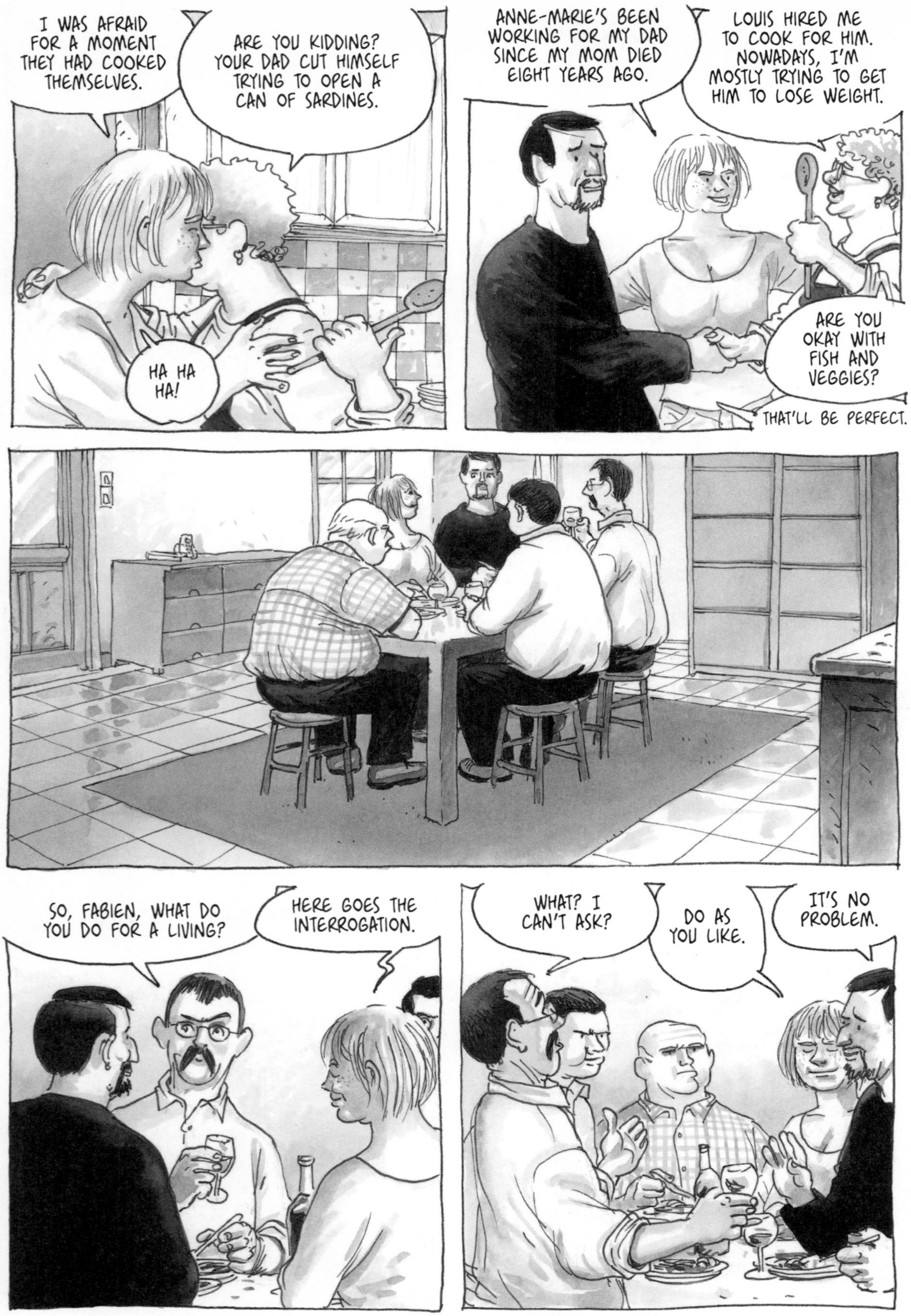
I WAS AFRAID FOR A MOMENT THEY HAD COOKED THEMSELVES.
ARE YOU KIDDING? YOUR DAD CUT HIMSELF TRYING TO OPEN A CAN OF SARDINES.
HA HA HA!
ANNE-MARIE'S BEEN WORKING FOR MY DAD SINCE MY MOM DIED EIGHT YEARS AGO.
LOUIS HIRED ME TO COOK FOR HIM. NOWADAYS, I'M MOSTLY TRYING TO GET HIM TO LOSE WEIGHT.
ARE YOU OKAY WITH FISH AND VEGGIES?
THAT'LL BE PERFECT.
SO, FABIEN, WHAT DO YOU DO FOR A LIVING?
HERE GOES THE INTERROGATION.
WHAT? I CAN'T ASK?
DO AS YOU LIKE.
IT'S NO PROBLEM.

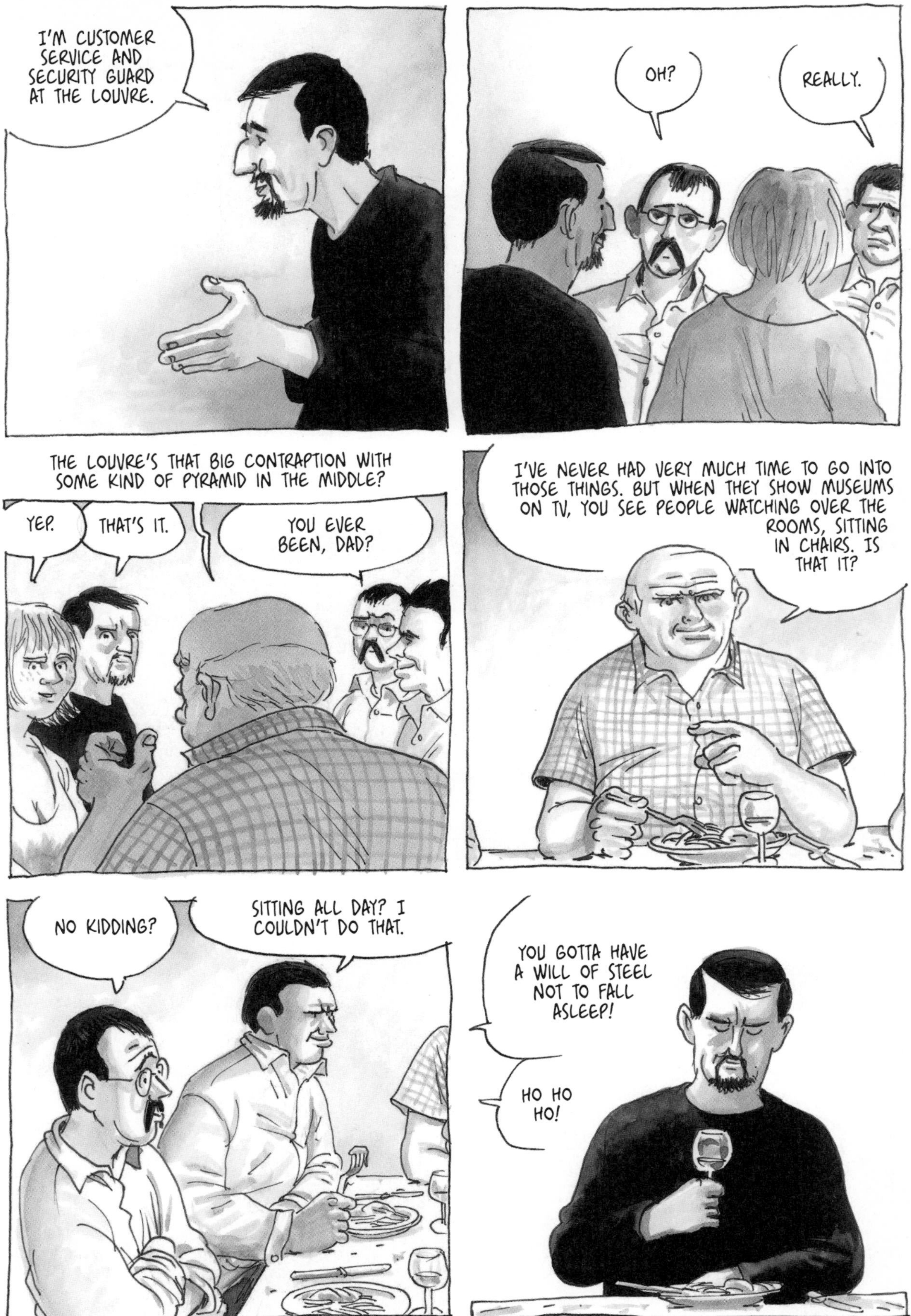
I'M CUSTOMER SERVICE AND SECURITY GUARD AT THE LOUVRE.
OH?
REALLY.
THE LOUVRE'S THAT BIG CONTRAPTION WITH SOME KIND OF PYRAMID IN THE MIDDLE?
YEP.
THAT'S IT.
YOU EVER BEEN, DAD?
I'VE NEVER HAD VERY MUCH TIME TO GO INTO THOSE THINGS. BUT WHEN THEY SHOW MUSEUMS ON TV, YOU SEE PEOPLE WATCHING OVER THE ROOMS, SITTING IN CHAIRS. IS THAT IT?
NO KIDDING?
SITTING ALL DAY? I COULDN'T DO THAT.
YOU GOTTA HAVE A WILL OF STEEL NOT TO FALL ASLEEP!
HO HO HO!

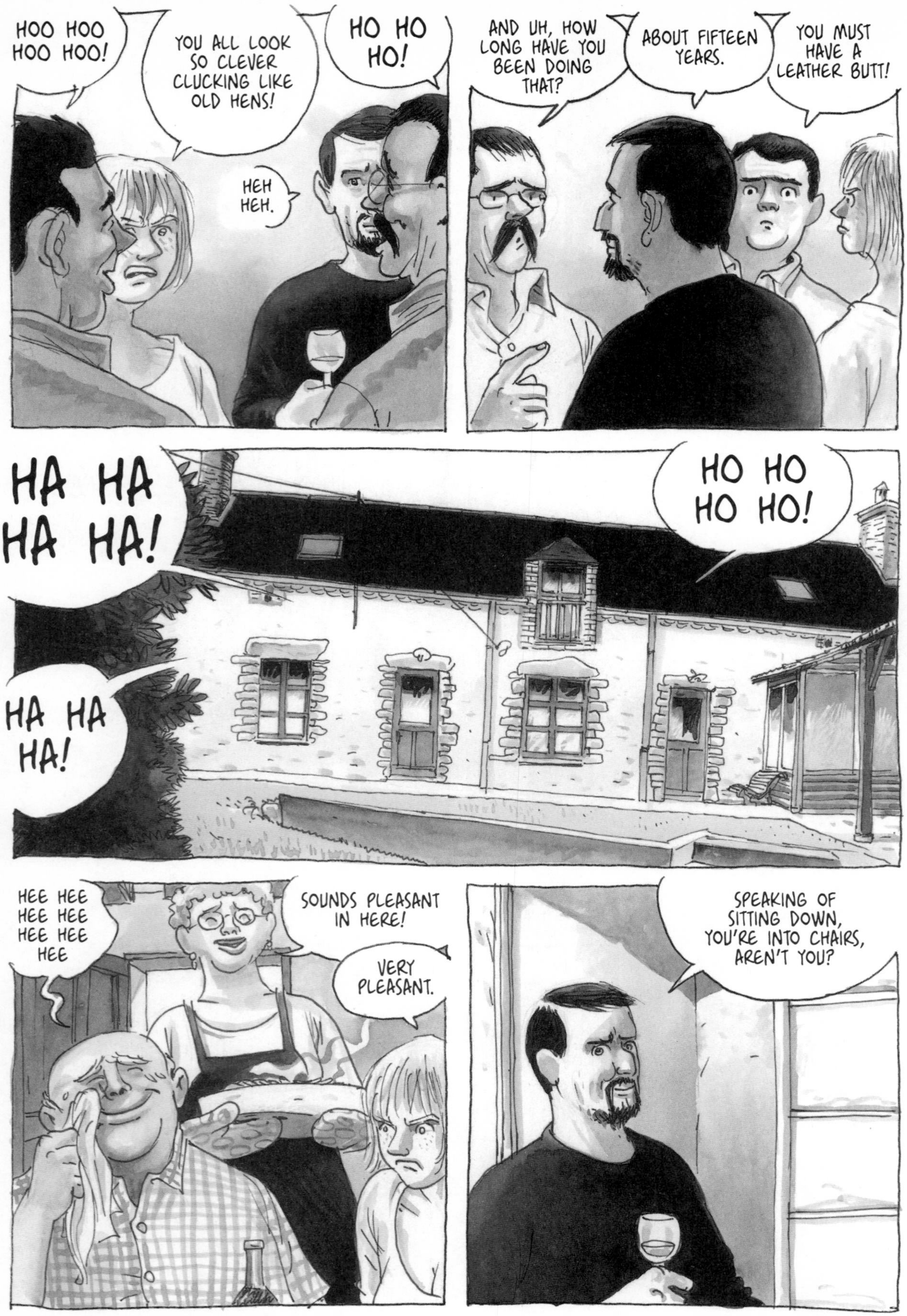
HOO HOO HOO HOO!
YOU ALL LOOK SO CLEVER CLUCKING LIKE OLD HENS!
HO HO HO!
HEH HEH.
AND UH, HOW LONG HAVE YOU BEEN DOING THAT?
ABOUT FIFTEEN YEARS.
YOU MUST HAVE A LEATHER BUTT!
HA HA HA HA!
HO HO HO HO!
HA HA HA!
HEE HEE HEE HEE HEE HEE HEE
SOUNDS PLEASANT IN HERE!
VERY PLEASANT.
SPEAKING OF SITTING DOWN, YOU'RE INTO CHAIRS, AREN'T YOU?

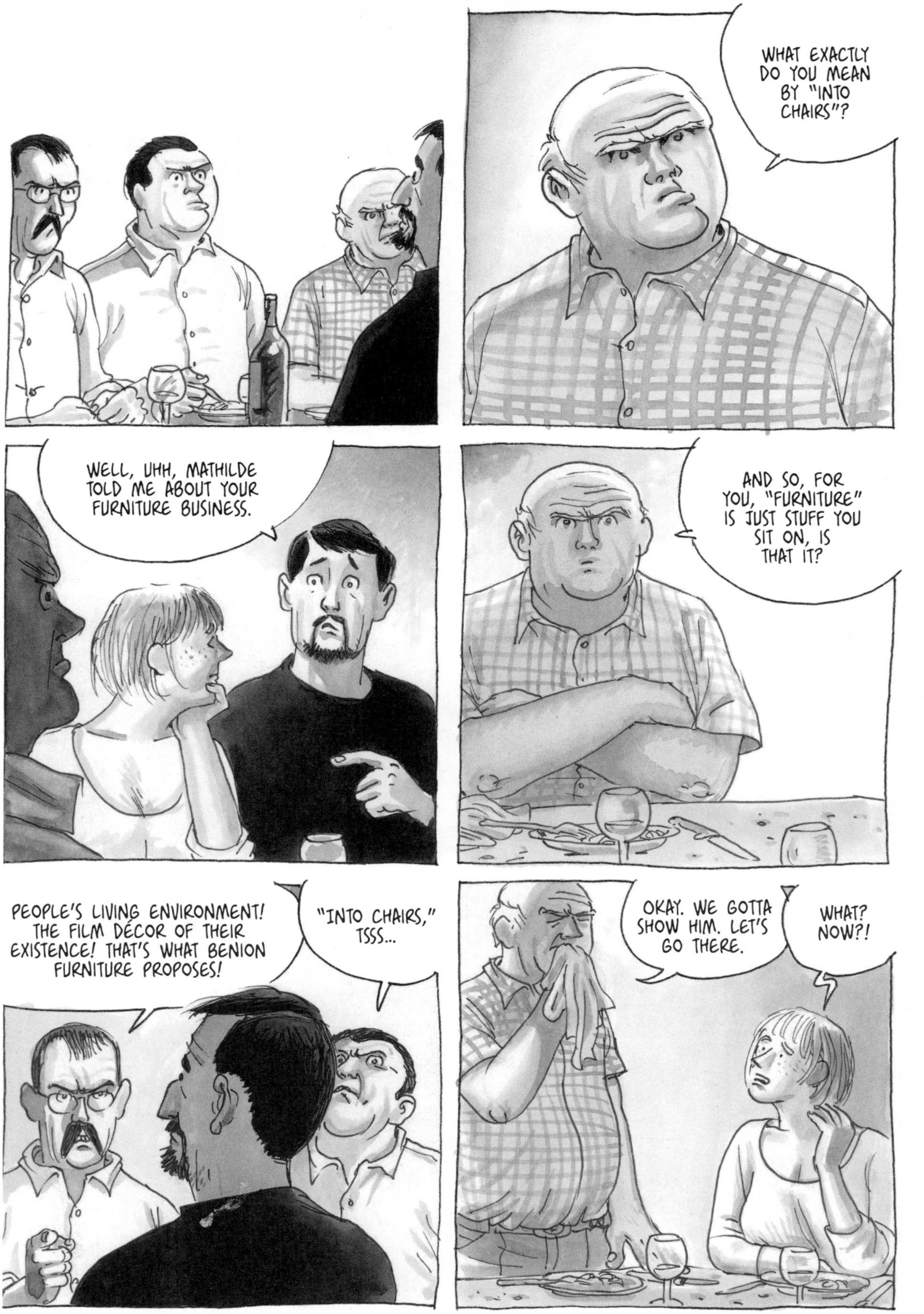
WHAT EXACTLY DO YOU MEAN BY "INTO CHAIRS"?
WELL, UHH, MATHILDE TOLD ME ABOUT YOUR FURNITURE BUSINESS.
AND SO, FOR YOU, "FURNITURE" IS JUST STUFF YOU SIT ON, IS THAT IT?
PEOPLE'S LIVING ENVIRONMENT! THE FILM DÉCOR OF THEIR EXISTENCE! THAT'S WHAT BENION FURNITURE PROPOSES!
"INTO CHAIRS," TSSS...
OKAY. WE GOTTA SHOW HIM. LET'S GO THERE.
WHAT? NOW?!

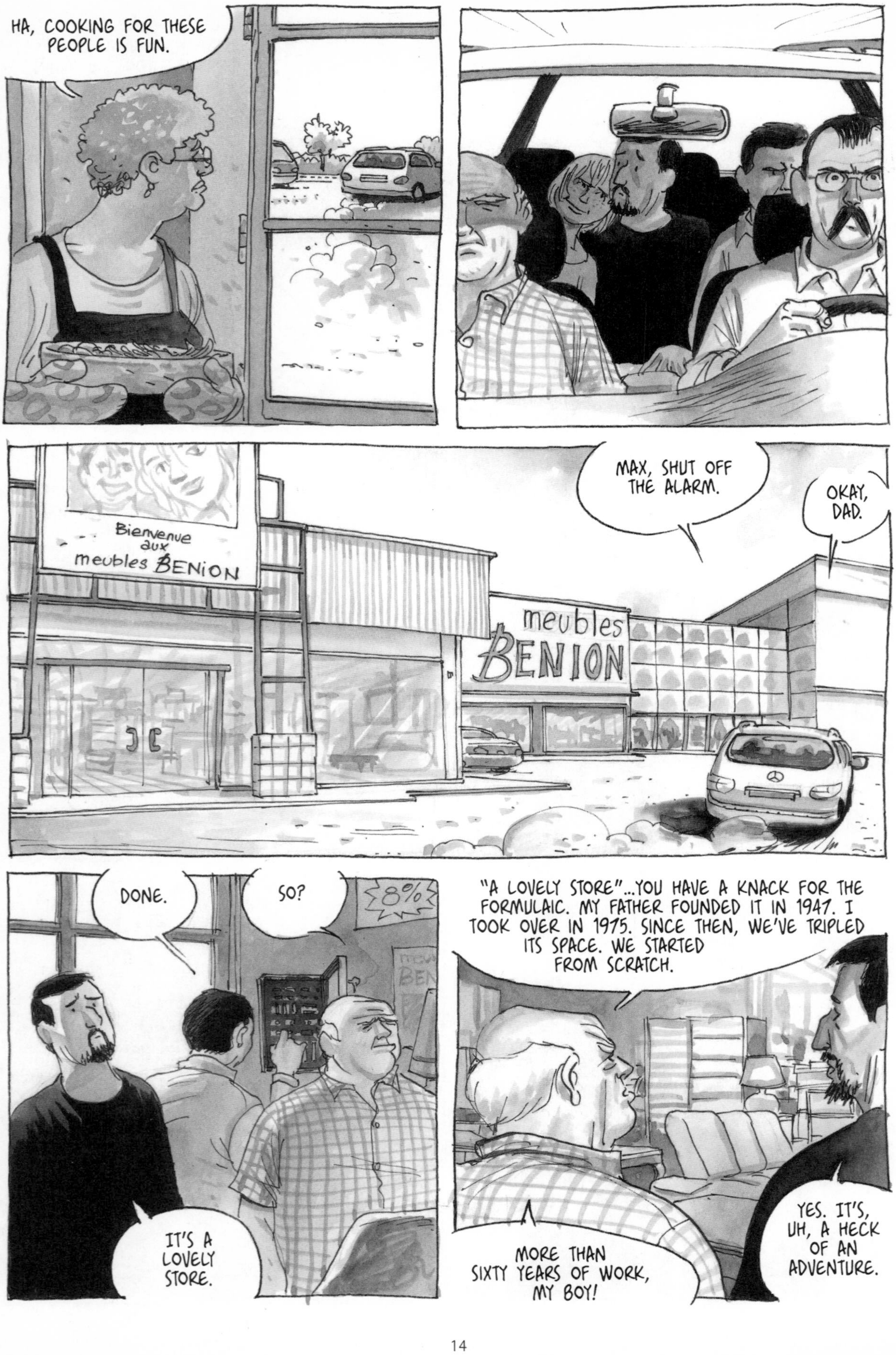

HA, COOKING FOR THESE PEOPLE IS FUN.
Bienvenue aux meubles BENION
meubles BENION
MAX, SHUT OFF THE ALARM.
OKAY, DAD.
DONE.
SO?
8%
IT'S A LOVELY STORE.
"A LOVELY STORE"...YOU HAVE A KNACK FOR THE FORMULAIC. MY FATHER FOUNDED IT IN 1947. I TOOK OVER IN 1975. SINCE THEN, WE'VE TRIPLED ITS SPACE. WE STARTED FROM SCRATCH.
MORE THAN SIXTY YEARS OF WORK, MY BOY!
YES. IT'S, UH, A HECK OF AN ADVENTURE.

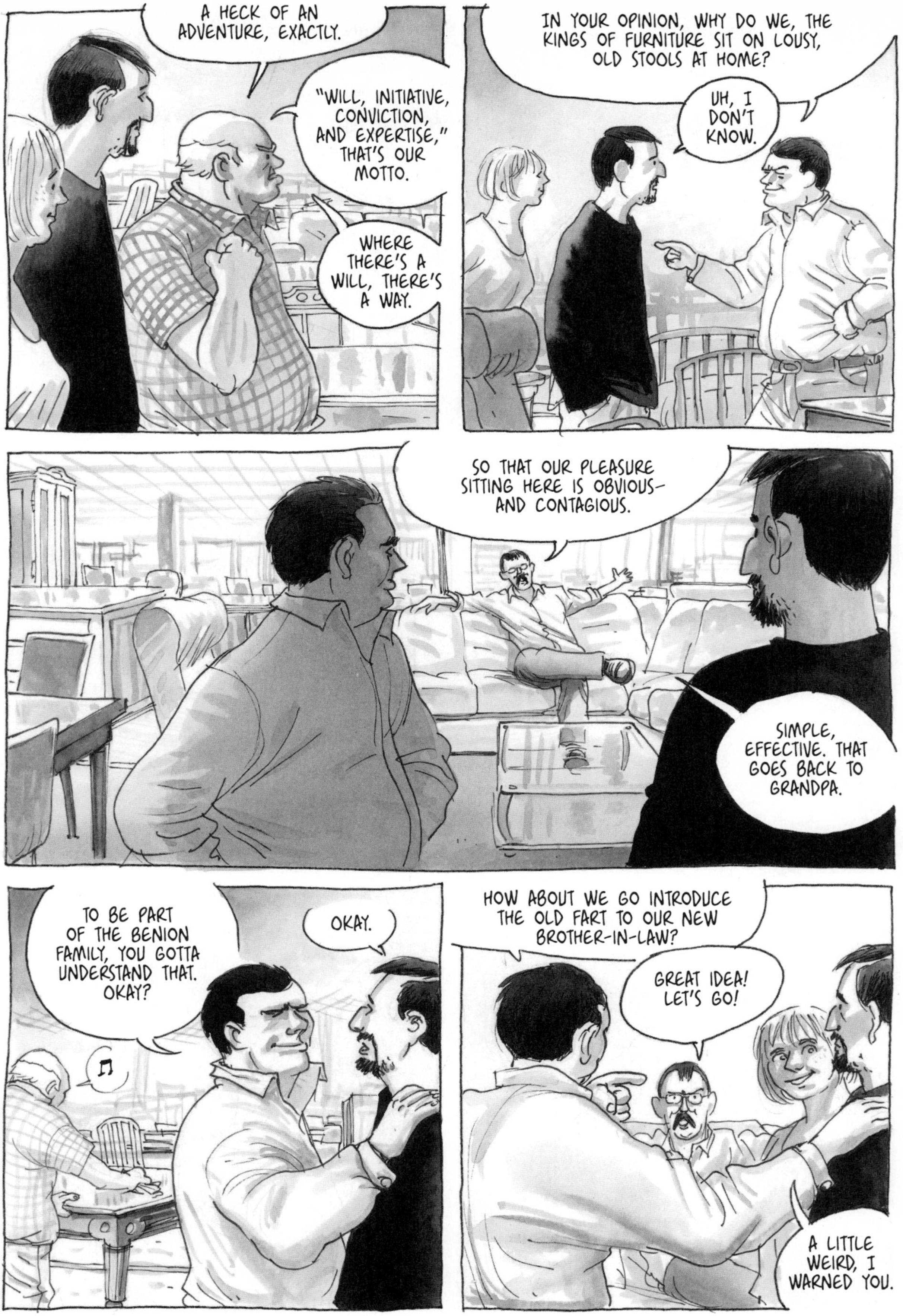
A HECK OF AN ADVENTURE, EXACTLY.
"WILL, INITIATIVE, CONVICTION, AND EXPERTISE," THAT'S OUR MOTTO.
WHERE THERE'S A WILL, THERE'S A WAY.
IN YOUR OPINION, WHY DO WE, THE KINGS OF FURNITURE SIT ON LOUSY, OLD STOOLS AT HOME?
UH, I DON'T KNOW.
SO THAT OUR PLEASURE SITTING HERE IS OBVIOUS–AND CONTAGIOUS.
SIMPLE, EFFECTIVE. THAT GOES BACK TO GRANDPA.
TO BE PART OF THE BENION FAMILY, YOU GOTTA UNDERSTAND THAT. OKAY?
OKAY.
♫
HOW ABOUT WE GO INTRODUCE THE OLD FART TO OUR NEW BROTHER-IN-LAW?
GREAT IDEA! LET'S GO!
A LITTLE WEIRD, I WARNED YOU.

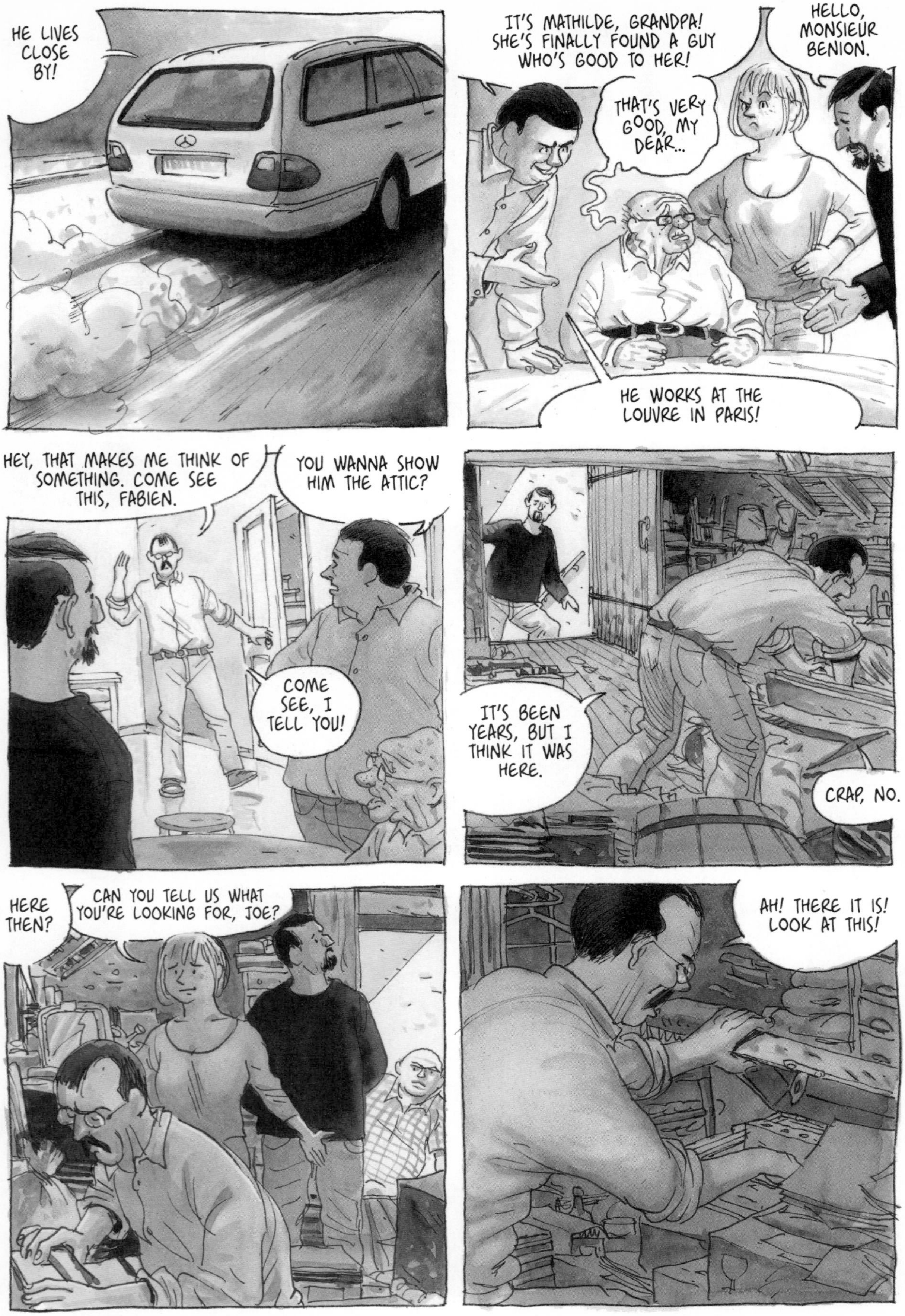
HE LIVES CLOSE BY!
IT'S MATHILDE, GRANDPA! SHE'S FINALLY FOUND A GUY WHO'S GOOD TO HER!
HELLO, MONSIEUR BENION.
THAT'S VERY GOOD, MY DEAR...
HE WORKS AT THE LOUVRE IN PARIS!
HEY, THAT MAKES ME THINK OF SOMETHING. COME SEE THIS, FABIEN.
YOU WANNA SHOW HIM THE ATTIC?
COME SEE, I TELL YOU!
IT'S BEEN YEARS, BUT I THINK IT WAS HERE.
CRAP, NO.
HERE THEN?
CAN YOU TELL US WHAT YOU'RE LOOKING FOR, JOE?
AH! THERE IT IS! LOOK AT THIS!

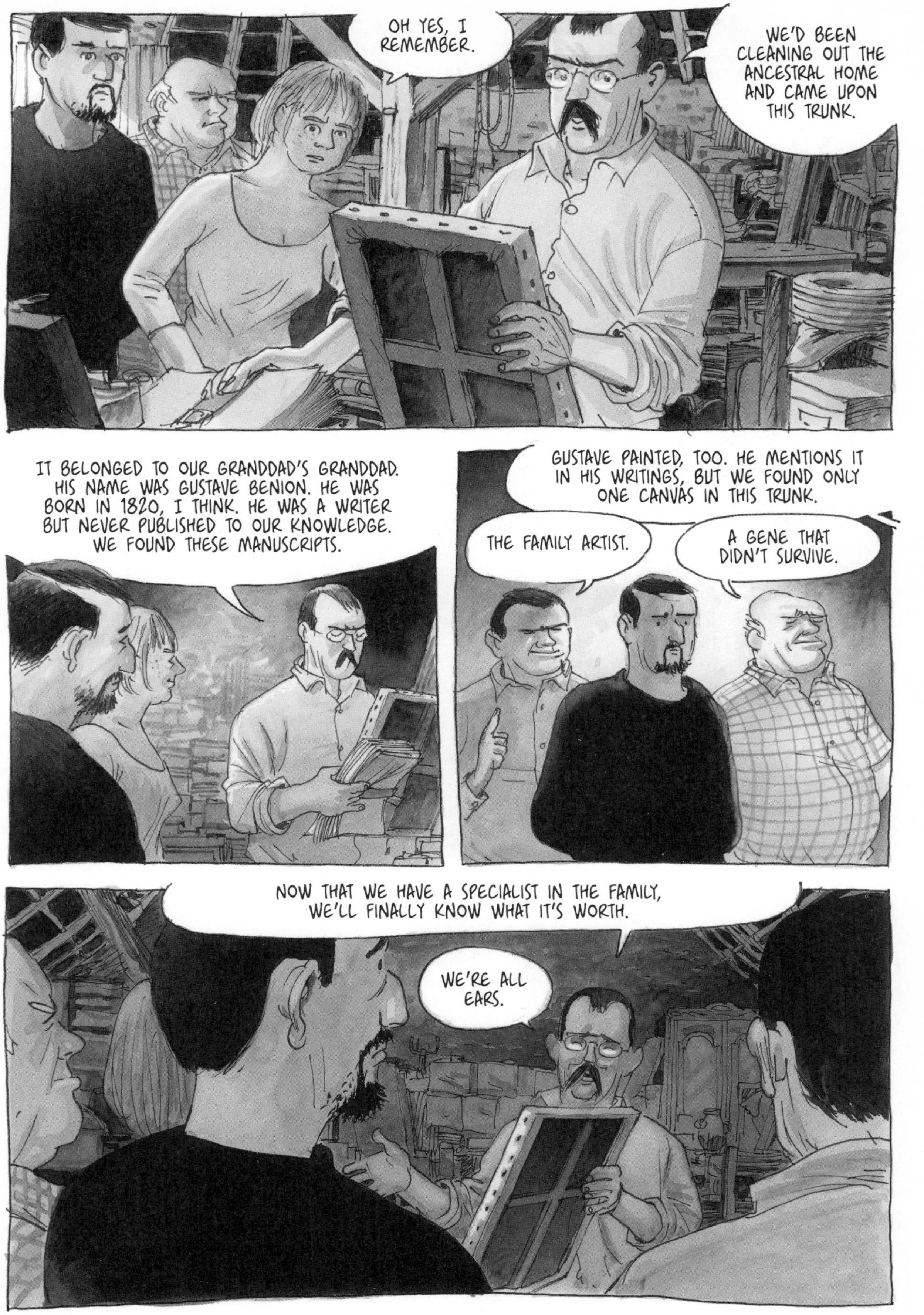
OH YES, I REMEMBER.
WE'D BEEN CLEANING OUT THE ANCESTRAL HOME AND CAME UPON THIS TRUNK.
IT BELONGED TO OUR GRANDDAD'S GRANDDAD. HIS NAME WAS GUSTAVE BENION. HE WAS BORN IN 1820, I THINK. HE WAS A WRITER BUT NEVER PUBLISHED TO OUR KNOWLEDGE. WE FOUND THESE MANUSCRIPTS.
GUSTAVE PAINTED, TOO. HE MENTIONS IT IN HIS WRITINGS, BUT WE FOUND ONLY ONE CANVAS IN THIS TRUNK.
THE FAMILY ARTIST.
A GENE THAT DIDN'T SURVIVE.
NOW THAT WE HAVE A SPECIALIST IN THE FAMILY, WE'LL FINALLY KNOW WHAT IT'S WORTH.
WE'RE ALL EARS.

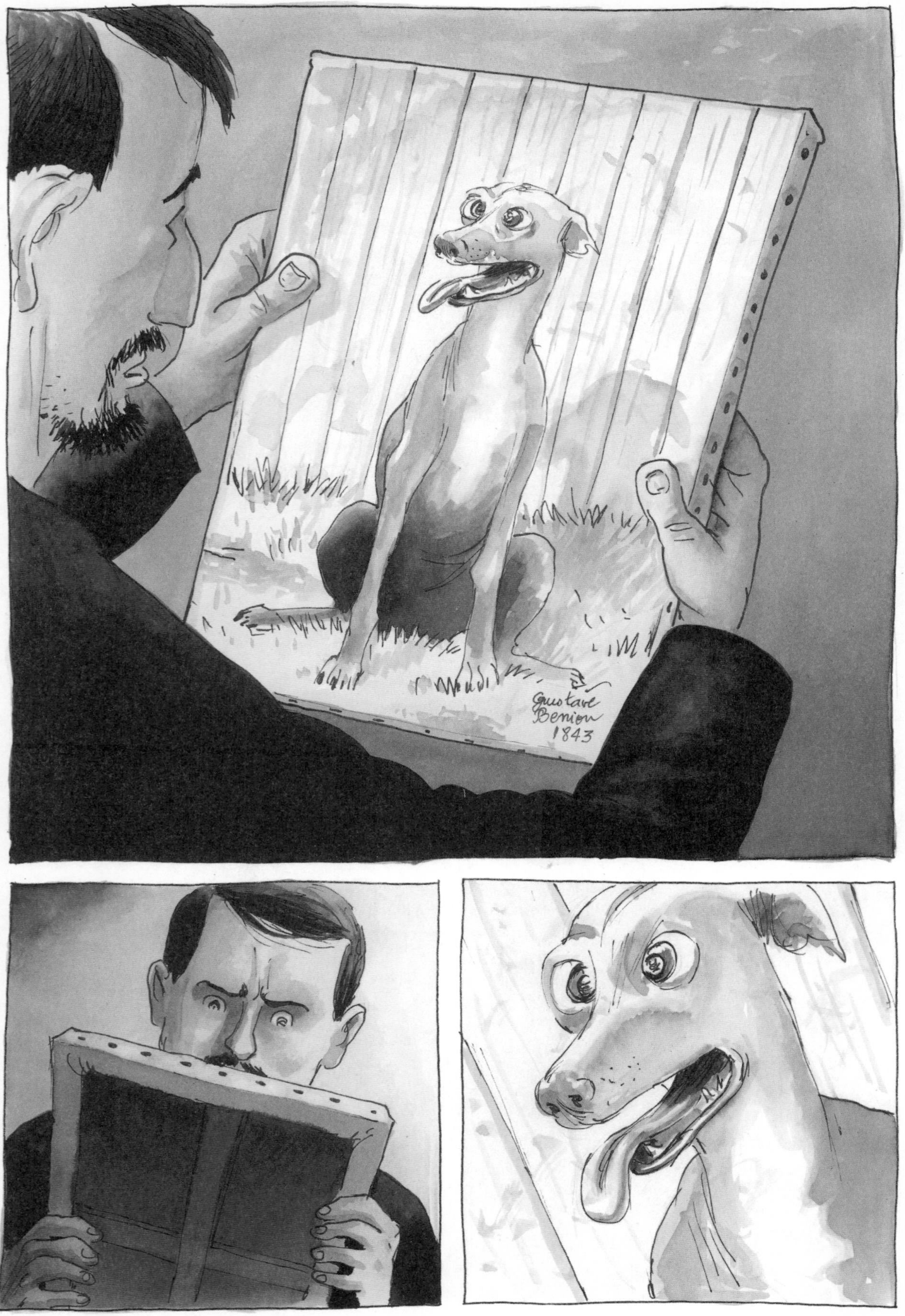
Gustave
Benion
1843

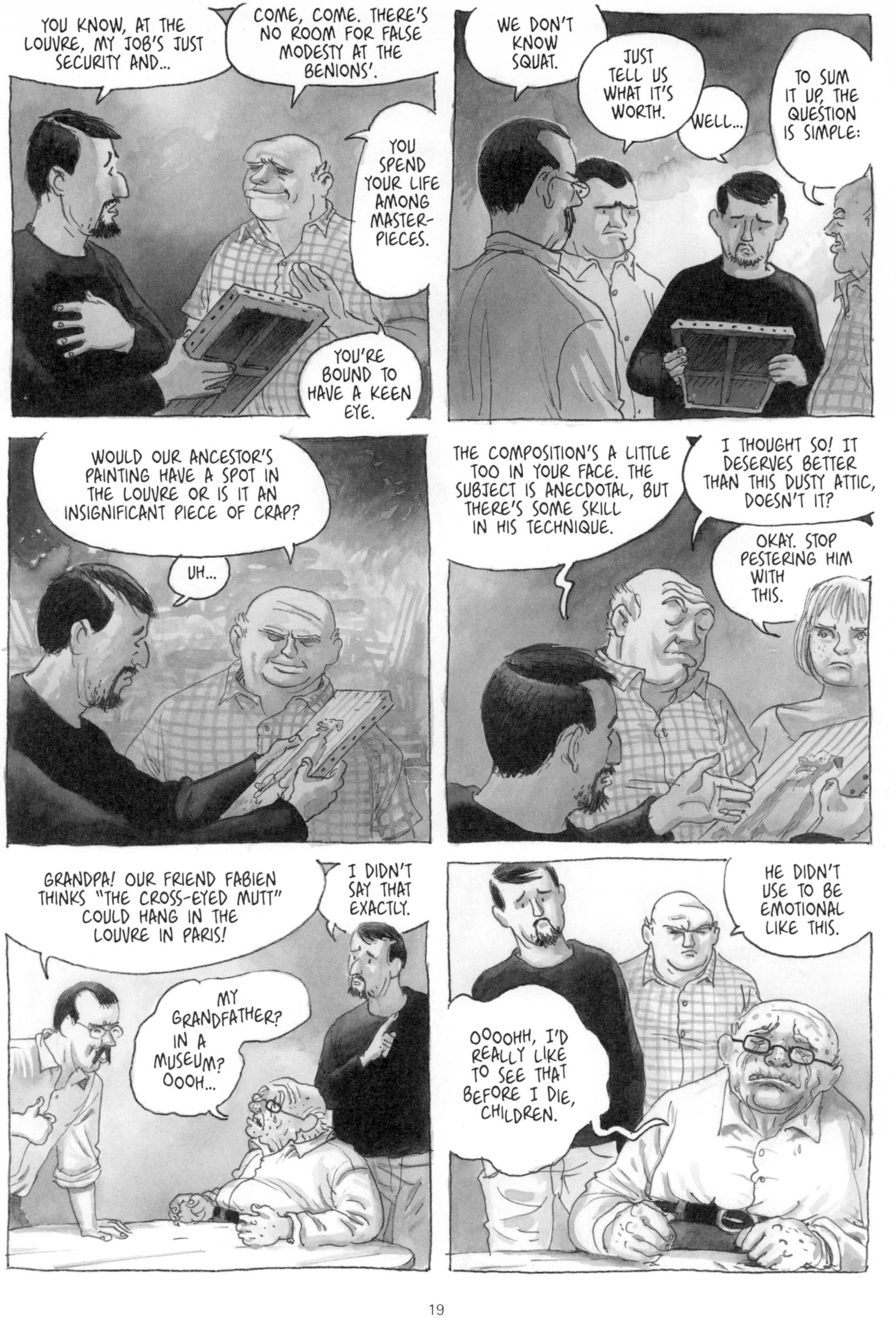
YOU KNOW, AT THE LOUVRE, MY JOB'S JUST SECURITY AND...
COME, COME. THERE'S NO ROOM FOR FALSE MODESTY AT THE BENIONS'.
YOU SPEND YOUR LIFE AMONG MASTER-PIECES.
YOU'RE BOUND TO HAVE A KEEN EYE.
WE DON'T KNOW SQUAT.
JUST TELL US WHAT IT'S WORTH.
WELL...
TO SUM IT UP, THE QUESTION IS SIMPLE:
WOULD OUR ANCESTOR'S PAINTING HAVE A SPOT IN THE LOUVRE OR IS IT AN INSIGNIFICANT PIECE OF CRAP?
UH...
THE COMPOSITION'S A LITTLE TOO IN YOUR FACE. THE SUBJECT IS ANECDOTAL, BUT THERE'S SOME SKILL IN HIS TECHNIQUE.
I THOUGHT SO! IT DESERVES BETTER THAN THIS DUSTY ATTIC, DOESN'T IT?
OKAY. STOP PESTERING HIM WITH THIS.
GRANDPA! OUR FRIEND FABIEN THINKS "THE CROSS-EYED MUTT" COULD HANG IN THE LOUVRE IN PARIS!
I DIDN'T SAY THAT EXACTLY.
MY GRANDFATHER? IN A MUSEUM? OOOH...
HE DIDN'T USE TO BE EMOTIONAL LIKE THIS.
OOOOHH, I'D REALLY LIKE TO SEE THAT BEFORE I DIE, CHILDREN.

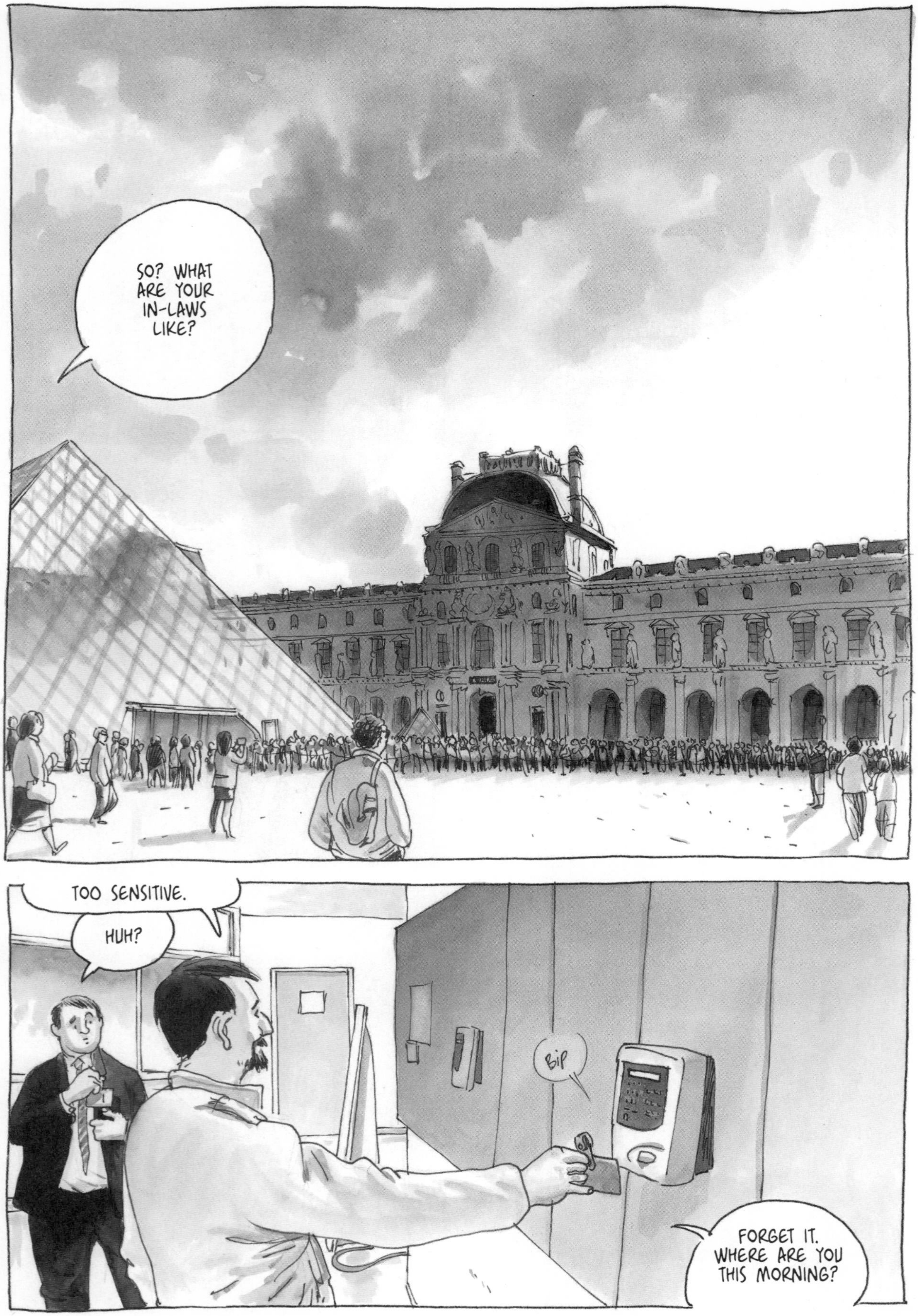
SO? WHAT ARE YOUR IN-LAWS LIKE?
TOO SENSITIVE.
HUH?
BIP
FORGET IT. WHERE ARE YOU THIS MORNING?

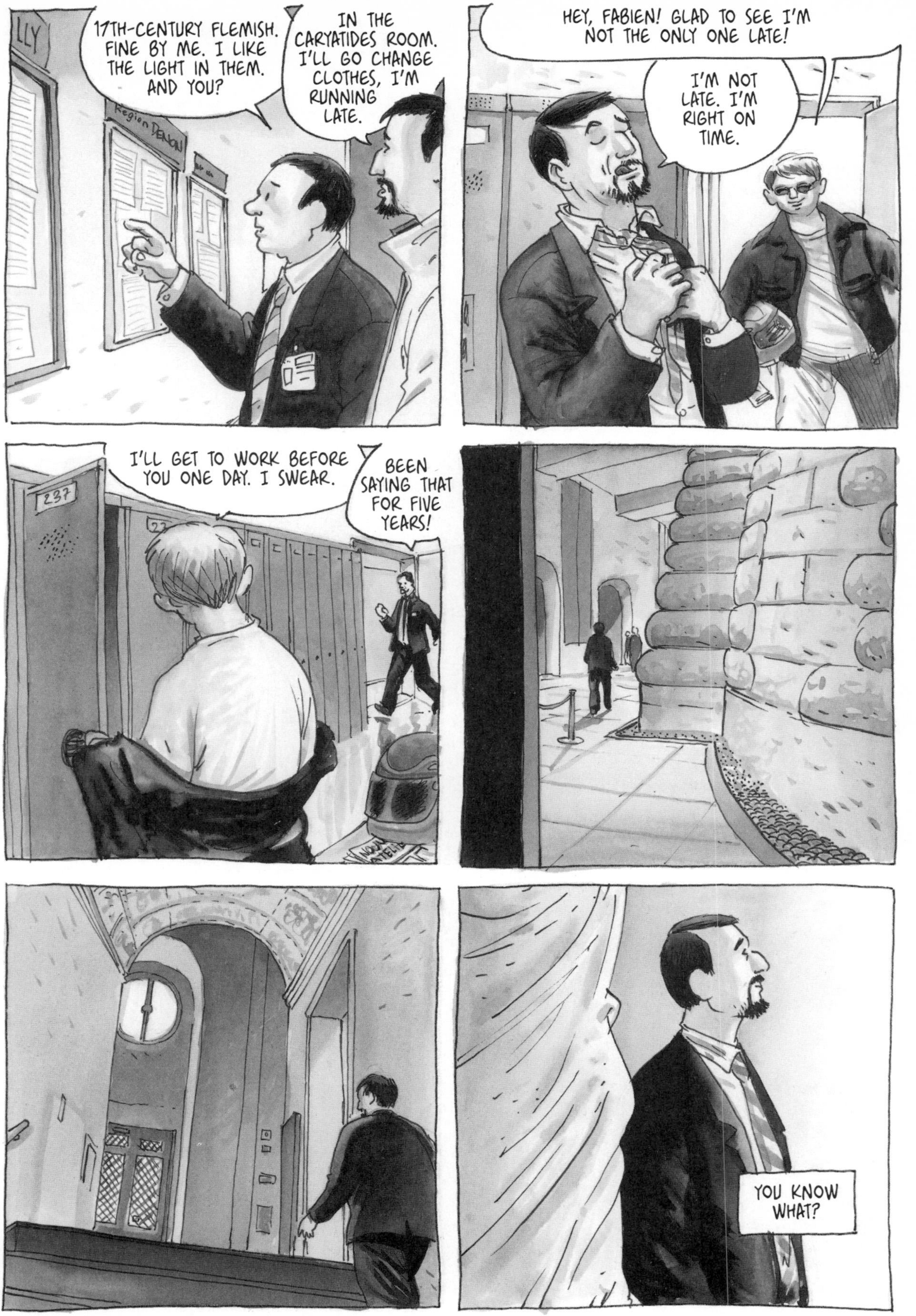
17TH-CENTURY FLEMISH. FINE BY ME. I LIKE THE LIGHT IN THEM. AND YOU?
IN THE CARYATIDES ROOM. I'LL GO CHANGE CLOTHES, I'M RUNNING LATE.
Région DENON
HEY, FABIEN! GLAD TO SEE I'M NOT THE ONLY ONE LATE!
I'M NOT LATE. I'M RIGHT ON TIME.
I'LL GET TO WORK BEFORE YOU ONE DAY. I SWEAR.
BEEN SAYING THAT FOR FIVE YEARS!
237
YOU KNOW WHAT?

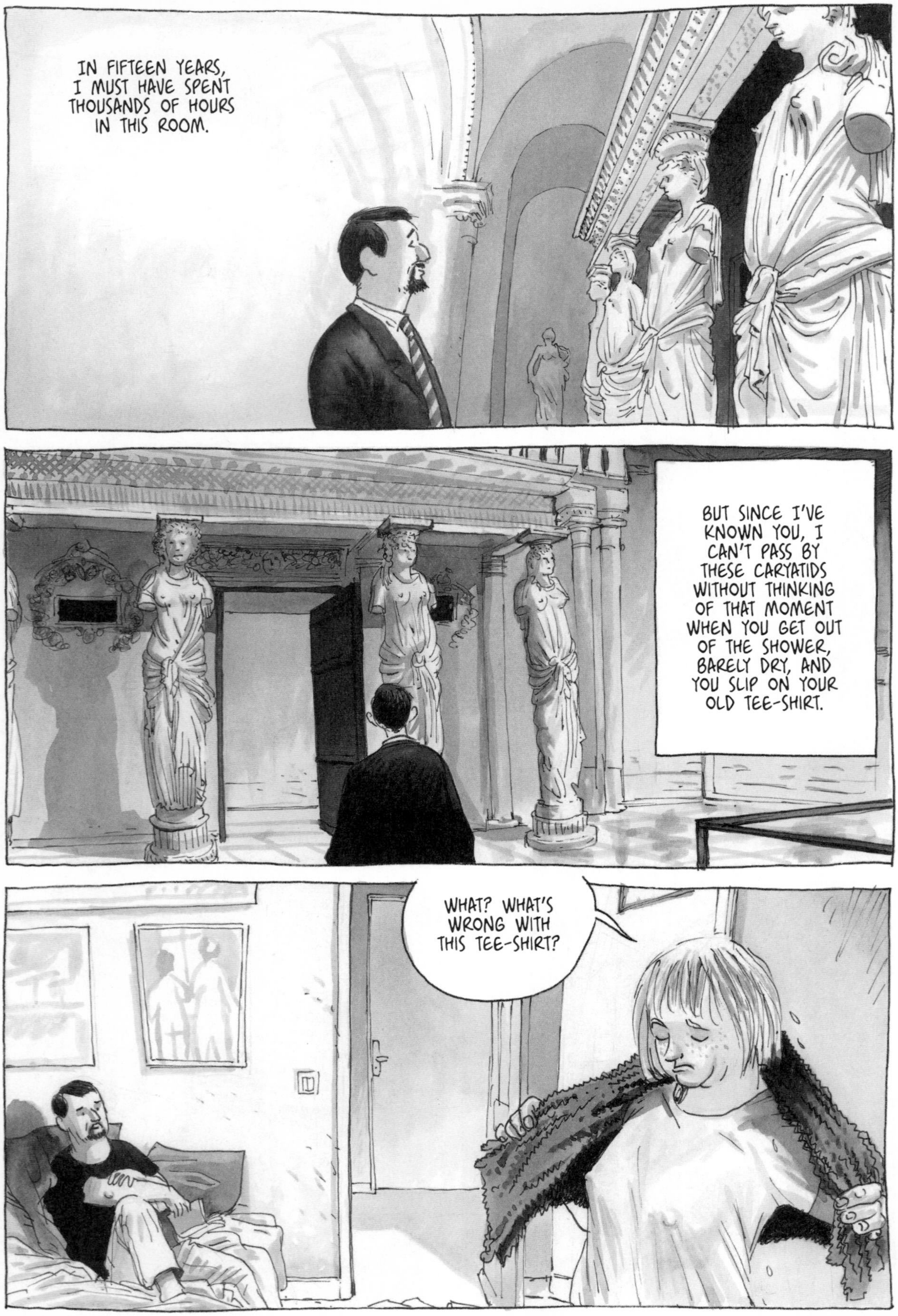
IN FIFTEEN YEARS, I MUST HAVE SPENT THOUSANDS OF HOURS IN THIS ROOM.
BUT SINCE I'VE KNOWN YOU, I CAN'T PASS BY THESE CARYATIDS WITHOUT THINKING OF THAT MOMENT WHEN YOU GET OUT OF THE SHOWER, BARELY DRY, AND YOU SLIP ON YOUR OLD TEE-SHIRT.
WHAT? WHAT'S WRONG WITH THIS TEE-SHIRT?

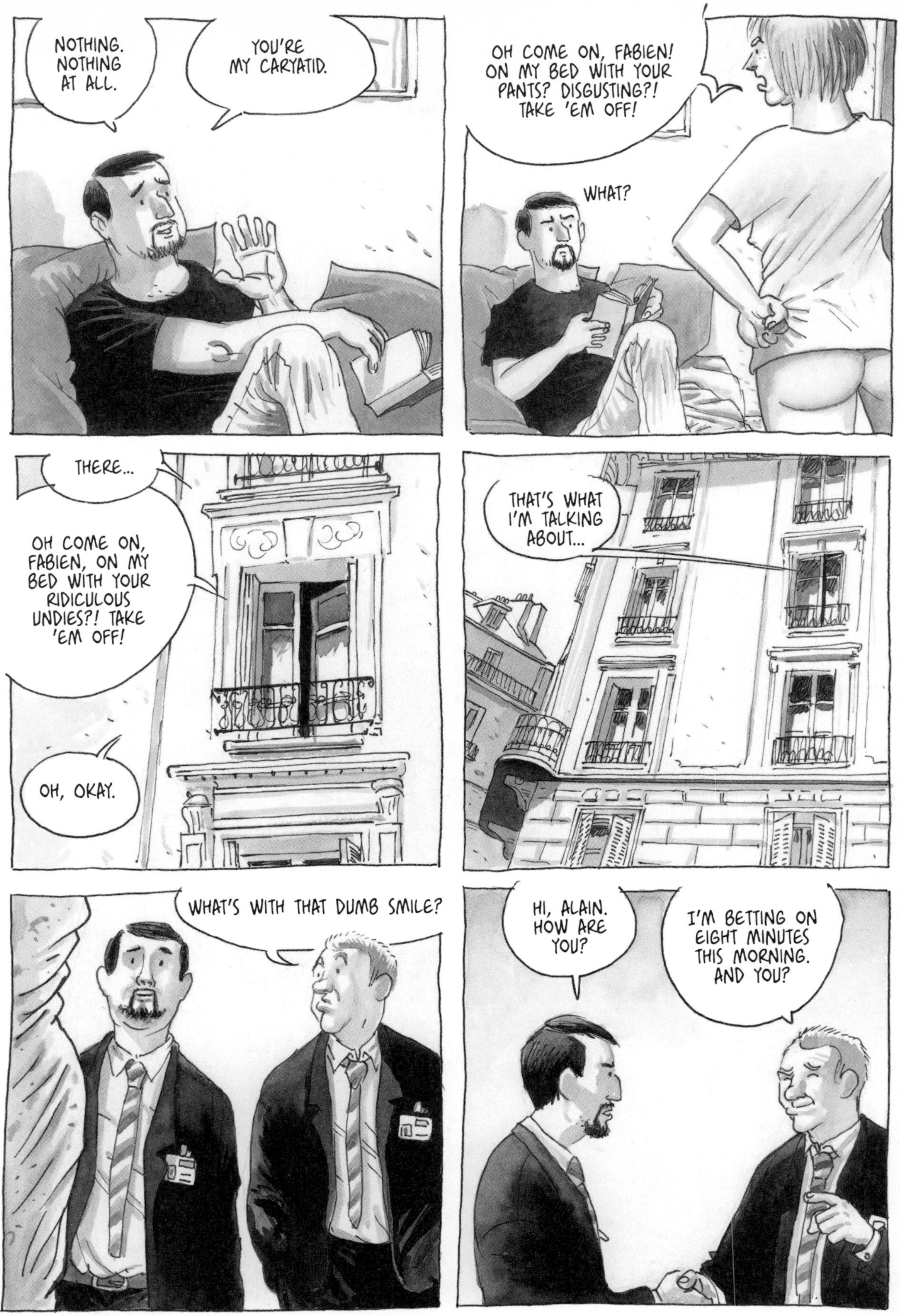
NOTHING. NOTHING AT ALL.
YOU'RE MY CARYATID.
OH COME ON, FABIEN! ON MY BED WITH YOUR PANTS? DISGUSTING?! TAKE 'EM OFF!
WHAT?
THERE...
OH COME ON, FABIEN, ON MY BED WITH YOUR RIDICULOUS UNDIES?! TAKE 'EM OFF!
OH, OKAY.
THAT'S WHAT I'M TALKING ABOUT...
WHAT'S WITH THAT DUMB SMILE?
HI, ALAIN. HOW ARE YOU?
I'M BETTING ON EIGHT MINUTES THIS MORNING. AND YOU?

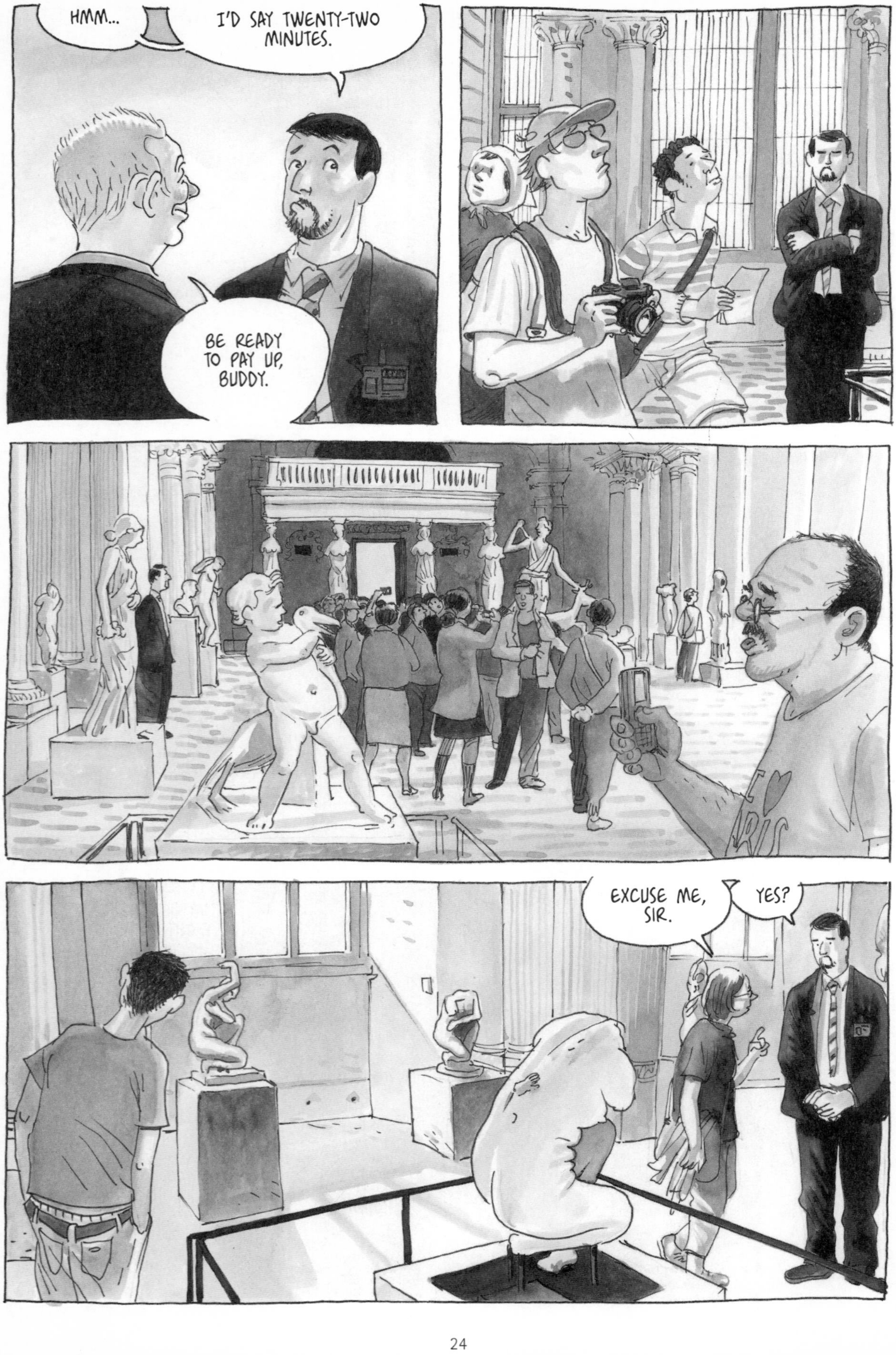
HMM...
I'D SAY TWENTY-TWO MINUTES.
BE READY TO PAY UP, BUDDY.
EXCUSE ME, SIR.
YES?

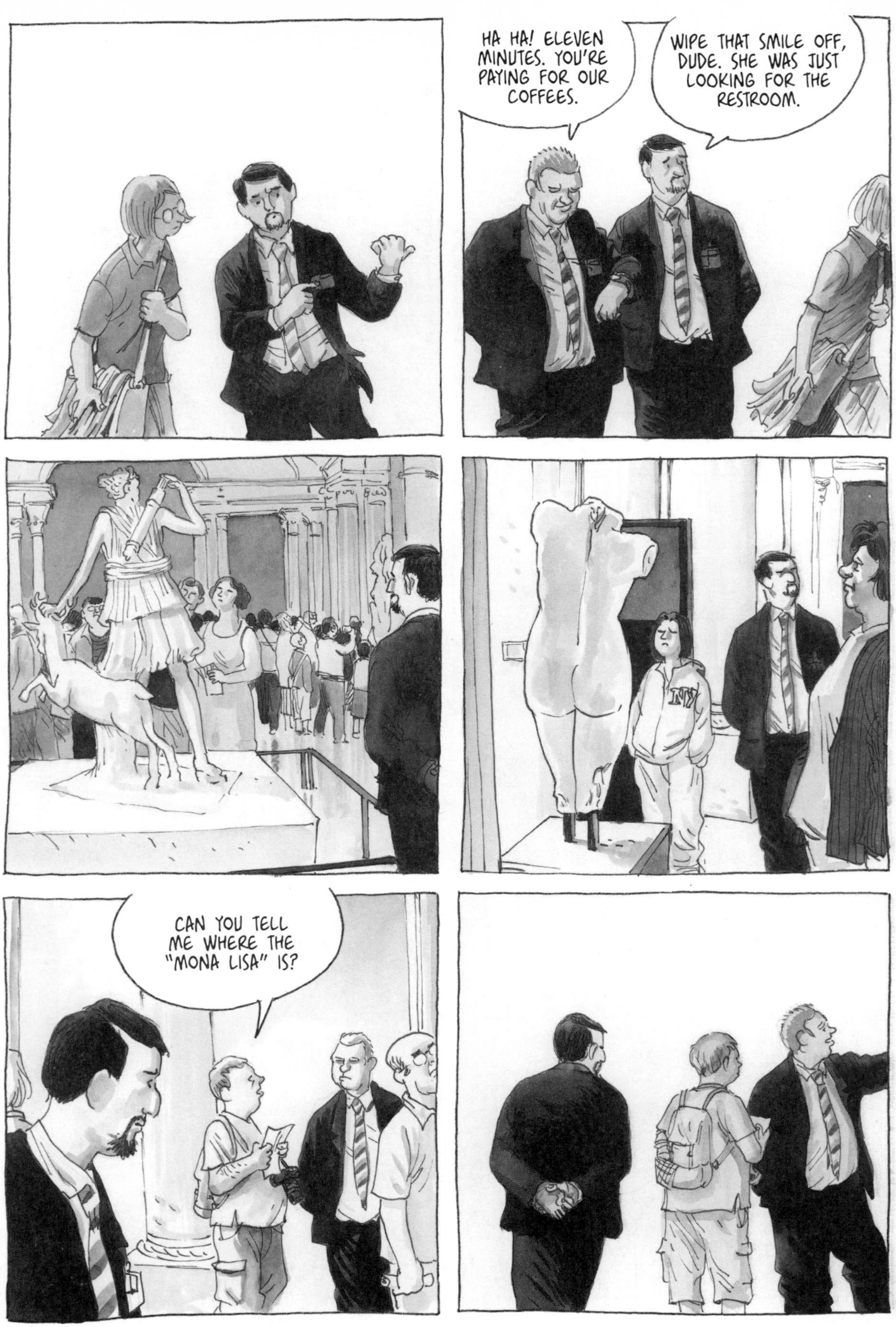
HA HA! ELEVEN MINUTES. YOU'RE PAYING FOR OUR COFFEES.
WIPE THAT SMILE OFF, DUDE. SHE WAS JUST LOOKING FOR THE RESTROOM.
NY
CAN YOU TELL ME WHERE THE "MONA LISA" IS?

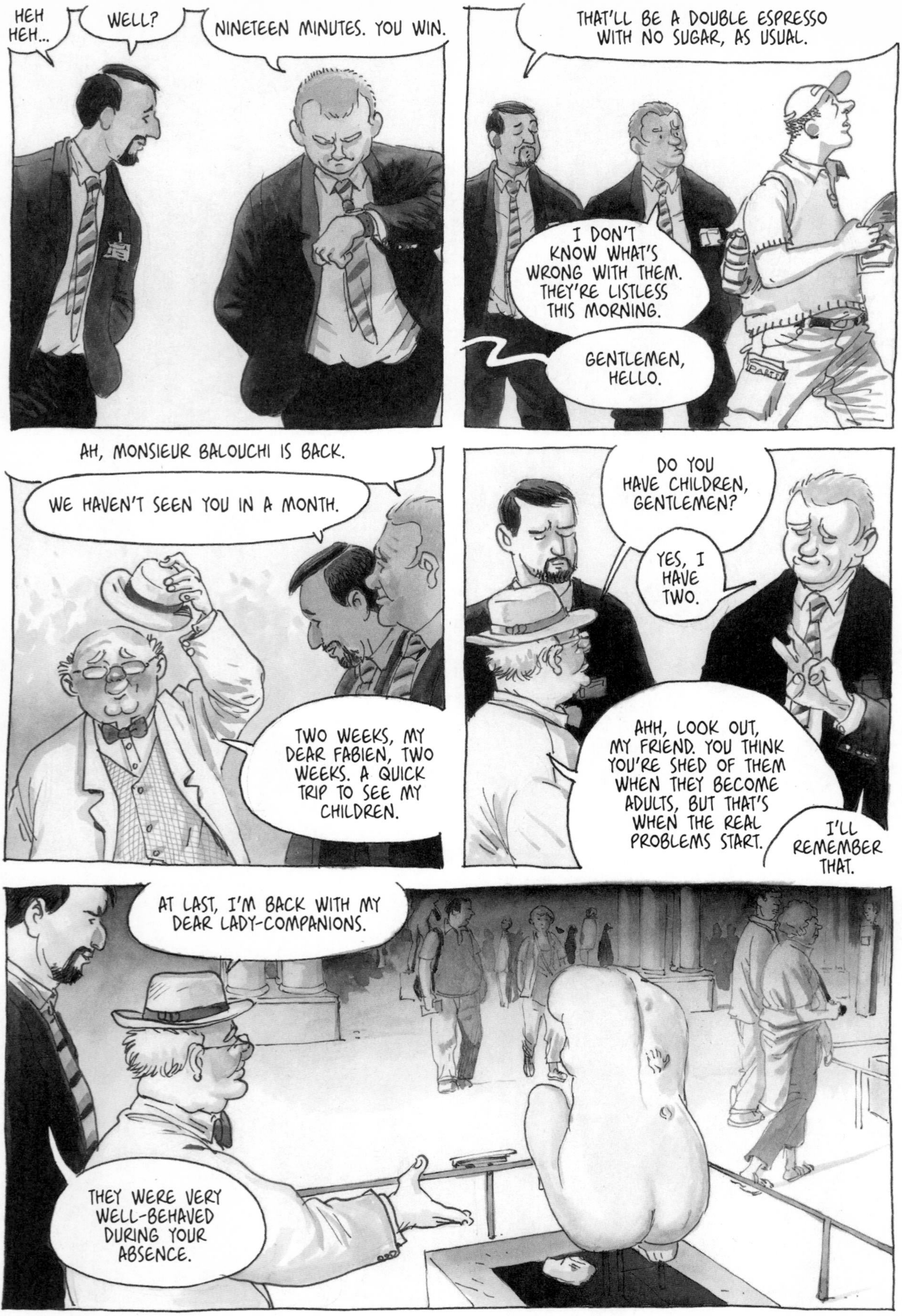
HEH HEH...
WELL?
NINETEEN MINUTES. YOU WIN.
THAT'LL BE A DOUBLE ESPRESSO WITH NO SUGAR, AS USUAL.
I DON'T KNOW WHAT'S WRONG WITH THEM. THEY'RE LISTLESS THIS MORNING.
GENTLEMEN, HELLO.
AH, MONSIEUR BALOUCHI IS BACK.
WE HAVEN'T SEEN YOU IN A MONTH.
TWO WEEKS, MY DEAR FABIEN, TWO WEEKS. A QUICK TRIP TO SEE MY CHILDREN.
DO YOU HAVE CHILDREN, GENTLEMEN?
YES, I HAVE TWO.
AHH, LOOK OUT, MY FRIEND. YOU THINK YOU'RE SHED OF THEM WHEN THEY BECOME ADULTS, BUT THAT'S WHEN THE REAL PROBLEMS START.
I'LL REMEMBER THAT.
AT LAST, I'M BACK WITH MY DEAR LADY-COMPANIONS.
THEY WERE VERY WELL-BEHAVED DURING YOUR ABSENCE.

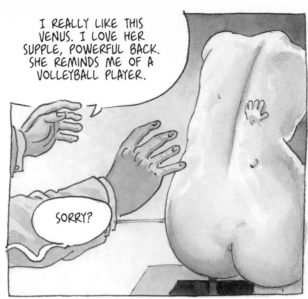

I REALLY LIKE THIS VENUS. I LOVE HER SUPPLE, POWERFUL BACK. SHE REMINDS ME OF A VOLLEYBALL PLAYER.

SORRY?

I'M TALKING ABOUT THOSE WOMEN ATHLETES WHO GET PHOTOGRAPHED AS A TEAM BEFORE THEIR MATCH. THE ONES IN THE FRONT ROW POSE WITH A KNEE ON THE GROUND. DO YOU SEE?

OH, YES, I SEE.

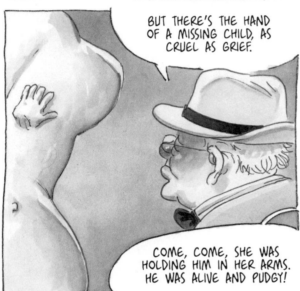

BUT THERE'S THE HAND OF A MISSING CHILD, AS CRUEL AS GRIEF.

COME, COME, SHE WAS HOLDING HIM IN HER ARMS. HE WAS ALIVE AND PUDGY!

YOU'RE RIGHT.

HOWEVER, THE ABSENCE OF THAT RASCAL REINFORCES THE LOVELY PRESENCE OF ITS MAMA.

TELL ME, MONSIEUR BALOUCHI...

HAVE YOU NEVER THOUGHT OF PROPOSING YOUR SERVICES TO THE MUSEUM AS A TOUR GUIDE?

NEVER! MY PLEASURE IS SELFISH!

OTHER LADY FRIENDS AWAIT ME. SEE YOU SOON, GENTLEMEN.

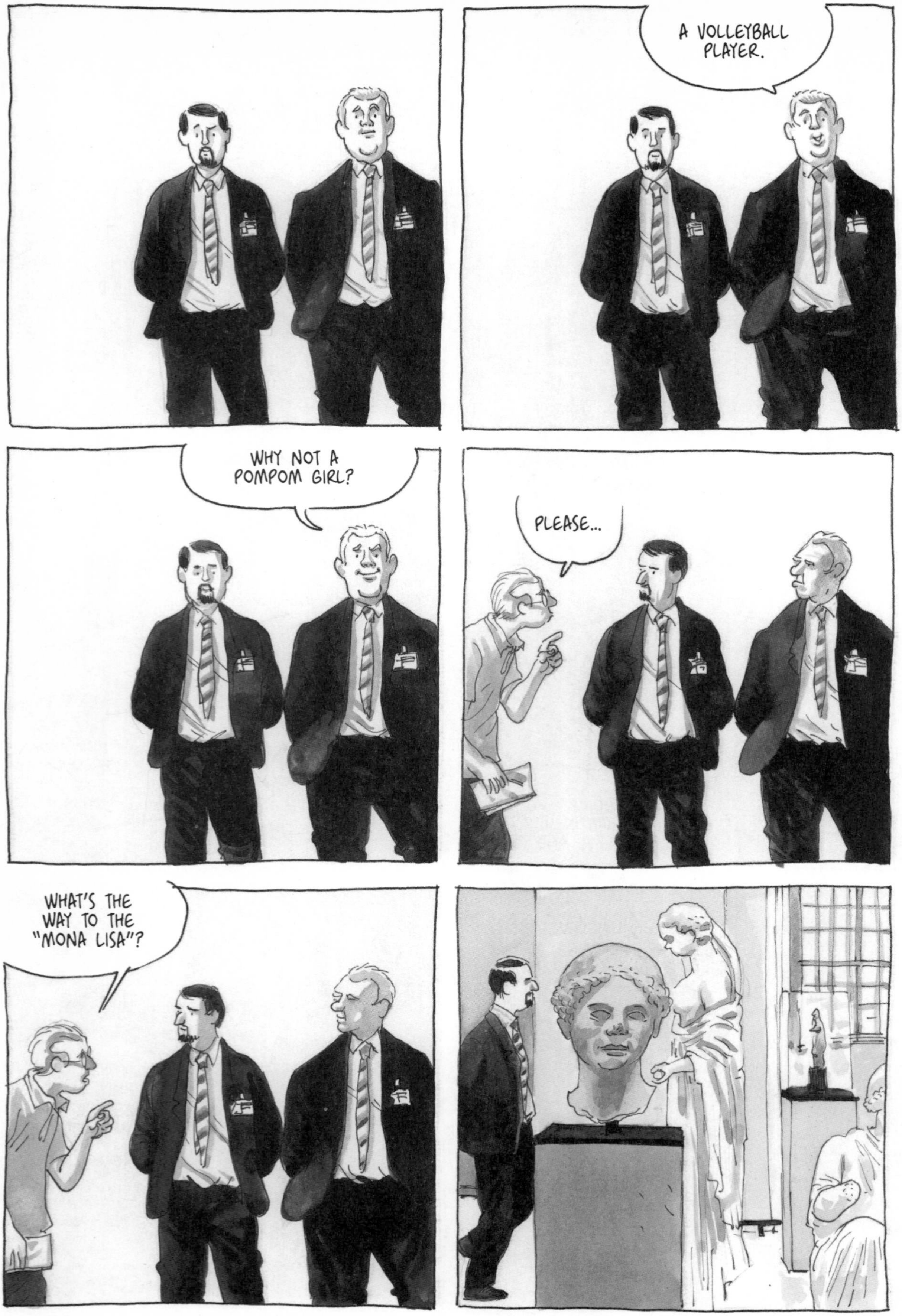
A VOLLEYBALL PLAYER.
WHY NOT A POMPOM GIRL?
PLEASE...
WHAT'S THE WAY TO THE "MONA LISA"?

Musée du Louvre
Entrée du personnel
YES, AN ORDINARY DAY, THAT'S ALL.

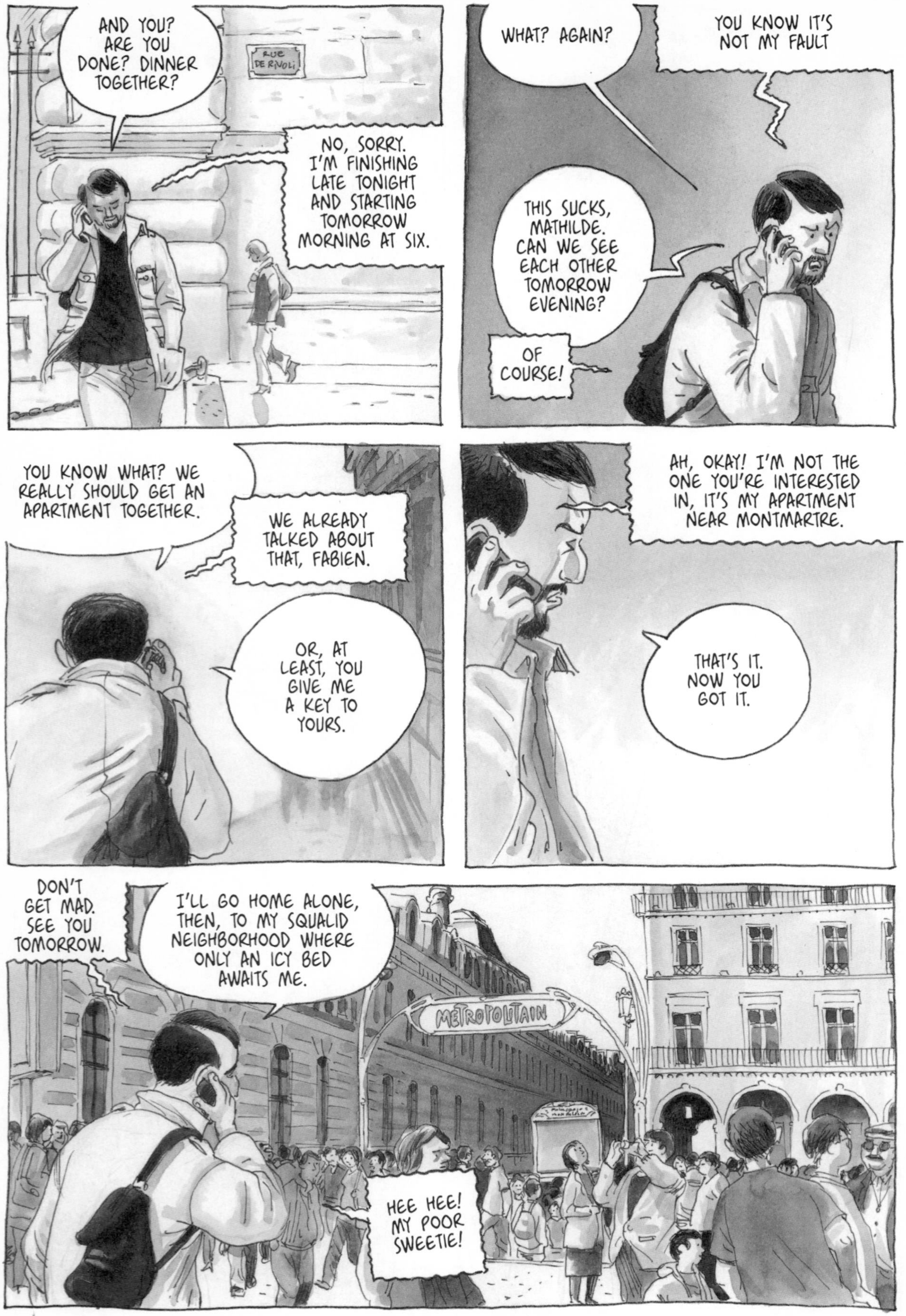
RUE DE RIVOLI
AND YOU? ARE YOU DONE? DINNER TOGETHER?
NO, SORRY. I'M FINISHING LATE TONIGHT AND STARTING TOMORROW MORNING AT SIX.
WHAT? AGAIN?
YOU KNOW IT'S NOT MY FAULT
THIS SUCKS, MATHILDE. CAN WE SEE EACH OTHER TOMORROW EVENING?
OF COURSE!
YOU KNOW WHAT? WE REALLY SHOULD GET AN APARTMENT TOGETHER.
WE ALREADY TALKED ABOUT THAT, FABIEN.
OR, AT LEAST, YOU GIVE ME A KEY TO YOURS.
AH, OKAY! I'M NOT THE ONE YOU'RE INTERESTED IN, IT'S MY APARTMENT NEAR MONTMARTRE.
THAT'S IT. NOW YOU GOT IT.
DON'T GET MAD. SEE YOU TOMORROW.
I'LL GO HOME ALONE, THEN, TO MY SQUALID NEIGHBORHOOD WHERE ONLY AN ICY BED AWAITS ME.
METROPOLITAIN
HEE HEE! MY POOR SWEETIE!

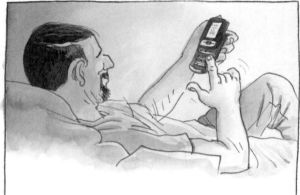

HELP, MATHILDE. I'M OVER AT SOME FRIENDS'. A HOT BLOND IS MAKING INDECENT PROPOSITIONS TO ME. NOT SURE I CAN RESIST. WISH ME LUCK.

I'LL BET MY OLD TEE-SHIRT YOU'RE SPRAWLING IN FRONT OF YOUR TV. I THINK I REMEMBER YOU HAVING AN "ICY BED" AT YOUR DISPOSAL. IT SHOULD COOL YOU DOWN. XOXOX.

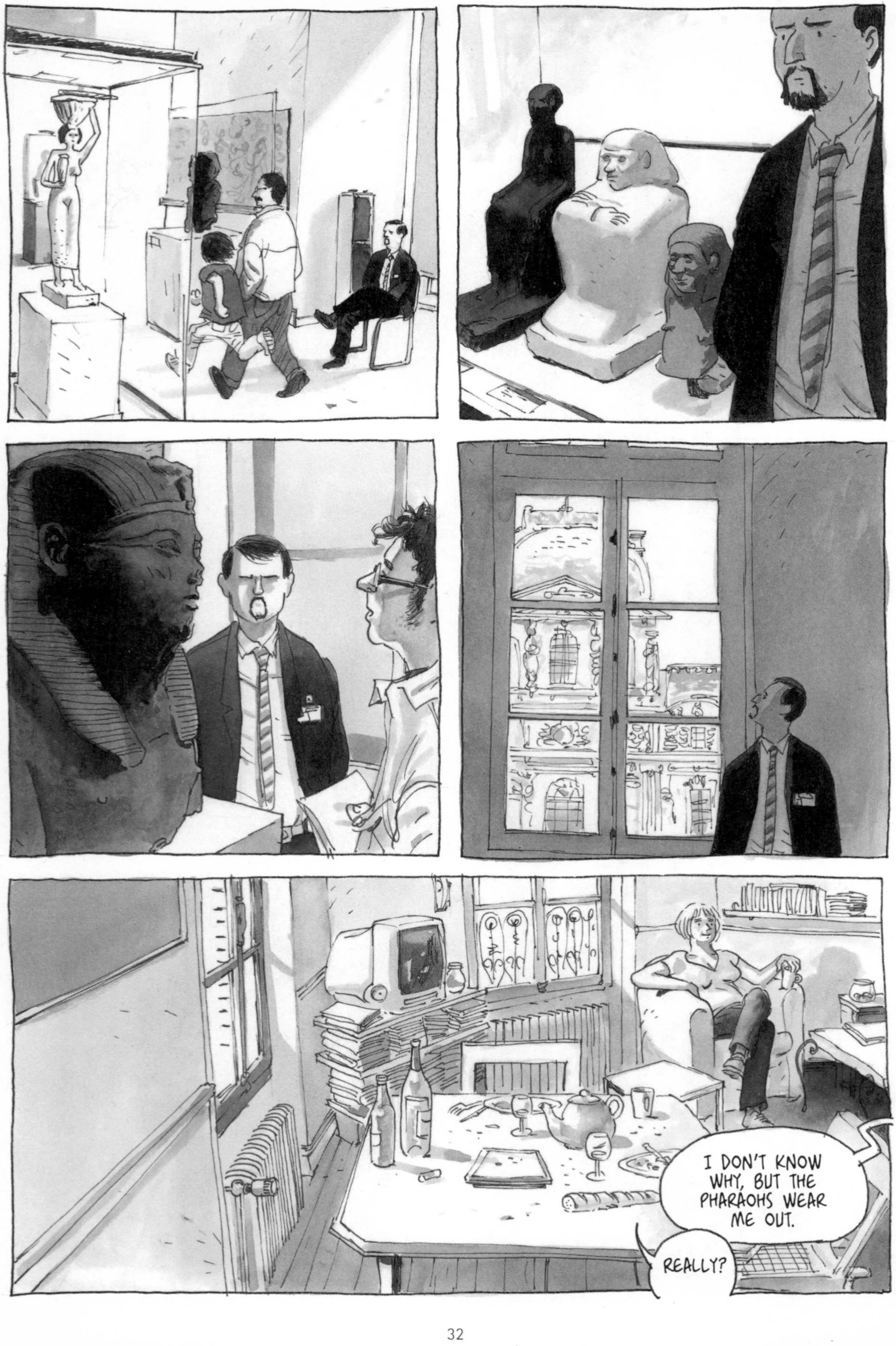
I DON'T KNOW WHY, BUT THE PHARAOHS WEAR ME OUT.
REALLY?

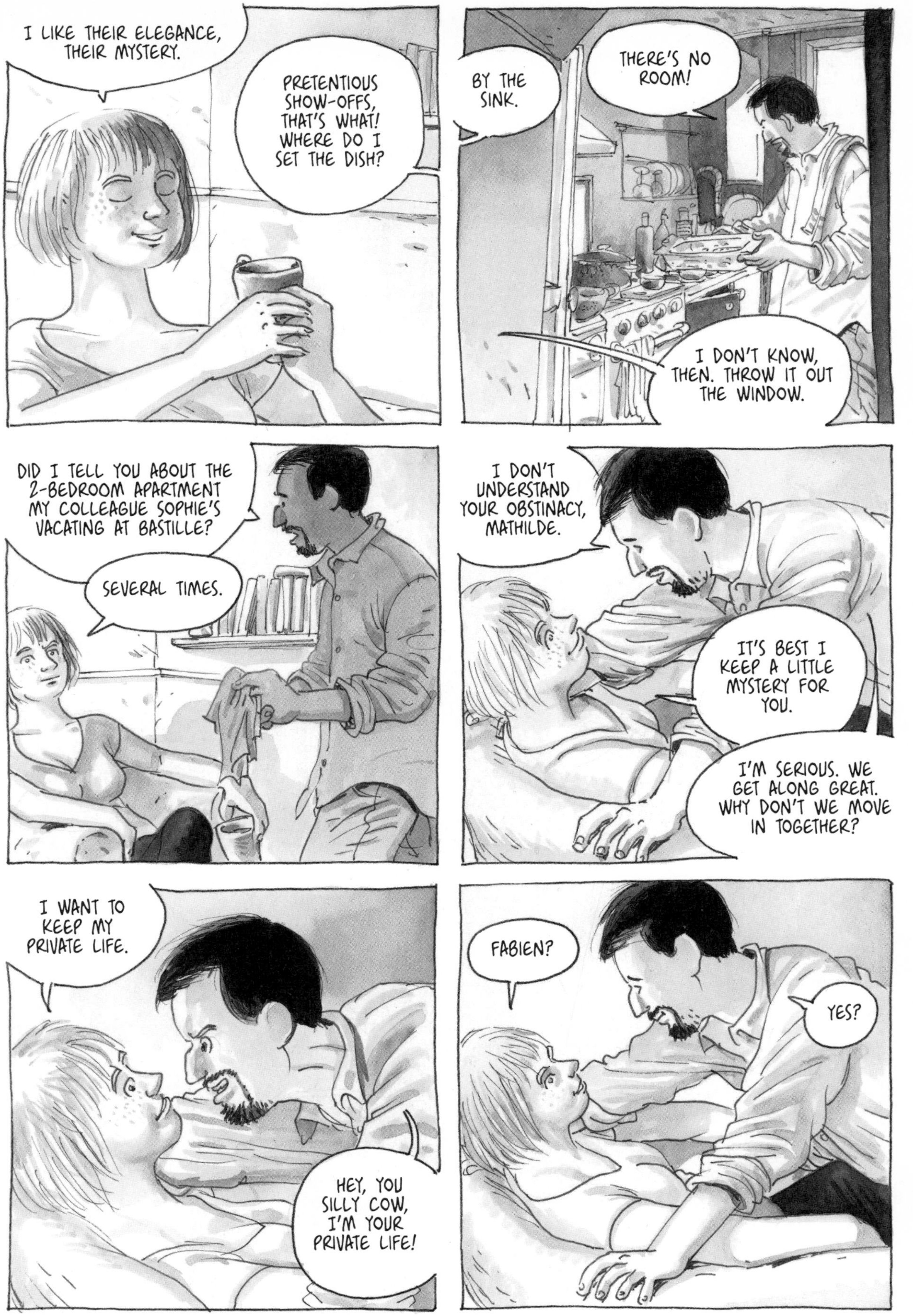
I LIKE THEIR ELEGANCE, THEIR MYSTERY.
PRETENTIOUS SHOW-OFFS, THAT'S WHAT! WHERE DO I SET THE DISH?
BY THE SINK.
THERE'S NO ROOM!
I DON'T KNOW, THEN. THROW IT OUT THE WINDOW.
DID I TELL YOU ABOUT THE 2-BEDROOM APARTMENT MY COLLEAGUE SOPHIE'S VACATING AT BASTILLE?
SEVERAL TIMES.
I DON'T UNDERSTAND YOUR OBSTINACY, MATHILDE.
IT'S BEST I KEEP A LITTLE MYSTERY FOR YOU.
I'M SERIOUS. WE GET ALONG GREAT. WHY DON'T WE MOVE IN TOGETHER?
I WANT TO KEEP MY PRIVATE LIFE.
HEY, YOU SILLY COW, I'M YOUR PRIVATE LIFE!
FABIEN?
YES?

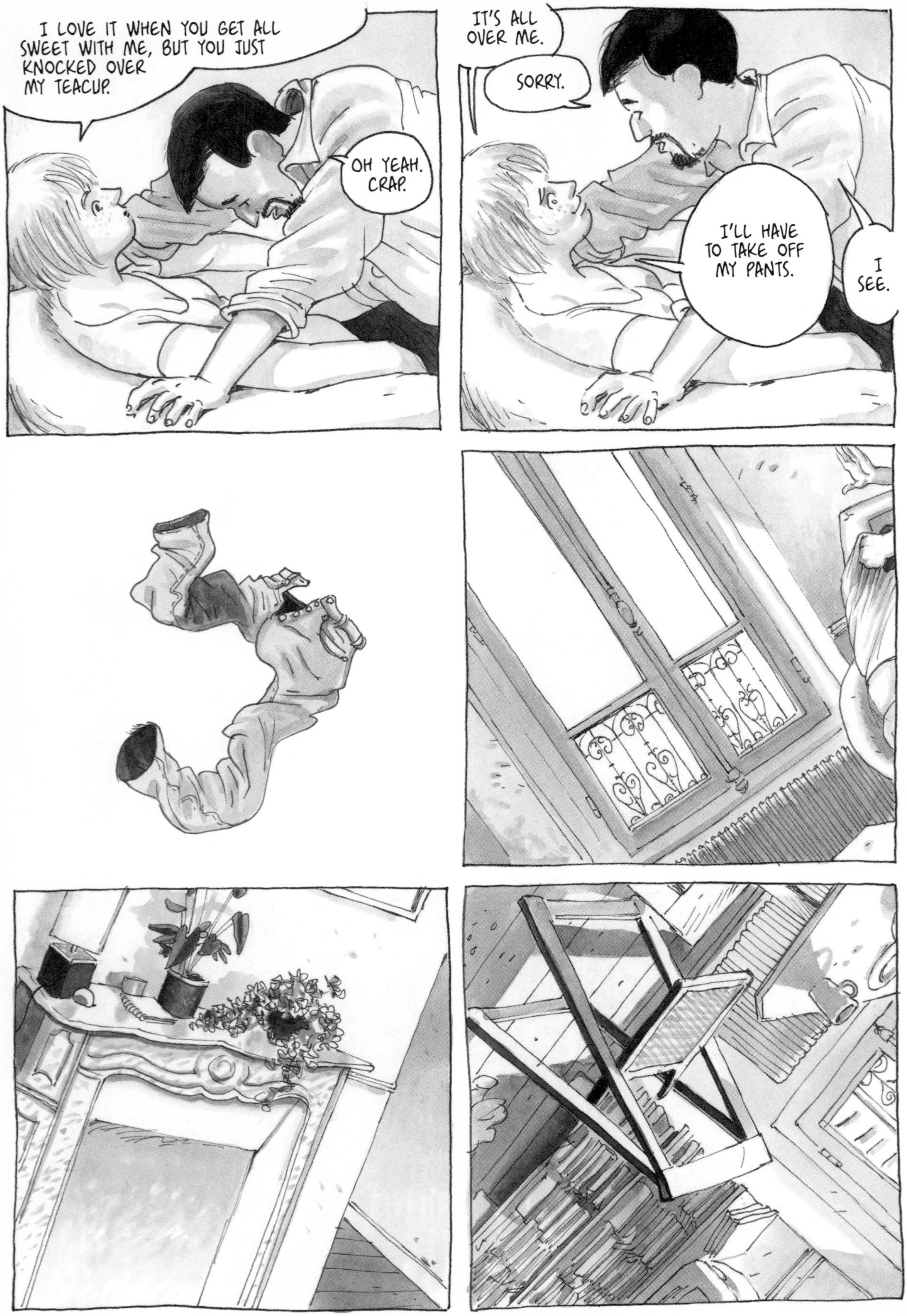
I LOVE IT WHEN YOU GET ALL SWEET WITH ME, BUT YOU JUST KNOCKED OVER MY TEACUP.
OH YEAH. CRAP.
IT'S ALL OVER ME.
SORRY.
I'LL HAVE TO TAKE OFF MY PANTS.
I SEE.

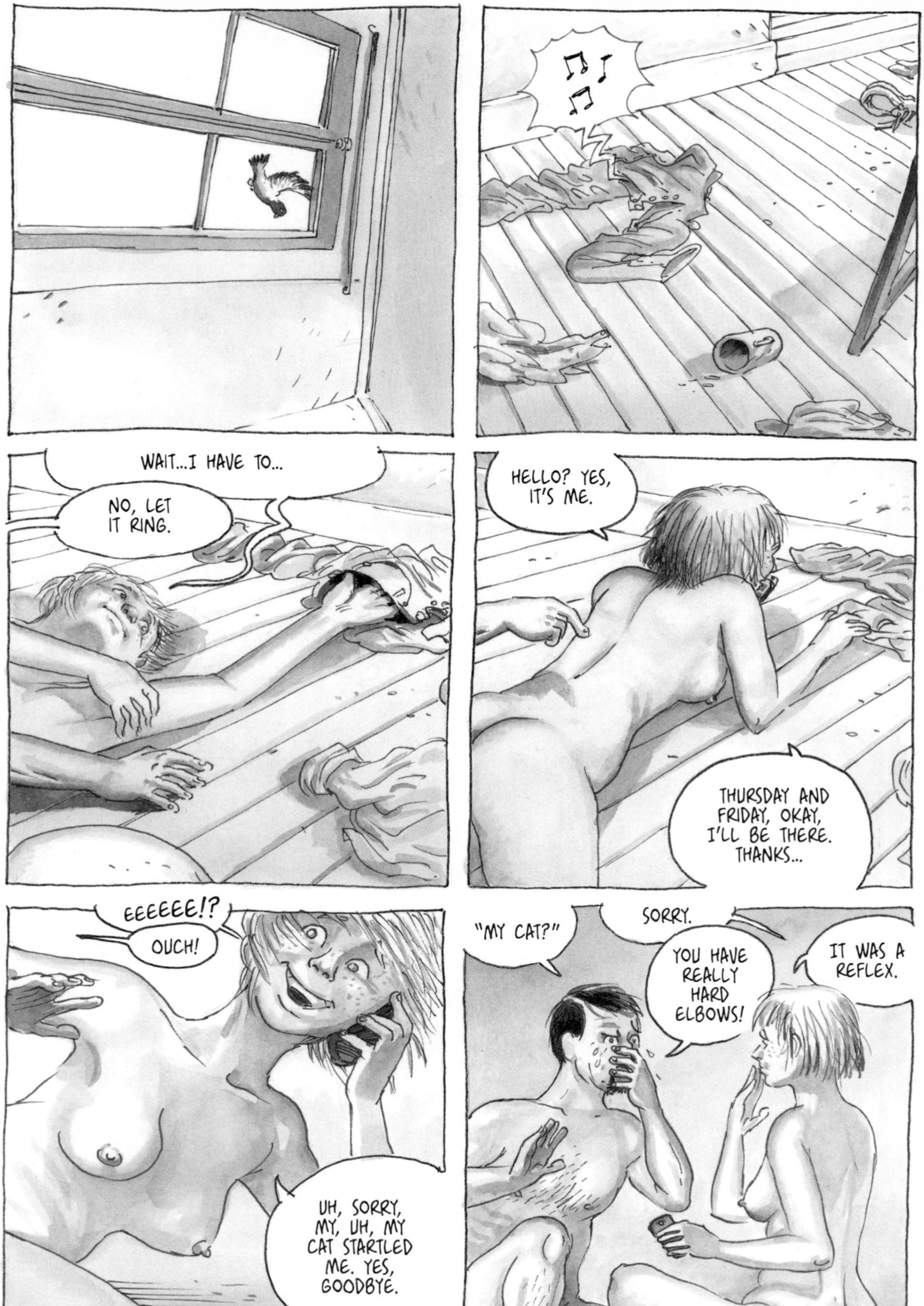
WAIT...I HAVE TO...
NO, LET IT RING.
HELLO? YES, IT'S ME.
THURSDAY AND FRIDAY, OKAY, I'LL BE THERE. THANKS...
EEEEEE!?
OUCH!
UH, SORRY, MY, UH, MY CAT STARTLED ME. YES, GOODBYE.
"MY CAT?"
SORRY.
YOU HAVE REALLY HARD ELBOWS!
IT WAS A REFLEX.

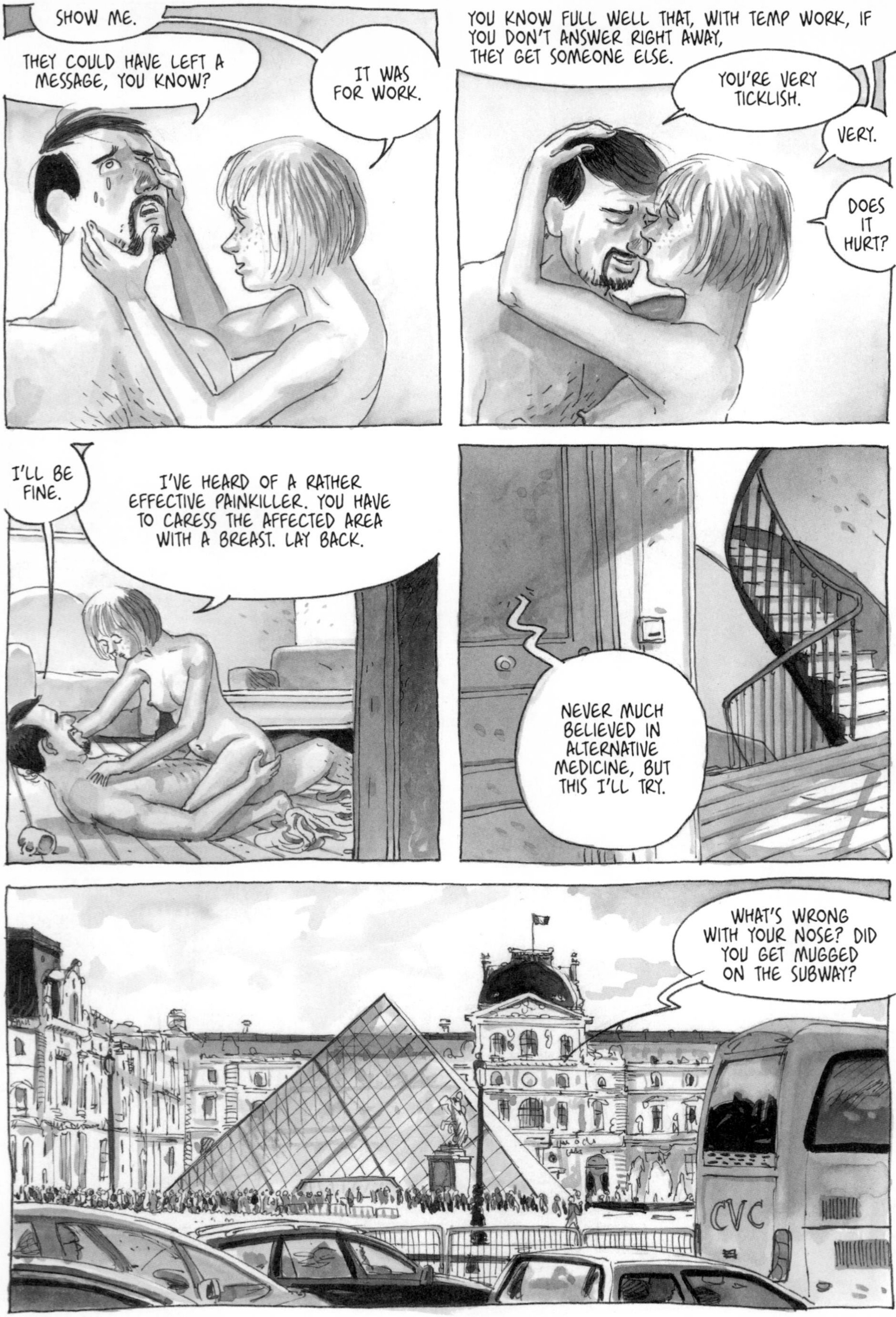
SHOW ME.
THEY COULD HAVE LEFT A MESSAGE, YOU KNOW?
IT WAS FOR WORK.
YOU KNOW FULL WELL THAT, WITH TEMP WORK, IF YOU DON'T ANSWER RIGHT AWAY, THEY GET SOMEONE ELSE.
YOU'RE VERY TICKLISH.
VERY.
DOES IT HURT?
I'LL BE FINE.
I'VE HEARD OF A RATHER EFFECTIVE PAINKILLER. YOU HAVE TO CARESS THE AFFECTED AREA WITH A BREAST. LAY BACK.
NEVER MUCH BELIEVED IN ALTERNATIVE MEDICINE, BUT THIS I'LL TRY.
WHAT'S WRONG WITH YOUR NOSE? DID YOU GET MUGGED ON THE SUBWAY?
CVC

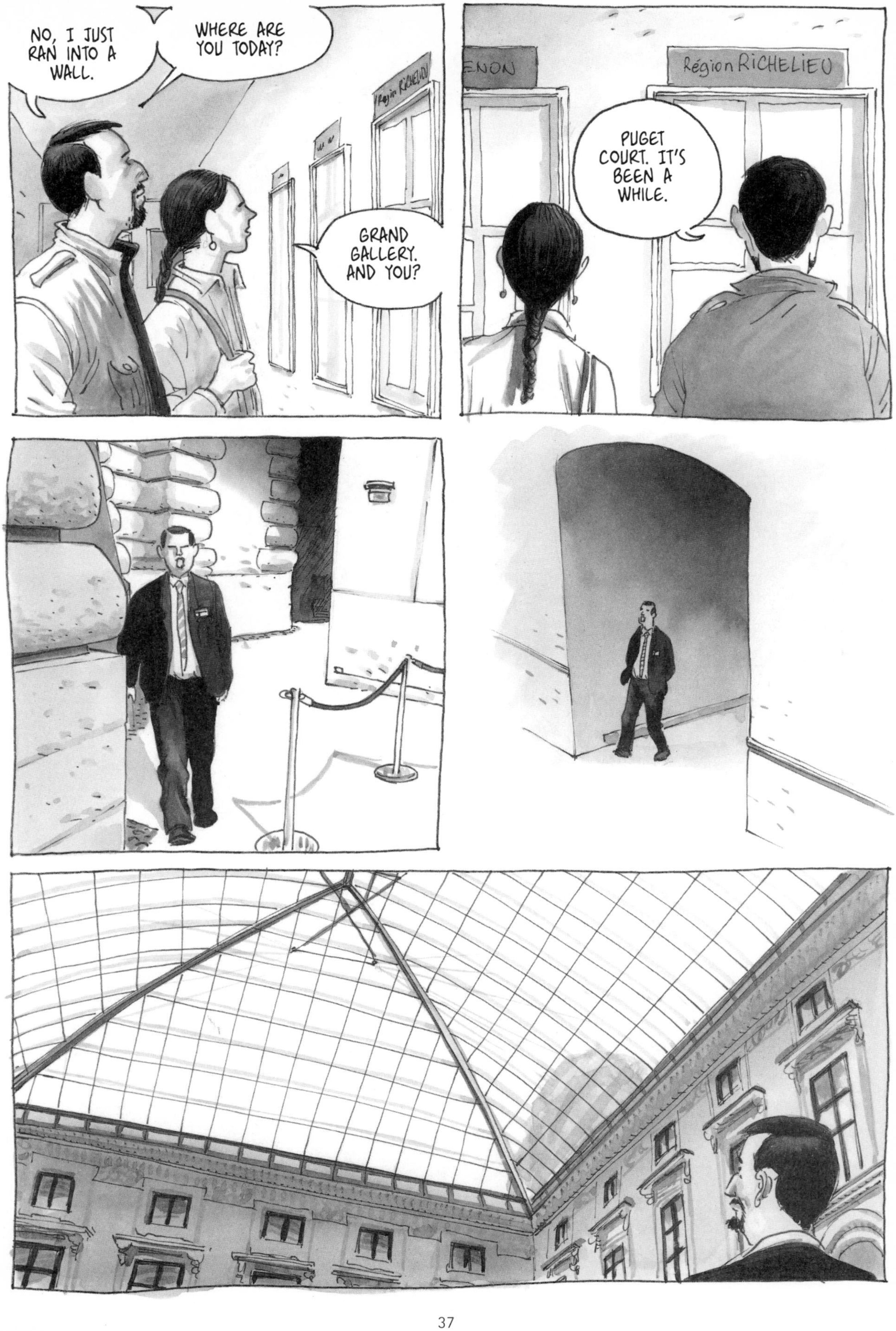
NO, I JUST RAN INTO A WALL.
WHERE ARE YOU TODAY?
Région RICHELIEU
GRAND GALLERY. AND YOU?
ENON
Région RICHELIEU
PUGET COURT. IT'S BEEN A WHILE.

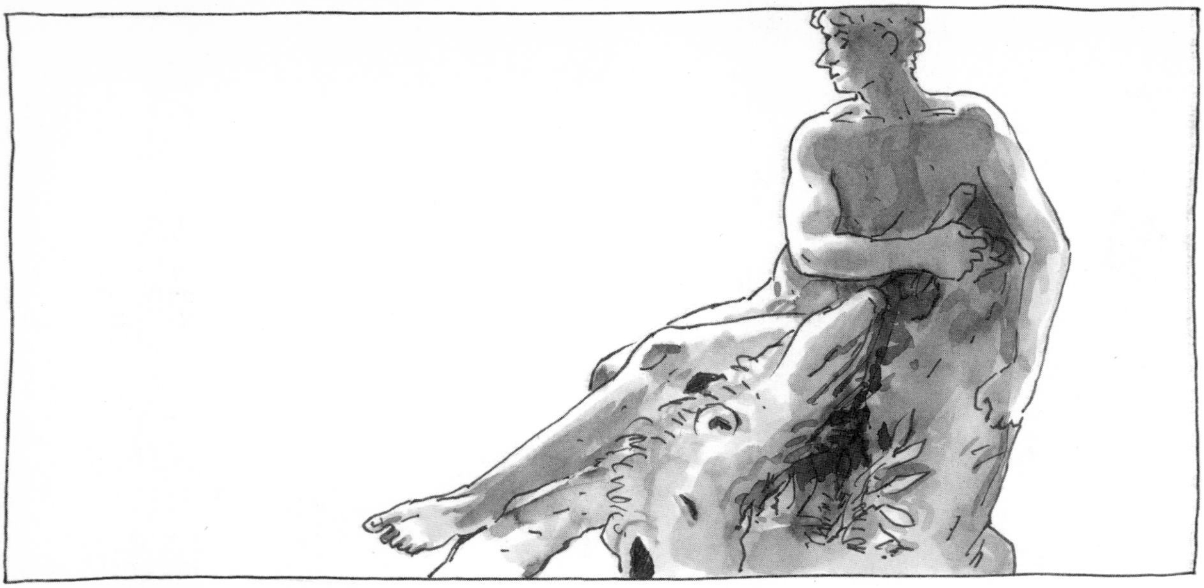
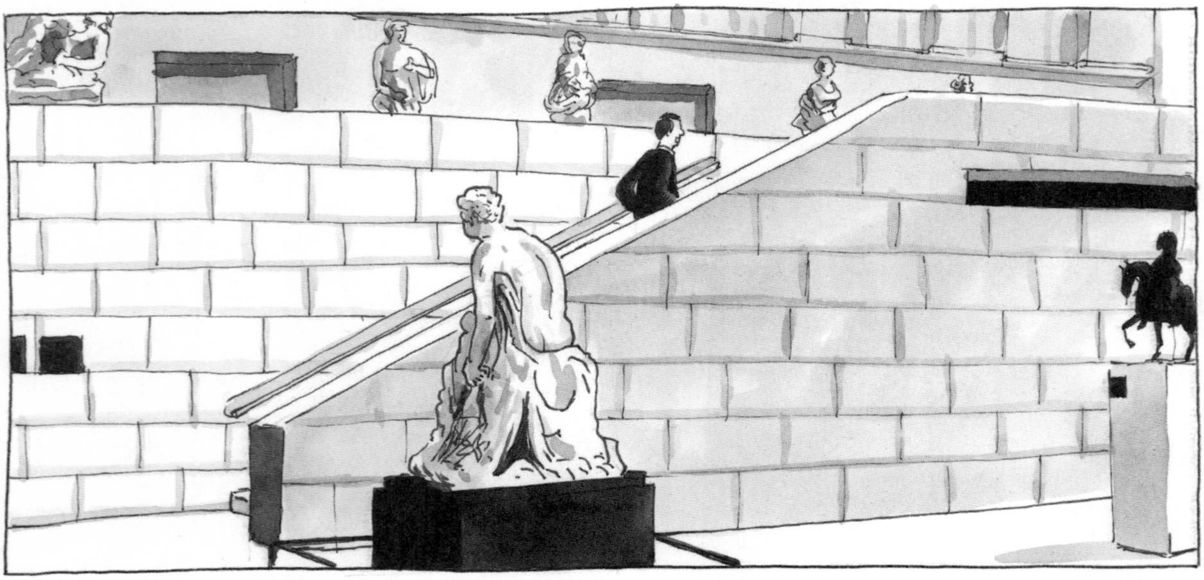
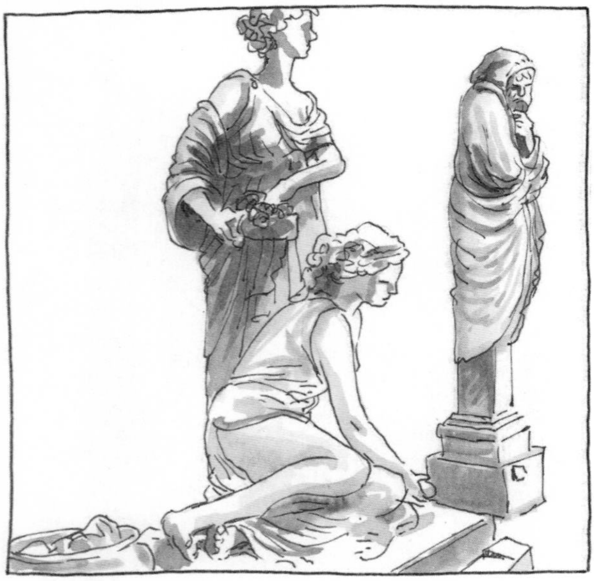
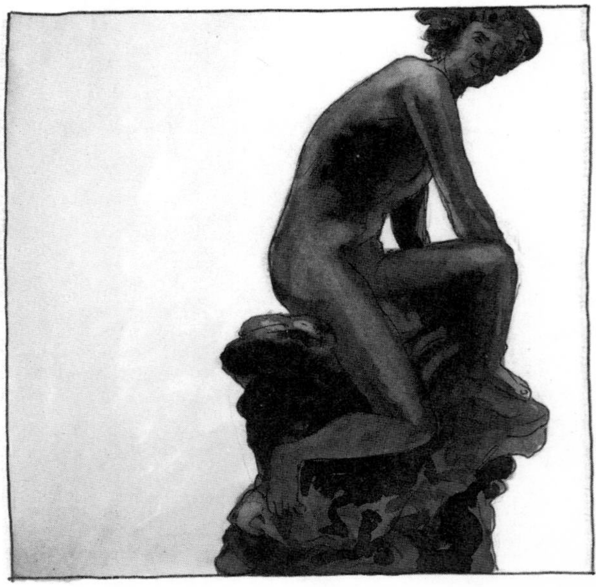

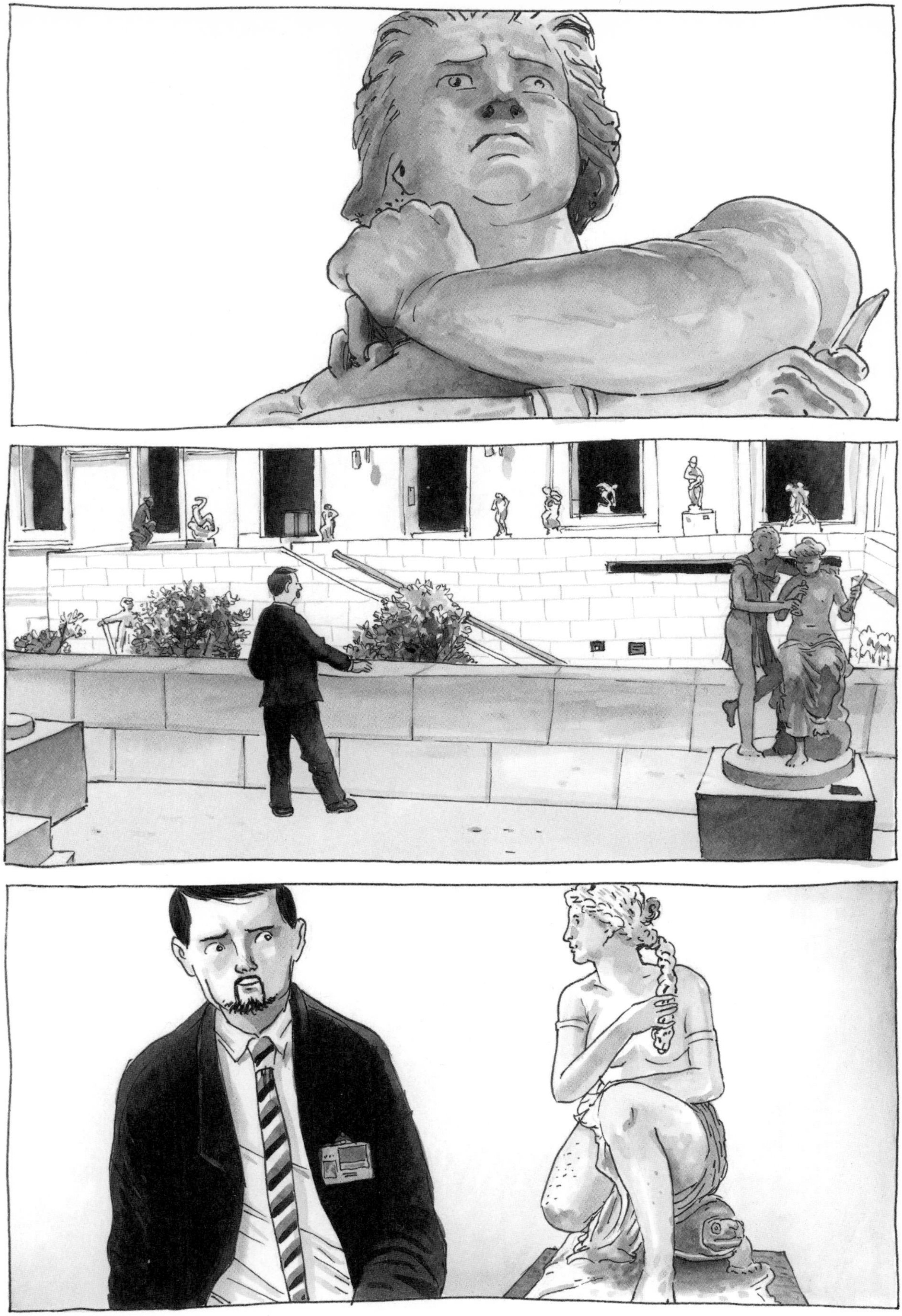

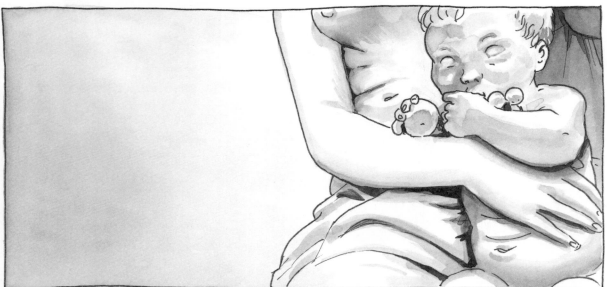

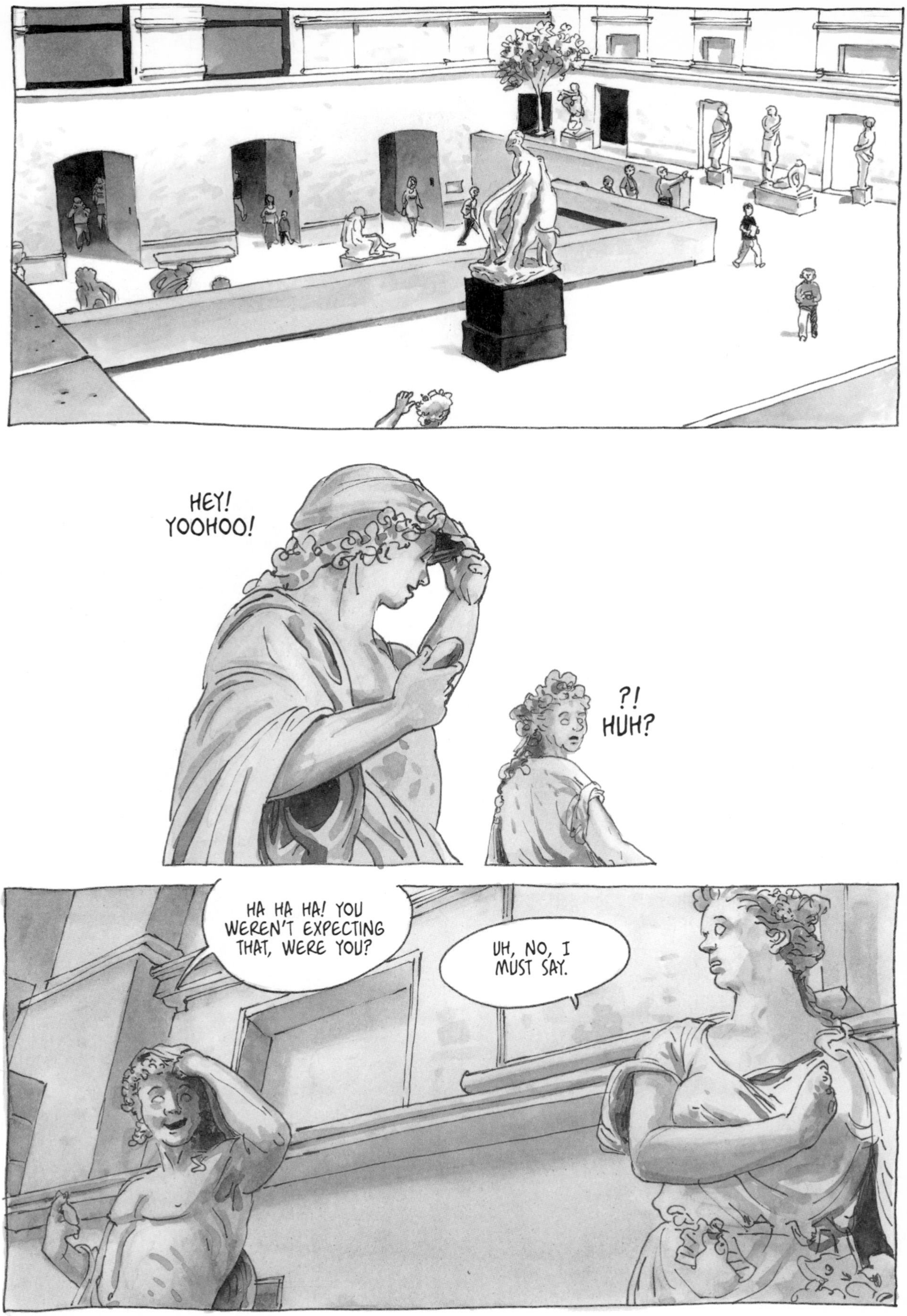
HEY!
YOOHOO!
?!
HUH?
HA HA HA! YOU WEREN'T EXPECTING THAT, WERE YOU?
UH, NO, I MUST SAY.

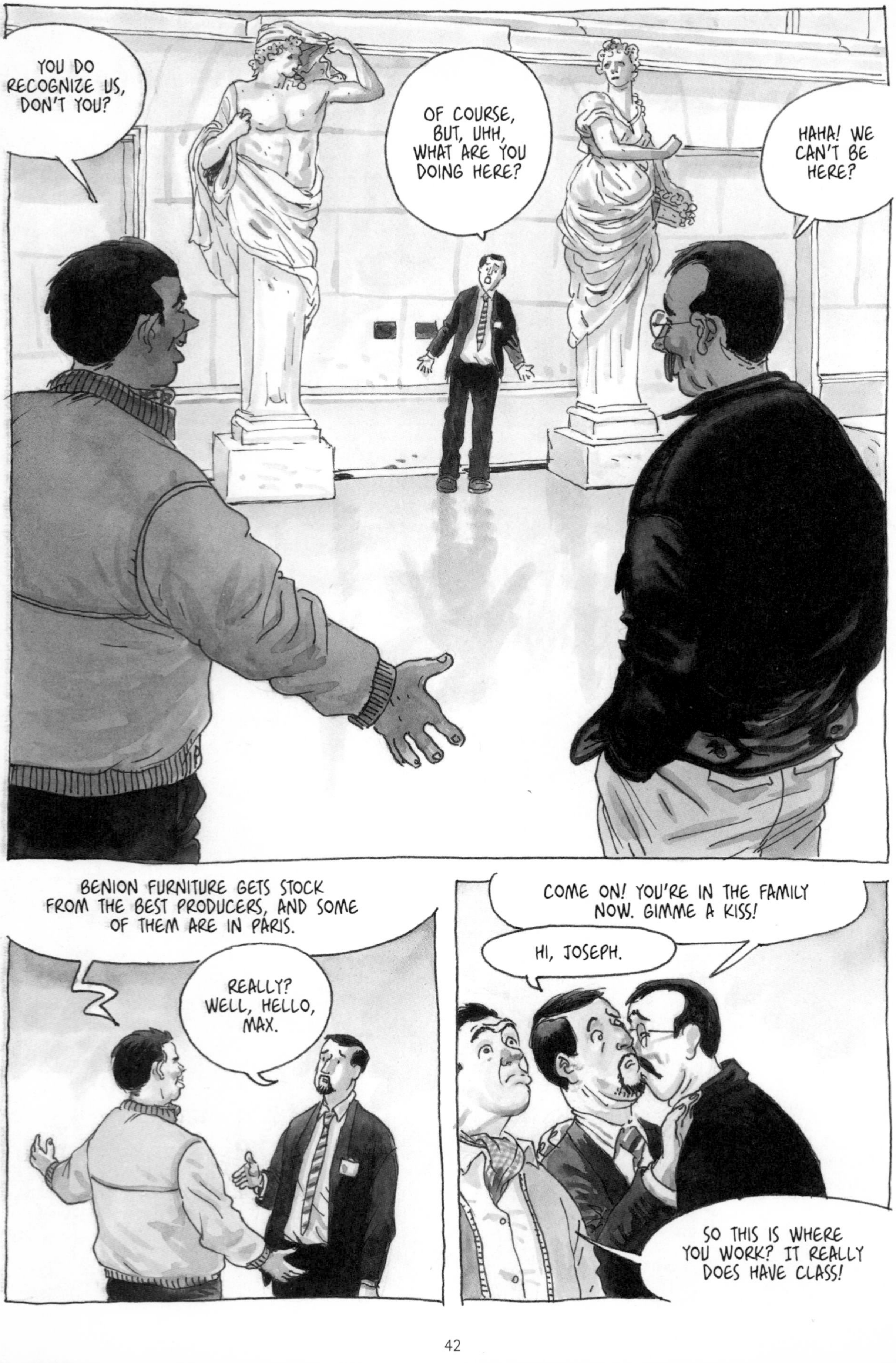
YOU DO RECOGNIZE US, DON'T YOU?
OF COURSE, BUT, UHH, WHAT ARE YOU DOING HERE?
HAHA! WE CAN'T BE HERE?
BENION FURNITURE GETS STOCK FROM THE BEST PRODUCERS, AND SOME OF THEM ARE IN PARIS.
REALLY? WELL, HELLO, MAX.
COME ON! YOU'RE IN THE FAMILY NOW. GIMME A KISS!
HI, JOSEPH.
SO THIS IS WHERE YOU WORK? IT REALLY DOES HAVE CLASS!

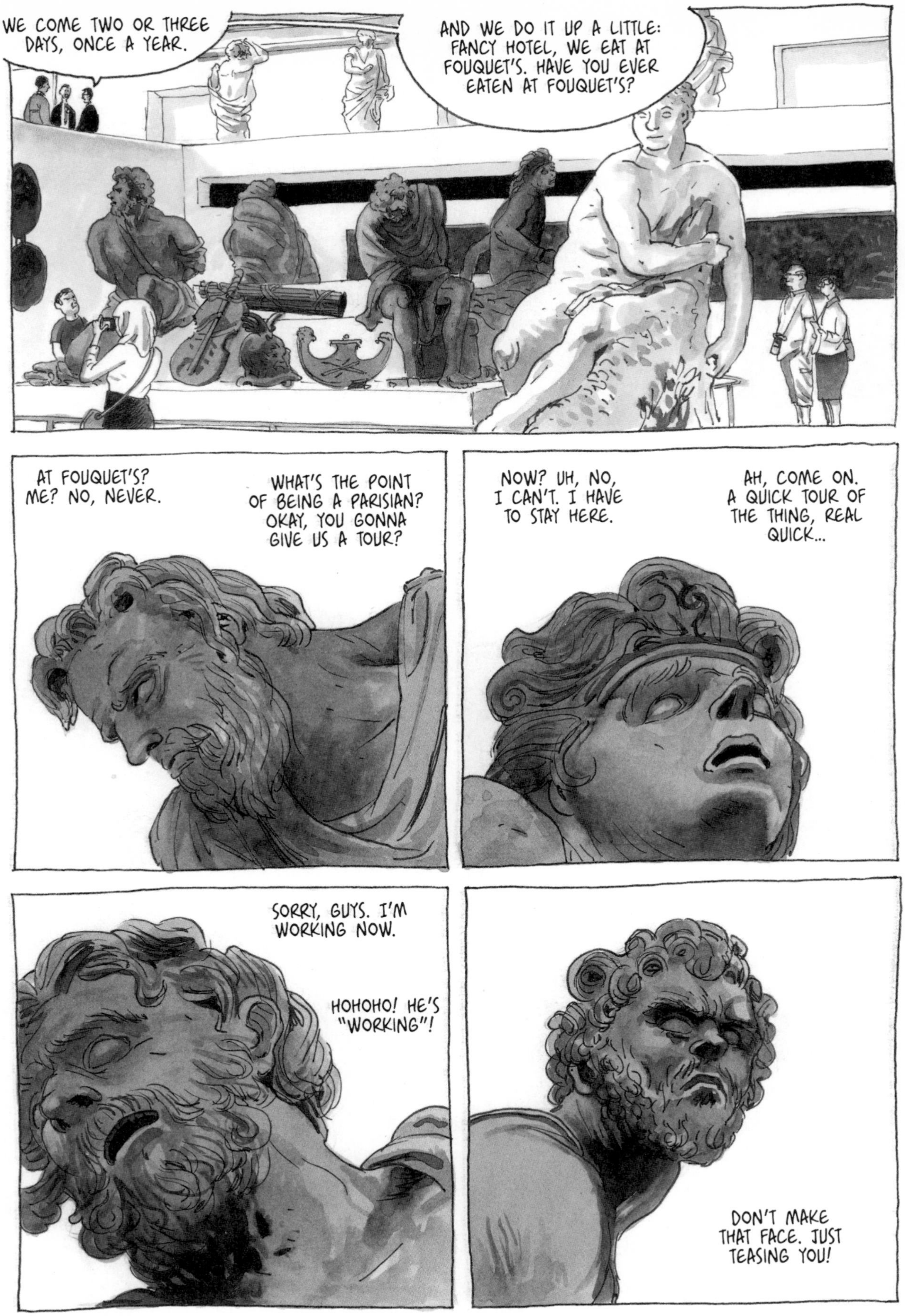
WE COME TWO OR THREE DAYS, ONCE A YEAR.
AND WE DO IT UP A LITTLE: FANCY HOTEL, WE EAT AT FOUQUET'S. HAVE YOU EVER EATEN AT FOUQUET'S?
AT FOUQUET'S? ME? NO, NEVER.
WHAT'S THE POINT OF BEING A PARISIAN? OKAY, YOU GONNA GIVE US A TOUR?
NOW? UH, NO, I CAN'T. I HAVE TO STAY HERE.
AH, COME ON. A QUICK TOUR OF THE THING, REAL QUICK...
SORRY, GUYS. I'M WORKING NOW.
HOHOHO! HE'S "WORKING"!
DON'T MAKE THAT FACE. JUST TEASING YOU!

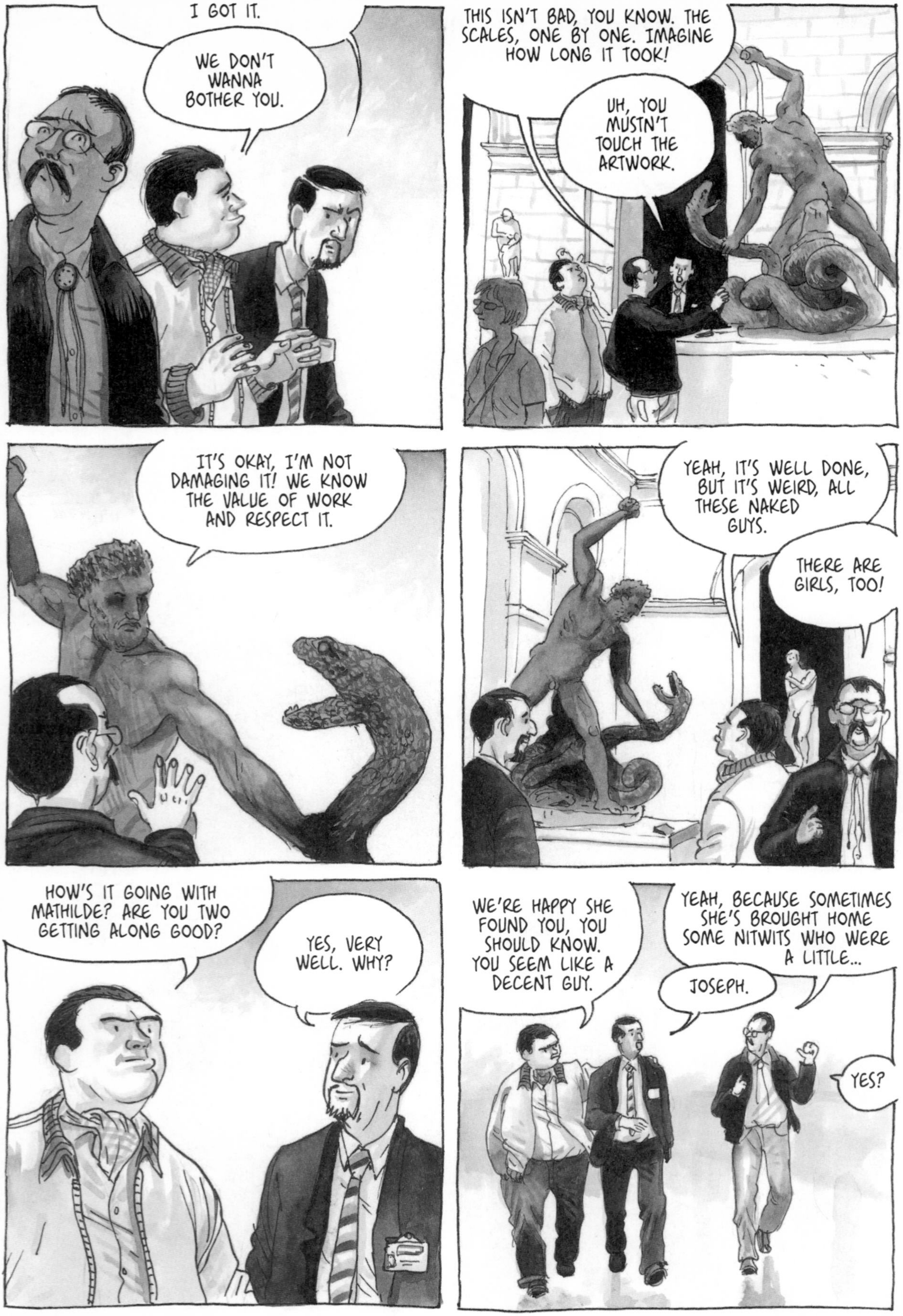
I GOT IT.
WE DON'T WANNA BOTHER YOU.
THIS ISN'T BAD, YOU KNOW. THE SCALES, ONE BY ONE. IMAGINE HOW LONG IT TOOK!
UH, YOU MUSTN'T TOUCH THE ARTWORK.
IT'S OKAY, I'M NOT DAMAGING IT! WE KNOW THE VALUE OF WORK AND RESPECT IT.
YEAH, IT'S WELL DONE, BUT IT'S WEIRD, ALL THESE NAKED GUYS.
THERE ARE GIRLS, TOO!
HOW'S IT GOING WITH MATHILDE? ARE YOU TWO GETTING ALONG GOOD?
YES, VERY WELL. WHY?
WE'RE HAPPY SHE FOUND YOU, YOU SHOULD KNOW. YOU SEEM LIKE A DECENT GUY.
YEAH, BECAUSE SOMETIMES SHE'S BROUGHT HOME SOME NITWITS WHO WERE A LITTLE...
JOSEPH.
YES?

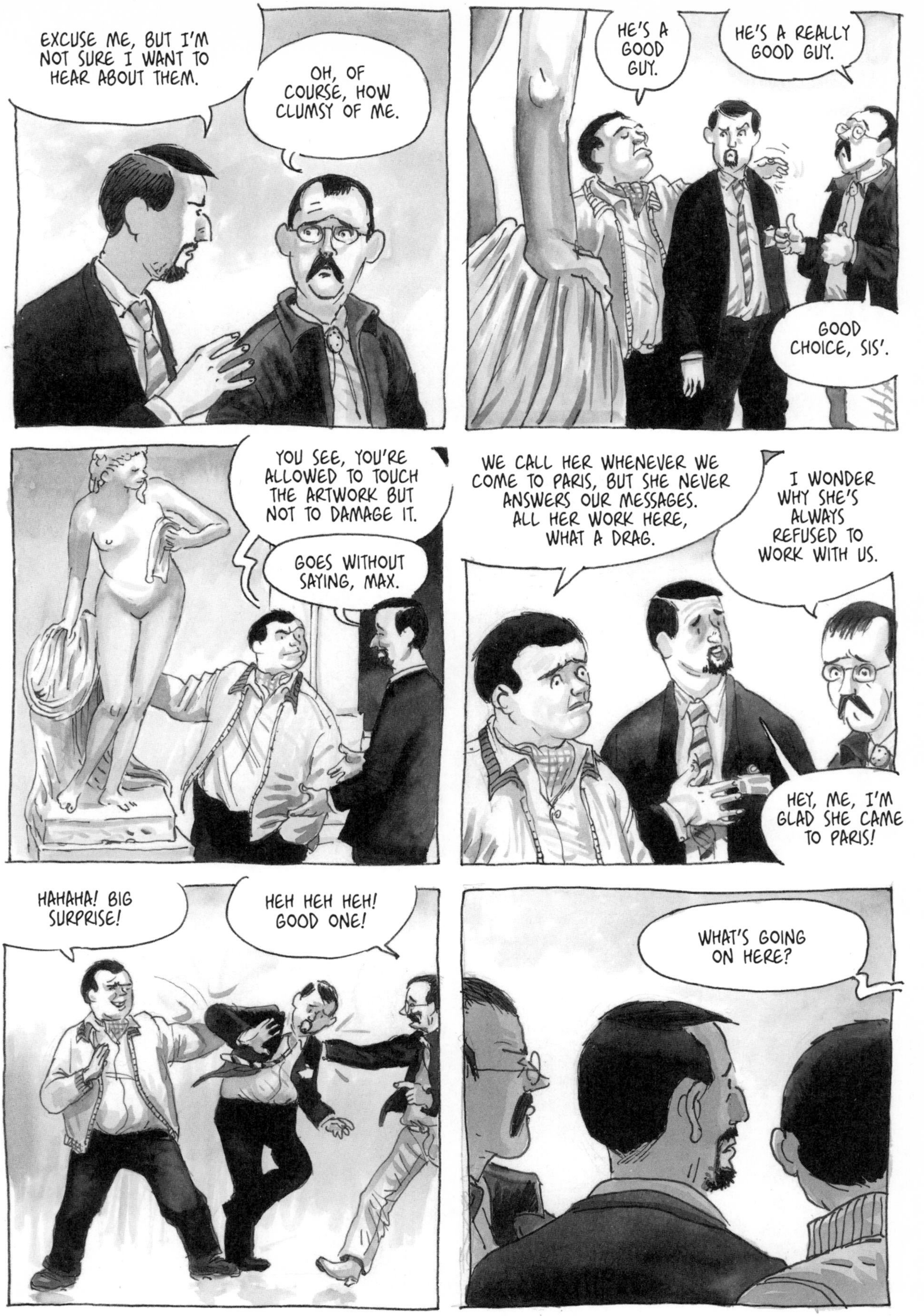
EXCUSE ME, BUT I'M NOT SURE I WANT TO HEAR ABOUT THEM.
OH, OF COURSE, HOW CLUMSY OF ME.
HE'S A GOOD GUY.
HE'S A REALLY GOOD GUY.
GOOD CHOICE, SIS'.
YOU SEE, YOU'RE ALLOWED TO TOUCH THE ARTWORK BUT NOT TO DAMAGE IT.
GOES WITHOUT SAYING, MAX.
WE CALL HER WHENEVER WE COME TO PARIS, BUT SHE NEVER ANSWERS OUR MESSAGES. ALL HER WORK HERE, WHAT A DRAG.
I WONDER WHY SHE'S ALWAYS REFUSED TO WORK WITH US.
HEY, ME, I'M GLAD SHE CAME TO PARIS!
HAHAHA! BIG SURPRISE!
HEH HEH HEH! GOOD ONE!
WHAT'S GOING ON HERE?

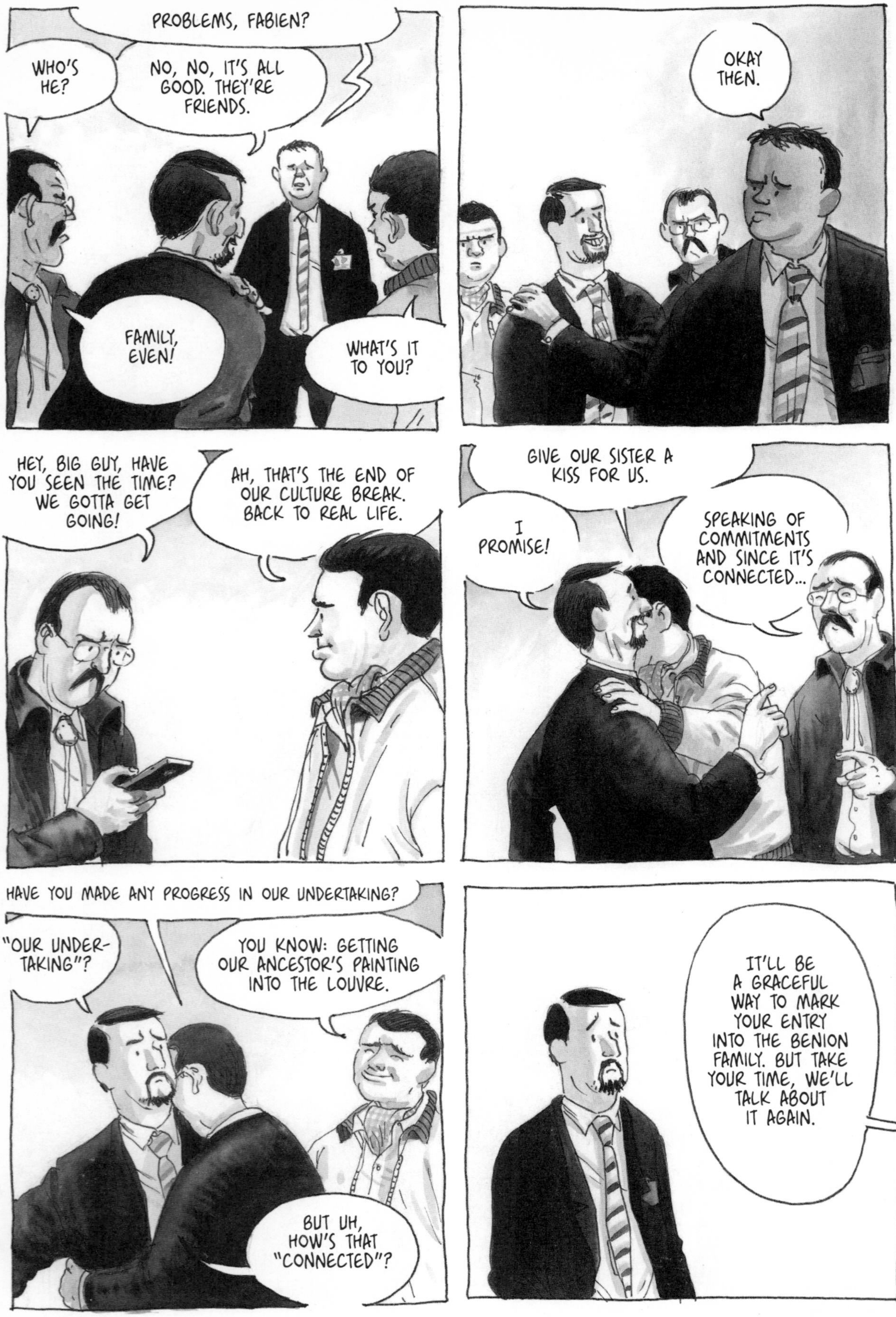
PROBLEMS, FABIEN?
WHO'S HE?
NO, NO, IT'S ALL GOOD. THEY'RE FRIENDS.
FAMILY, EVEN!
WHAT'S IT TO YOU?
OKAY THEN.
HEY, BIG GUY, HAVE YOU SEEN THE TIME? WE GOTTA GET GOING!
AH, THAT'S THE END OF OUR CULTURE BREAK. BACK TO REAL LIFE.
GIVE OUR SISTER A KISS FOR US.
I PROMISE!
SPEAKING OF COMMITMENTS AND SINCE IT'S CONNECTED...
HAVE YOU MADE ANY PROGRESS IN OUR UNDERTAKING?
"OUR UNDER-TAKING"?
YOU KNOW: GETTING OUR ANCESTOR'S PAINTING INTO THE LOUVRE.
BUT UH, HOW'S THAT "CONNECTED"?
IT'LL BE A GRACEFUL WAY TO MARK YOUR ENTRY INTO THE BENION FAMILY. BUT TAKE YOUR TIME, WE'LL TALK ABOUT IT AGAIN.

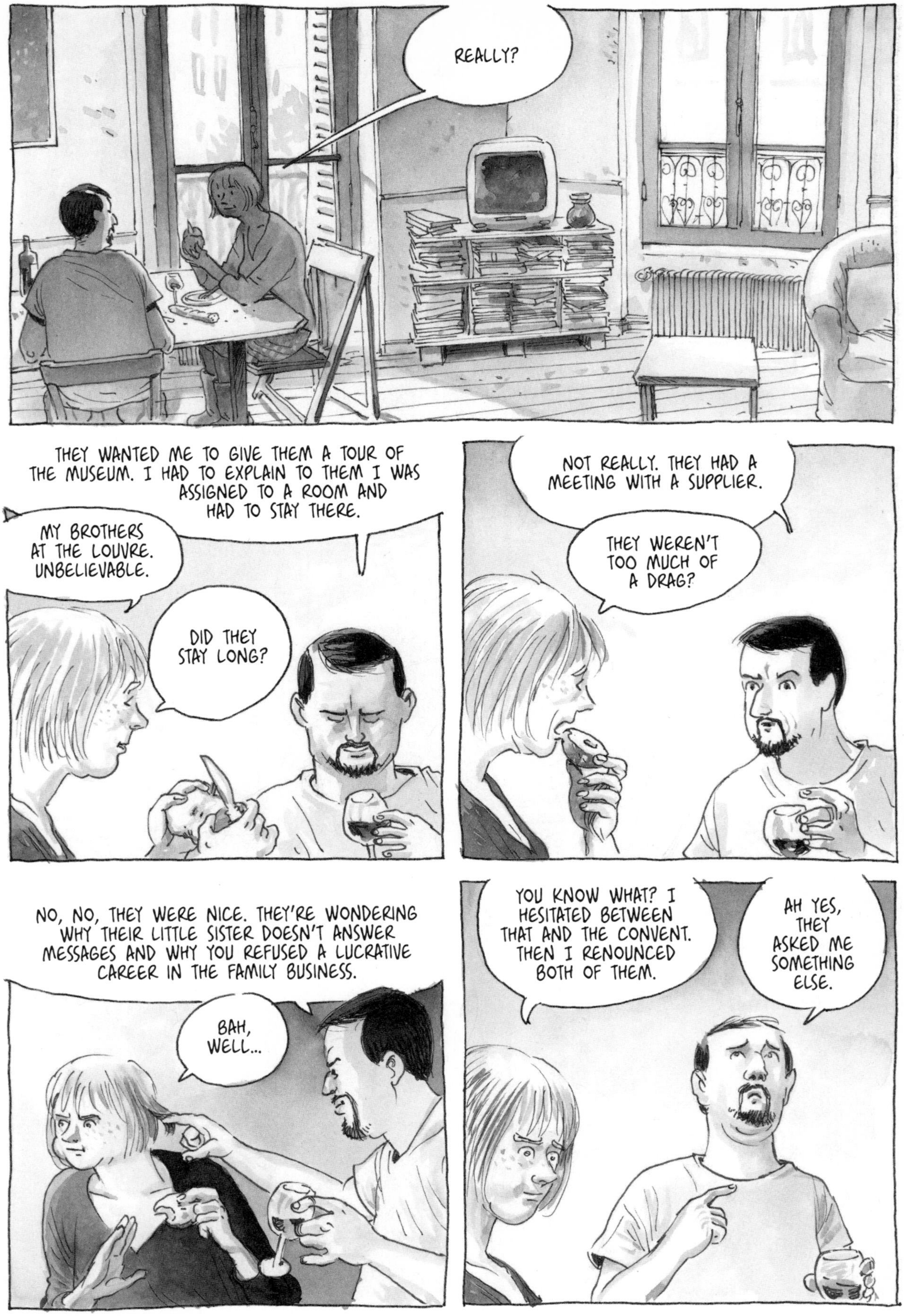
REALLY?
THEY WANTED ME TO GIVE THEM A TOUR OF THE MUSEUM. I HAD TO EXPLAIN TO THEM I WAS ASSIGNED TO A ROOM AND HAD TO STAY THERE.
MY BROTHERS AT THE LOUVRE. UNBELIEVABLE.
DID THEY STAY LONG?
NOT REALLY. THEY HAD A MEETING WITH A SUPPLIER.
THEY WEREN'T TOO MUCH OF A DRAG?
NO, NO, THEY WERE NICE. THEY'RE WONDERING WHY THEIR LITTLE SISTER DOESN'T ANSWER MESSAGES AND WHY YOU REFUSED A LUCRATIVE CAREER IN THE FAMILY BUSINESS.
BAH, WELL...
YOU KNOW WHAT? I HESITATED BETWEEN THAT AND THE CONVENT. THEN I RENOUNCED BOTH OF THEM.
AH YES, THEY ASKED ME SOMETHING ELSE.

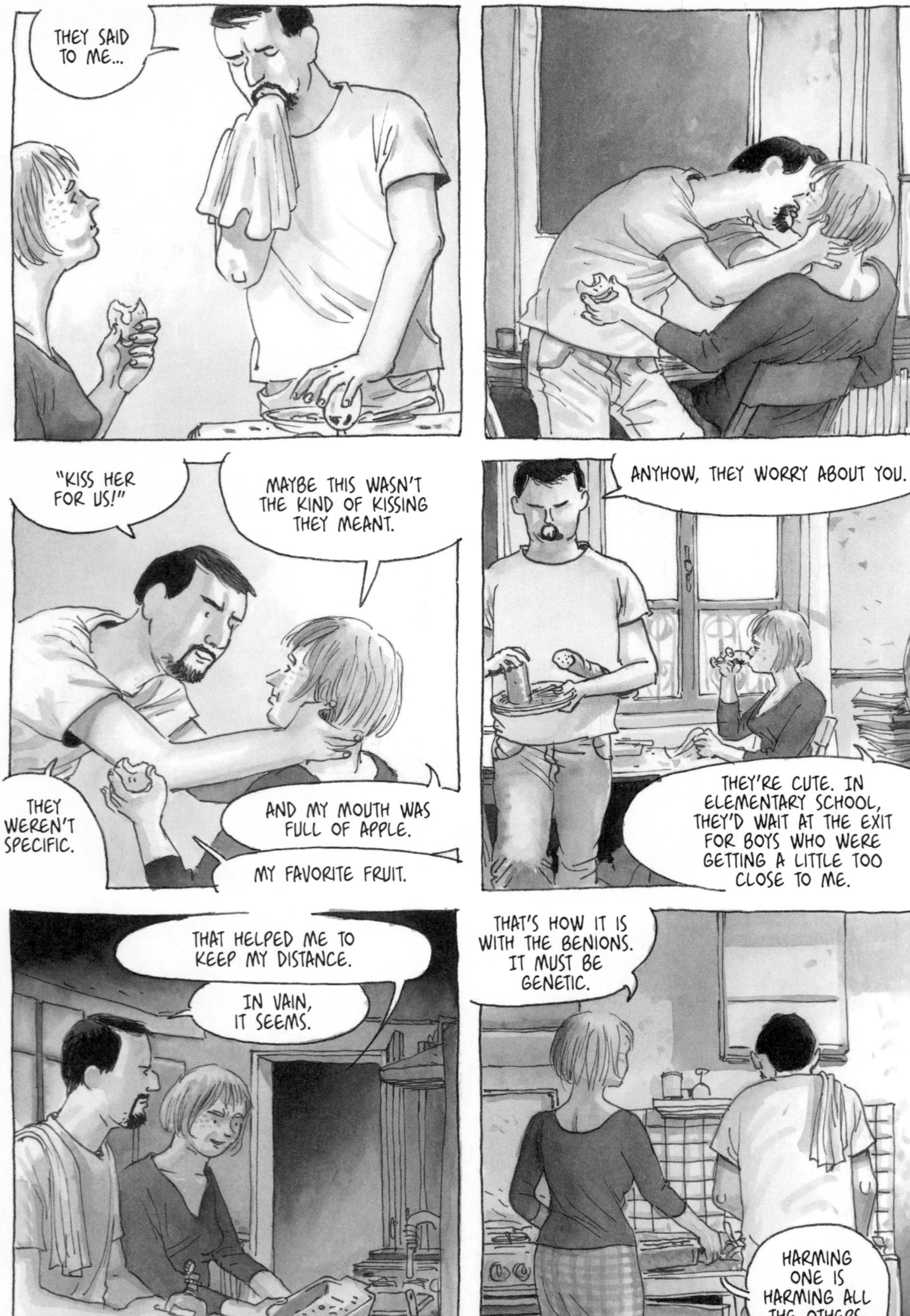
THEY SAID TO ME...
"KISS HER FOR US!"
MAYBE THIS WASN'T THE KIND OF KISSING THEY MEANT.
THEY WEREN'T SPECIFIC.
AND MY MOUTH WAS FULL OF APPLE.
MY FAVORITE FRUIT.
ANYHOW, THEY WORRY ABOUT YOU.
THEY'RE CUTE. IN ELEMENTARY SCHOOL, THEY'D WAIT AT THE EXIT FOR BOYS WHO WERE GETTING A LITTLE TOO CLOSE TO ME.
THAT HELPED ME TO KEEP MY DISTANCE.
IN VAIN, IT SEEMS.
THAT'S HOW IT IS WITH THE BENIONS. IT MUST BE GENETIC.
HARMING ONE IS HARMING ALL THE OTHERS.

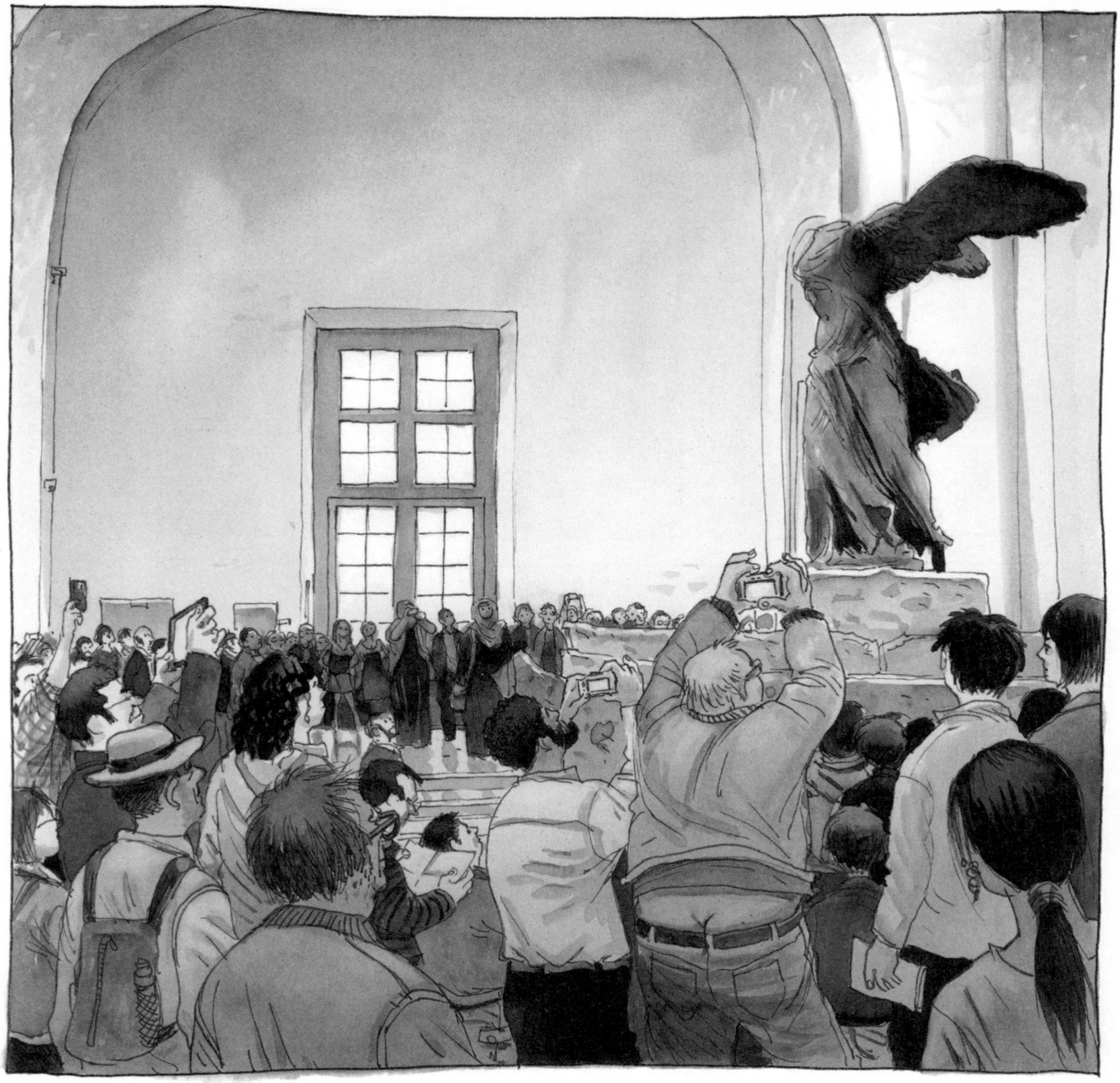

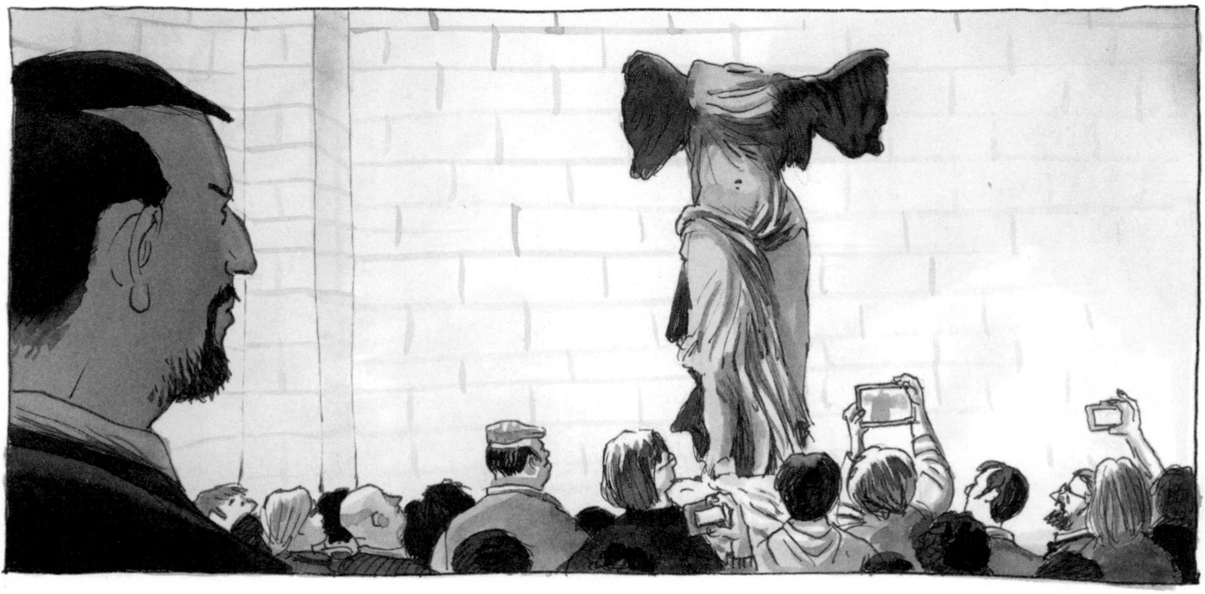

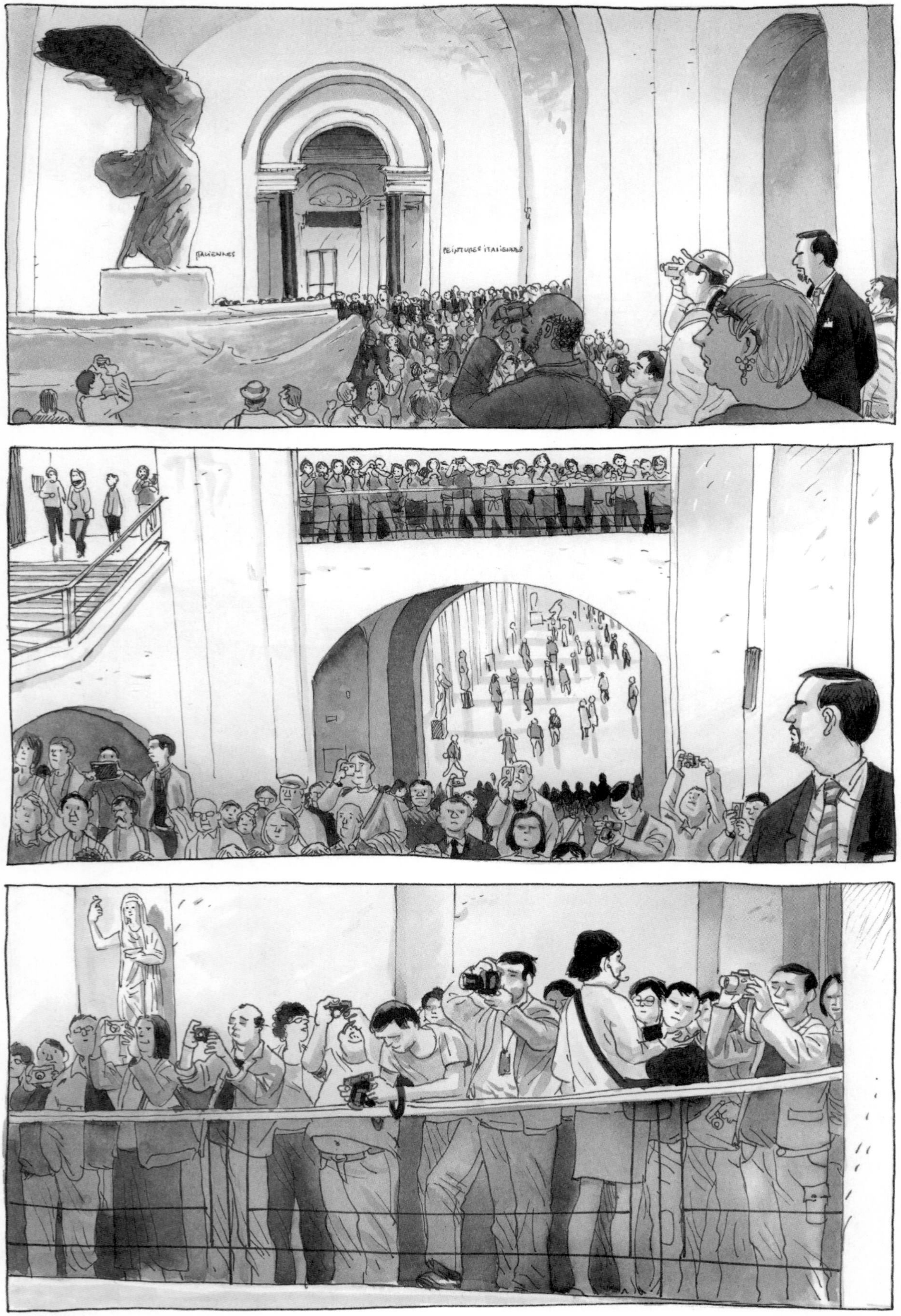

ITALIENNES
PEINTURES ITALIENNES

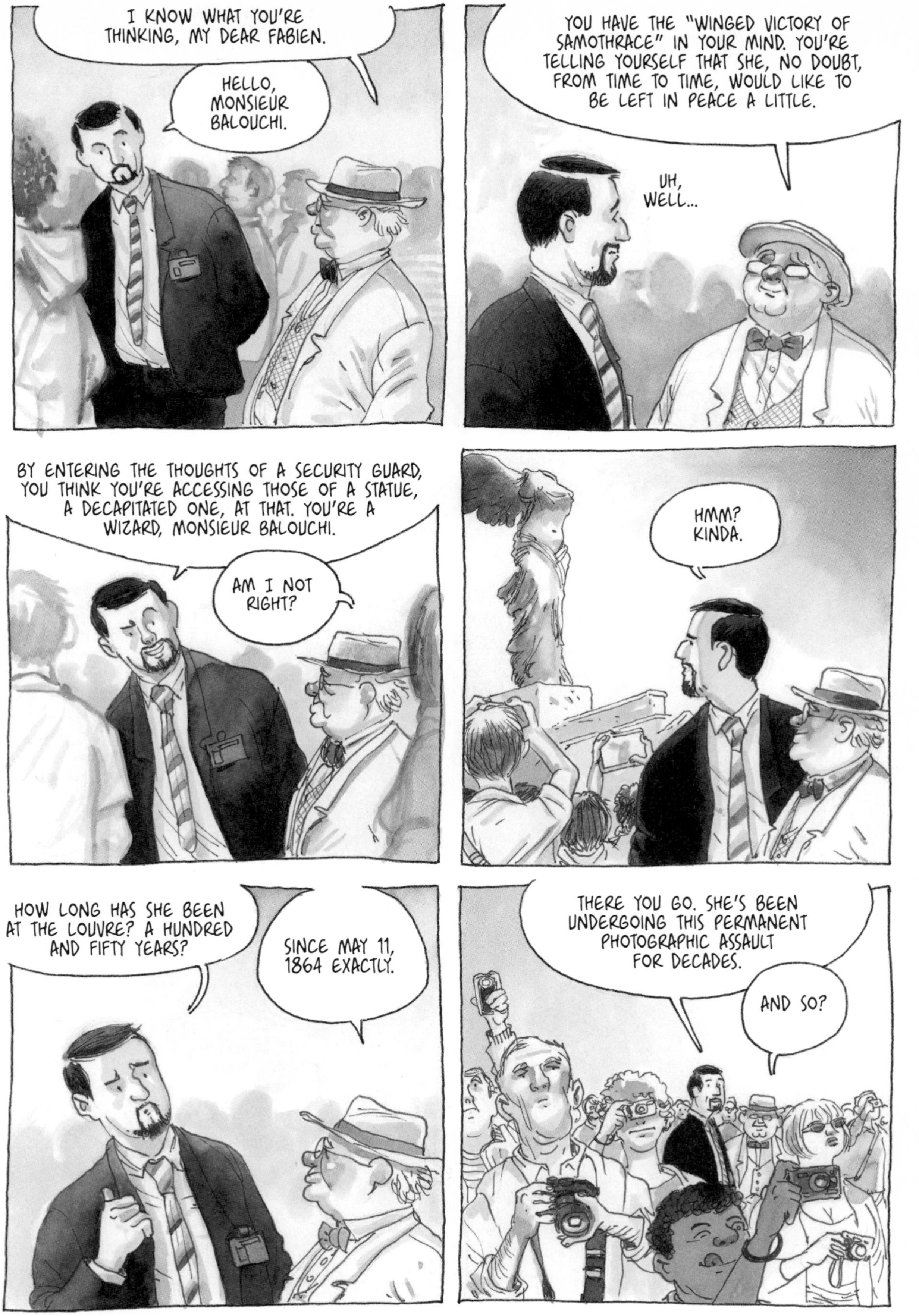
I KNOW WHAT YOU'RE THINKING, MY DEAR FABIEN.
HELLO, MONSIEUR BALOUCHI.
YOU HAVE THE "WINGED VICTORY OF SAMOTHRACE" IN YOUR MIND. YOU'RE TELLING YOURSELF THAT SHE, NO DOUBT, FROM TIME TO TIME, WOULD LIKE TO BE LEFT IN PEACE A LITTLE.
UH, WELL...
BY ENTERING THE THOUGHTS OF A SECURITY GUARD, YOU THINK YOU'RE ACCESSING THOSE OF A STATUE, A DECAPITATED ONE, AT THAT. YOU'RE A WIZARD, MONSIEUR BALOUCHI.
AM I NOT RIGHT?
HMM? KINDA.
HOW LONG HAS SHE BEEN AT THE LOUVRE? A HUNDRED AND FIFTY YEARS?
SINCE MAY 11, 1864 EXACTLY.
THERE YOU GO. SHE'S BEEN UNDERGOING THIS PERMANENT PHOTOGRAPHIC ASSAULT FOR DECADES.
AND SO?

SO THEN, FROM THE BIG WHATSIT WITH GUSSETS TO THE LATEST DIGITAL TABLET, SHE'S SEEN IT ALL. SHE MUST KNOW A THING OR TWO ABOUT PHOTOGRAPHY, THAT'S WHAT I SAY.

HEE HEE HEE!

AND TO BE FRANK, I'VE OFTEN WONDERED WHAT MYSTERIOUS REFLEX PUSHES PEOPLE TO REDO THE UMPTEENTH PHOTO OF A STATUE PICTURED MILLIONS OF TIMES OVER IN THOUSANDS OF BOOKS AROUND THE WORLD.

YOU KNOW WHAT I WOULD LIKE?

FROM TIME TO TIME, I WISH PEOPLE WOULD TURN AROUND AND GIVE A LITTLE ATTENTION TO...

...THE LADY'S HAND...

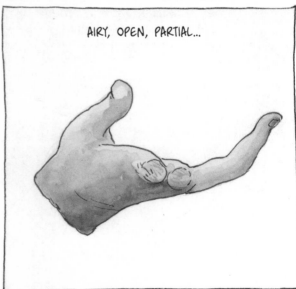

AIRY, OPEN, PARTIAL...

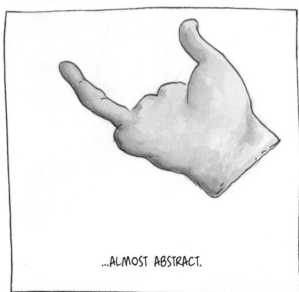

...ALMOST ABSTRACT.

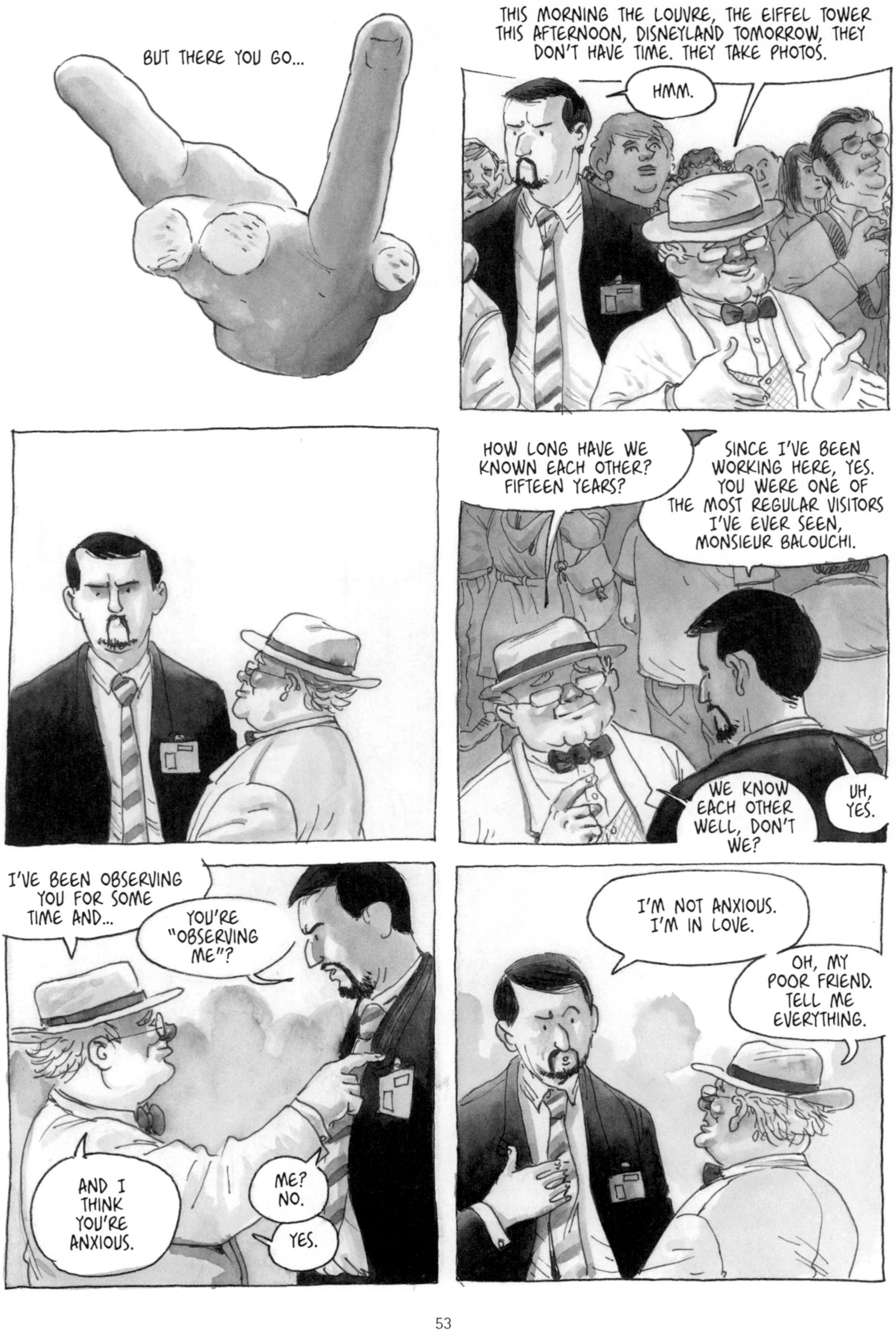

BUT THERE YOU GO...
THIS MORNING THE LOUVRE, THE EIFFEL TOWER THIS AFTERNOON, DISNEYLAND TOMORROW, THEY DON'T HAVE TIME. THEY TAKE PHOTOS.
HMM.
HOW LONG HAVE WE KNOWN EACH OTHER? FIFTEEN YEARS?
SINCE I'VE BEEN WORKING HERE, YES. YOU WERE ONE OF THE MOST REGULAR VISITORS I'VE EVER SEEN, MONSIEUR BALOUCHI.
WE KNOW EACH OTHER WELL, DON'T WE?
UH, YES.
I'VE BEEN OBSERVING YOU FOR SOME TIME AND...
YOU'RE "OBSERVING ME"?
AND I THINK YOU'RE ANXIOUS.
ME? NO.
YES.
I'M NOT ANXIOUS. I'M IN LOVE.
OH, MY POOR FRIEND. TELL ME EVERYTHING.

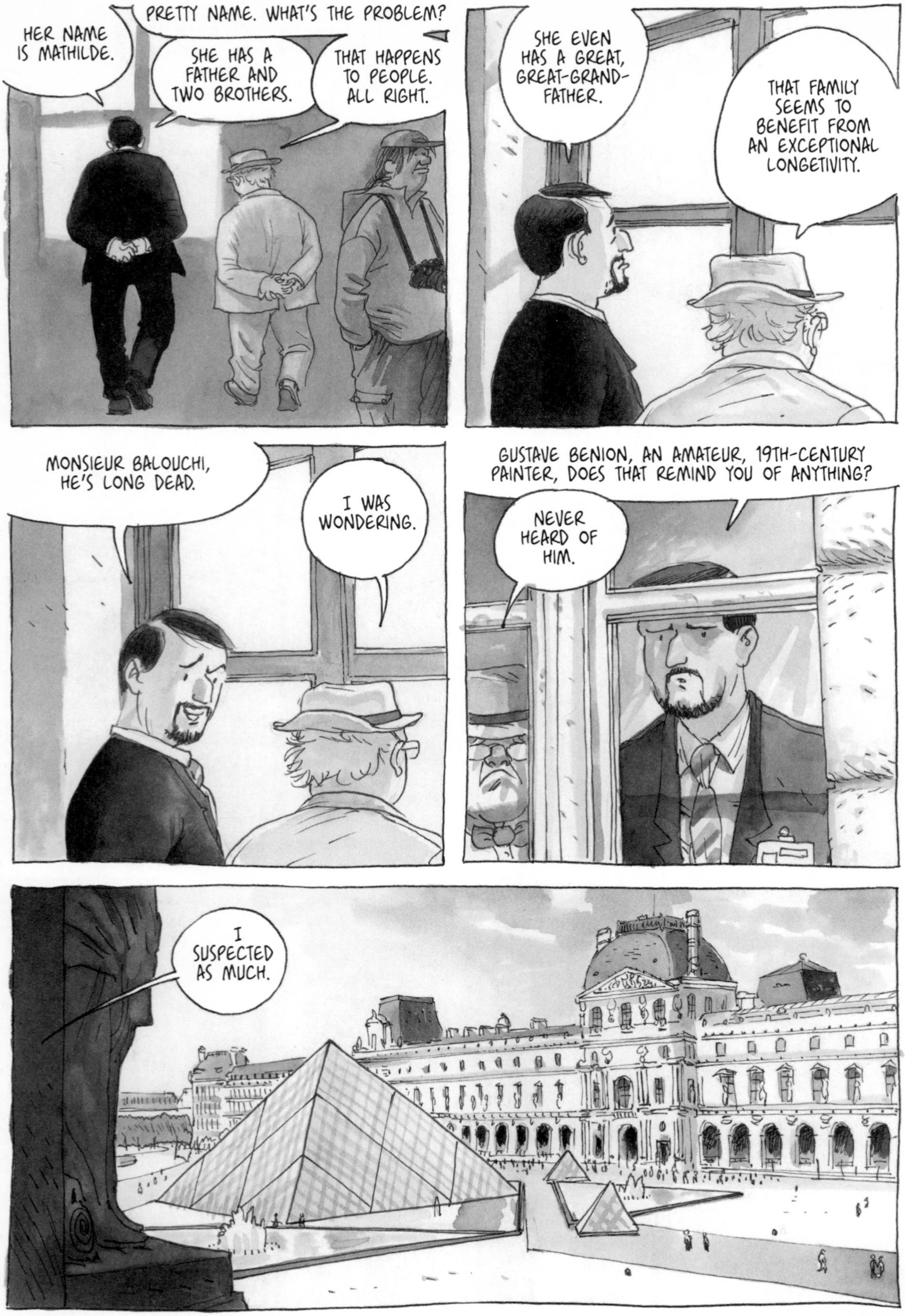
HER NAME IS MATHILDE.
PRETTY NAME. WHAT'S THE PROBLEM?
SHE HAS A FATHER AND TWO BROTHERS.
THAT HAPPENS TO PEOPLE. ALL RIGHT.
SHE EVEN HAS A GREAT, GREAT-GRAND-FATHER.
THAT FAMILY SEEMS TO BENEFIT FROM AN EXCEPTIONAL LONGETIVITY.
MONSIEUR BALOUCHI, HE'S LONG DEAD.
I WAS WONDERING.
GUSTAVE BENION, AN AMATEUR, 19TH-CENTURY PAINTER, DOES THAT REMIND YOU OF ANYTHING?
NEVER HEARD OF HIM.
I SUSPECTED AS MUCH.

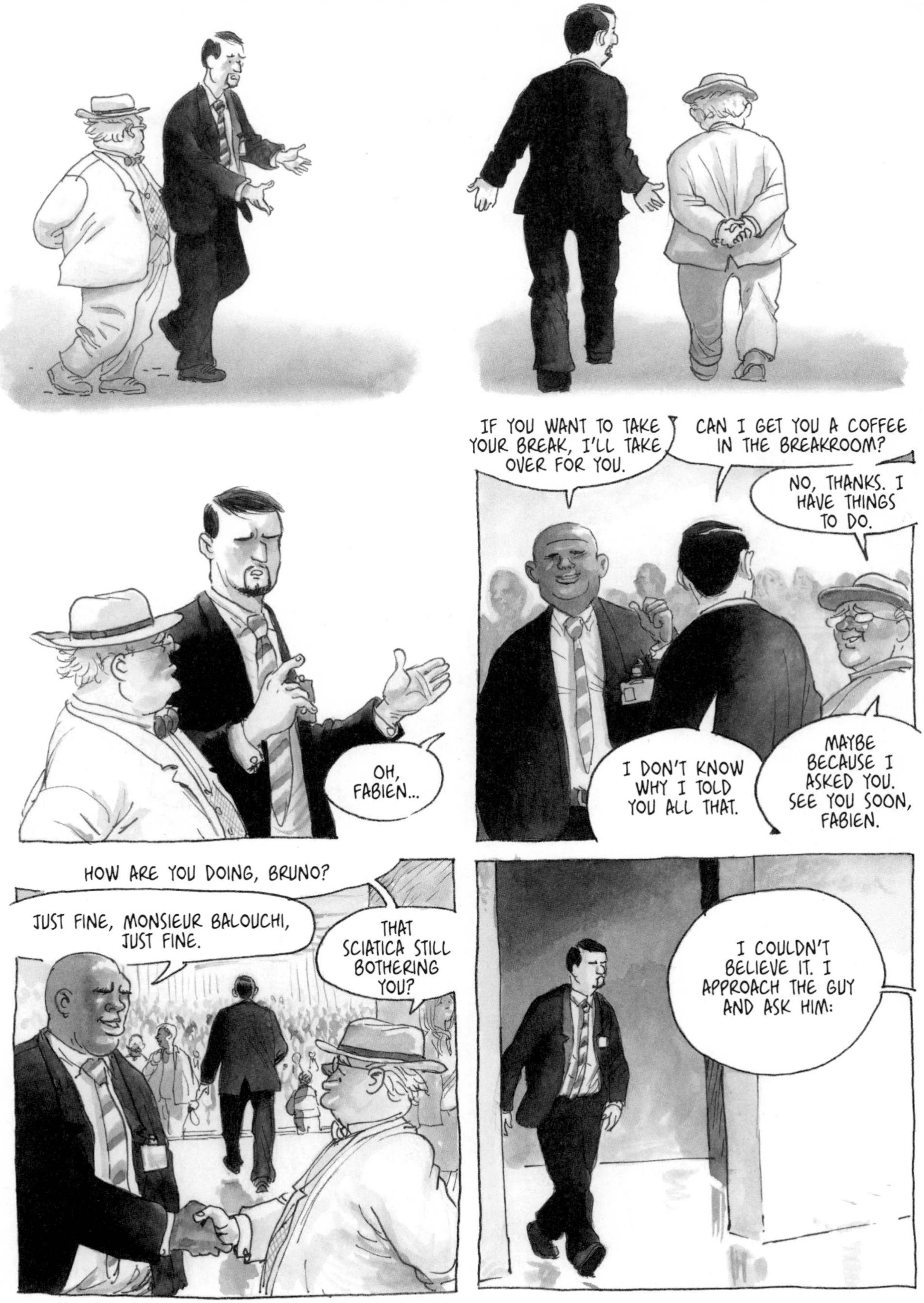

IF YOU WANT TO TAKE YOUR BREAK, I'LL TAKE OVER FOR YOU.
CAN I GET YOU A COFFEE IN THE BREAKROOM?
NO, THANKS. I HAVE THINGS TO DO.
OH, FABIEN...
I DON'T KNOW WHY I TOLD YOU ALL THAT.
MAYBE BECAUSE I ASKED YOU. SEE YOU SOON, FABIEN.
HOW ARE YOU DOING, BRUNO?
JUST FINE, MONSIEUR BALOUCHI, JUST FINE.
THAT SCIATICA STILL BOTHERING YOU?
I COULDN'T BELIEVE IT. I APPROACH THE GUY AND ASK HIM:

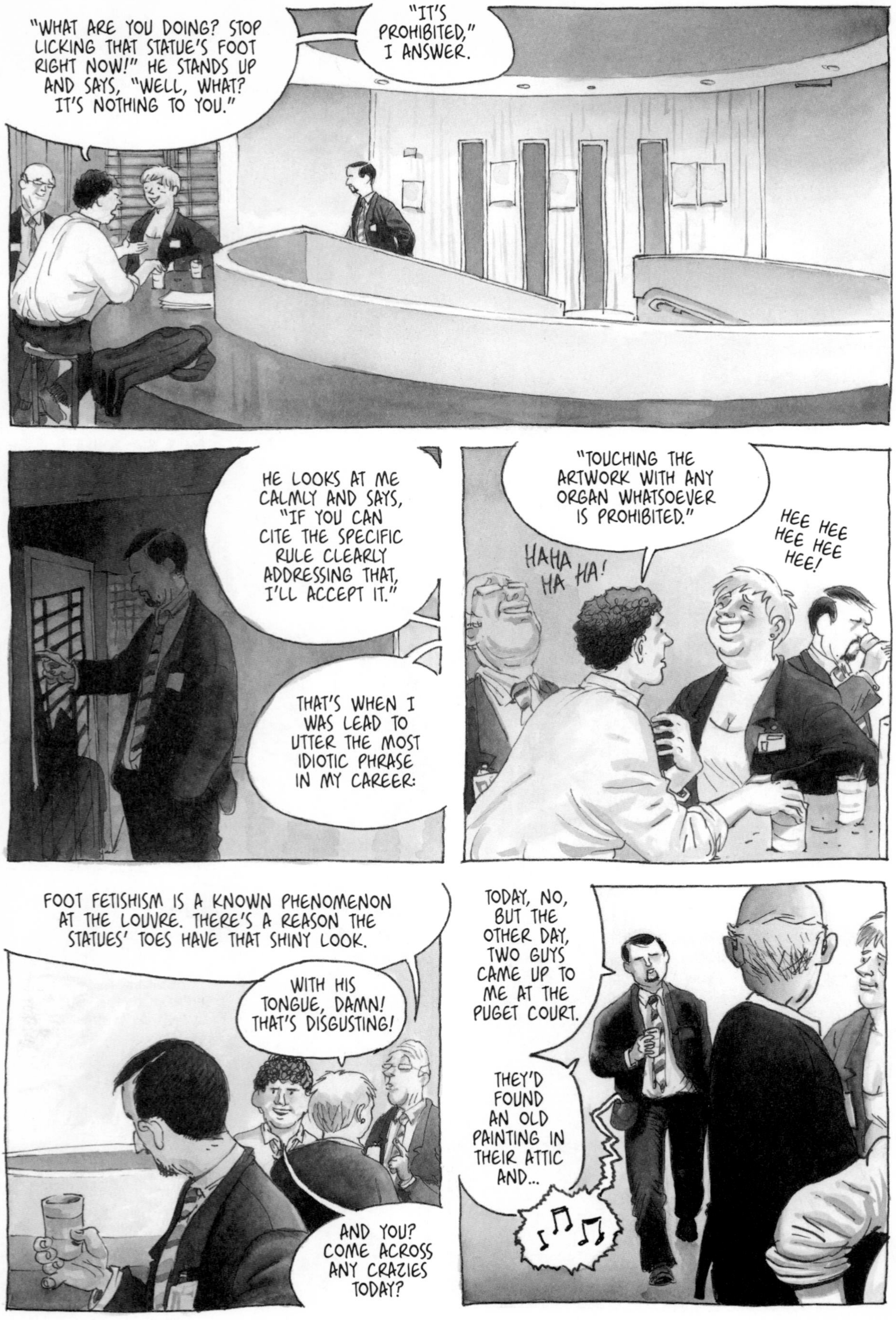
"WHAT ARE YOU DOING? STOP LICKING THAT STATUE'S FOOT RIGHT NOW!" HE STANDS UP AND SAYS, "WELL, WHAT? IT'S NOTHING TO YOU."
"IT'S PROHIBITED," I ANSWER.
HE LOOKS AT ME CALMLY AND SAYS, "IF YOU CAN CITE THE SPECIFIC RULE CLEARLY ADDRESSING THAT, I'LL ACCEPT IT."
THAT'S WHEN I WAS LEAD TO UTTER THE MOST IDIOTIC PHRASE IN MY CAREER:
"TOUCHING THE ARTWORK WITH ANY ORGAN WHATSOEVER IS PROHIBITED."
HAHA HA HA!
HEE HEE HEE HEE HEE!
FOOT FETISHISM IS A KNOWN PHENOMENON AT THE LOUVRE. THERE'S A REASON THE STATUES' TOES HAVE THAT SHINY LOOK.
WITH HIS TONGUE, DAMN! THAT'S DISGUSTING!
AND YOU? COME ACROSS ANY CRAZIES TODAY?
TODAY, NO, BUT THE OTHER DAY, TWO GUYS CAME UP TO ME AT THE PUGET COURT.
THEY'D FOUND AN OLD PAINTING IN THEIR ATTIC AND...

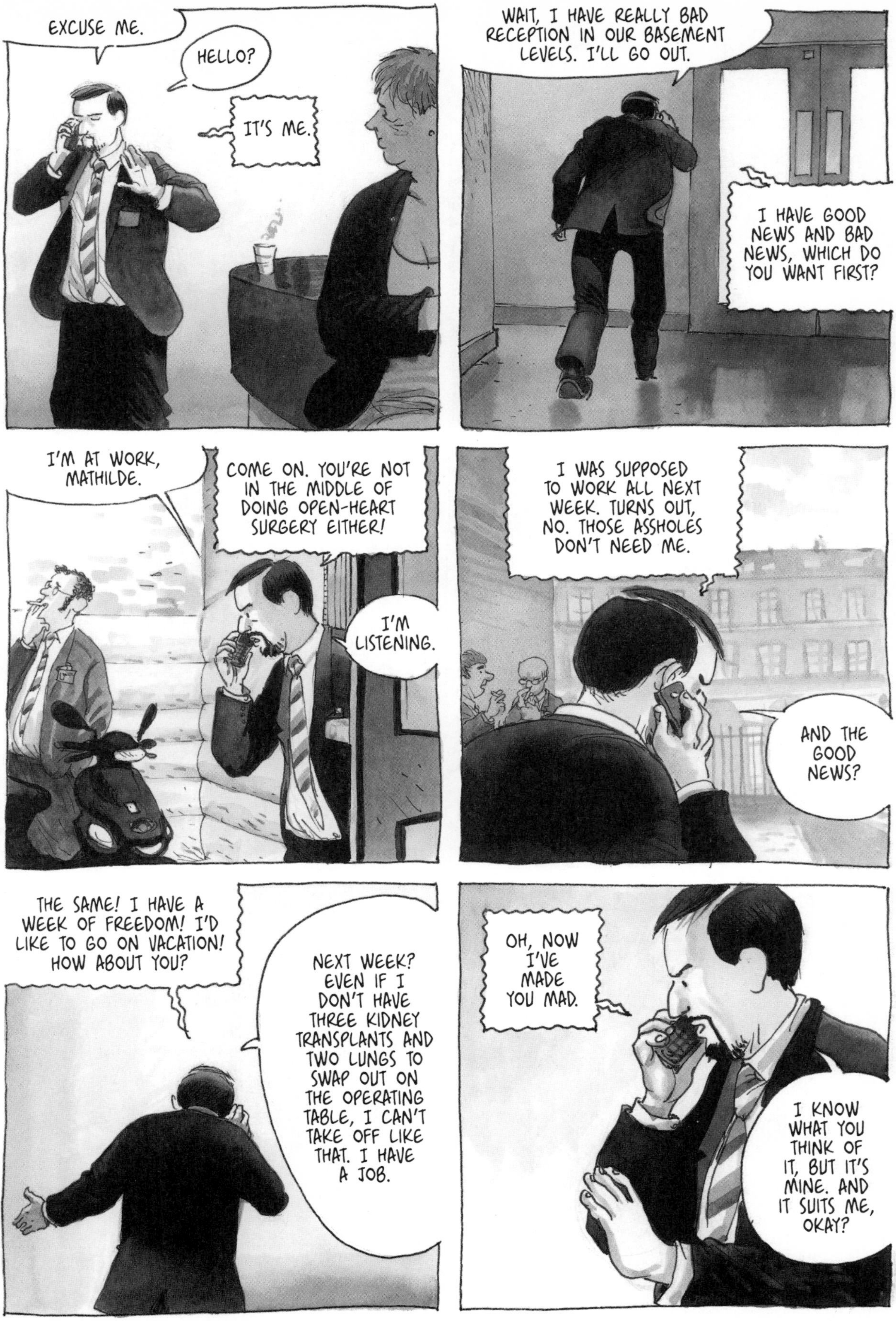
EXCUSE ME.
HELLO?
IT'S ME.
WAIT, I HAVE REALLY BAD RECEPTION IN OUR BASEMENT LEVELS. I'LL GO OUT.
I HAVE GOOD NEWS AND BAD NEWS, WHICH DO YOU WANT FIRST?
I'M AT WORK, MATHILDE.
COME ON. YOU'RE NOT IN THE MIDDLE OF DOING OPEN-HEART SURGERY EITHER!
I'M LISTENING.
I WAS SUPPOSED TO WORK ALL NEXT WEEK. TURNS OUT, NO. THOSE ASSHOLES DON'T NEED ME.
AND THE GOOD NEWS?
THE SAME! I HAVE A WEEK OF FREEDOM! I'D LIKE TO GO ON VACATION! HOW ABOUT YOU?
NEXT WEEK? EVEN IF I DON'T HAVE THREE KIDNEY TRANSPLANTS AND TWO LUNGS TO SWAP OUT ON THE OPERATING TABLE, I CAN'T TAKE OFF LIKE THAT. I HAVE A JOB.
OH, NOW I'VE MADE YOU MAD.
I KNOW WHAT YOU THINK OF IT, BUT IT'S MINE. AND IT SUITS ME, OKAY?

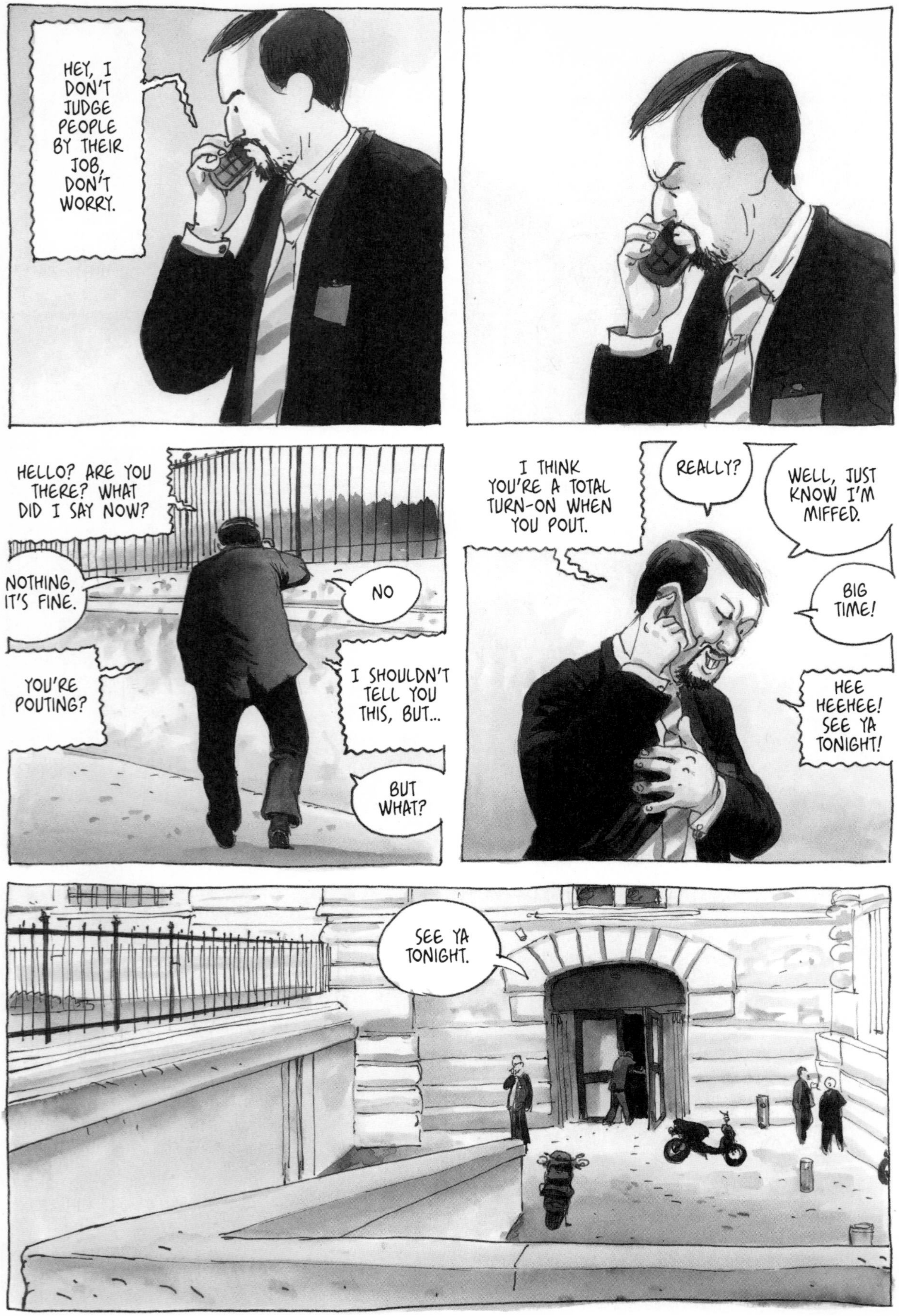
HEY, I DON'T JUDGE PEOPLE BY THEIR JOB, DON'T WORRY.
HELLO? ARE YOU THERE? WHAT DID I SAY NOW?
NOTHING, IT'S FINE.
NO
YOU'RE POUTING?
I SHOULDN'T TELL YOU THIS, BUT...
BUT WHAT?
I THINK YOU'RE A TOTAL TURN-ON WHEN YOU POUT.
REALLY?
WELL, JUST KNOW I'M MIFFED.
BIG TIME!
HEE HEEHEE! SEE YA TONIGHT!
SEE YA TONIGHT.

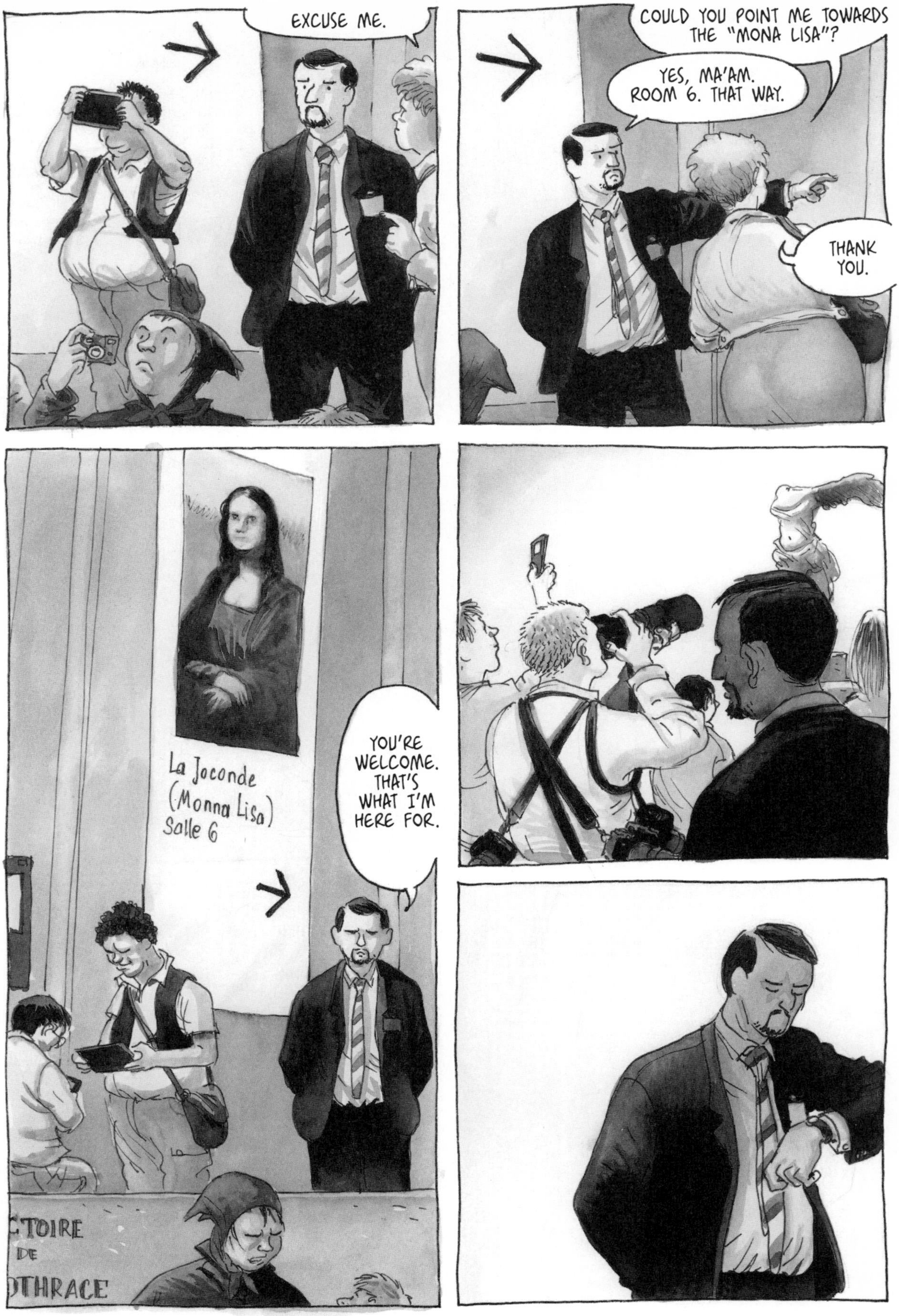
EXCUSE ME.
COULD YOU POINT ME TOWARDS THE "MONA LISA"?
YES, MA'AM. ROOM 6. THAT WAY.
THANK YOU.
La Joconde (Monna Lisa) Salle 6
YOU'RE WELCOME. THAT'S WHAT I'M HERE FOR.
CTOIRE DE OTHRACE

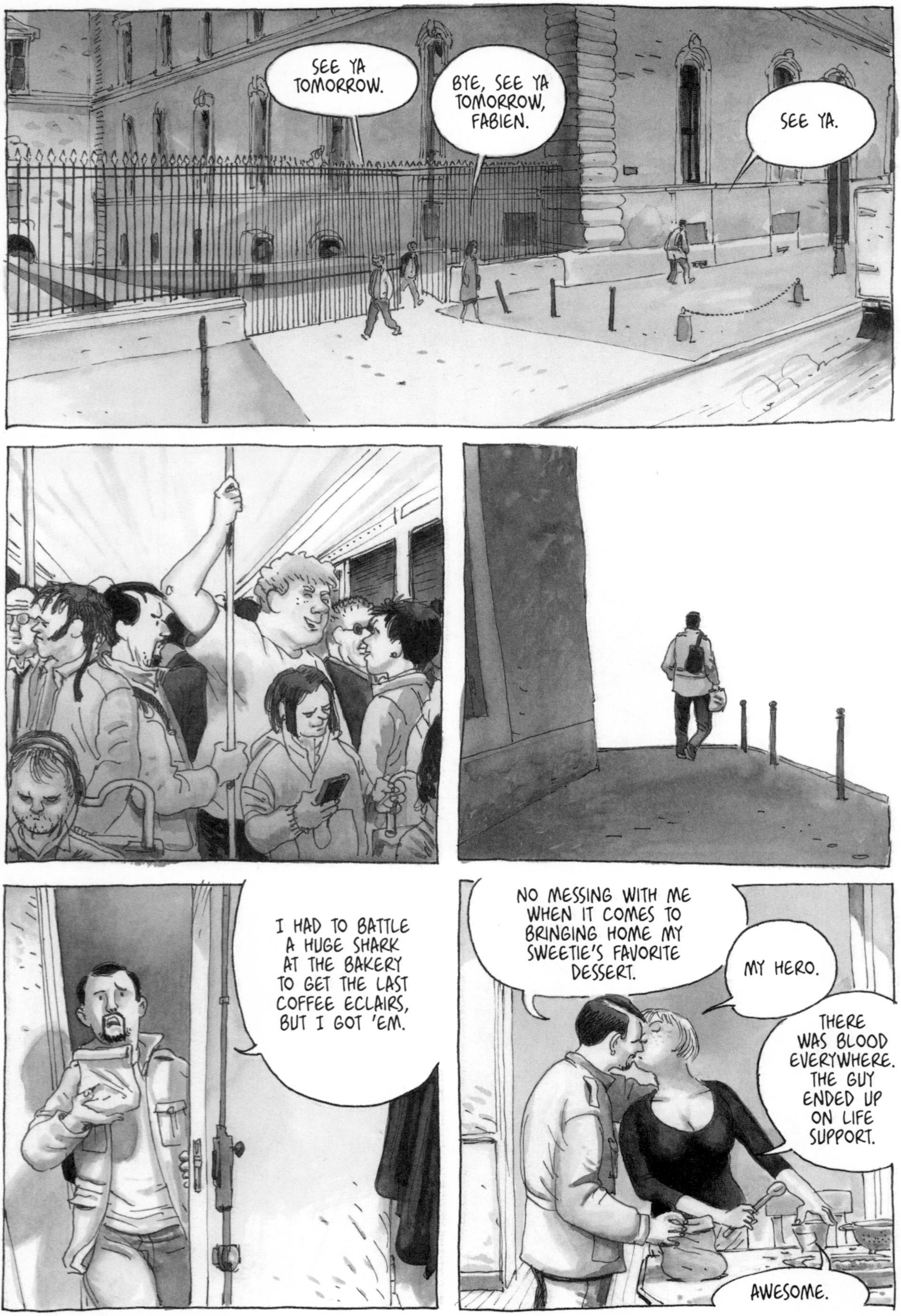
SEE YA TOMORROW.
BYE, SEE YA TOMORROW, FABIEN.
SEE YA.
I HAD TO BATTLE A HUGE SHARK AT THE BAKERY TO GET THE LAST COFFEE ECLAIRS, BUT I GOT 'EM.
NO MESSING WITH ME WHEN IT COMES TO BRINGING HOME MY SWEETIE'S FAVORITE DESSERT.
MY HERO.
THERE WAS BLOOD EVERYWHERE. THE GUY ENDED UP ON LIFE SUPPORT.
AWESOME.

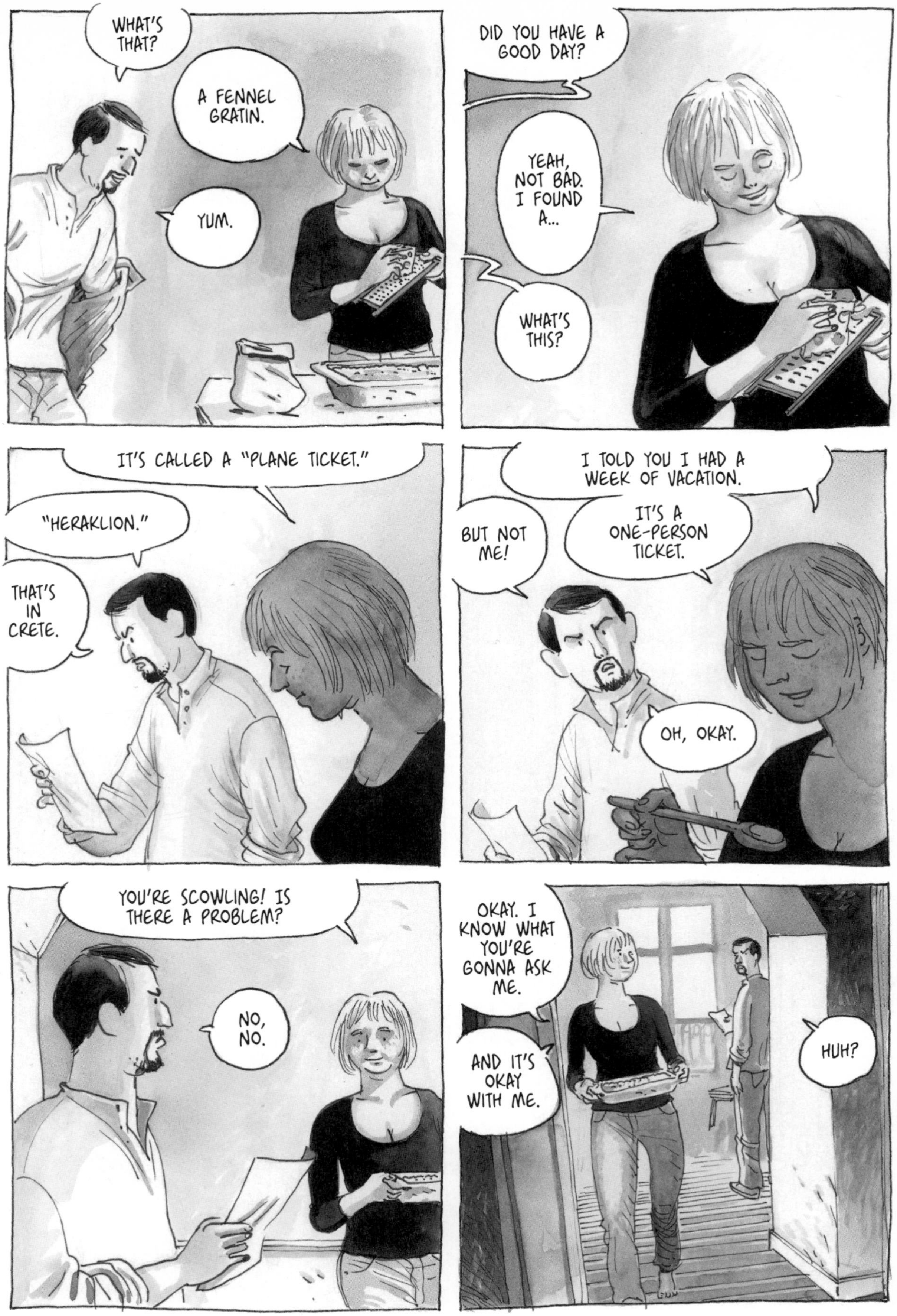
WHAT'S THAT?
A FENNEL GRATIN.
YUM.
DID YOU HAVE A GOOD DAY?
YEAH, NOT BAD. I FOUND A...
WHAT'S THIS?
IT'S CALLED A "PLANE TICKET."
"HERAKLION."
THAT'S IN CRETE.
I TOLD YOU I HAD A WEEK OF VACATION.
BUT NOT ME!
IT'S A ONE-PERSON TICKET.
OH, OKAY.
YOU'RE SCOWLING! IS THERE A PROBLEM?
NO, NO.
OKAY. I KNOW WHAT YOU'RE GONNA ASK ME.
AND IT'S OKAY WITH ME.
HUH?

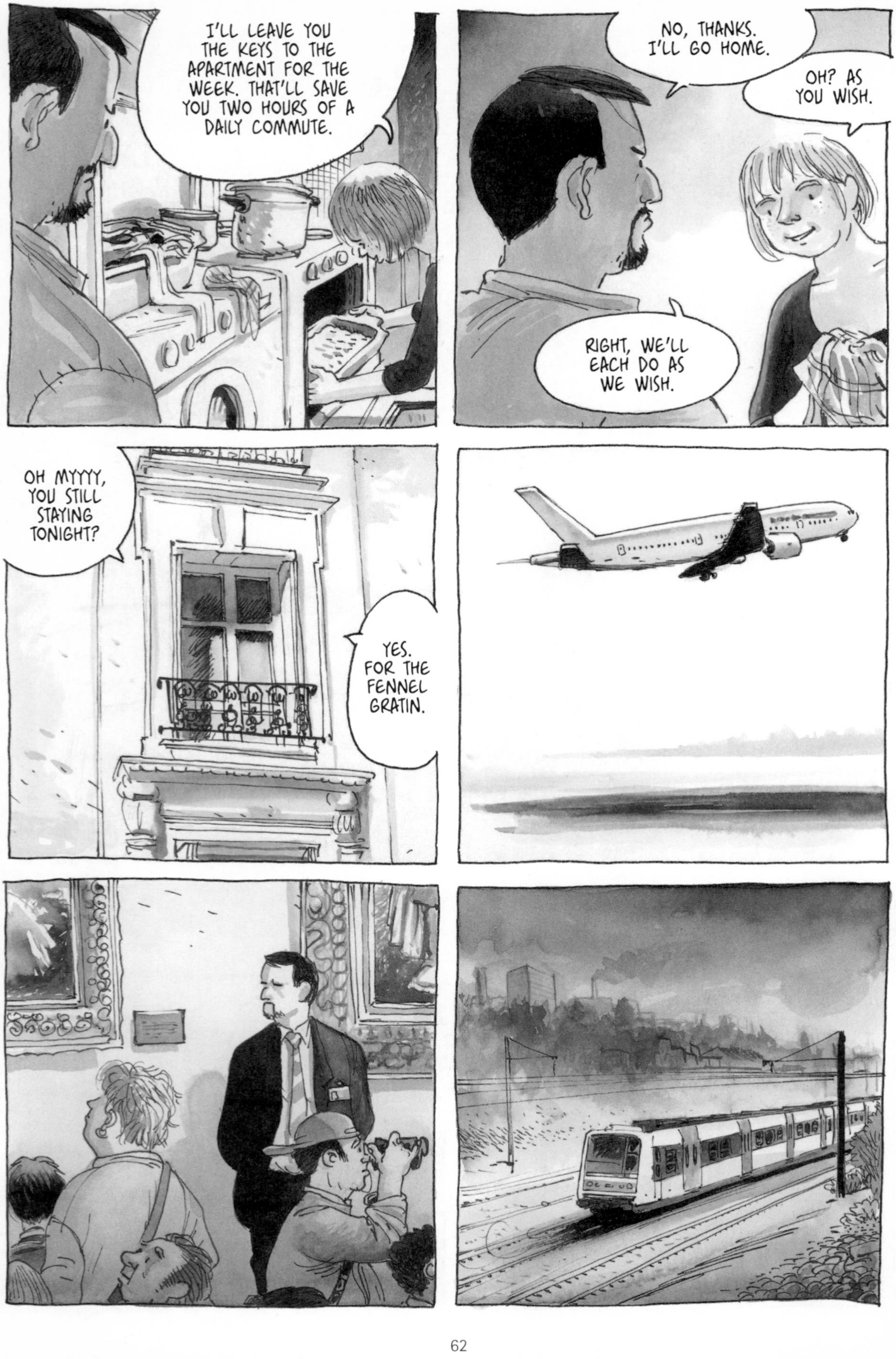
I'LL LEAVE YOU THE KEYS TO THE APARTMENT FOR THE WEEK. THAT'LL SAVE YOU TWO HOURS OF A DAILY COMMUTE.
NO, THANKS. I'LL GO HOME.
OH? AS YOU WISH.
RIGHT, WE'LL EACH DO AS WE WISH.
OH MYYYY, YOU STILL STAYING TONIGHT?
YES. FOR THE FENNEL GRATIN.

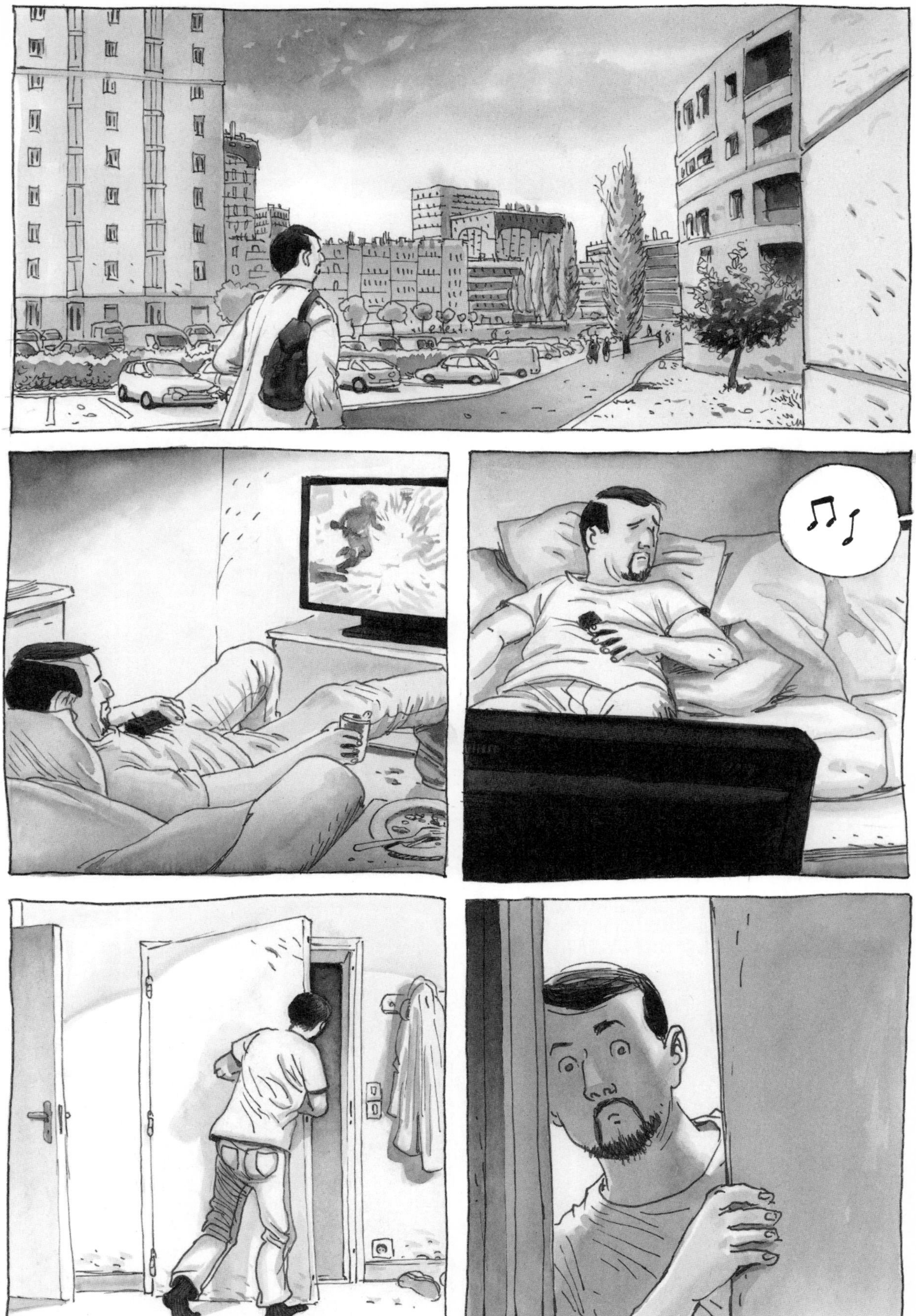

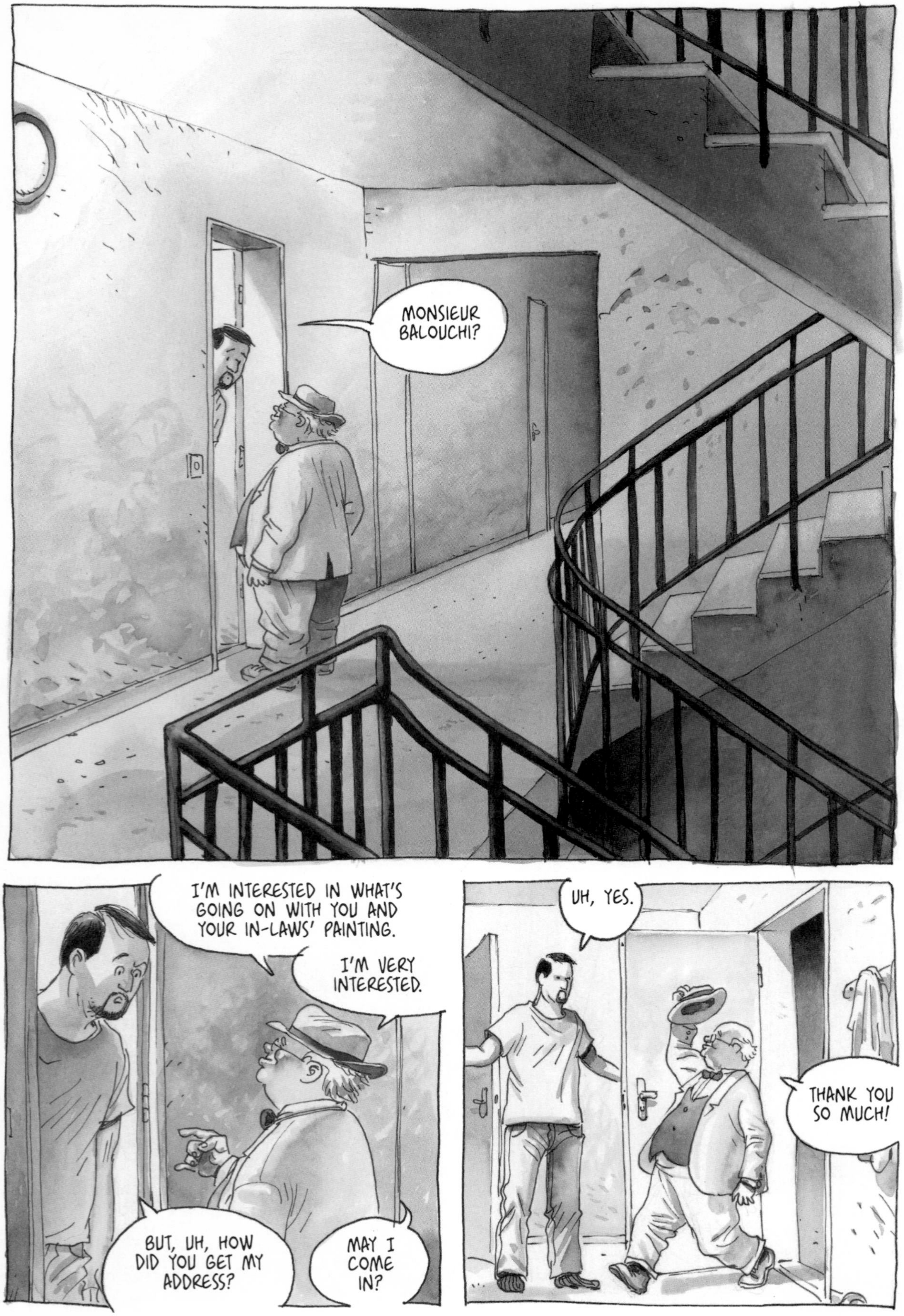
MONSIEUR BALOUCHI?
I'M INTERESTED IN WHAT'S GOING ON WITH YOU AND YOUR IN-LAWS' PAINTING.
I'M VERY INTERESTED.
BUT, UH, HOW DID YOU GET MY ADDRESS?
MAY I COME IN?
UH, YES.
THANK YOU SO MUCH!

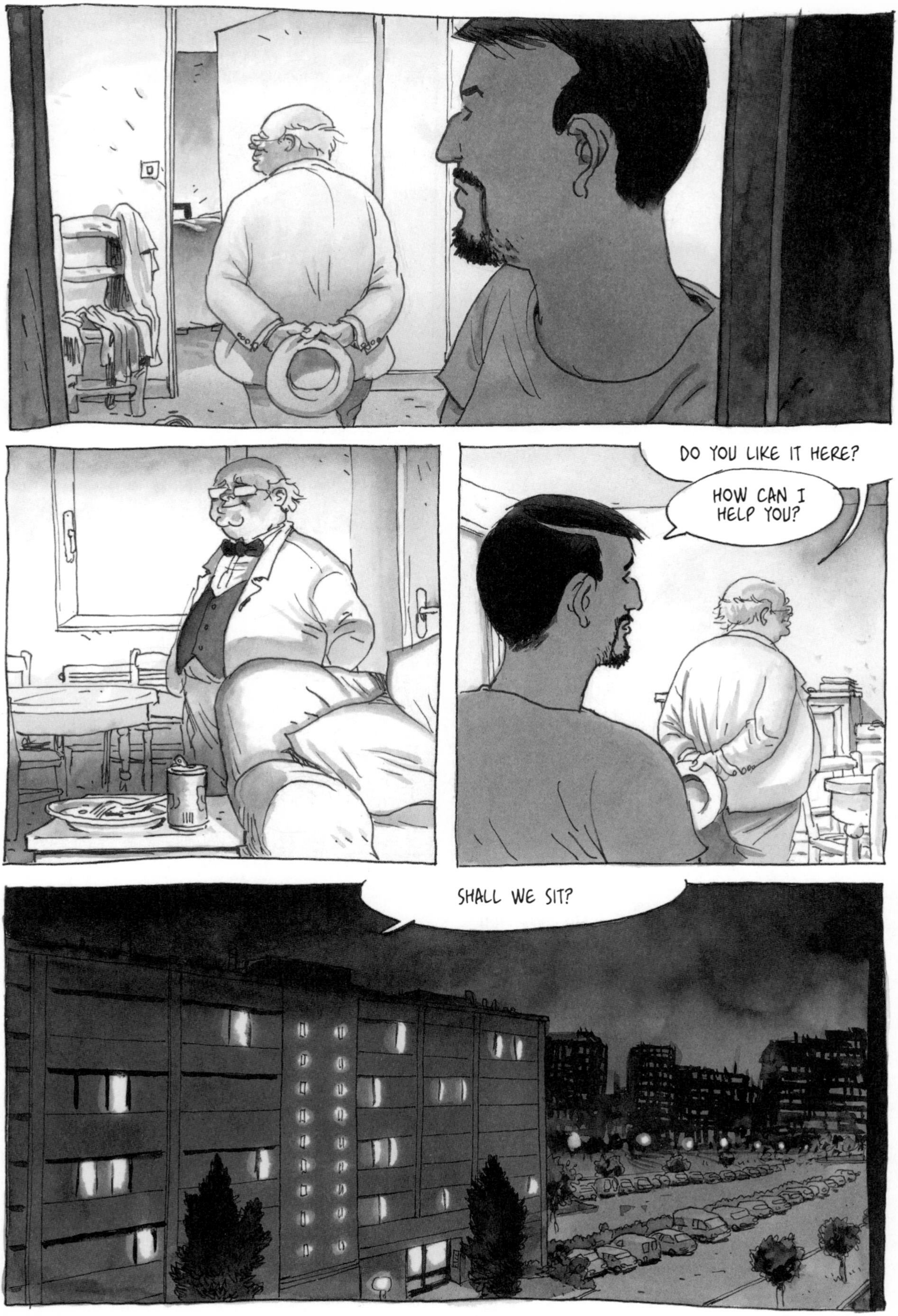
DO YOU LIKE IT HERE?
HOW CAN I HELP YOU?
SHALL WE SIT?

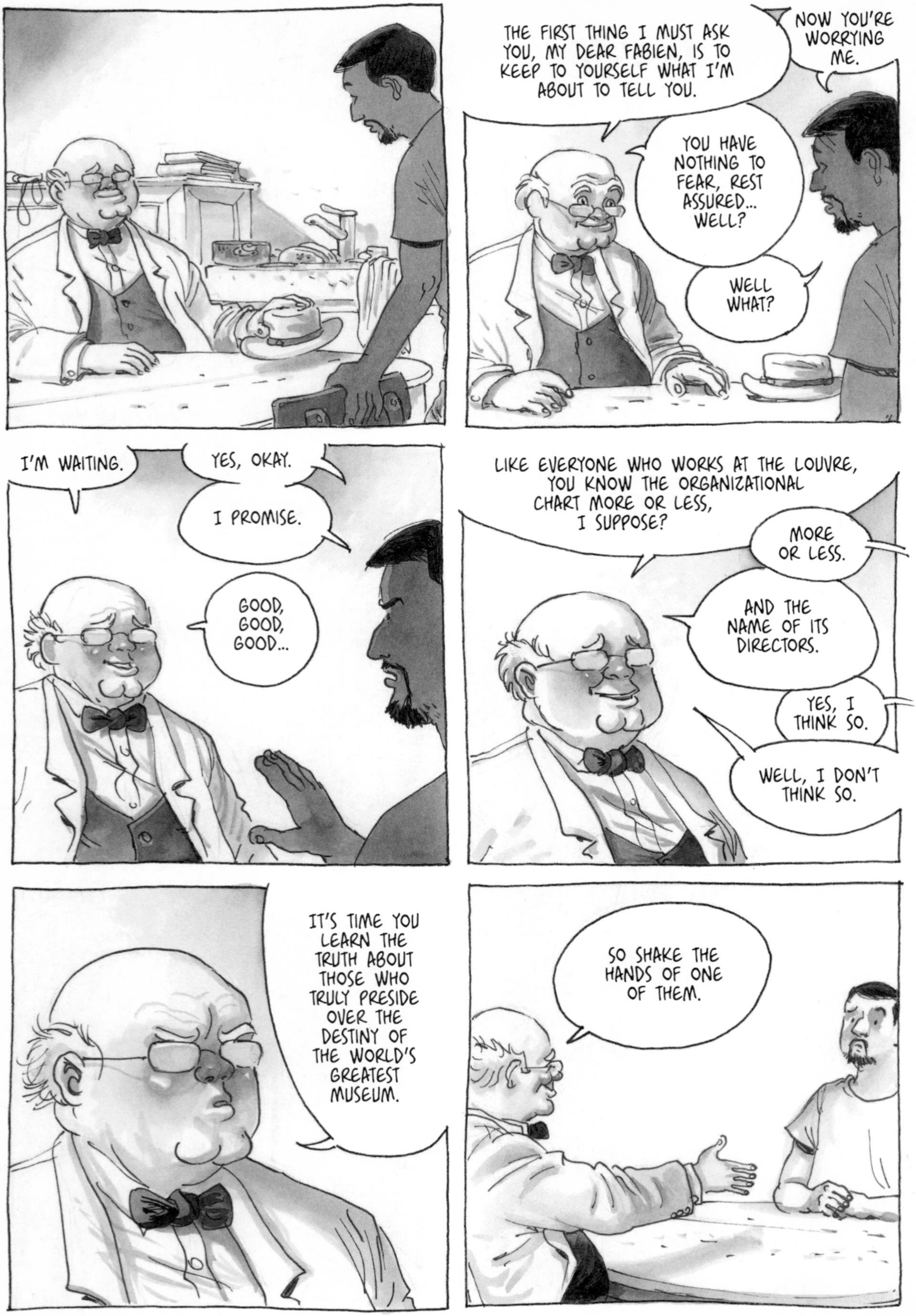
THE FIRST THING I MUST ASK YOU, MY DEAR FABIEN, IS TO KEEP TO YOURSELF WHAT I'M ABOUT TO TELL YOU.
NOW YOU'RE WORRYING ME.
YOU HAVE NOTHING TO FEAR, REST ASSURED... WELL?
WELL WHAT?
I'M WAITING.
YES, OKAY.
I PROMISE.
GOOD, GOOD, GOOD...
LIKE EVERYONE WHO WORKS AT THE LOUVRE, YOU KNOW THE ORGANIZATIONAL CHART MORE OR LESS, I SUPPOSE?
MORE OR LESS.
AND THE NAME OF ITS DIRECTORS.
YES, I THINK SO.
WELL, I DON'T THINK SO.
IT'S TIME YOU LEARN THE TRUTH ABOUT THOSE WHO TRULY PRESIDE OVER THE DESTINY OF THE WORLD'S GREATEST MUSEUM.
SO SHAKE THE HANDS OF ONE OF THEM.

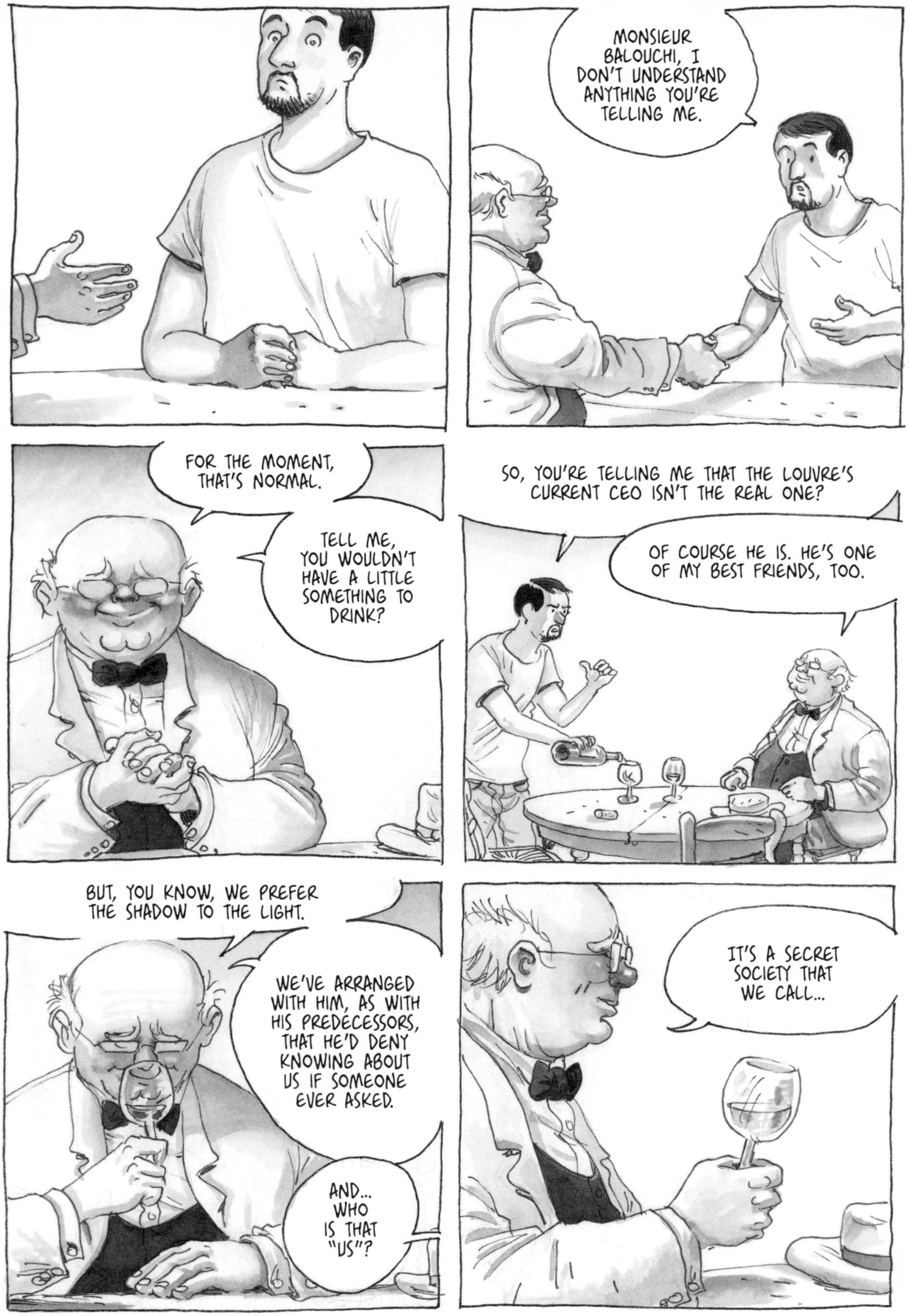
MONSIEUR BALOUCHI, I DON'T UNDERSTAND ANYTHING YOU'RE TELLING ME.
FOR THE MOMENT, THAT'S NORMAL.
TELL ME, YOU WOULDN'T HAVE A LITTLE SOMETHING TO DRINK?
SO, YOU'RE TELLING ME THAT THE LOUVRE'S CURRENT CEO ISN'T THE REAL ONE?
OF COURSE HE IS. HE'S ONE OF MY BEST FRIENDS, TOO.
BUT, YOU KNOW, WE PREFER THE SHADOW TO THE LIGHT.
WE'VE ARRANGED WITH HIM, AS WITH HIS PREDECESSORS, THAT HE'D DENY KNOWING ABOUT US IF SOMEONE EVER ASKED.
AND... WHO IS THAT "US"?
IT'S A SECRET SOCIETY THAT WE CALL...

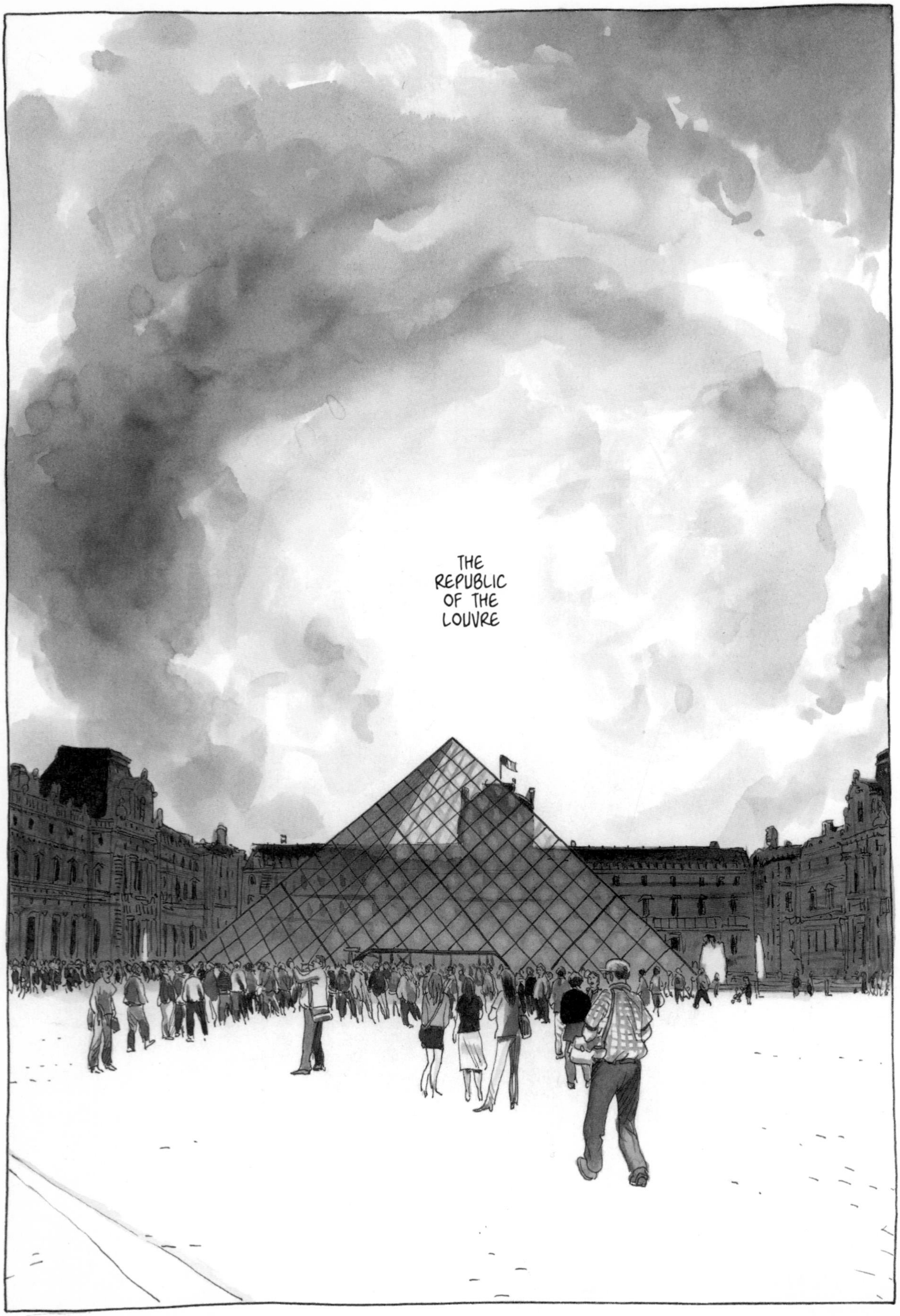
THE REPUBLIC OF THE LOUVRE

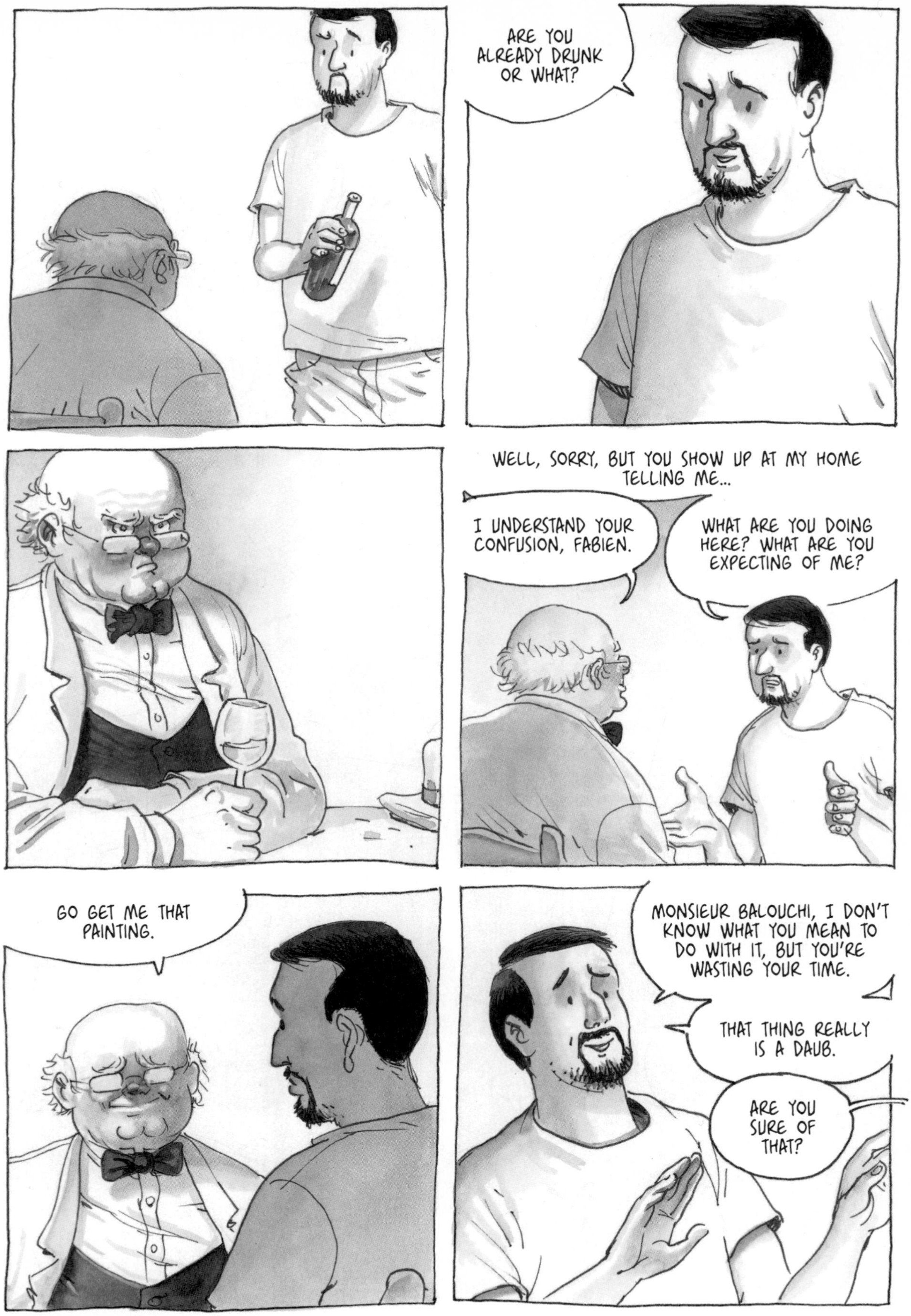
ARE YOU ALREADY DRUNK OR WHAT?
WELL, SORRY, BUT YOU SHOW UP AT MY HOME TELLING ME...
I UNDERSTAND YOUR CONFUSION, FABIEN.
WHAT ARE YOU DOING HERE? WHAT ARE YOU EXPECTING OF ME?
GO GET ME THAT PAINTING.
MONSIEUR BALOUCHI, I DON'T KNOW WHAT YOU MEAN TO DO WITH IT, BUT YOU'RE WASTING YOUR TIME.
THAT THING REALLY IS A DAUB.
ARE YOU SURE OF THAT?

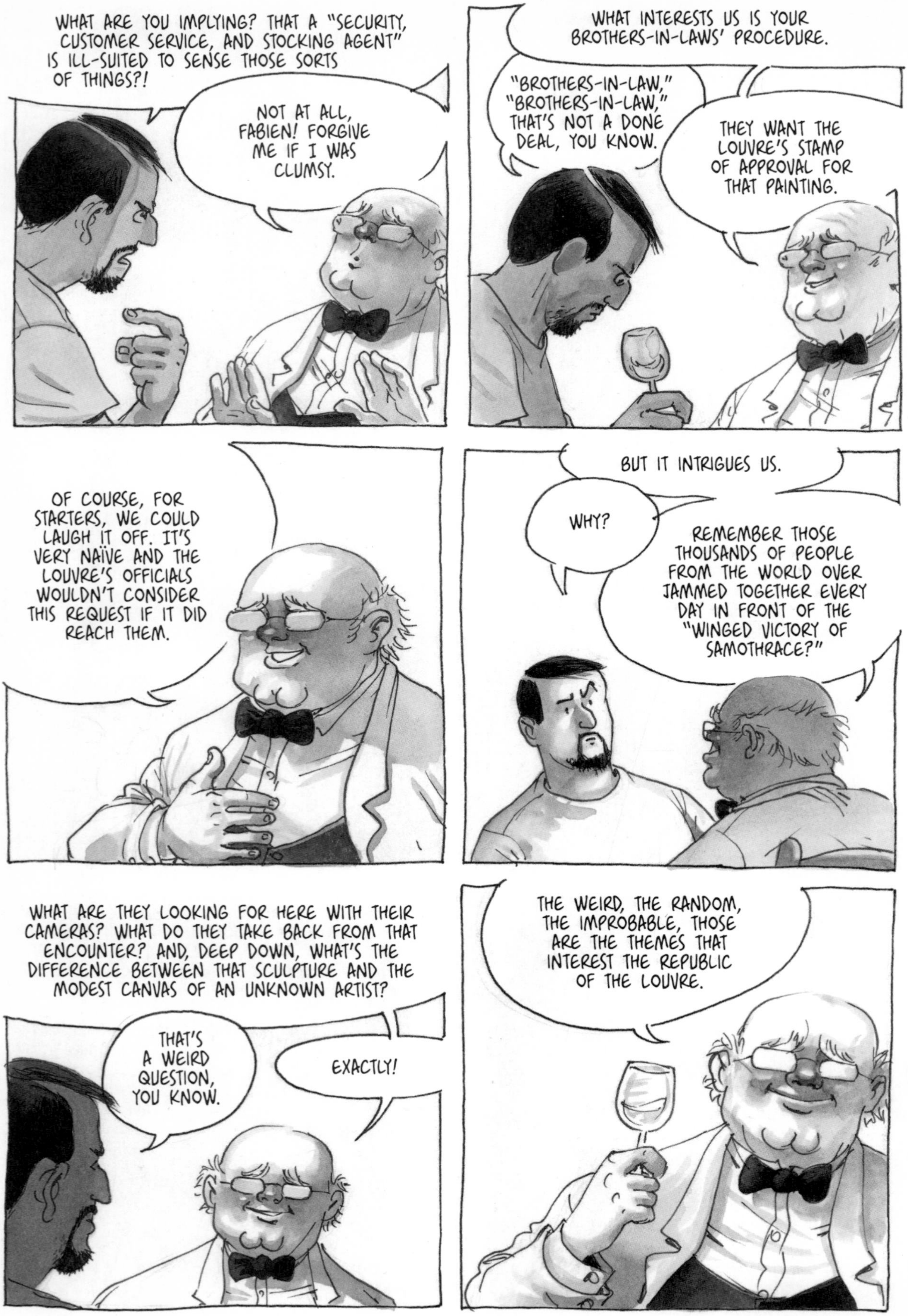
WHAT ARE YOU IMPLYING? THAT A "SECURITY, CUSTOMER SERVICE, AND STOCKING AGENT" IS ILL-SUITED TO SENSE THOSE SORTS OF THINGS?!
NOT AT ALL, FABIEN! FORGIVE ME IF I WAS CLUMSY.
WHAT INTERESTS US IS YOUR BROTHERS-IN-LAWS' PROCEDURE.
"BROTHERS-IN-LAW," "BROTHERS-IN-LAW," THAT'S NOT A DONE DEAL, YOU KNOW.
THEY WANT THE LOUVRE'S STAMP OF APPROVAL FOR THAT PAINTING.
OF COURSE, FOR STARTERS, WE COULD LAUGH IT OFF. IT'S VERY NAÏVE AND THE LOUVRE'S OFFICIALS WOULDN'T CONSIDER THIS REQUEST IF IT DID REACH THEM.
BUT IT INTRIGUES US.
WHY?
REMEMBER THOSE THOUSANDS OF PEOPLE FROM THE WORLD OVER JAMMED TOGETHER EVERY DAY IN FRONT OF THE "WINGED VICTORY OF SAMOTHRACE?"
WHAT ARE THEY LOOKING FOR HERE WITH THEIR CAMERAS? WHAT DO THEY TAKE BACK FROM THAT ENCOUNTER? AND, DEEP DOWN, WHAT'S THE DIFFERENCE BETWEEN THAT SCULPTURE AND THE MODEST CANVAS OF AN UNKNOWN ARTIST?
THAT'S A WEIRD QUESTION, YOU KNOW.
EXACTLY!
THE WEIRD, THE RANDOM, THE IMPROBABLE, THOSE ARE THE THEMES THAT INTEREST THE REPUBLIC OF THE LOUVRE.

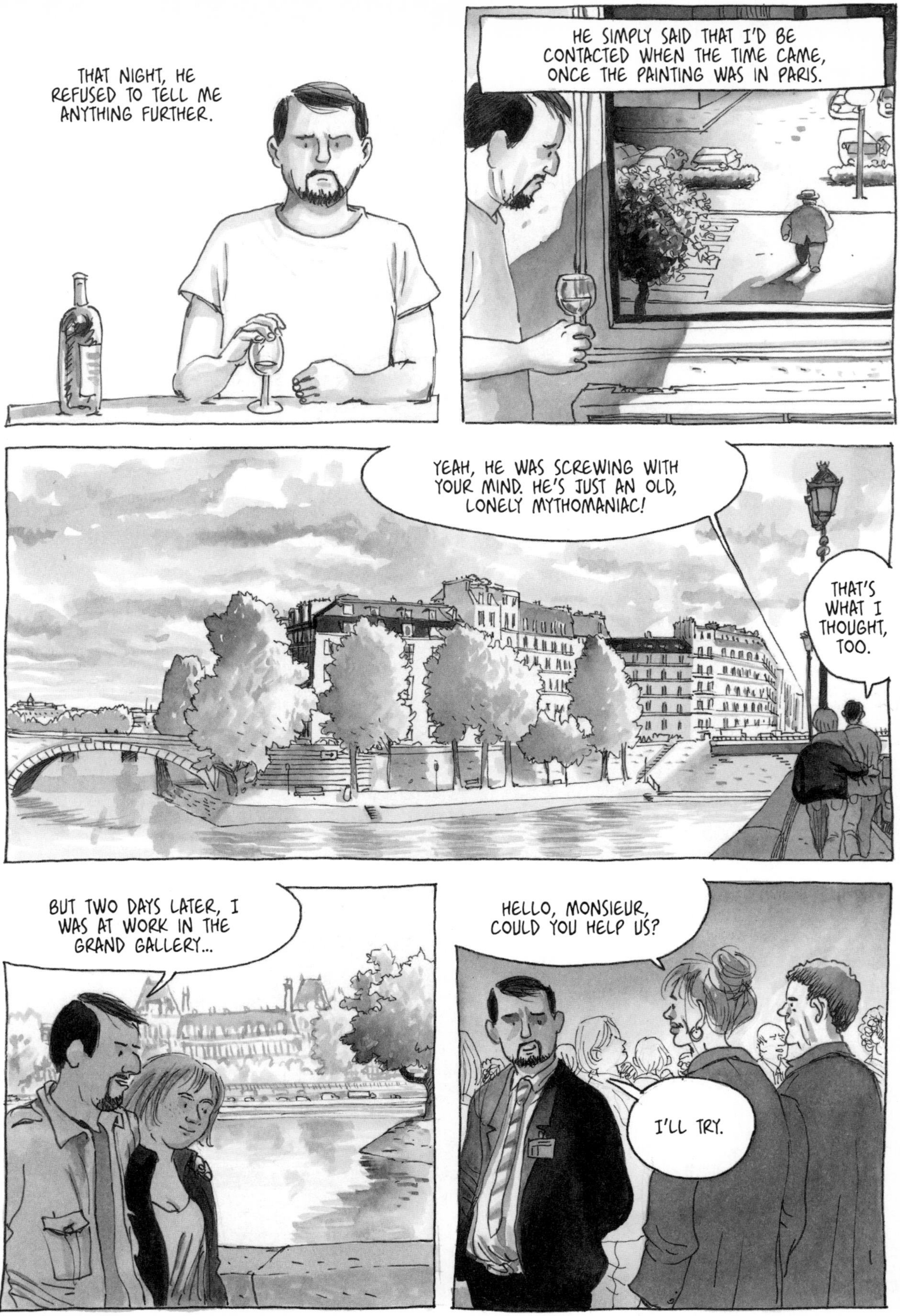
THAT NIGHT, HE REFUSED TO TELL ME ANYTHING FURTHER.
HE SIMPLY SAID THAT I'D BE CONTACTED WHEN THE TIME CAME, ONCE THE PAINTING WAS IN PARIS.
YEAH, HE WAS SCREWING WITH YOUR MIND. HE'S JUST AN OLD, LONELY MYTHOMANIAC!
THAT'S WHAT I THOUGHT, TOO.
BUT TWO DAYS LATER, I WAS AT WORK IN THE GRAND GALLERY...
HELLO, MONSIEUR, COULD YOU HELP US?
I'LL TRY.

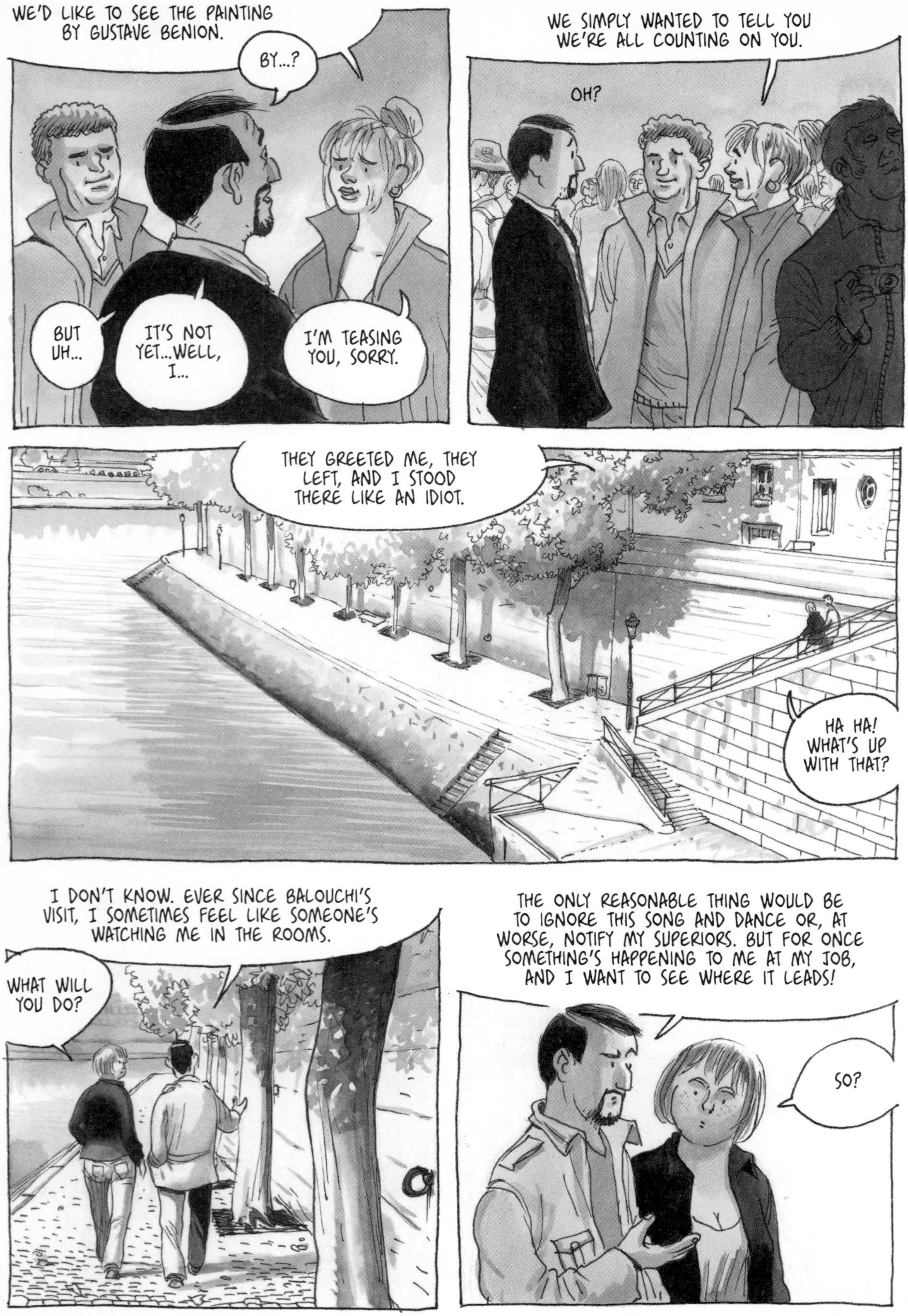
WE'D LIKE TO SEE THE PAINTING BY GUSTAVE BENION.
BY...?
BUT UH...
IT'S NOT YET...WELL, I...
I'M TEASING YOU, SORRY.
WE SIMPLY WANTED TO TELL YOU WE'RE ALL COUNTING ON YOU.
OH?
THEY GREETED ME, THEY LEFT, AND I STOOD THERE LIKE AN IDIOT.
HA HA! WHAT'S UP WITH THAT?
I DON'T KNOW. EVER SINCE BALOUCHI'S VISIT, I SOMETIMES FEEL LIKE SOMEONE'S WATCHING ME IN THE ROOMS.
WHAT WILL YOU DO?
THE ONLY REASONABLE THING WOULD BE TO IGNORE THIS SONG AND DANCE OR, AT WORSE, NOTIFY MY SUPERIORS. BUT FOR ONCE SOMETHING'S HAPPENING TO ME AT MY JOB, AND I WANT TO SEE WHERE IT LEADS!
SO?

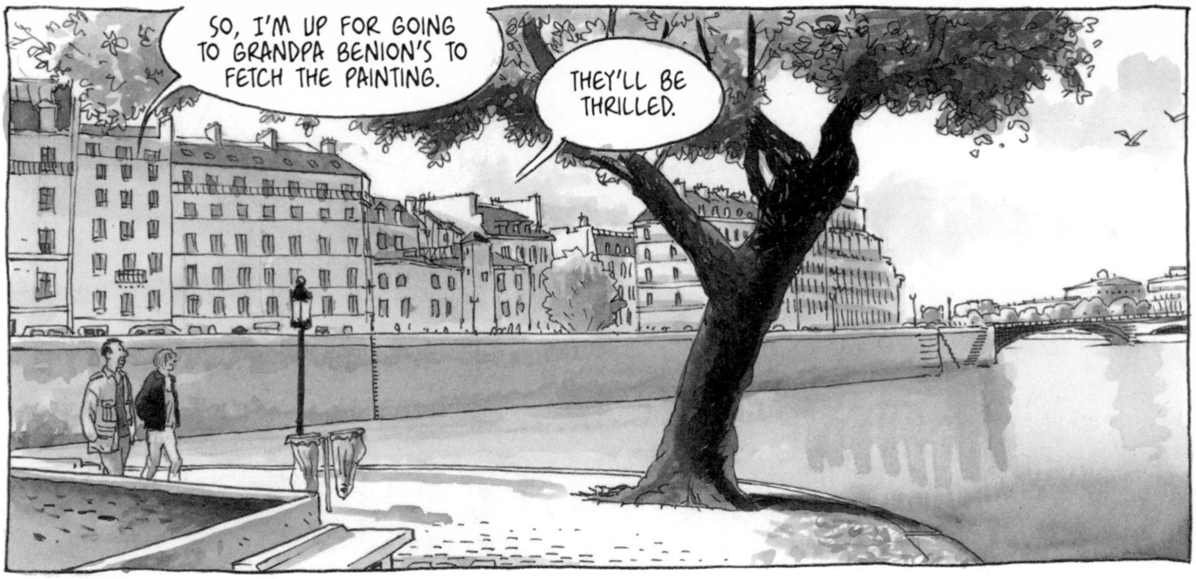
SO, I'M UP FOR GOING TO GRANDPA BENION'S TO FETCH THE PAINTING.
THEY'LL BE THRILLED.

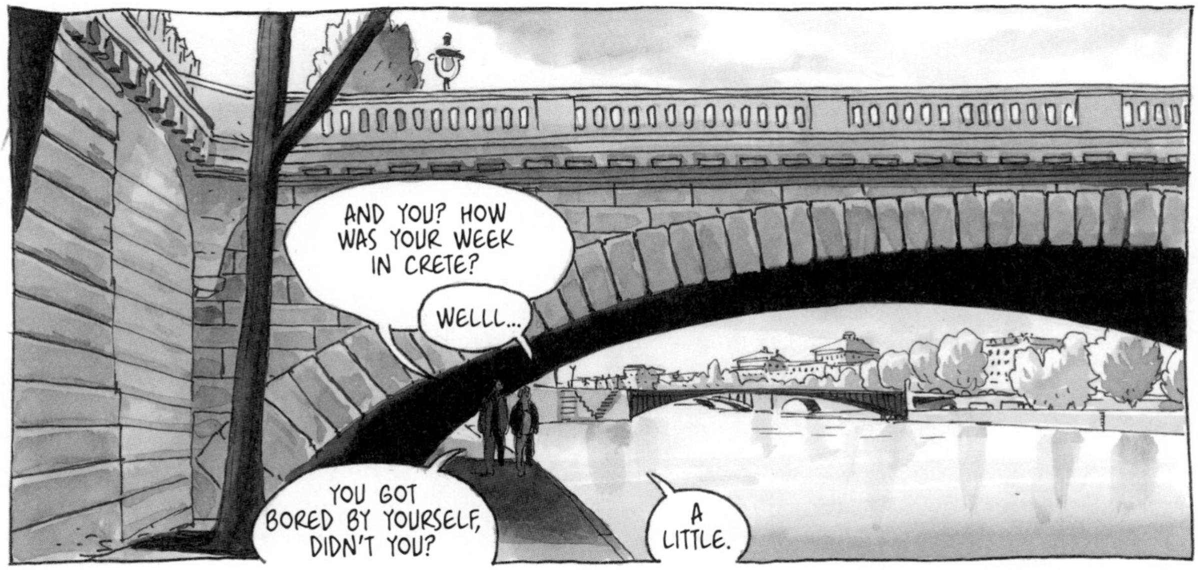
AND YOU? HOW WAS YOUR WEEK IN CRETE?
WELLL...
YOU GOT BORED BY YOURSELF, DIDN'T YOU?
A LITTLE.

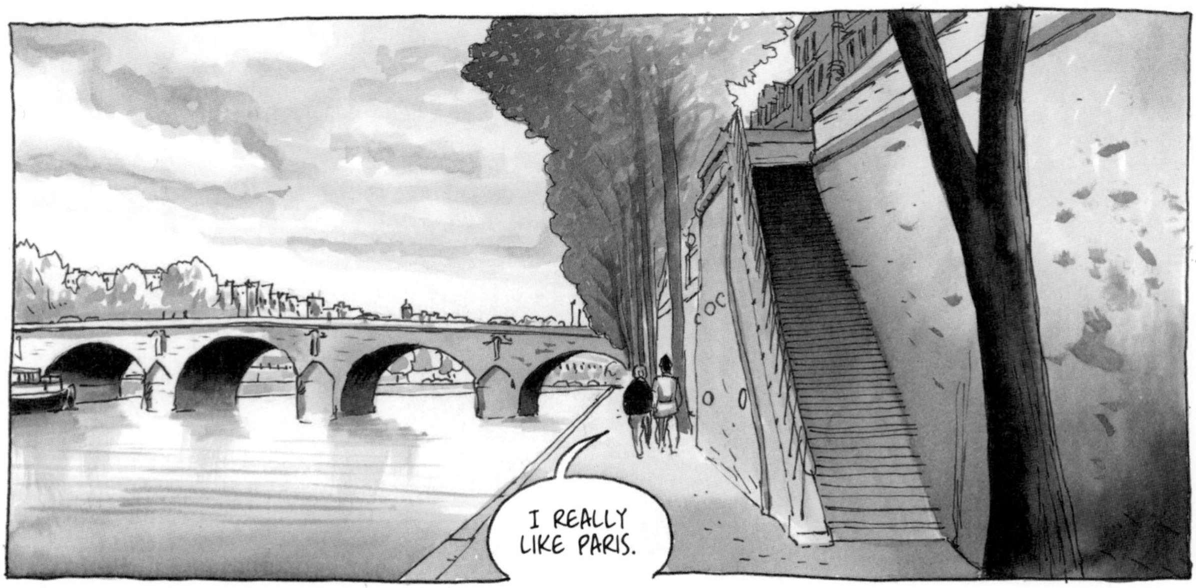
I REALLY LIKE PARIS.

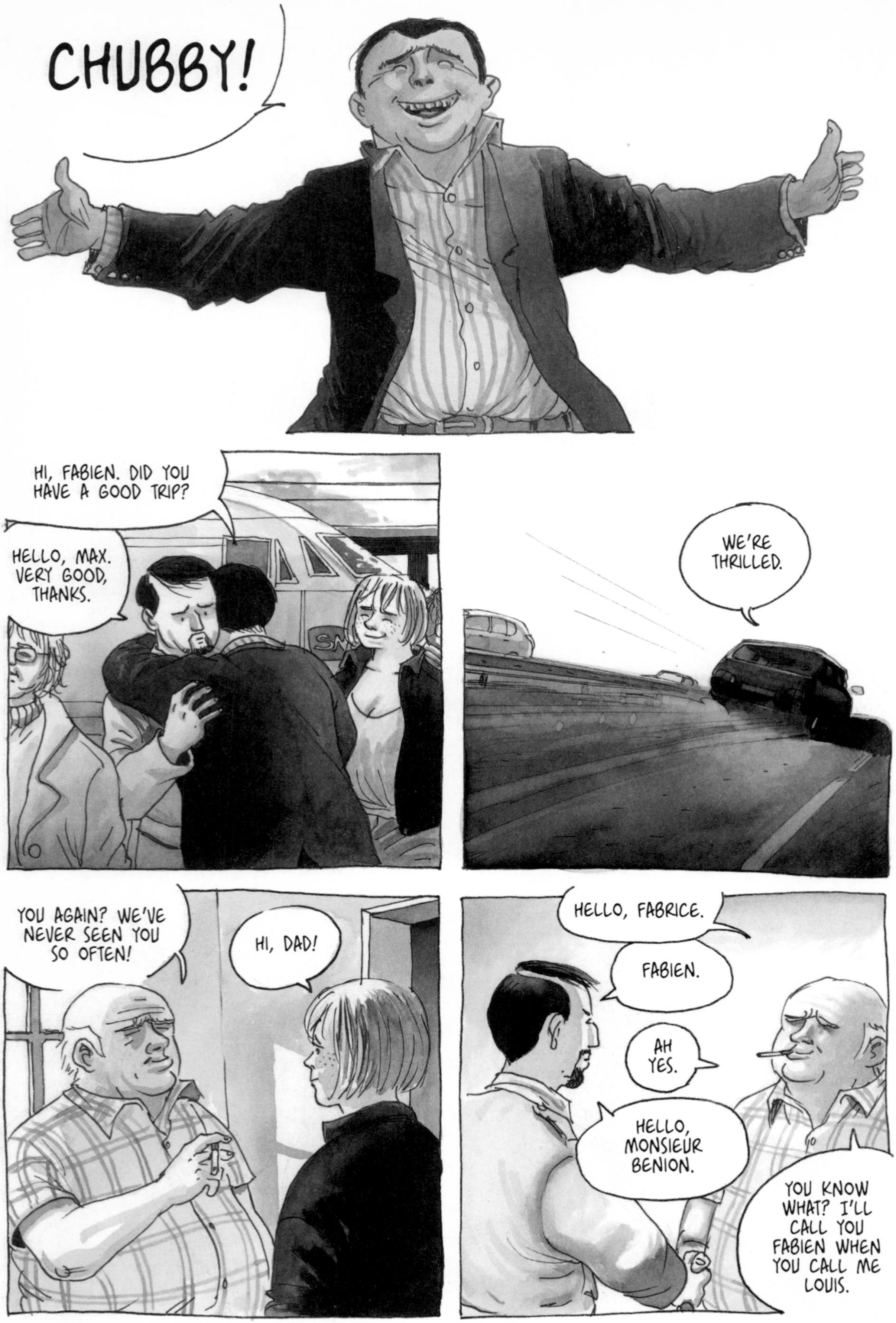
CHUBBY!
HI, FABIEN. DID YOU HAVE A GOOD TRIP?
HELLO, MAX. VERY GOOD, THANKS.
WE'RE THRILLED.
YOU AGAIN? WE'VE NEVER SEEN YOU SO OFTEN!
HI, DAD!
HELLO, FABRICE.
FABIEN.
AH YES.
HELLO, MONSIEUR BENION.
YOU KNOW WHAT? I'LL CALL YOU FABIEN WHEN YOU CALL ME LOUIS.

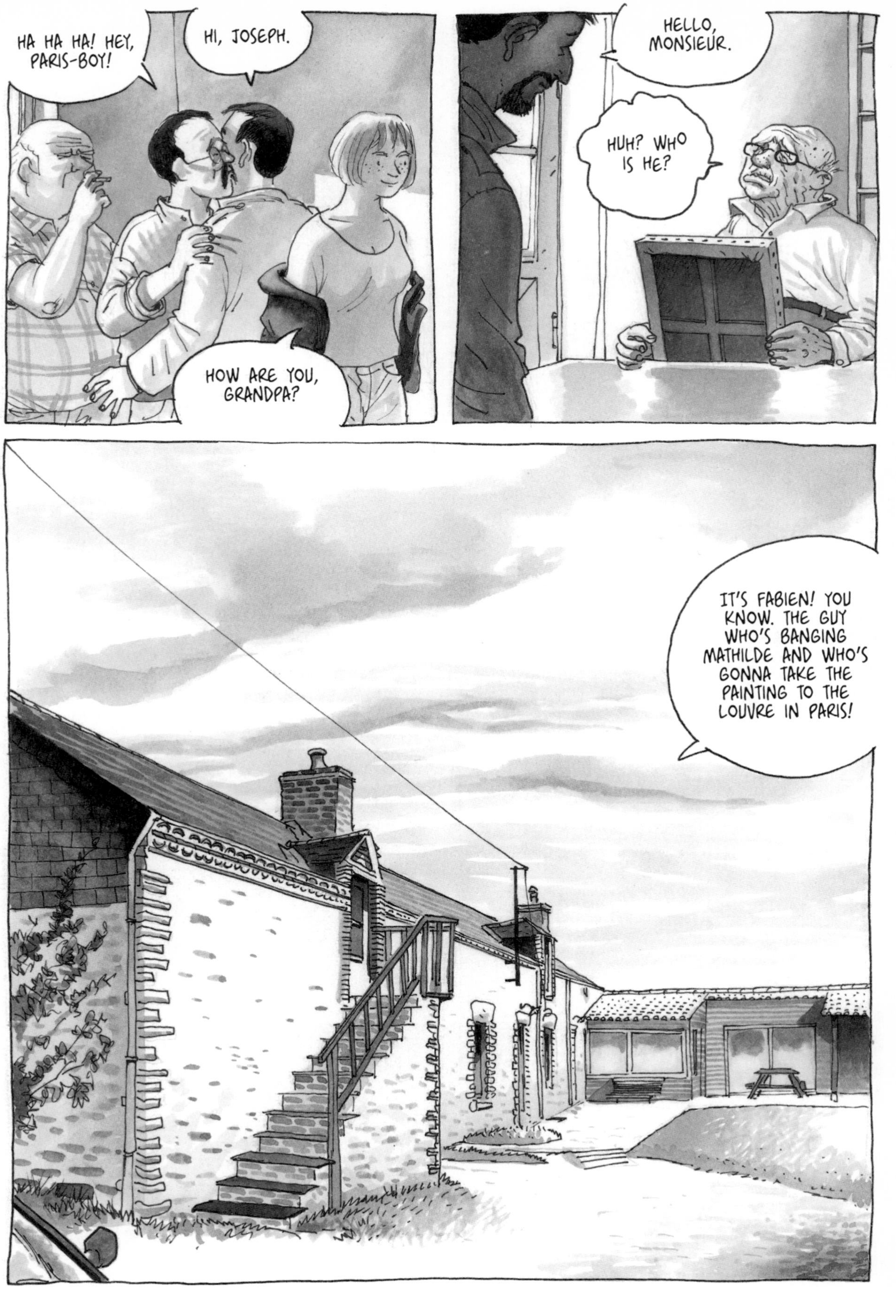
HA HA HA! HEY, PARIS-BOY!
HI, JOSEPH.
HOW ARE YOU, GRANDPA?
HELLO, MONSIEUR.
HUH? WHO IS HE?
IT'S FABIEN! YOU KNOW. THE GUY WHO'S BANGING MATHILDE AND WHO'S GONNA TAKE THE PAINTING TO THE LOUVRE IN PARIS!

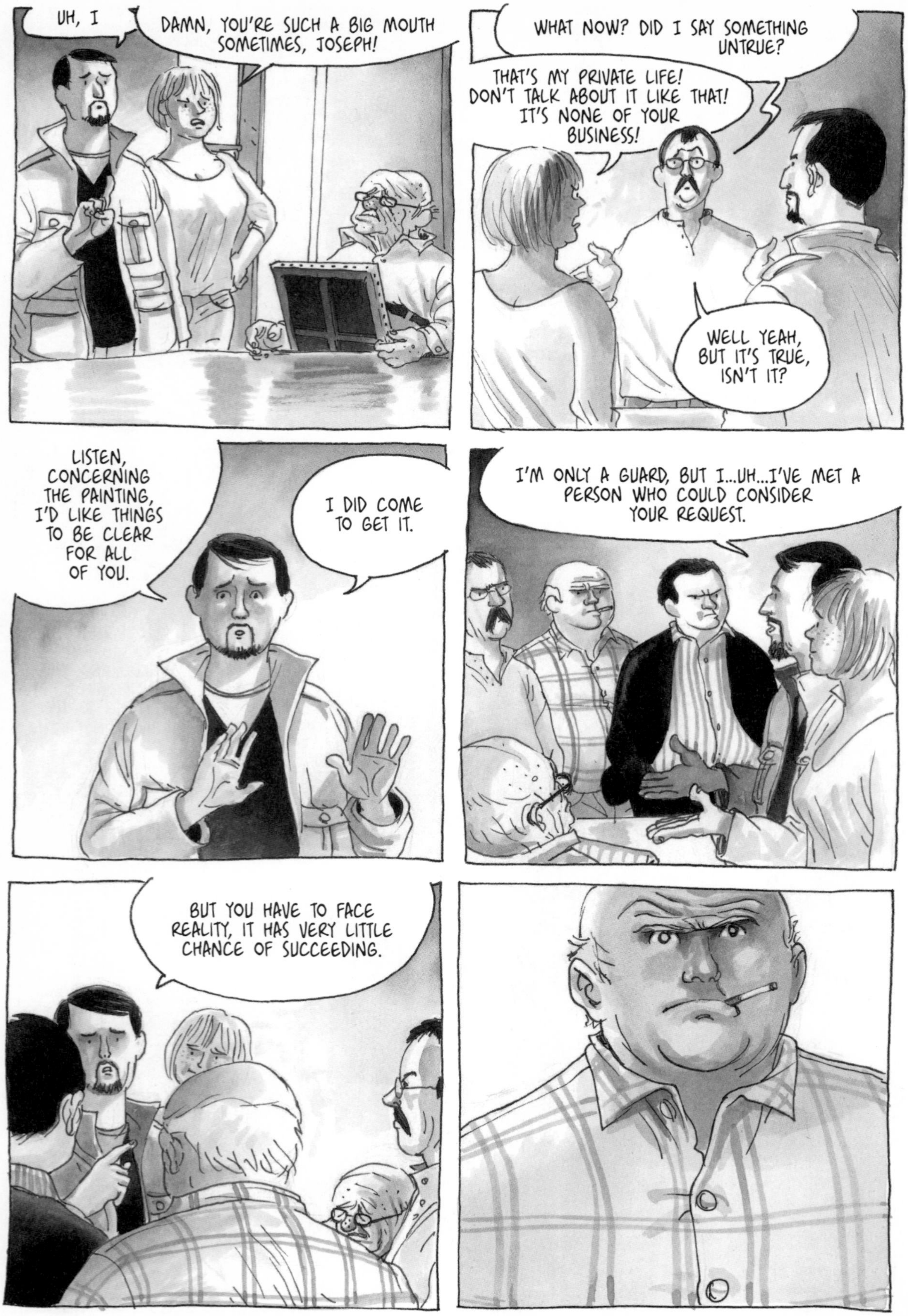
UH, I
DAMN, YOU'RE SUCH A BIG MOUTH SOMETIMES, JOSEPH!
WHAT NOW? DID I SAY SOMETHING UNTRUE?
THAT'S MY PRIVATE LIFE! DON'T TALK ABOUT IT LIKE THAT! IT'S NONE OF YOUR BUSINESS!
WELL YEAH, BUT IT'S TRUE, ISN'T IT?
LISTEN, CONCERNING THE PAINTING, I'D LIKE THINGS TO BE CLEAR FOR ALL OF YOU.
I DID COME TO GET IT.
I'M ONLY A GUARD, BUT I...UH...I'VE MET A PERSON WHO COULD CONSIDER YOUR REQUEST.
BUT YOU HAVE TO FACE REALITY, IT HAS VERY LITTLE CHANCE OF SUCCEEDING.

I GET IT.

IT'S FAIR GAME.

HOW MUCH?

SORRY?

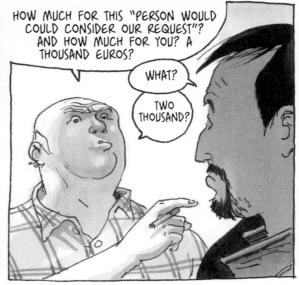

HOW MUCH FOR THIS "PERSON WOULD COULD CONSIDER OUR REQUEST"? AND HOW MUCH FOR YOU? A THOUSAND EUROS?

WHAT?

TWO THOUSAND?

NO! NOBODY'S DEMANDING MONEY! YOU'RE COMPLETELY MISTAKEN, LOUIS!

I'M NOT DOING IT FOR THAT!

BESIDES WE'RE GIVING HIM OUR SISTER. THAT SEEMS EQUITABLE TO ME.

HOLY COW! WHAT A HARDNOSED NEGOTIATOR!

HA HA HA HA HA HA

AS YOU CAN SEE, WE WERE LUCKY TO HAVE MET. I COULD HAVE FLED MUCH FARTHER AWAY THAN PARIS.

CHILDREN...

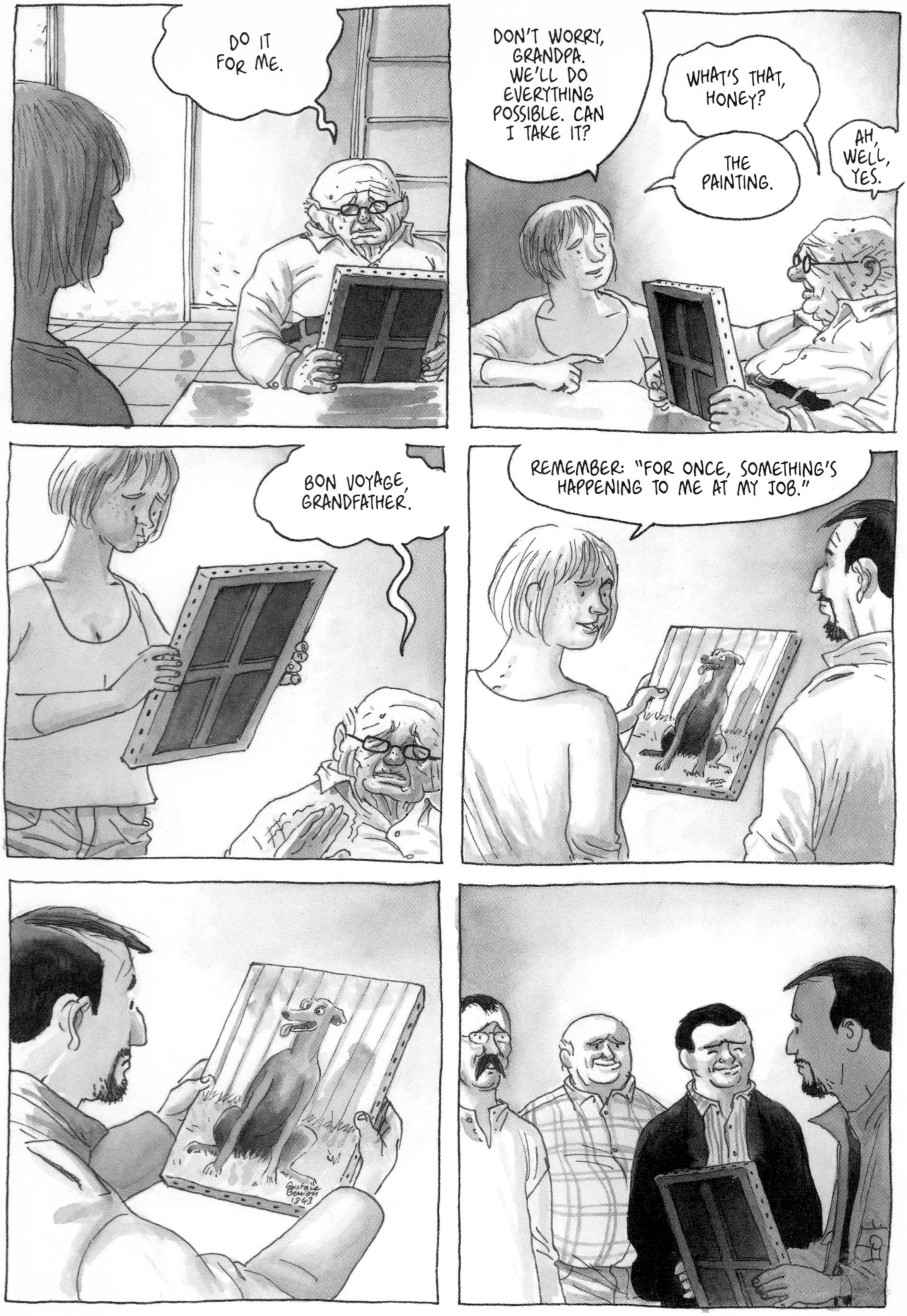
DO IT FOR ME.
DON'T WORRY, GRANDPA. WE'LL DO EVERYTHING POSSIBLE. CAN I TAKE IT?
WHAT'S THAT, HONEY?
THE PAINTING.
AH, WELL, YES.
BON VOYAGE, GRANDFATHER.
REMEMBER: "FOR ONCE, SOMETHING'S HAPPENING TO ME AT MY JOB."

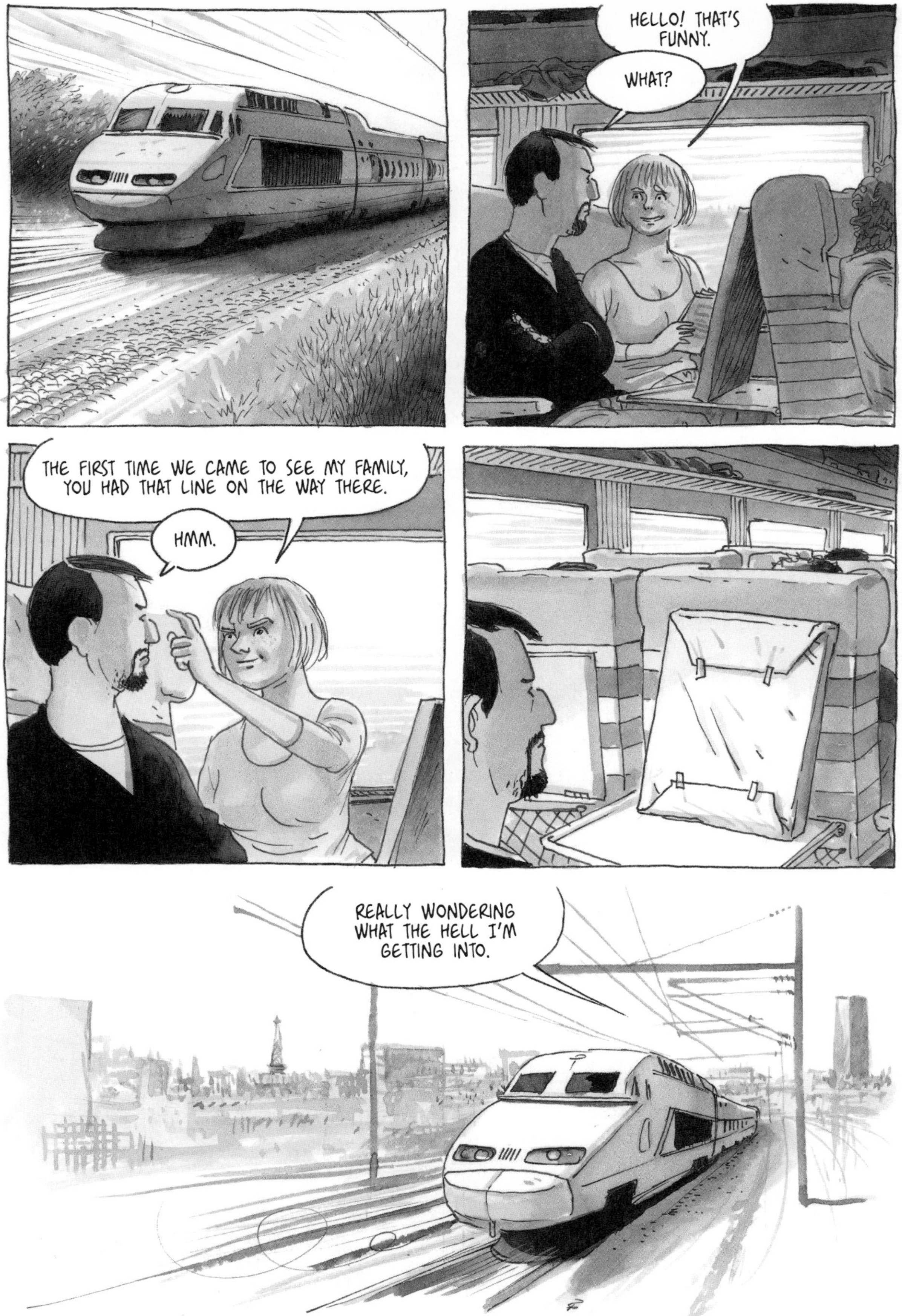
HELLO! THAT'S FUNNY.
WHAT?
THE FIRST TIME WE CAME TO SEE MY FAMILY, YOU HAD THAT LINE ON THE WAY THERE.
HMM.
REALLY WONDERING WHAT THE HELL I'M GETTING INTO.

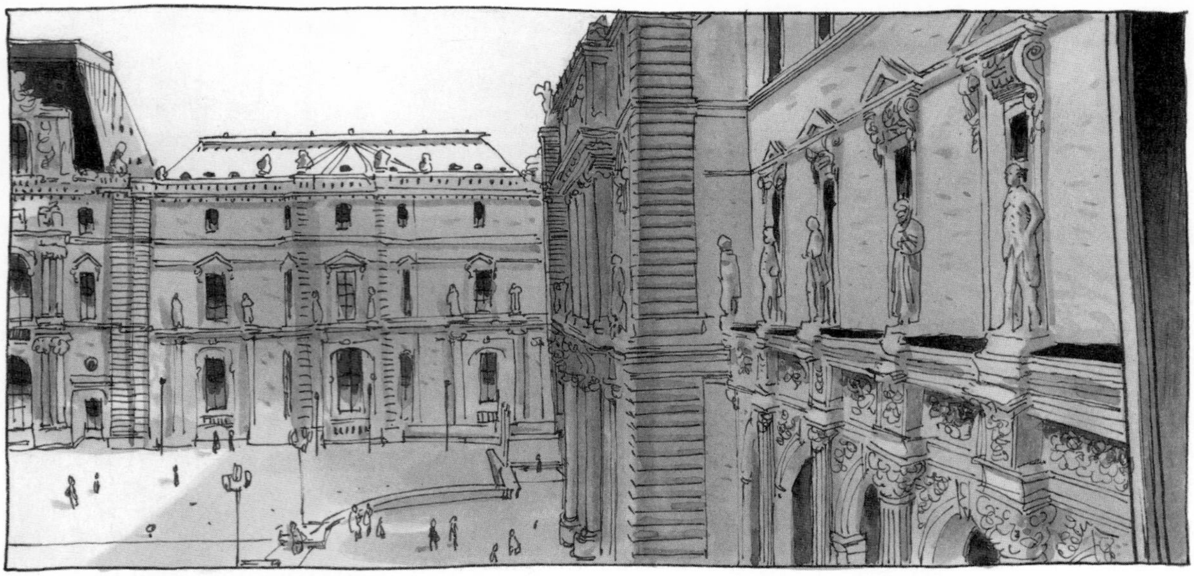

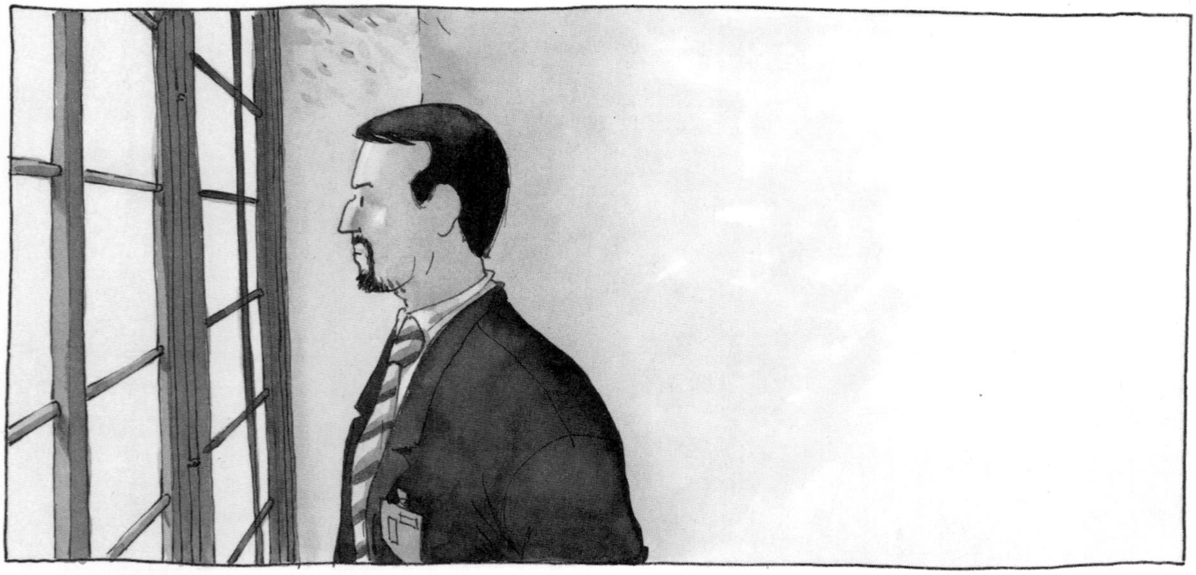

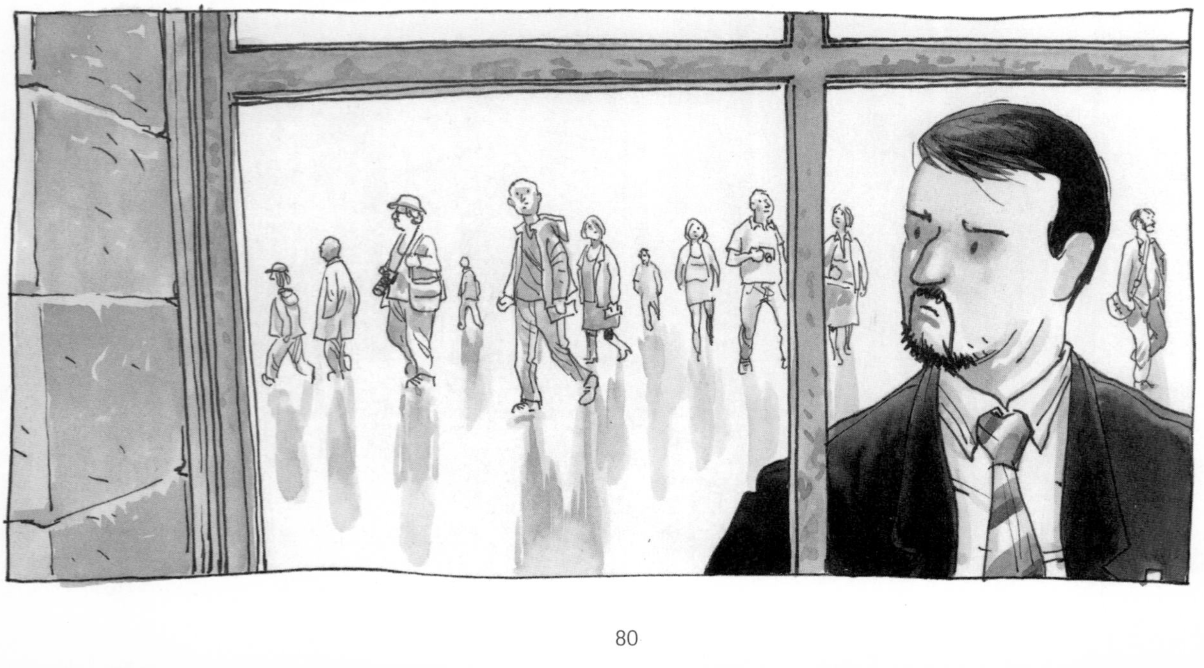

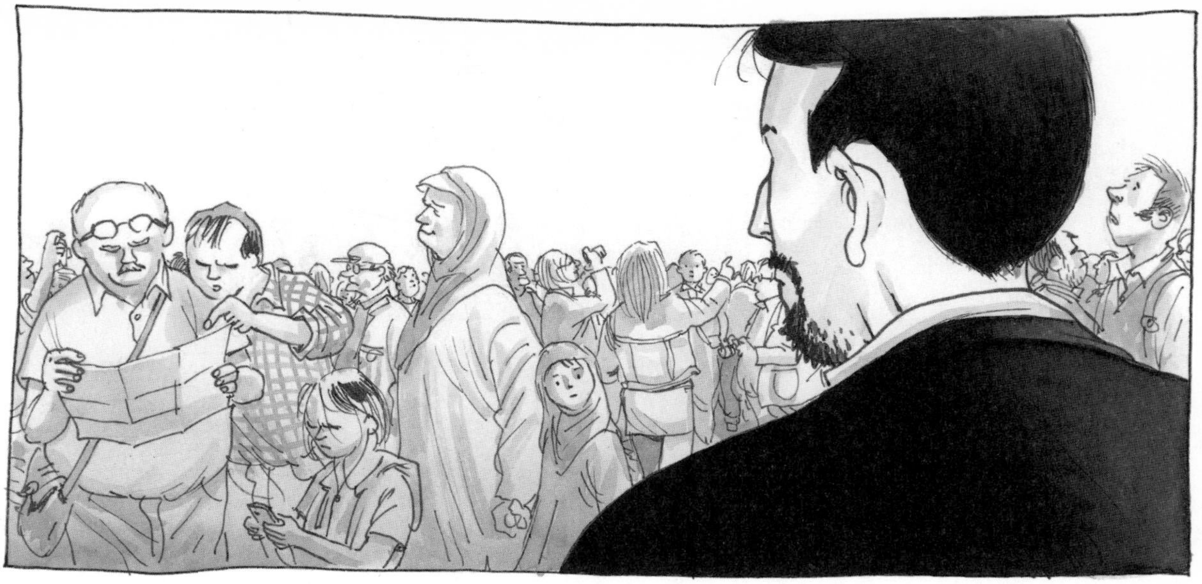

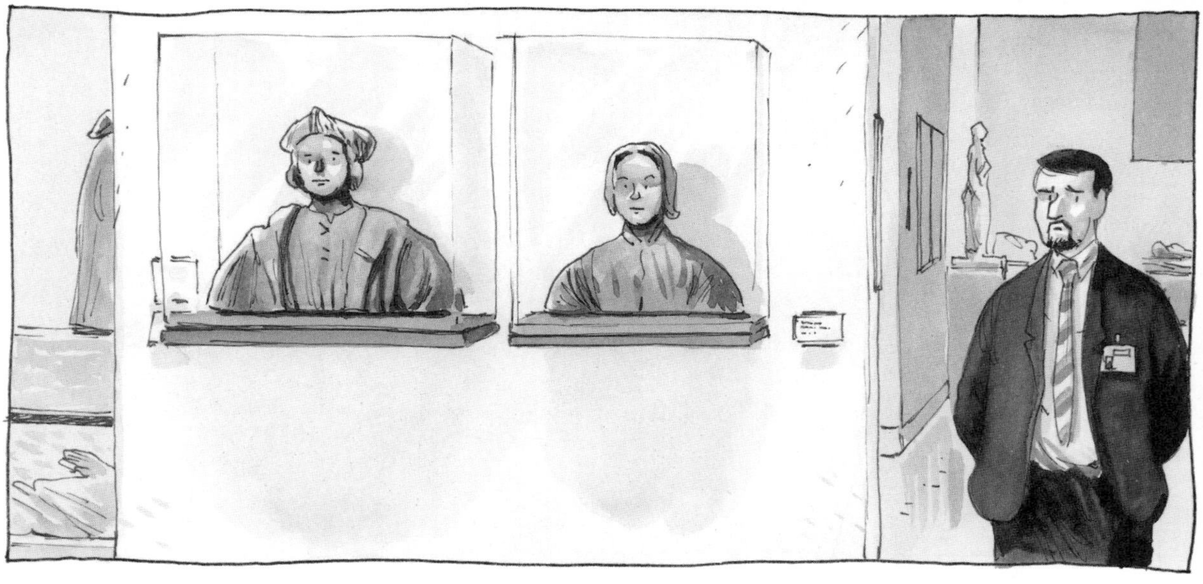

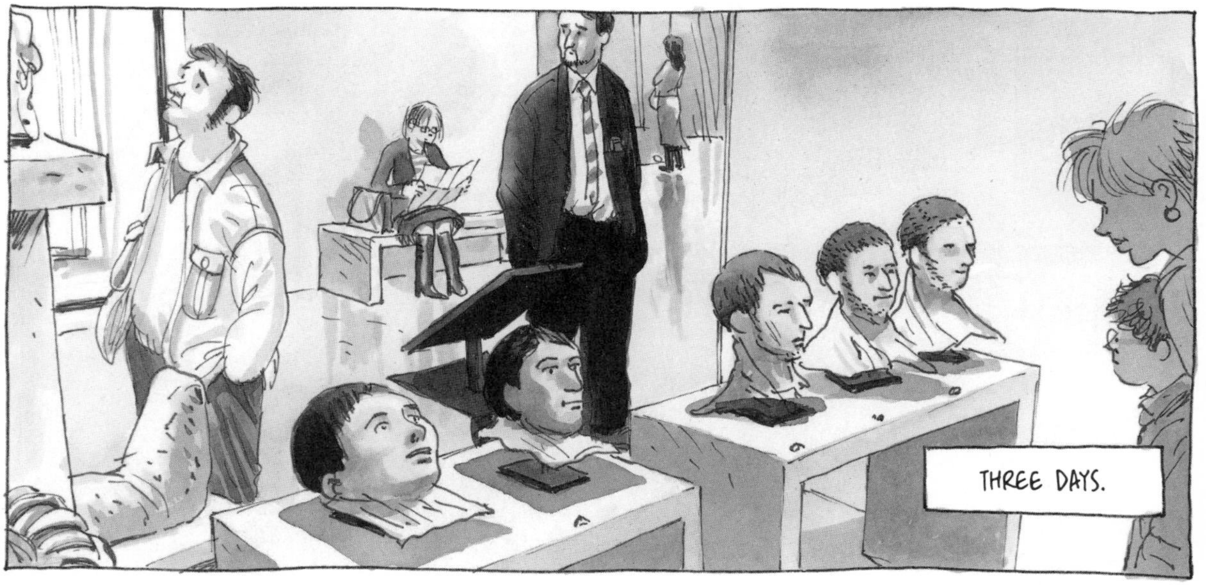
THREE DAYS.

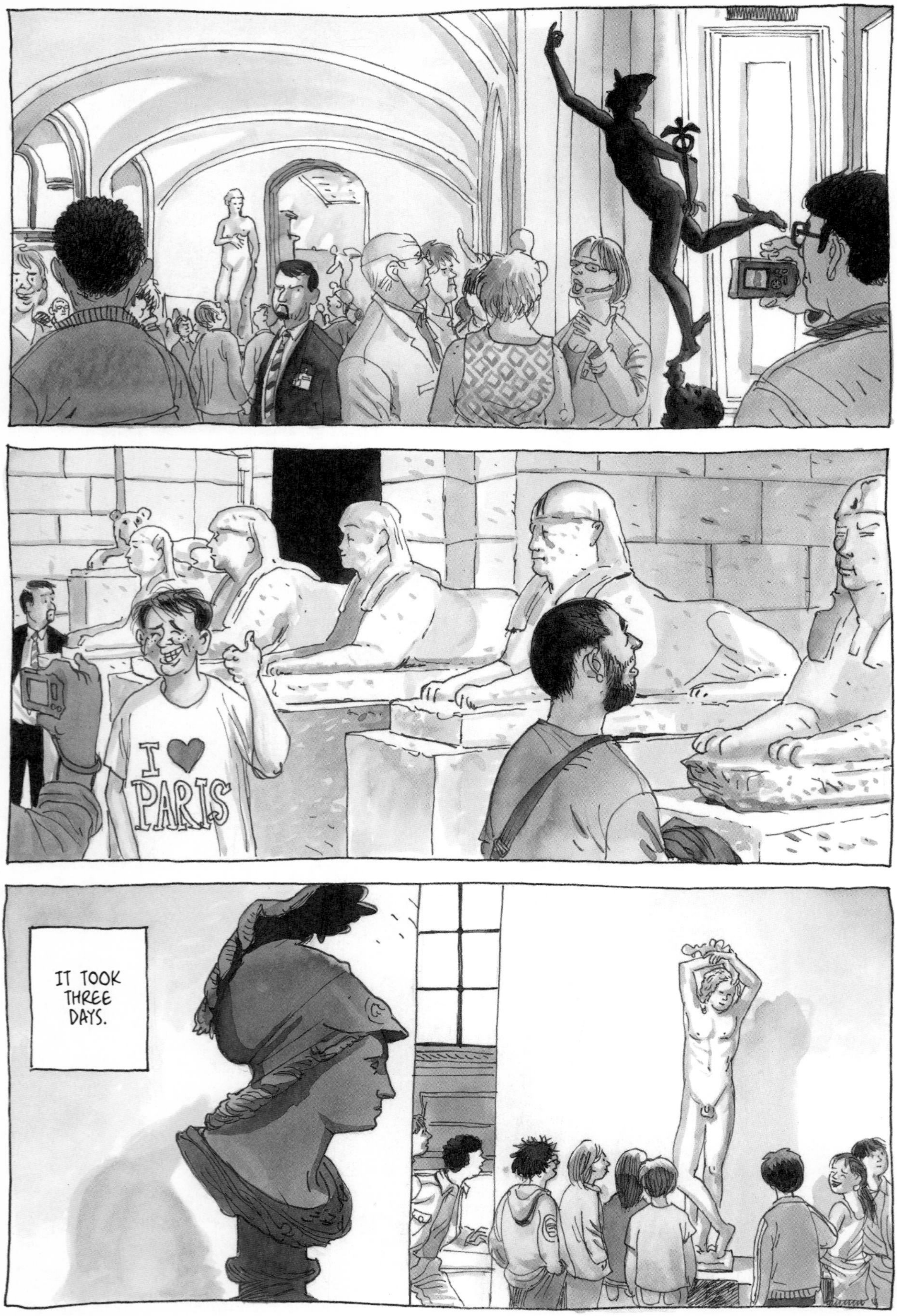
I ♥ PARIS
IT TOOK THREE DAYS.

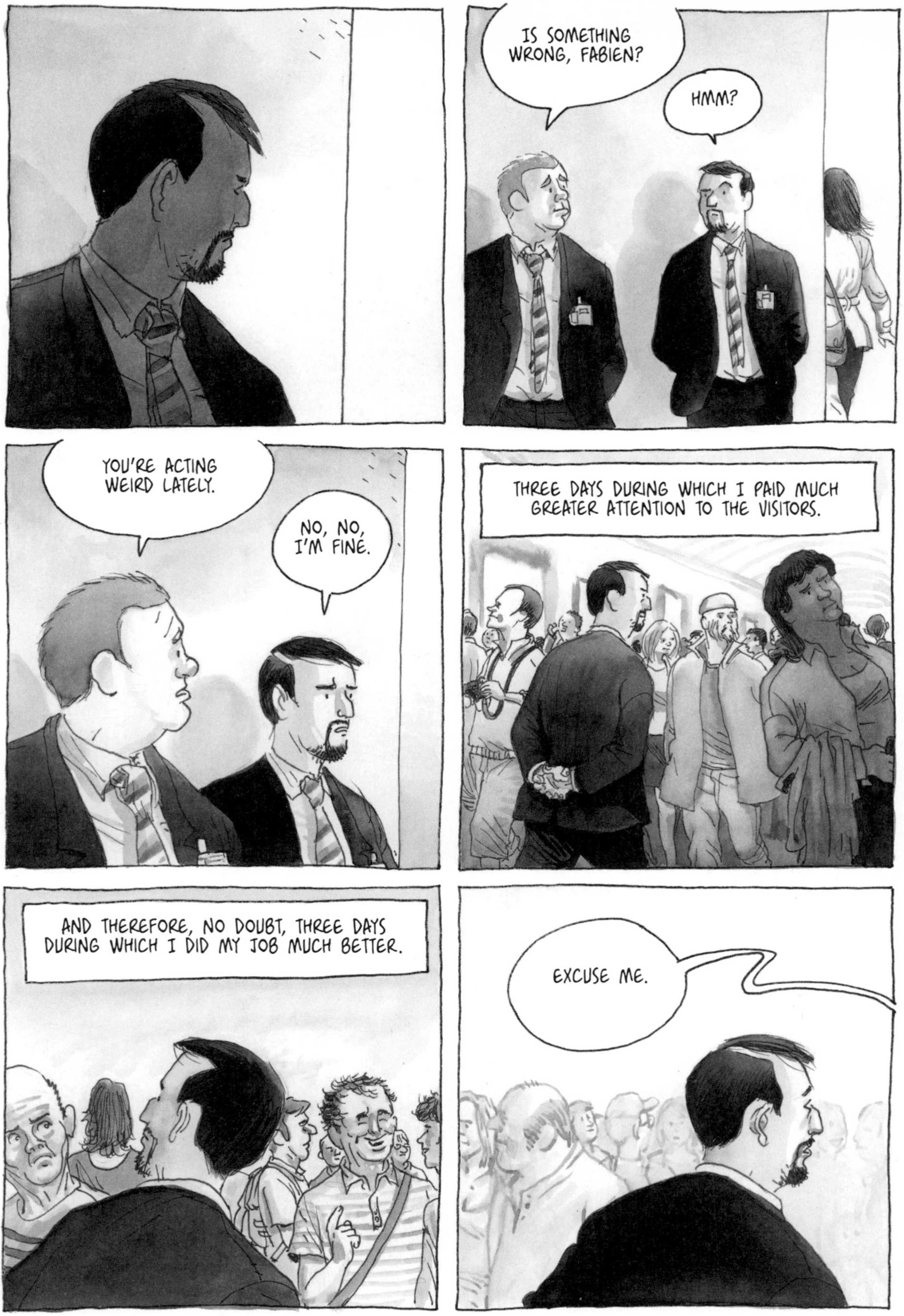
IS SOMETHING WRONG, FABIEN?
HMM?
YOU'RE ACTING WEIRD LATELY.
NO, NO, I'M FINE.
THREE DAYS DURING WHICH I PAID MUCH GREATER ATTENTION TO THE VISITORS.
AND THEREFORE, NO DOUBT, THREE DAYS DURING WHICH I DID MY JOB MUCH BETTER.
EXCUSE ME.

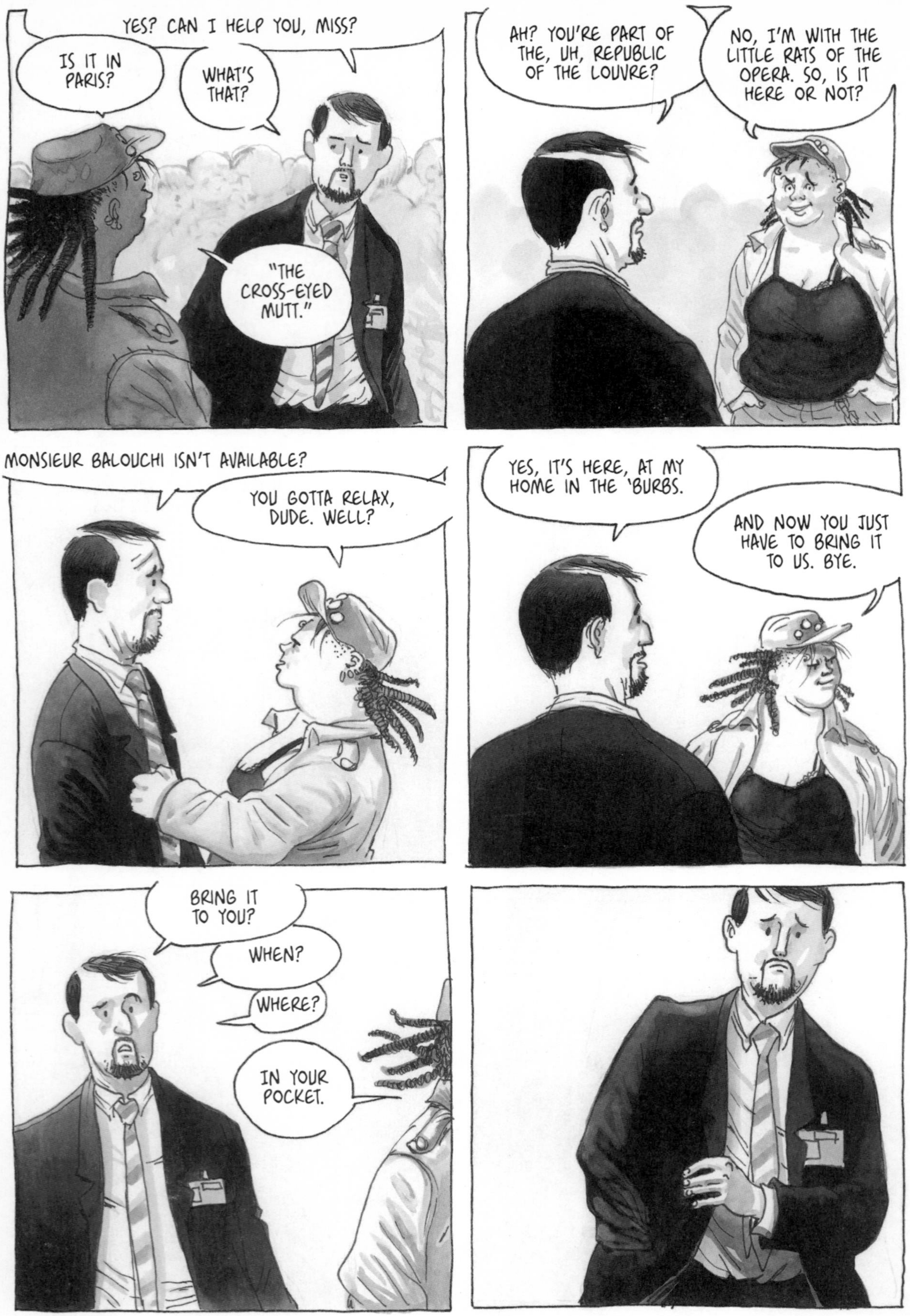
YES? CAN I HELP YOU, MISS?
IS IT IN PARIS?
WHAT'S THAT?
"THE CROSS-EYED MUTT."
AH? YOU'RE PART OF THE, UH, REPUBLIC OF THE LOUVRE?
NO, I'M WITH THE LITTLE RATS OF THE OPERA. SO, IS IT HERE OR NOT?
MONSIEUR BALOUCHI ISN'T AVAILABLE?
YOU GOTTA RELAX, DUDE. WELL?
YES, IT'S HERE, AT MY HOME IN THE 'BURBS.
AND NOW YOU JUST HAVE TO BRING IT TO US. BYE.
BRING IT TO YOU?
WHEN?
WHERE?
IN YOUR POCKET.

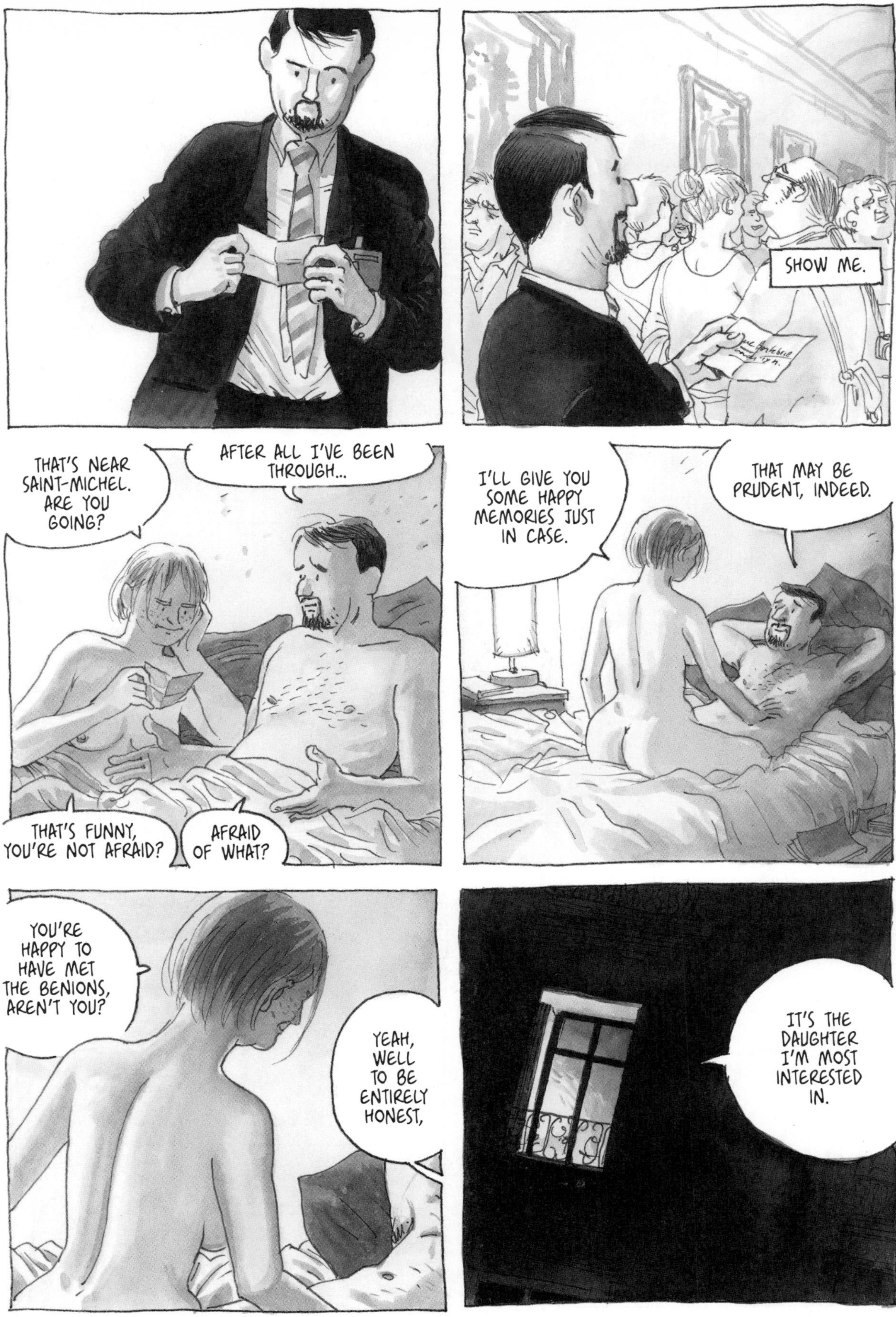
SHOW ME.
THAT'S NEAR SAINT-MICHEL. ARE YOU GOING?
AFTER ALL I'VE BEEN THROUGH...
THAT'S FUNNY, YOU'RE NOT AFRAID?
AFRAID OF WHAT?
I'LL GIVE YOU SOME HAPPY MEMORIES JUST IN CASE.
THAT MAY BE PRUDENT, INDEED.
YOU'RE HAPPY TO HAVE MET THE BENIONS, AREN'T YOU?
YEAH, WELL TO BE ENTIRELY HONEST,
IT'S THE DAUGHTER I'M MOST INTERESTED IN.

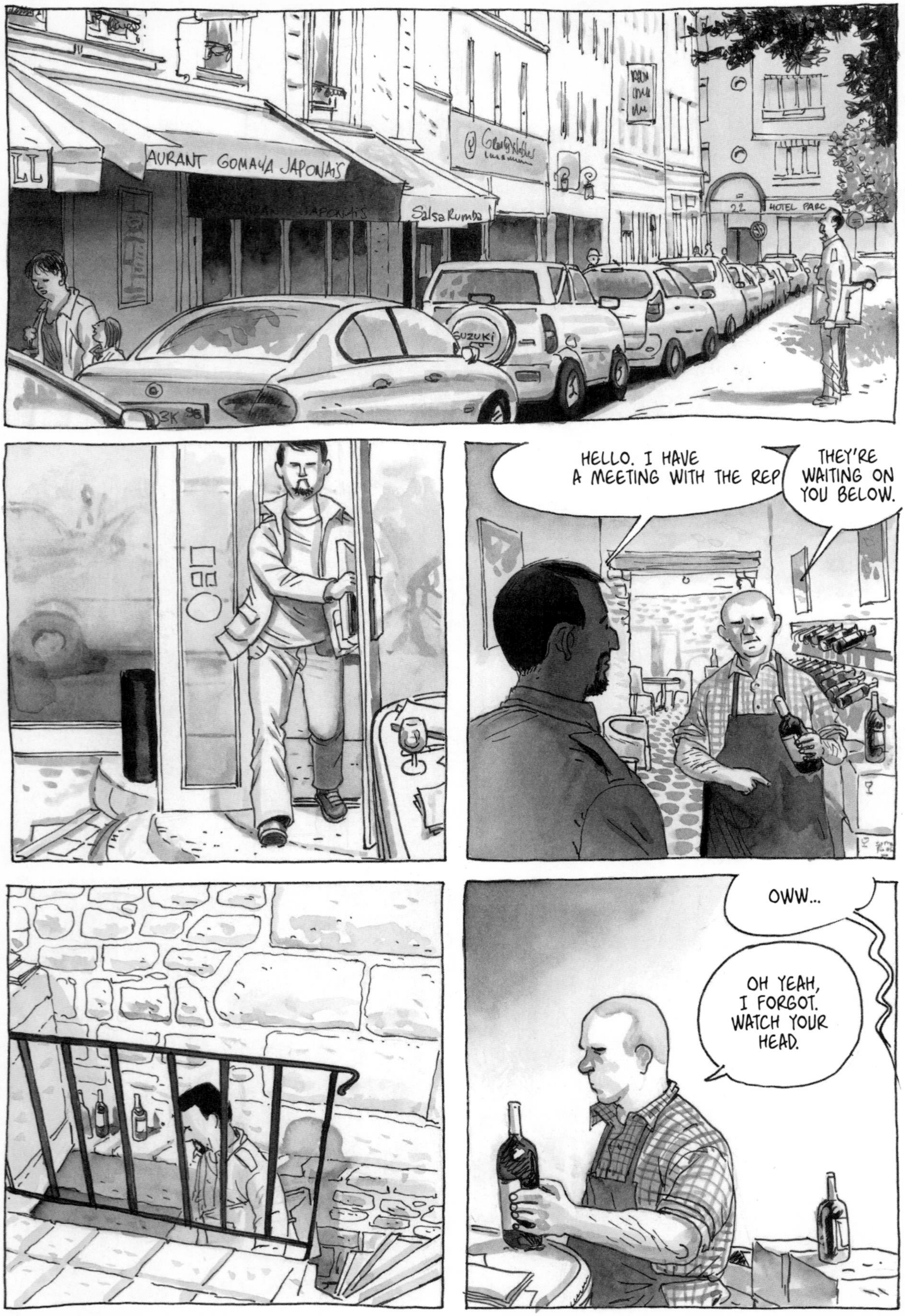
AURANT GOMAYA JAPONAIS
Salsa Rumba
HOTEL PARC
HELLO. I HAVE A MEETING WITH THE REP
THEY'RE WAITING ON YOU BELOW.
OWW...
OH YEAH, I FORGOT. WATCH YOUR HEAD.

MY DEAR FABIEN, WELCOME!

HELLO, MONSIEUR BALOUCHI.

RELAX. YOU'RE AMONG FRIENDS HERE.

HELLO, EVERYONE.

SET THE PAINTING ON THAT TABLE.

SHOULD I UNWRAP IT NOW?

PLEASE.

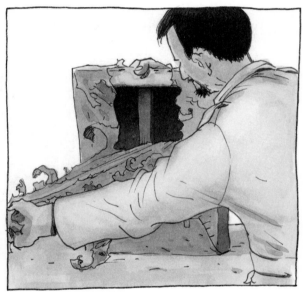

THERE.

87

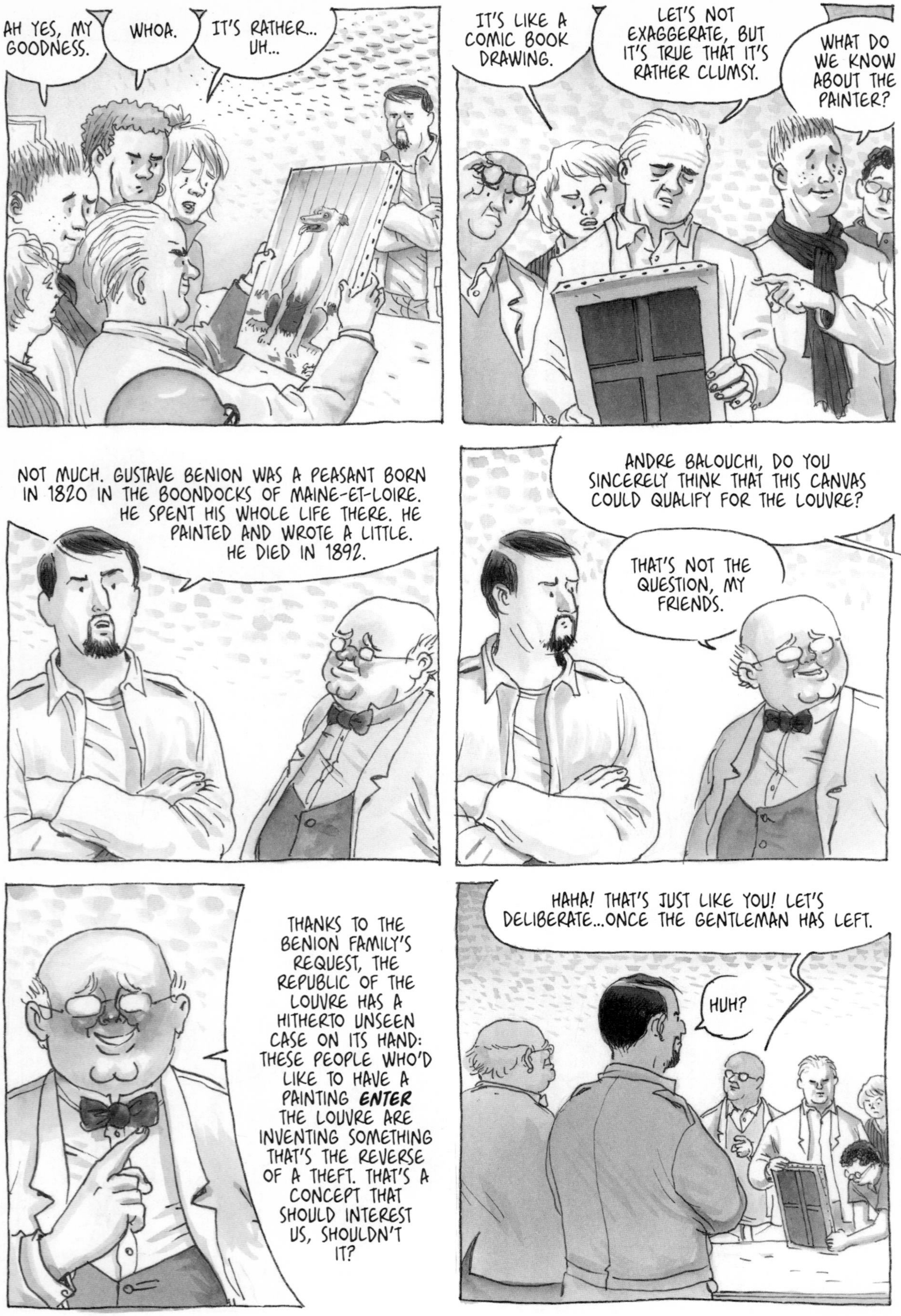
AH YES, MY GOODNESS.
WHOA.
IT'S RATHER... UH...
IT'S LIKE A COMIC BOOK DRAWING.
LET'S NOT EXAGGERATE, BUT IT'S TRUE THAT IT'S RATHER CLUMSY.
WHAT DO WE KNOW ABOUT THE PAINTER?
NOT MUCH. GUSTAVE BENION WAS A PEASANT BORN IN 1820 IN THE BOONDOCKS OF MAINE-ET-LOIRE. HE SPENT HIS WHOLE LIFE THERE. HE PAINTED AND WROTE A LITTLE. HE DIED IN 1892.
ANDRE BALOUCHI, DO YOU SINCERELY THINK THAT THIS CANVAS COULD QUALIFY FOR THE LOUVRE?
THAT'S NOT THE QUESTION, MY FRIENDS.
THANKS TO THE BENION FAMILY'S REQUEST, THE REPUBLIC OF THE LOUVRE HAS A HITHERTO UNSEEN CASE ON ITS HAND: THESE PEOPLE WHO'D LIKE TO HAVE A PAINTING ENTER THE LOUVRE ARE INVENTING SOMETHING THAT'S THE REVERSE OF A THEFT. THAT'S A CONCEPT THAT SHOULD INTEREST US, SHOULDN'T IT?
HAHA! THAT'S JUST LIKE YOU! LET'S DELIBERATE...ONCE THE GENTLEMAN HAS LEFT.
HUH?

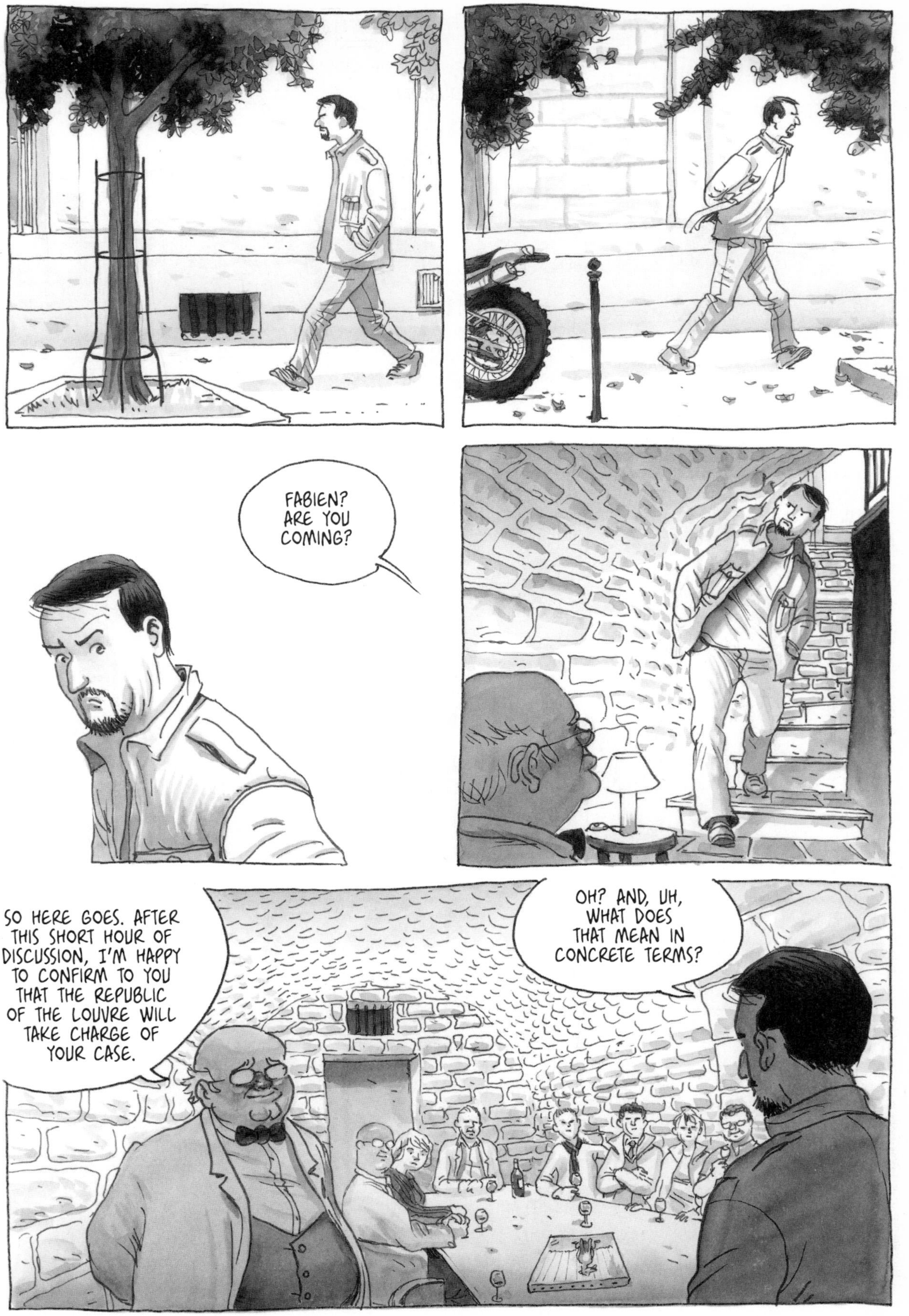
FABIEN? ARE YOU COMING?
SO HERE GOES. AFTER THIS SHORT HOUR OF DISCUSSION, I'M HAPPY TO CONFIRM TO YOU THAT THE REPUBLIC OF THE LOUVRE WILL TAKE CHARGE OF YOUR CASE.
OH? AND, UH, WHAT DOES THAT MEAN IN CONCRETE TERMS?

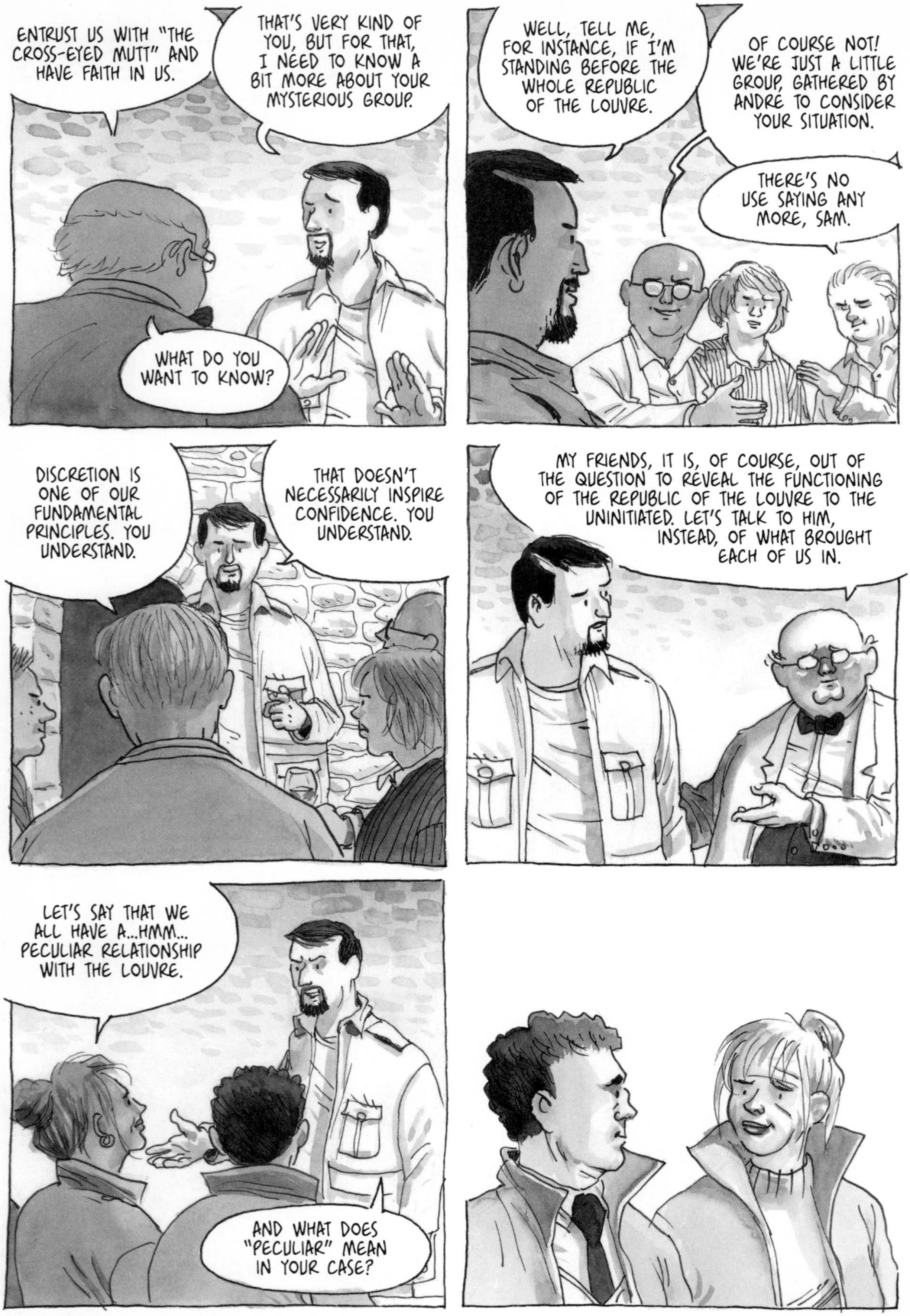
ENTRUST US WITH "THE CROSS-EYED MUTT" AND HAVE FAITH IN US.
THAT'S VERY KIND OF YOU, BUT FOR THAT, I NEED TO KNOW A BIT MORE ABOUT YOUR MYSTERIOUS GROUP.
WHAT DO YOU WANT TO KNOW?
WELL, TELL ME, FOR INSTANCE, IF I'M STANDING BEFORE THE WHOLE REPUBLIC OF THE LOUVRE.
OF COURSE NOT! WE'RE JUST A LITTLE GROUP, GATHERED BY ANDRE TO CONSIDER YOUR SITUATION.
THERE'S NO USE SAYING ANY MORE, SAM.
DISCRETION IS ONE OF OUR FUNDAMENTAL PRINCIPLES. YOU UNDERSTAND.
THAT DOESN'T NECESSARILY INSPIRE CONFIDENCE. YOU UNDERSTAND.
MY FRIENDS, IT IS, OF COURSE, OUT OF THE QUESTION TO REVEAL THE FUNCTIONING OF THE REPUBLIC OF THE LOUVRE TO THE UNINITIATED. LET'S TALK TO HIM, INSTEAD, OF WHAT BROUGHT EACH OF US IN.
LET'S SAY THAT WE ALL HAVE A...HMM... PECULIAR RELATIONSHIP WITH THE LOUVRE.
AND WHAT DOES "PECULIAR" MEAN IN YOUR CASE?

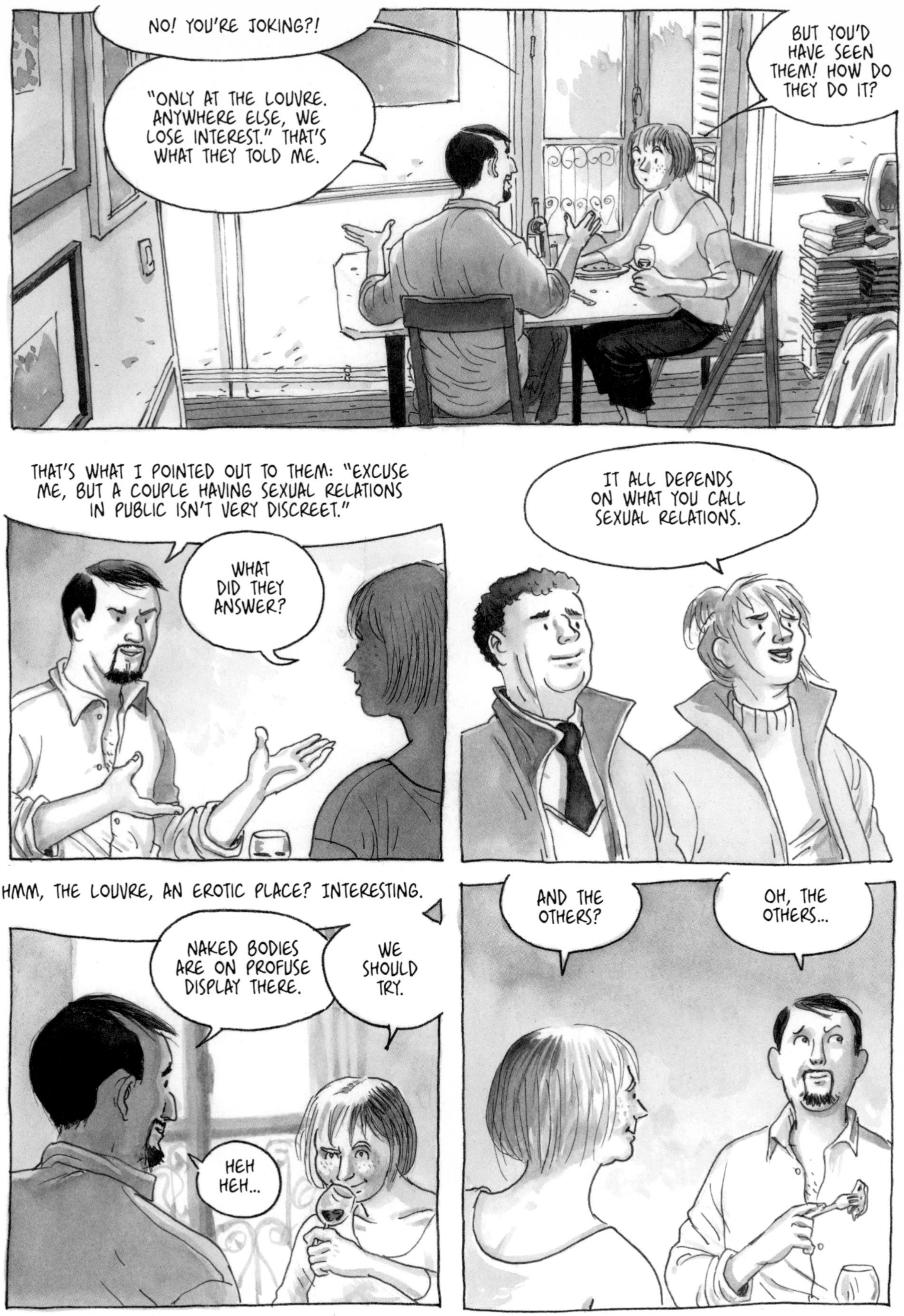

NO! YOU'RE JOKING?!
"ONLY AT THE LOUVRE. ANYWHERE ELSE, WE LOSE INTEREST." THAT'S WHAT THEY TOLD ME.
BUT YOU'D HAVE SEEN THEM! HOW DO THEY DO IT?
THAT'S WHAT I POINTED OUT TO THEM: "EXCUSE ME, BUT A COUPLE HAVING SEXUAL RELATIONS IN PUBLIC ISN'T VERY DISCREET."
WHAT DID THEY ANSWER?
IT ALL DEPENDS ON WHAT YOU CALL SEXUAL RELATIONS.
HMM, THE LOUVRE, AN EROTIC PLACE? INTERESTING.
NAKED BODIES ARE ON PROFUSE DISPLAY THERE.
WE SHOULD TRY.
HEH HEH...
AND THE OTHERS?
OH, THE OTHERS...

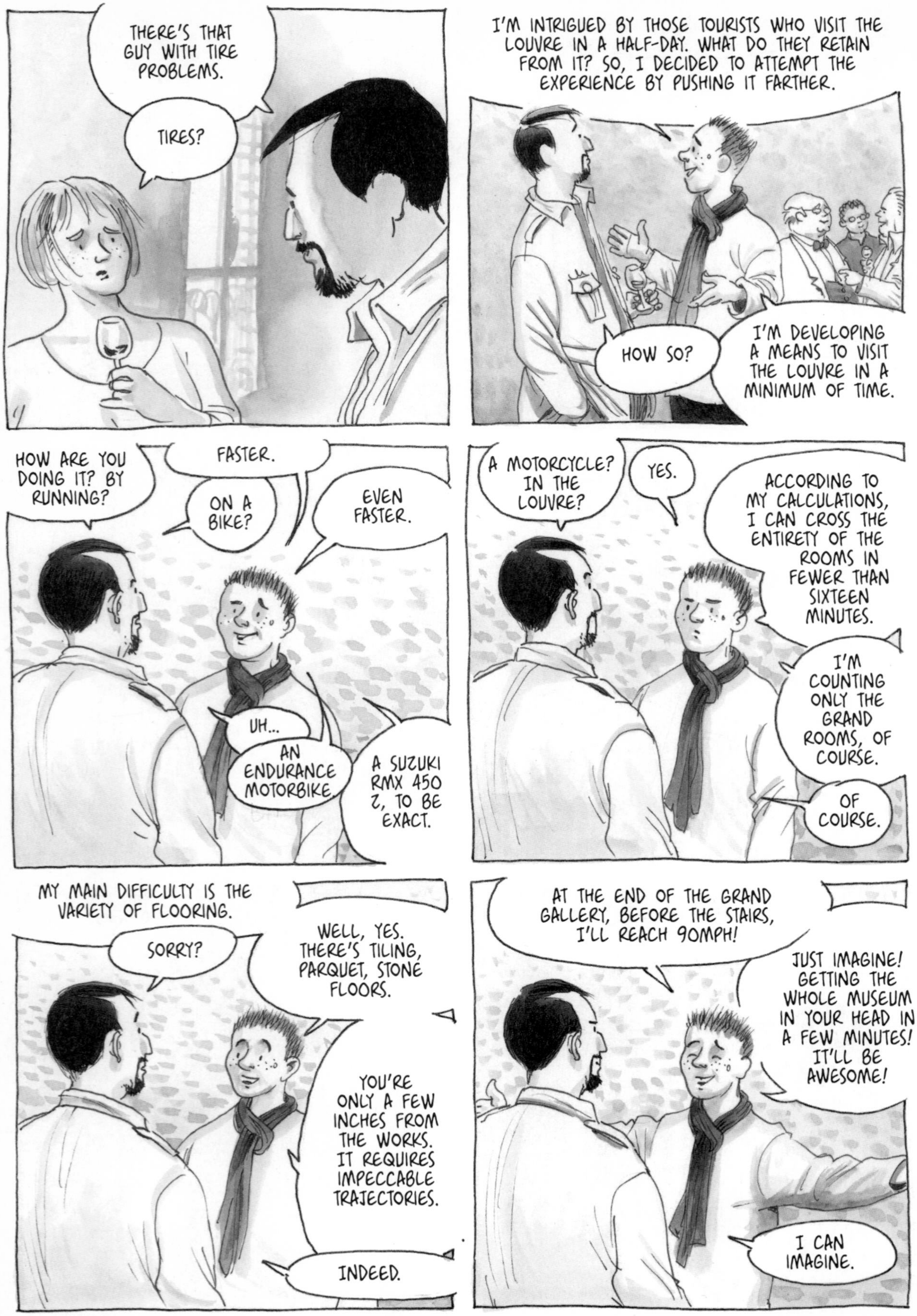
THERE'S THAT GUY WITH TIRE PROBLEMS.
TIRES?
I'M INTRIGUED BY THOSE TOURISTS WHO VISIT THE LOUVRE IN A HALF-DAY. WHAT DO THEY RETAIN FROM IT? SO, I DECIDED TO ATTEMPT THE EXPERIENCE BY PUSHING IT FARTHER.
HOW SO?
I'M DEVELOPING A MEANS TO VISIT THE LOUVRE IN A MINIMUM OF TIME.
HOW ARE YOU DOING IT? BY RUNNING?
FASTER.
ON A BIKE?
EVEN FASTER.
UH...
AN ENDURANCE MOTORBIKE.
A SUZUKI RMX 450 Z, TO BE EXACT.
A MOTORCYCLE? IN THE LOUVRE?
YES.
ACCORDING TO MY CALCULATIONS, I CAN CROSS THE ENTIRETY OF THE ROOMS IN FEWER THAN SIXTEEN MINUTES.
I'M COUNTING ONLY THE GRAND ROOMS, OF COURSE.
OF COURSE.
MY MAIN DIFFICULTY IS THE VARIETY OF FLOORING.
SORRY?
WELL, YES. THERE'S TILING, PARQUET, STONE FLOORS.
YOU'RE ONLY A FEW INCHES FROM THE WORKS. IT REQUIRES IMPECCABLE TRAJECTORIES.
INDEED.
AT THE END OF THE GRAND GALLERY, BEFORE THE STAIRS, I'LL REACH 90MPH!
JUST IMAGINE! GETTING THE WHOLE MUSEUM IN YOUR HEAD IN A FEW MINUTES! IT'LL BE AWESOME!
I CAN IMAGINE.

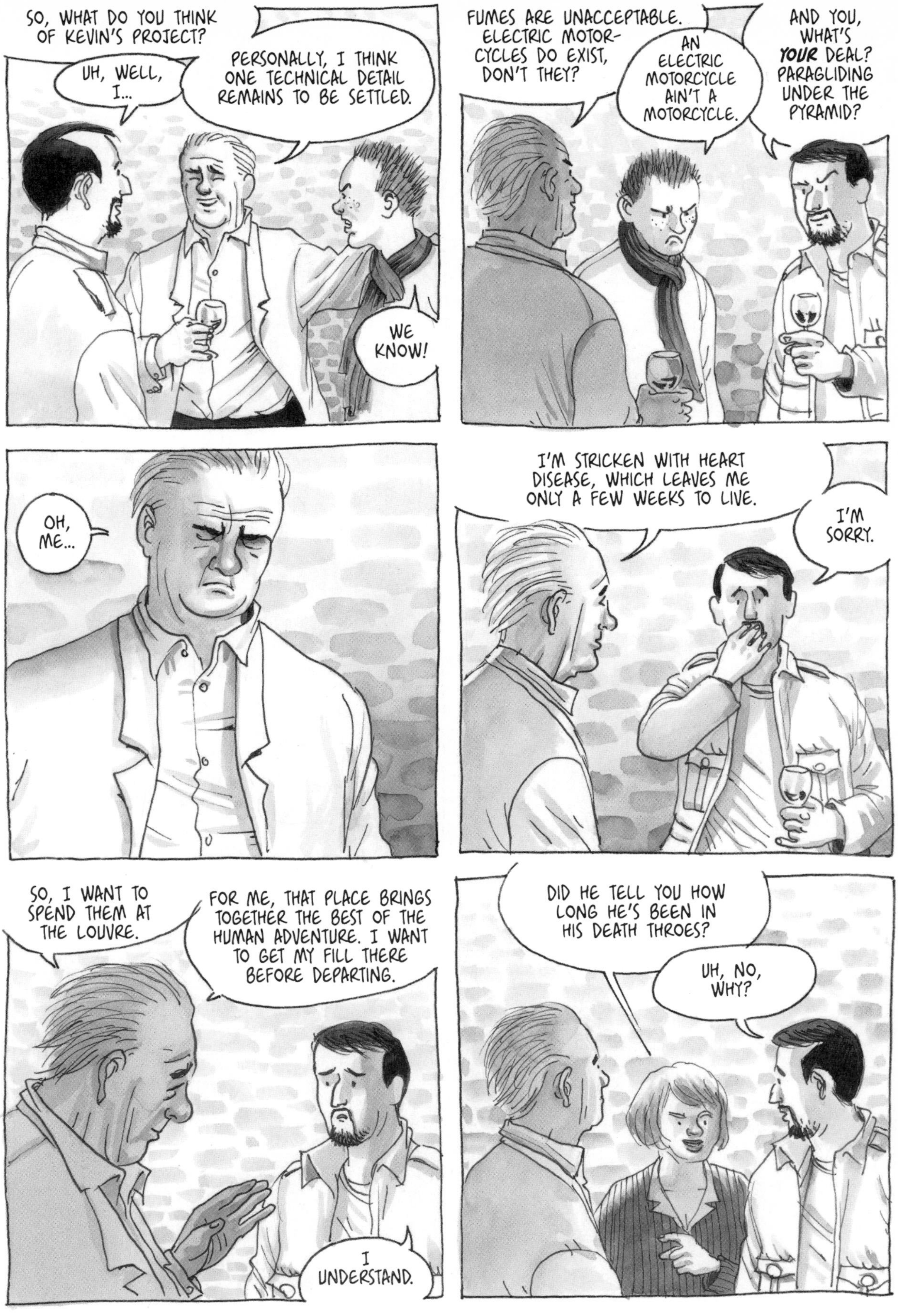
SO, WHAT DO YOU THINK OF KEVIN'S PROJECT?
UH, WELL, I...
PERSONALLY, I THINK ONE TECHNICAL DETAIL REMAINS TO BE SETTLED.
WE KNOW!
FUMES ARE UNACCEPTABLE. ELECTRIC MOTOR-CYCLES DO EXIST, DON'T THEY?
AN ELECTRIC MOTORCYCLE AIN'T A MOTORCYCLE.
AND YOU, WHAT'S **YOUR** DEAL? PARAGLIDING UNDER THE PYRAMID?
OH, ME...
I'M STRICKEN WITH HEART DISEASE, WHICH LEAVES ME ONLY A FEW WEEKS TO LIVE.
I'M SORRY.
SO, I WANT TO SPEND THEM AT THE LOUVRE.
FOR ME, THAT PLACE BRINGS TOGETHER THE BEST OF THE HUMAN ADVENTURE. I WANT TO GET MY FILL THERE BEFORE DEPARTING.
I UNDERSTAND.
DID HE TELL YOU HOW LONG HE'S BEEN IN HIS DEATH THROES?
UH, NO, WHY?

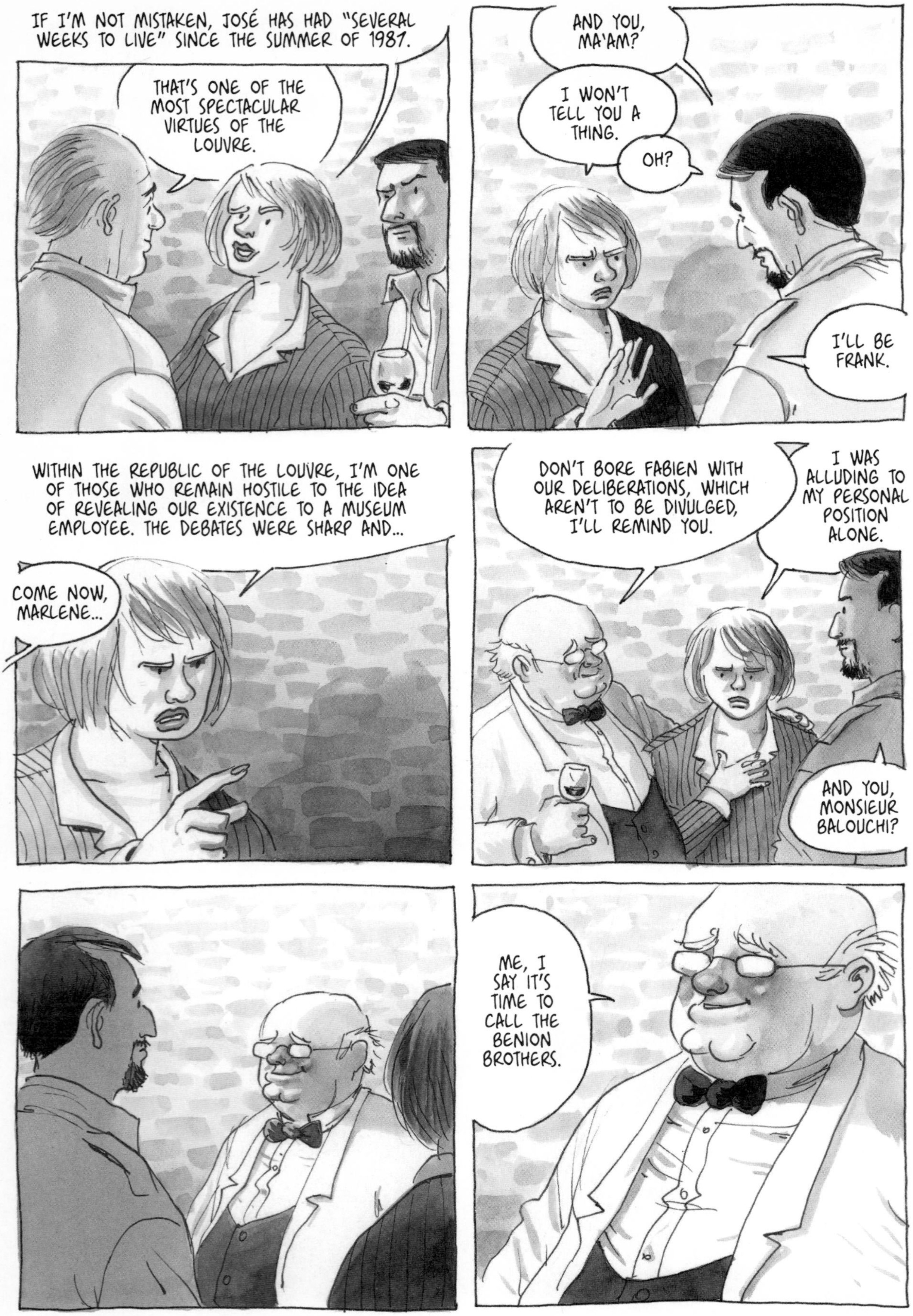
IF I'M NOT MISTAKEN, JOSÉ HAS HAD "SEVERAL WEEKS TO LIVE" SINCE THE SUMMER OF 1987.
THAT'S ONE OF THE MOST SPECTACULAR VIRTUES OF THE LOUVRE.
AND YOU, MA'AM?
I WON'T TELL YOU A THING.
OH?
I'LL BE FRANK.
WITHIN THE REPUBLIC OF THE LOUVRE, I'M ONE OF THOSE WHO REMAIN HOSTILE TO THE IDEA OF REVEALING OUR EXISTENCE TO A MUSEUM EMPLOYEE. THE DEBATES WERE SHARP AND...
COME NOW, MARLENE...
DON'T BORE FABIEN WITH OUR DELIBERATIONS, WHICH AREN'T TO BE DIVULGED, I'LL REMIND YOU.
I WAS ALLUDING TO MY PERSONAL POSITION ALONE.
AND YOU, MONSIEUR BALOUCHI?
ME, I SAY IT'S TIME TO CALL THE BENION BROTHERS.

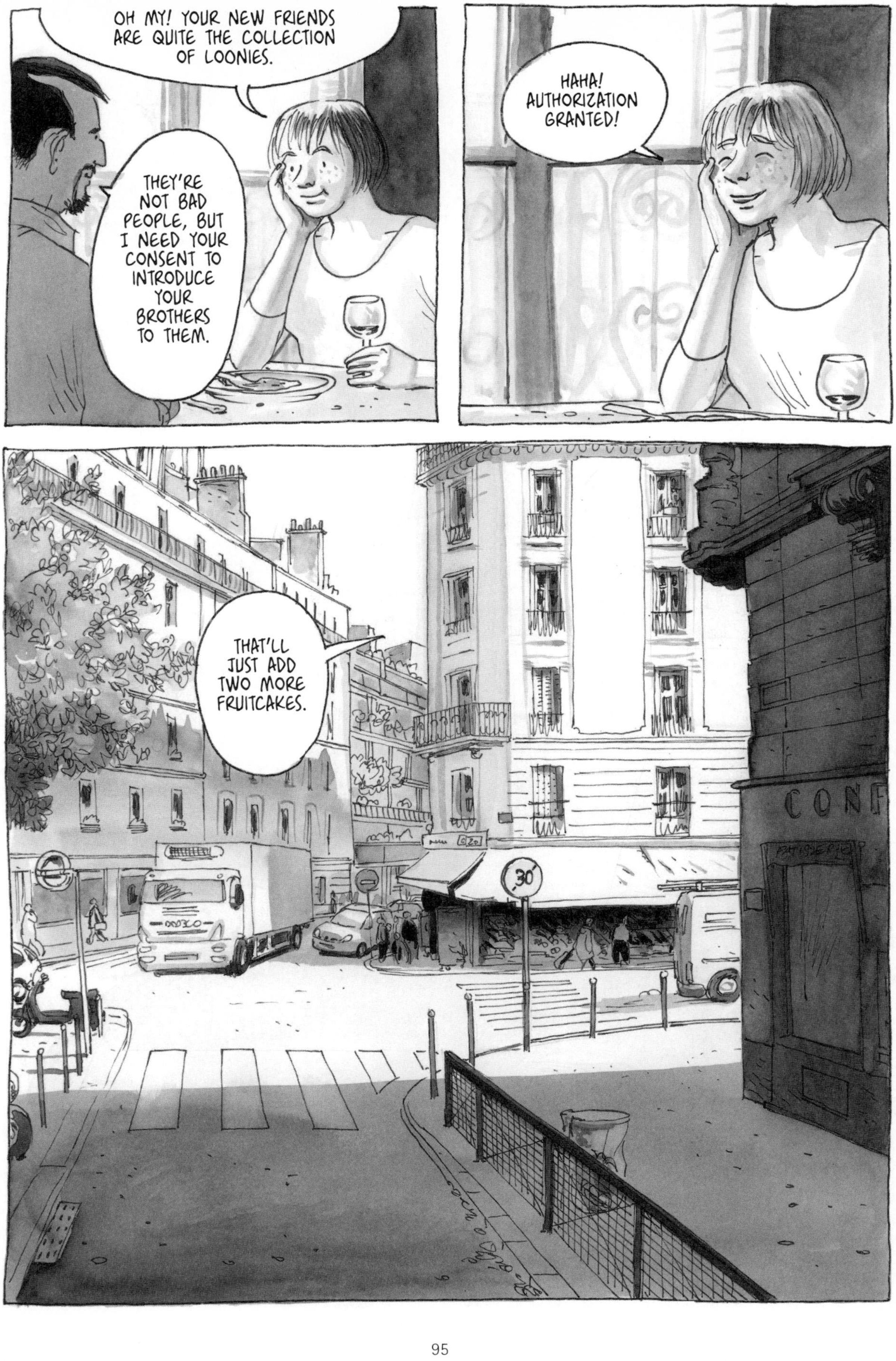
OH MY! YOUR NEW FRIENDS ARE QUITE THE COLLECTION OF LOONIES.
THEY'RE NOT BAD PEOPLE, BUT I NEED YOUR CONSENT TO INTRODUCE YOUR BROTHERS TO THEM.
HAHA! AUTHORIZATION GRANTED!
THAT'LL JUST ADD TWO MORE FRUITCAKES.
30
CONF

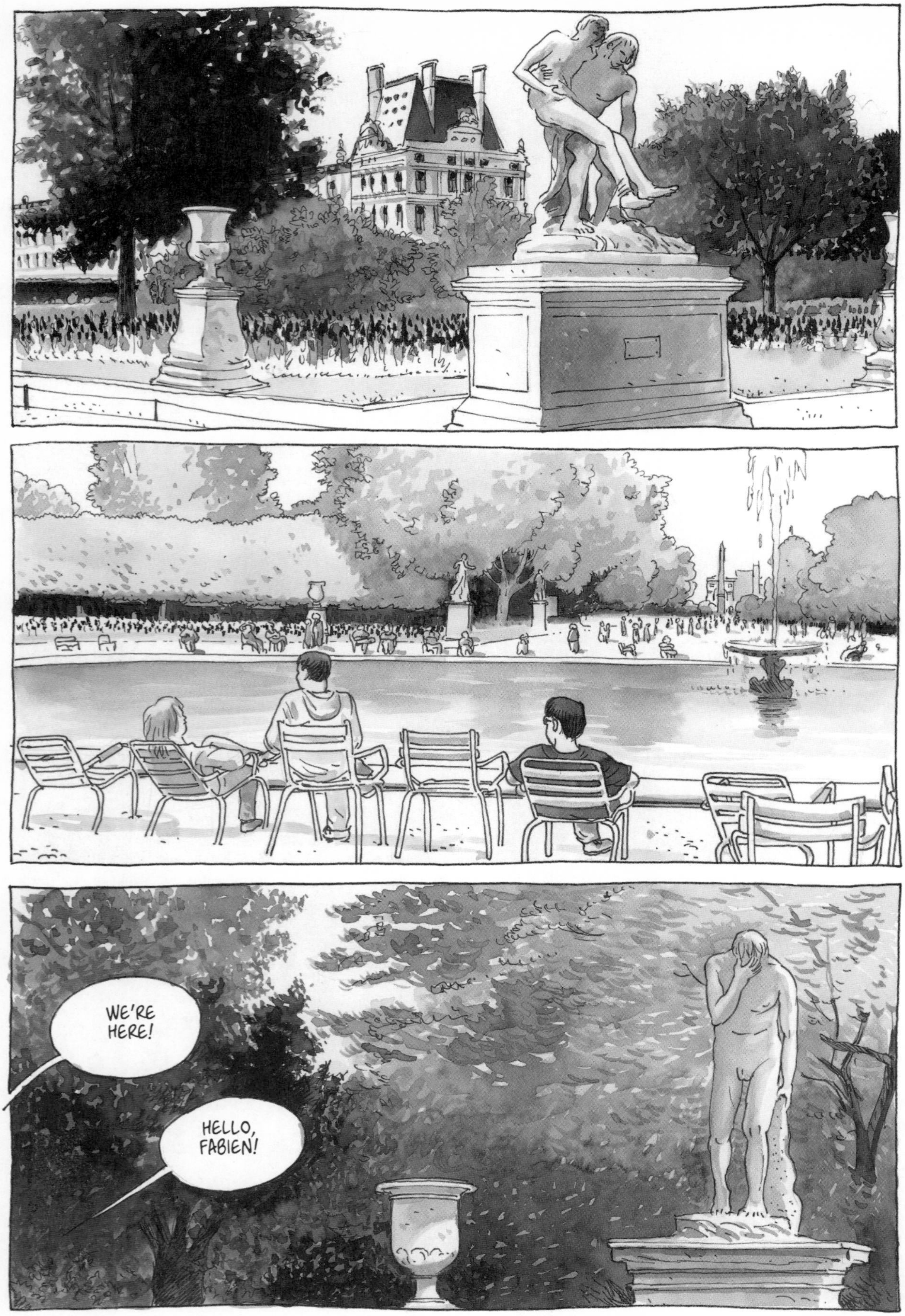
WE'RE HERE!
HELLO, FABIEN!

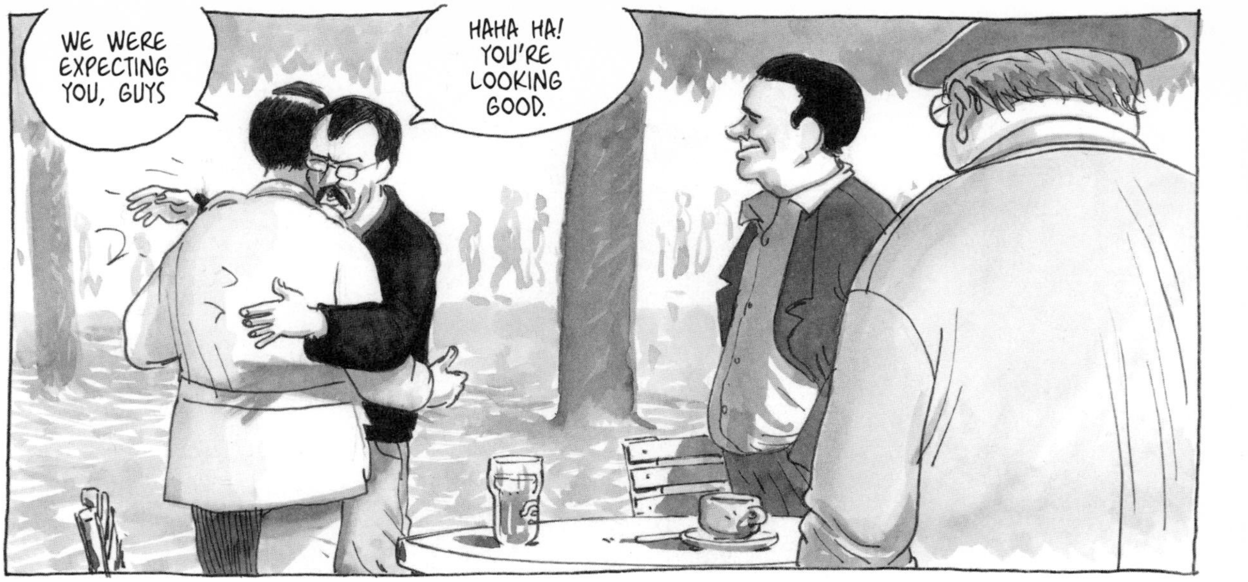
WE WERE EXPECTING YOU, GUYS
HAHA HA! YOU'RE LOOKING GOOD.

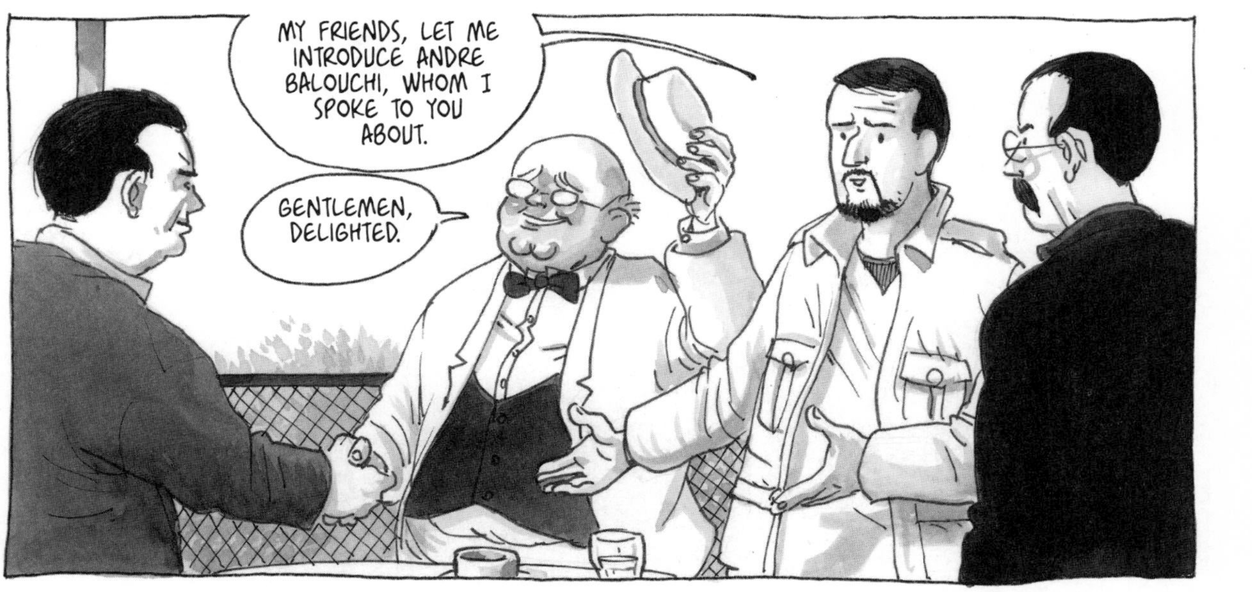
MY FRIENDS, LET ME INTRODUCE ANDRE BALOUCHI, WHOM I SPOKE TO YOU ABOUT.
GENTLEMEN, DELIGHTED.

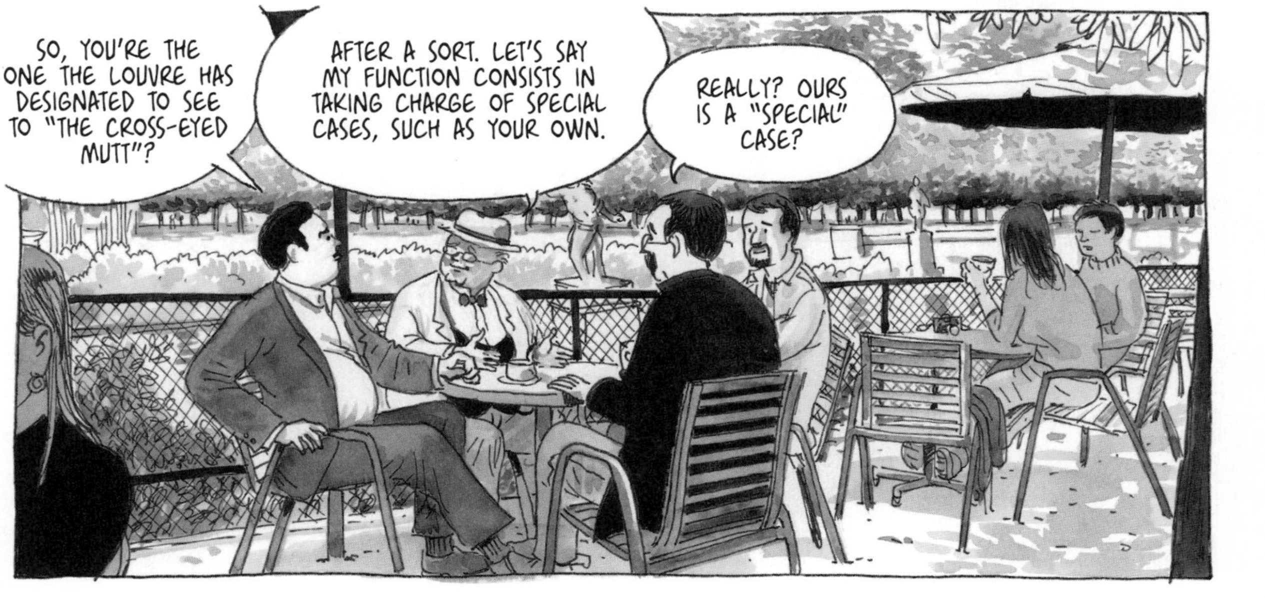
SO, YOU'RE THE ONE THE LOUVRE HAS DESIGNATED TO SEE TO "THE CROSS-EYED MUTT"?
AFTER A SORT. LET'S SAY MY FUNCTION CONSISTS IN TAKING CHARGE OF SPECIAL CASES, SUCH AS YOUR OWN.
REALLY? OURS IS A "SPECIAL" CASE?

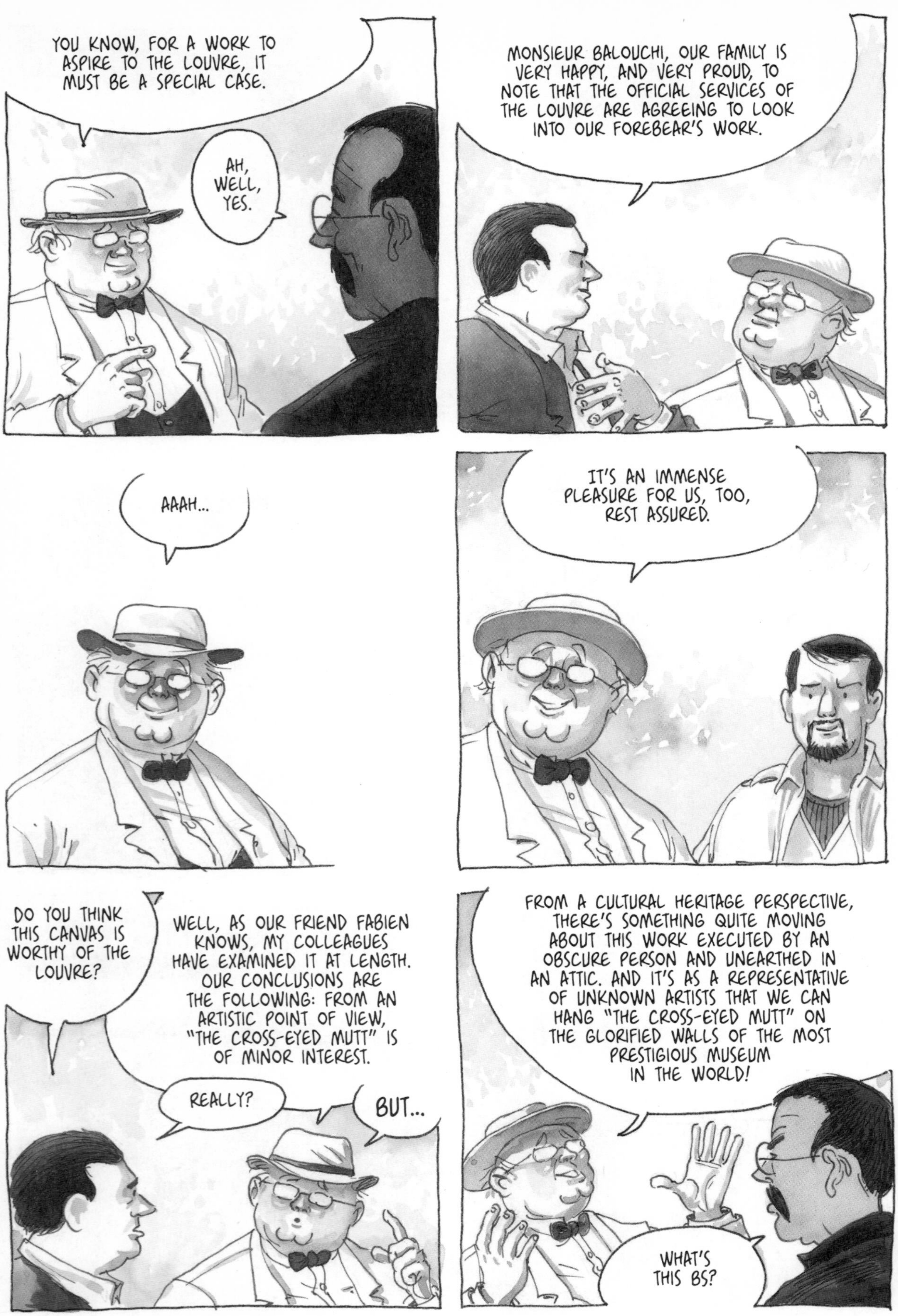

YOU KNOW, FOR A WORK TO ASPIRE TO THE LOUVRE, IT MUST BE A SPECIAL CASE.
AH, WELL, YES.
MONSIEUR BALOUCHI, OUR FAMILY IS VERY HAPPY, AND VERY PROUD, TO NOTE THAT THE OFFICIAL SERVICES OF THE LOUVRE ARE AGREEING TO LOOK INTO OUR FOREBEAR'S WORK.
AAAH...
IT'S AN IMMENSE PLEASURE FOR US, TOO, REST ASSURED.
DO YOU THINK THIS CANVAS IS WORTHY OF THE LOUVRE?
WELL, AS OUR FRIEND FABIEN KNOWS, MY COLLEAGUES HAVE EXAMINED IT AT LENGTH. OUR CONCLUSIONS ARE THE FOLLOWING: FROM AN ARTISTIC POINT OF VIEW, "THE CROSS-EYED MUTT" IS OF MINOR INTEREST.
REALLY?
BUT...
FROM A CULTURAL HERITAGE PERSPECTIVE, THERE'S SOMETHING QUITE MOVING ABOUT THIS WORK EXECUTED BY AN OBSCURE PERSON AND UNEARTHED IN AN ATTIC. AND IT'S AS A REPRESENTATIVE OF UNKNOWN ARTISTS THAT WE CAN HANG "THE CROSS-EYED MUTT" ON THE GLORIFIED WALLS OF THE MOST PRESTIGIOUS MUSEUM IN THE WORLD!
WHAT'S THIS BS?

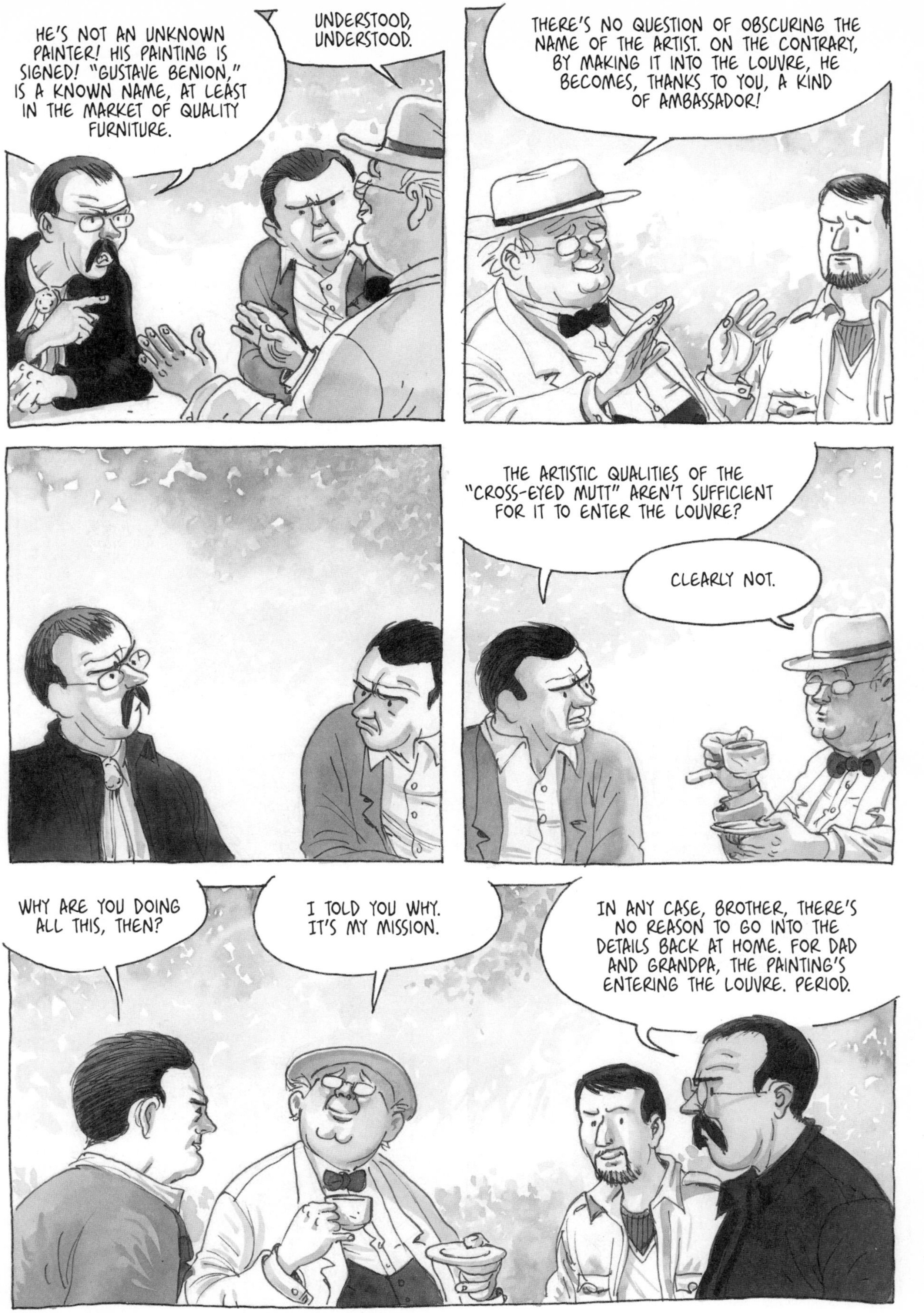
HE'S NOT AN UNKNOWN PAINTER! HIS PAINTING IS SIGNED! "GUSTAVE BENION," IS A KNOWN NAME, AT LEAST IN THE MARKET OF QUALITY FURNITURE.
UNDERSTOOD, UNDERSTOOD.
THERE'S NO QUESTION OF OBSCURING THE NAME OF THE ARTIST. ON THE CONTRARY, BY MAKING IT INTO THE LOUVRE, HE BECOMES, THANKS TO YOU, A KIND OF AMBASSADOR!
THE ARTISTIC QUALITIES OF THE "CROSS-EYED MUTT" AREN'T SUFFICIENT FOR IT TO ENTER THE LOUVRE?
CLEARLY NOT.
WHY ARE YOU DOING ALL THIS, THEN?
I TOLD YOU WHY. IT'S MY MISSION.
IN ANY CASE, BROTHER, THERE'S NO REASON TO GO INTO THE DETAILS BACK AT HOME. FOR DAD AND GRANDPA, THE PAINTING'S ENTERING THE LOUVRE. PERIOD.

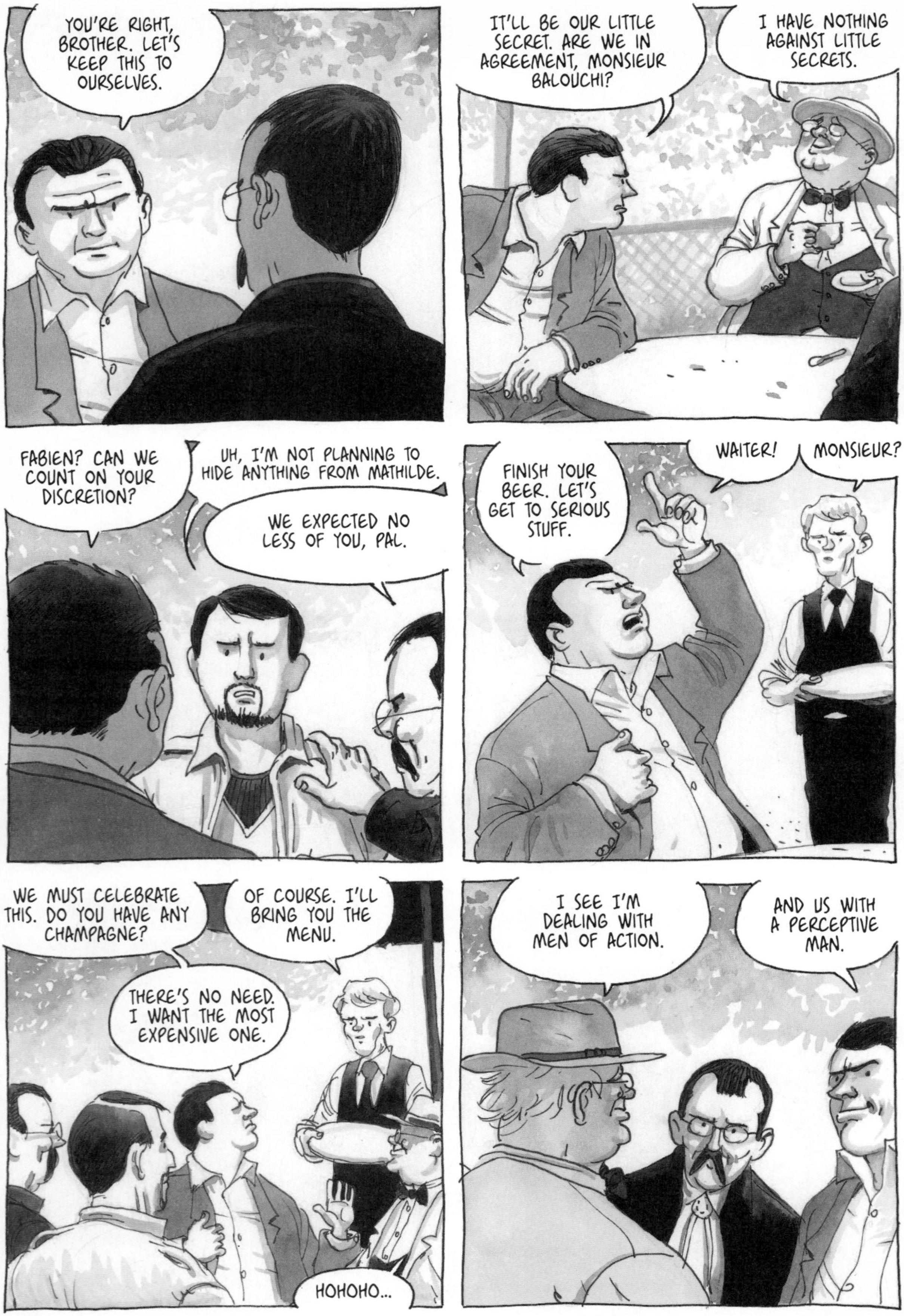
YOU'RE RIGHT, BROTHER. LET'S KEEP THIS TO OURSELVES.
IT'LL BE OUR LITTLE SECRET. ARE WE IN AGREEMENT, MONSIEUR BALOUCHI?
I HAVE NOTHING AGAINST LITTLE SECRETS.
FABIEN? CAN WE COUNT ON YOUR DISCRETION?
UH, I'M NOT PLANNING TO HIDE ANYTHING FROM MATHILDE.
WE EXPECTED NO LESS OF YOU, PAL.
FINISH YOUR BEER. LET'S GET TO SERIOUS STUFF.
WAITER!
MONSIEUR?
WE MUST CELEBRATE THIS. DO YOU HAVE ANY CHAMPAGNE?
OF COURSE. I'LL BRING YOU THE MENU.
THERE'S NO NEED. I WANT THE MOST EXPENSIVE ONE.
HOHOHO...
I SEE I'M DEALING WITH MEN OF ACTION.
AND US WITH A PERCEPTIVE MAN.

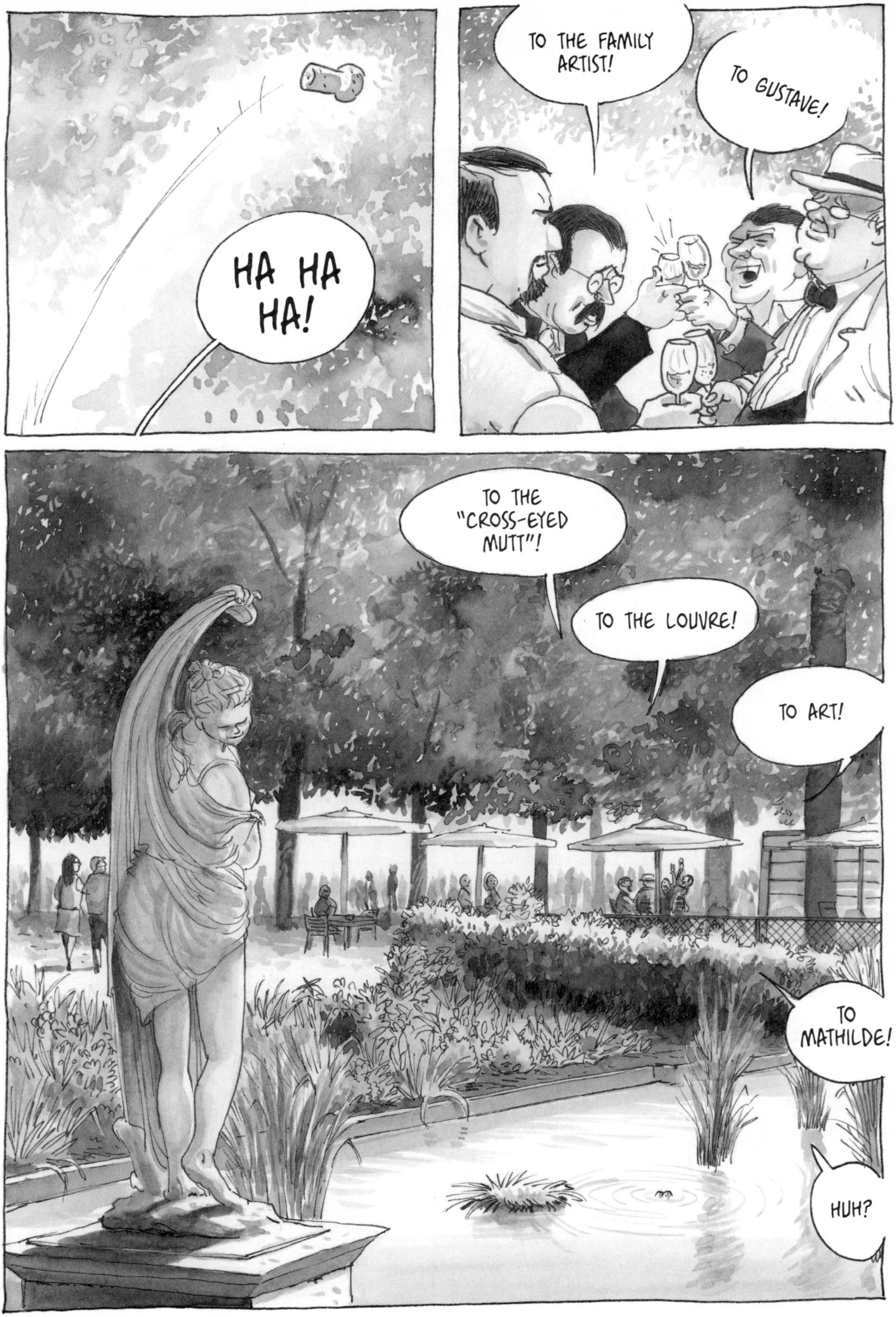
HA HA HA!
TO THE FAMILY ARTIST!
TO GUSTAVE!
TO THE "CROSS-EYED MUTT"!
TO THE LOUVRE!
TO ART!
TO MATHILDE!
HUH?

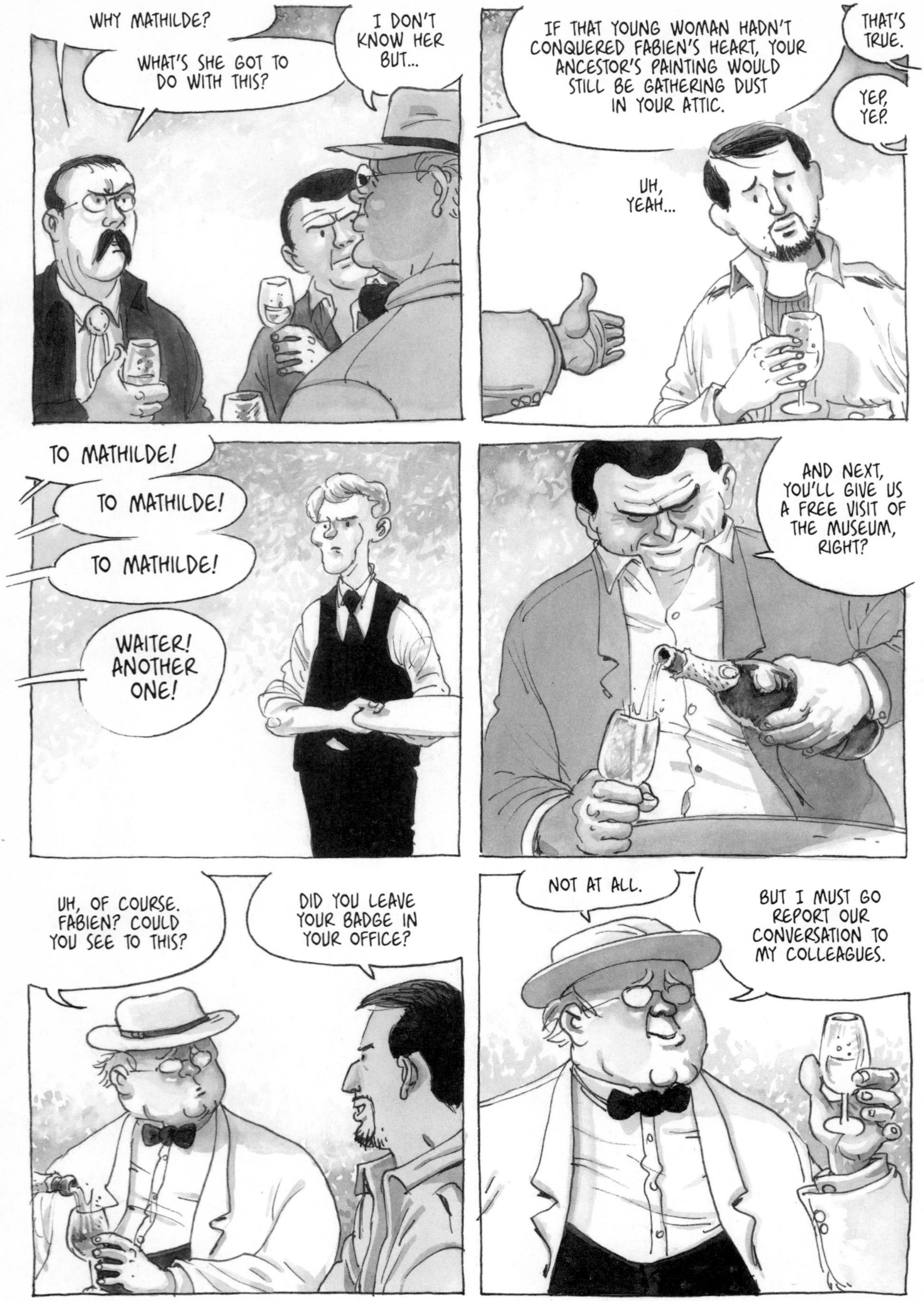
WHY MATHILDE?
WHAT'S SHE GOT TO DO WITH THIS?
I DON'T KNOW HER BUT...
IF THAT YOUNG WOMAN HADN'T CONQUERED FABIEN'S HEART, YOUR ANCESTOR'S PAINTING WOULD STILL BE GATHERING DUST IN YOUR ATTIC.
THAT'S TRUE.
YEP, YEP.
UH, YEAH...
TO MATHILDE!
TO MATHILDE!
TO MATHILDE!
WAITER! ANOTHER ONE!
AND NEXT, YOU'LL GIVE US A FREE VISIT OF THE MUSEUM, RIGHT?
UH, OF COURSE. FABIEN? COULD YOU SEE TO THIS?
DID YOU LEAVE YOUR BADGE IN YOUR OFFICE?
NOT AT ALL.
BUT I MUST GO REPORT OUR CONVERSATION TO MY COLLEAGUES.

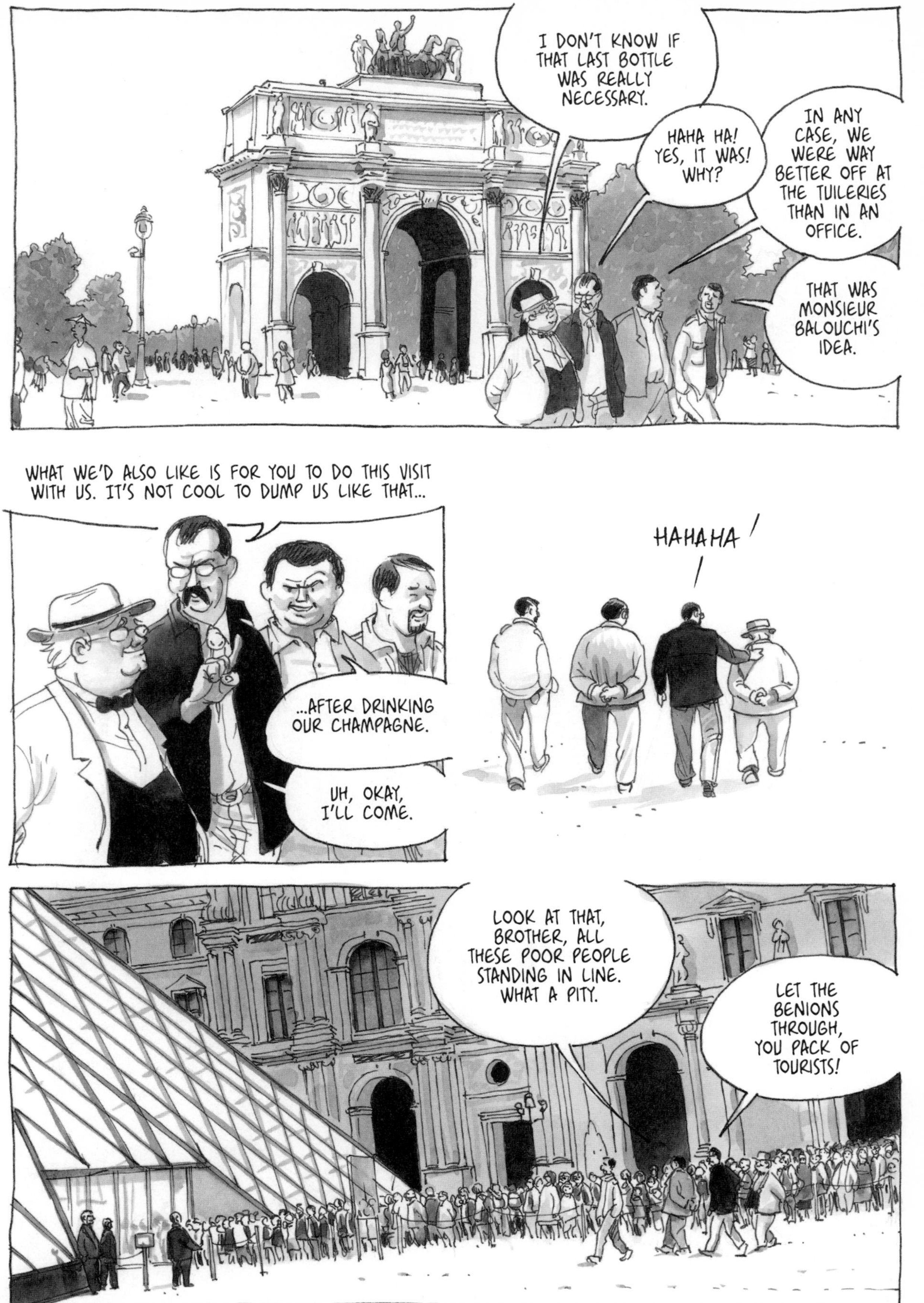
I DON'T KNOW IF THAT LAST BOTTLE WAS REALLY NECESSARY.
HAHA HA! YES, IT WAS! WHY?
IN ANY CASE, WE WERE WAY BETTER OFF AT THE TUILERIES THAN IN AN OFFICE.
THAT WAS MONSIEUR BALOUCHI'S IDEA.
WHAT WE'D ALSO LIKE IS FOR YOU TO DO THIS VISIT WITH US. IT'S NOT COOL TO DUMP US LIKE THAT...
...AFTER DRINKING OUR CHAMPAGNE.
UH, OKAY, I'LL COME.
HAHAHA
THAT WAS
LOOK AT THAT, BROTHER, ALL THESE POOR PEOPLE STANDING IN LINE. WHAT A PITY.
LET THE BENIONS THROUGH, YOU PACK OF TOURISTS!

HELLO, THERE ARE FOUR OF US.
GO AHEAD.
SORTIE
HOW'S IT FLYING?
GOOD JOB, KIDS!
OKAY, WHAT DO YOU WANT TO SEE? THE "MONA LISA"?
NO, WE DON'T CARE.
WE'LL TRUST YOU.

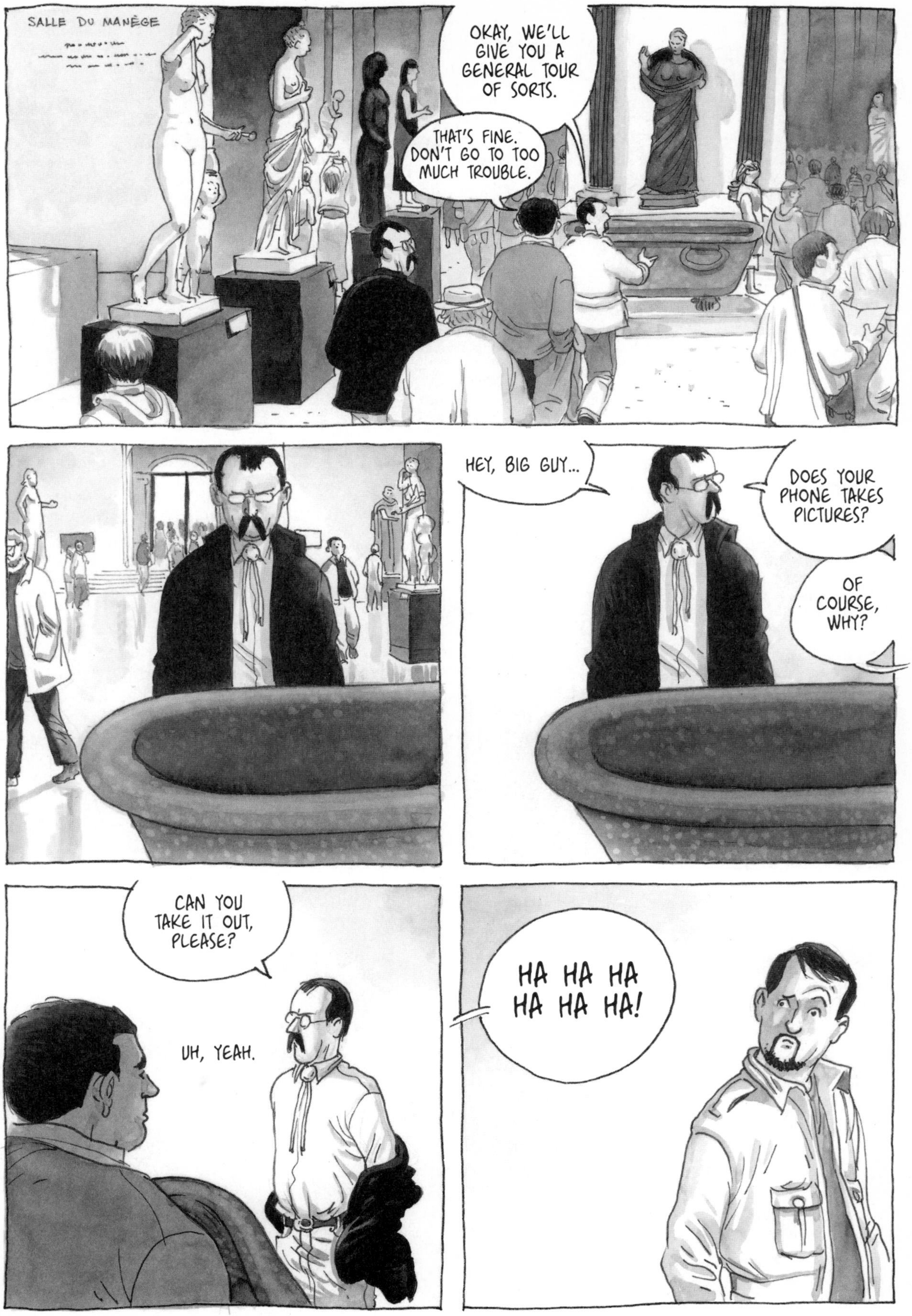
SALLE DU MANÈGE
OKAY, WE'LL GIVE YOU A GENERAL TOUR OF SORTS.
THAT'S FINE. DON'T GO TO TOO MUCH TROUBLE.
HEY, BIG GUY...
DOES YOUR PHONE TAKES PICTURES?
OF COURSE, WHY?
CAN YOU TAKE IT OUT, PLEASE?
UH, YEAH.
HA HA HA HA HA HA!

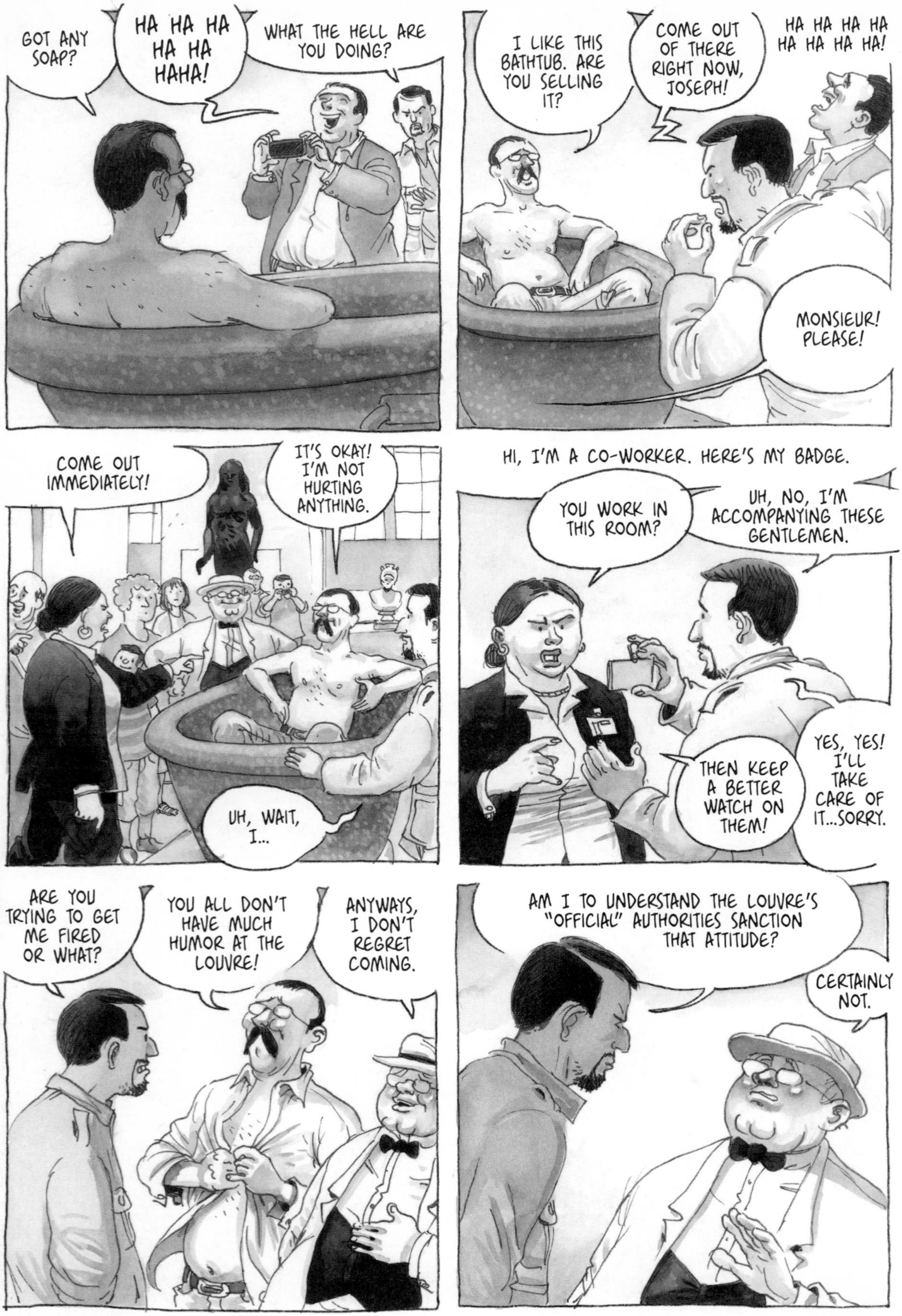

GOT ANY SOAP?
HA HA HA HA HA HAHA!
WHAT THE HELL ARE YOU DOING?
I LIKE THIS BATHTUB. ARE YOU SELLING IT?
COME OUT OF THERE RIGHT NOW, JOSEPH!
HA HA HA HA HA HA HA HA!
MONSIEUR! PLEASE!
COME OUT IMMEDIATELY!
IT'S OKAY! I'M NOT HURTING ANYTHING.
UH, WAIT, I...
HI, I'M A CO-WORKER. HERE'S MY BADGE.
YOU WORK IN THIS ROOM?
UH, NO, I'M ACCOMPANYING THESE GENTLEMEN.
THEN KEEP A BETTER WATCH ON THEM!
YES, YES! I'LL TAKE CARE OF IT...SORRY.
ARE YOU TRYING TO GET ME FIRED OR WHAT?
YOU ALL DON'T HAVE MUCH HUMOR AT THE LOUVRE!
ANYWAYS, I DON'T REGRET COMING.
AM I TO UNDERSTAND THE LOUVRE'S "OFFICIAL" AUTHORITIES SANCTION THAT ATTITUDE?
CERTAINLY NOT.

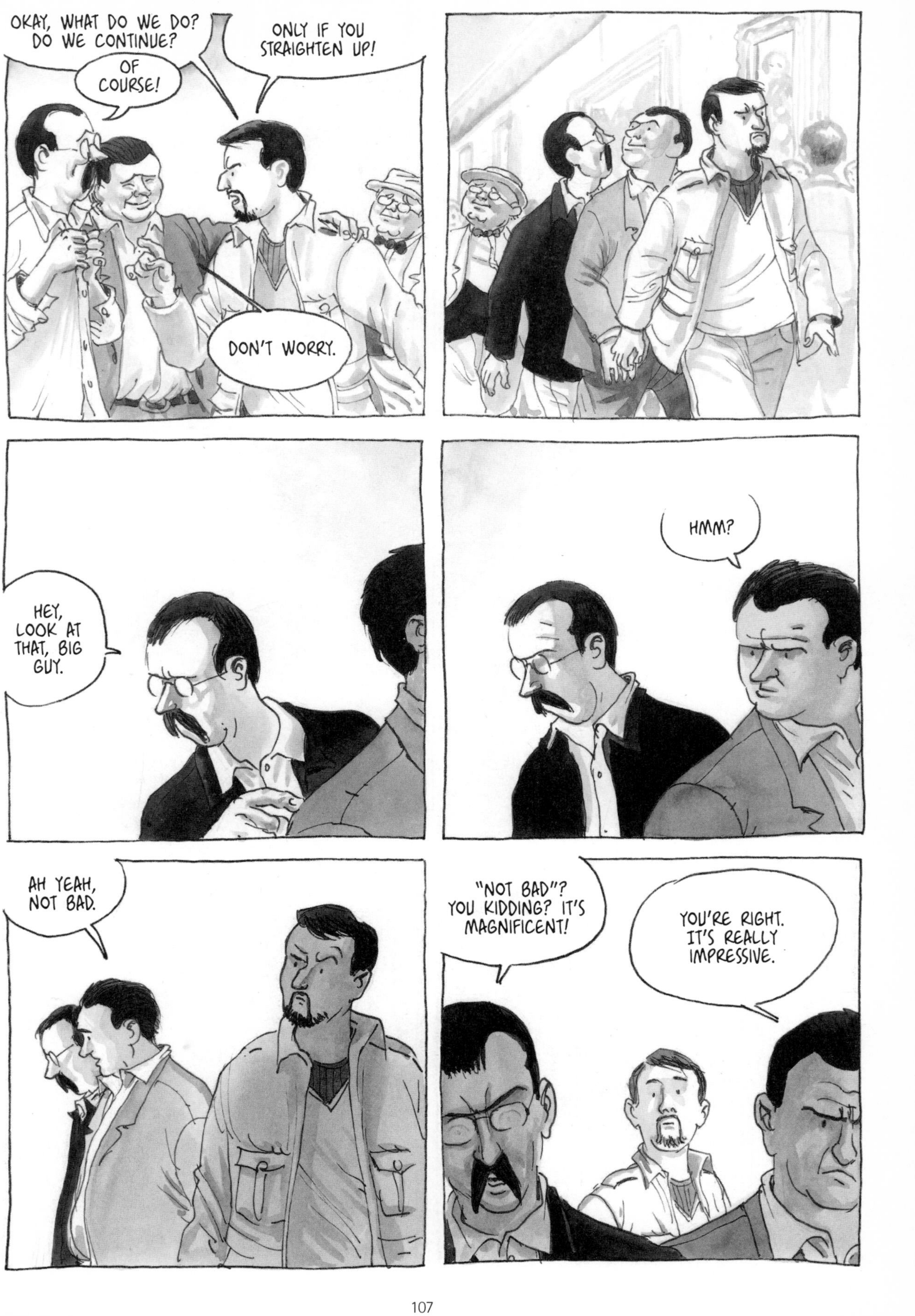
OKAY, WHAT DO WE DO? DO WE CONTINUE?
OF COURSE!
ONLY IF YOU STRAIGHTEN UP!
DON'T WORRY.
HEY, LOOK AT THAT, BIG GUY.
HMM?
AH YEAH, NOT BAD.
"NOT BAD"? YOU KIDDING? IT'S MAGNIFICENT!
YOU'RE RIGHT. IT'S REALLY IMPRESSIVE.

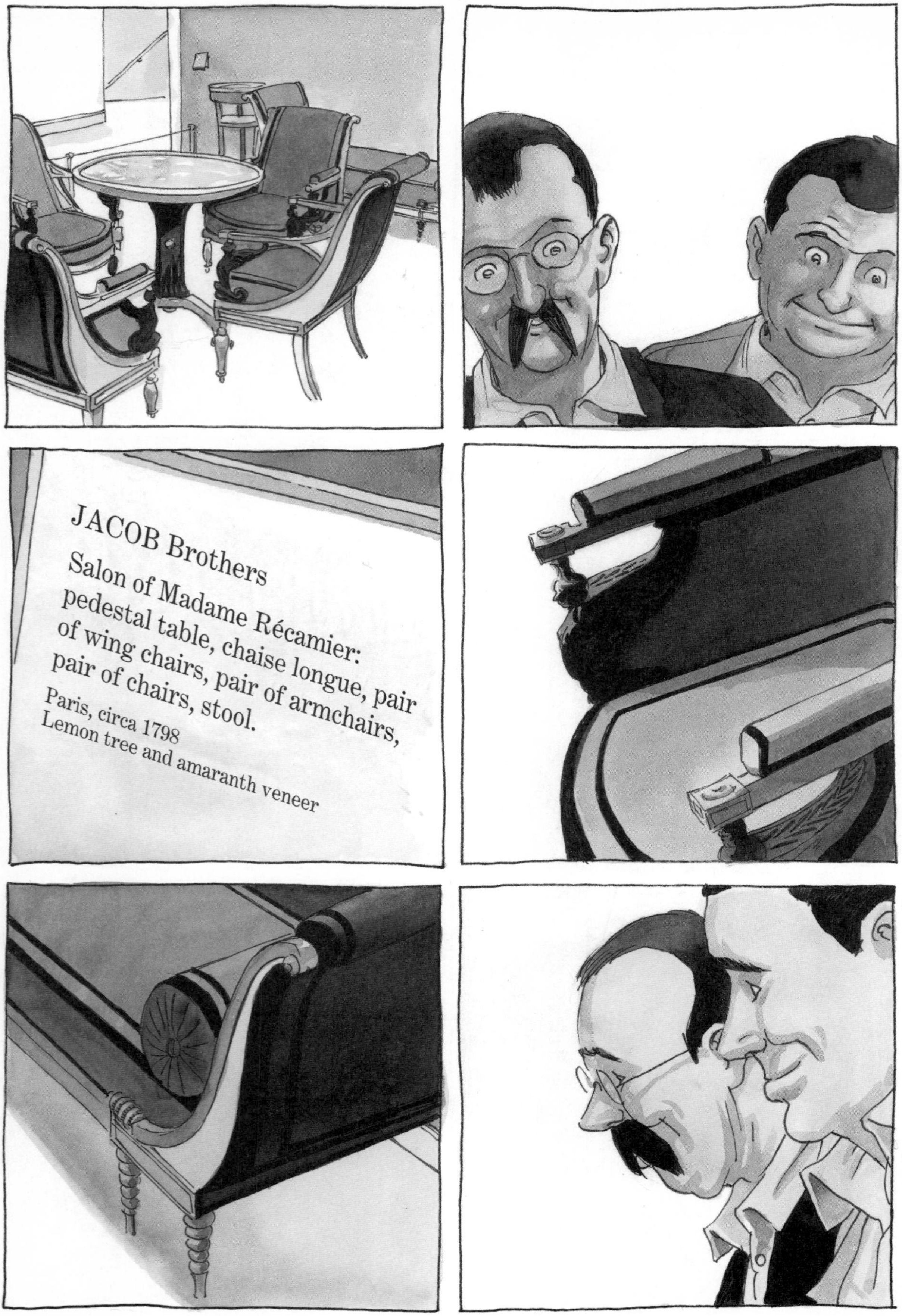
JACOB Brothers
Salon of Madame Récamier: pedestal table, chaise longue, pair of wing chairs, pair of armchairs, pair of chairs, stool.
Paris, circa 1798
Lemon tree and amaranth veneer

YOU COULD HAVE TOLD US, FABIEN.

WHAT'S THAT?

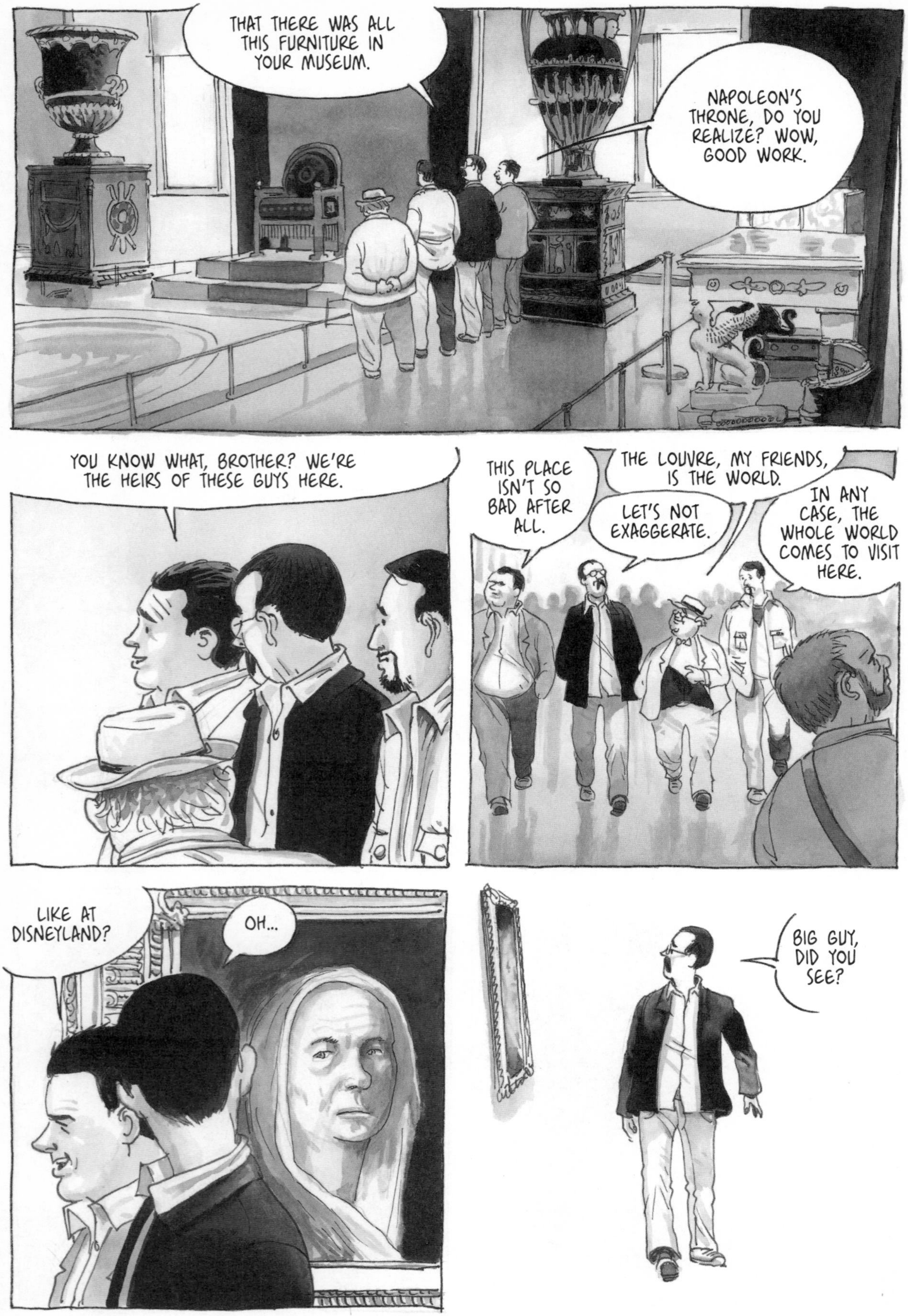
THAT THERE WAS ALL THIS FURNITURE IN YOUR MUSEUM.
NAPOLEON'S THRONE, DO YOU REALIZE? WOW, GOOD WORK.
YOU KNOW WHAT, BROTHER? WE'RE THE HEIRS OF THESE GUYS HERE.
THIS PLACE ISN'T SO BAD AFTER ALL.
THE LOUVRE, MY FRIENDS, IS THE WORLD.
LET'S NOT EXAGGERATE.
IN ANY CASE, THE WHOLE WORLD COMES TO VISIT HERE.
LIKE AT DISNEYLAND?
OH...
BIG GUY, DID YOU SEE?

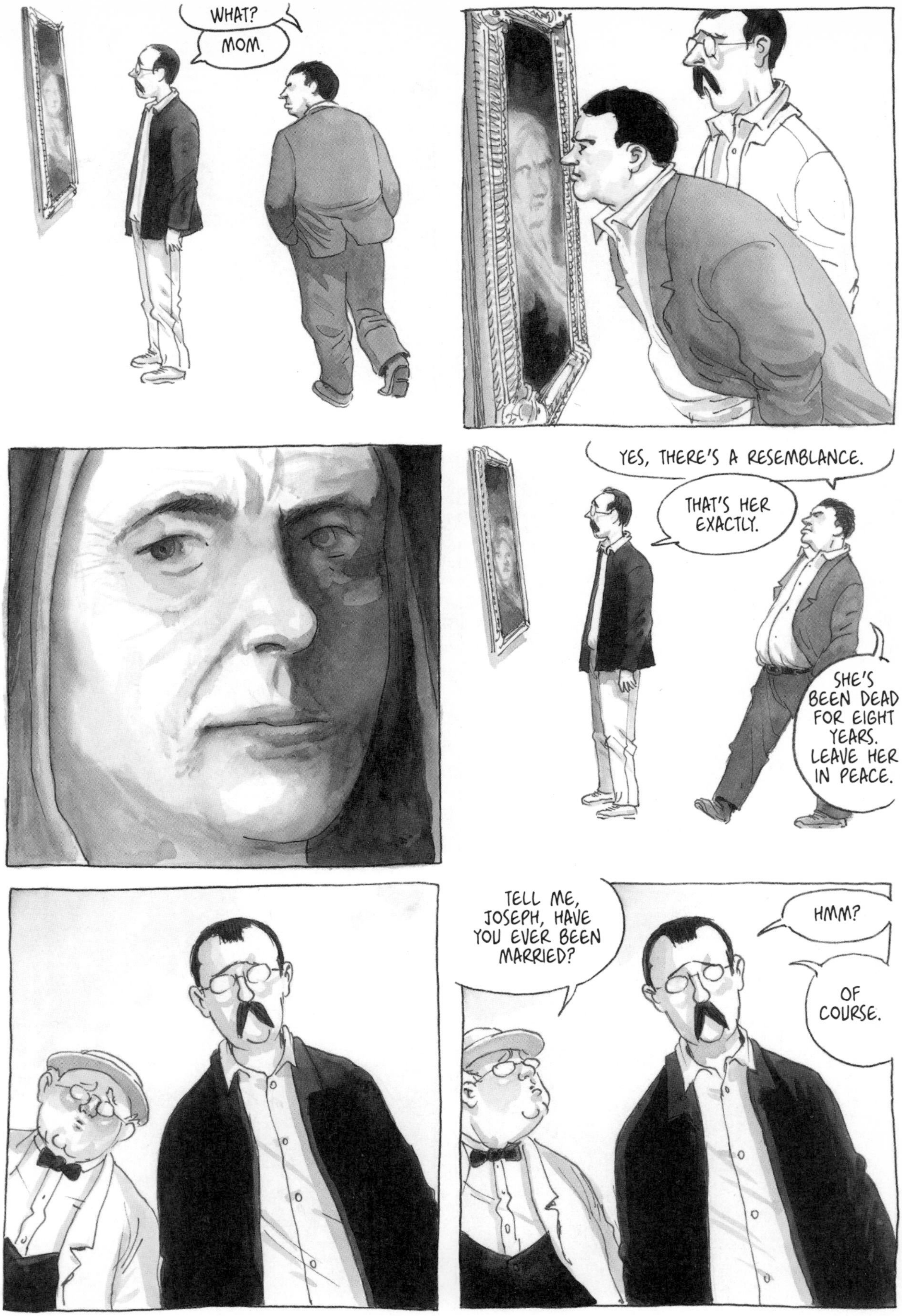
WHAT?
MOM.
YES, THERE'S A RESEMBLANCE.
THAT'S HER EXACTLY.
SHE'S BEEN DEAD FOR EIGHT YEARS. LEAVE HER IN PEACE.
TELL ME, JOSEPH, HAVE YOU EVER BEEN MARRIED?
HMM?
OF COURSE.

WE'VE BEEN MARRIED SINCE OUR TEENS, TO *BENION FURNITURE!*

HA HA HA!

AND YOU?

WHAT, ME?

MARRIED?

I THINK SO, YES.

SORRY?

COME SEE.

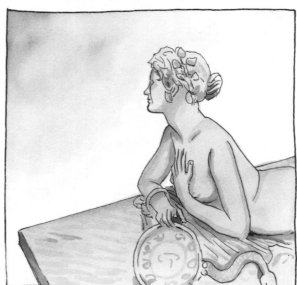

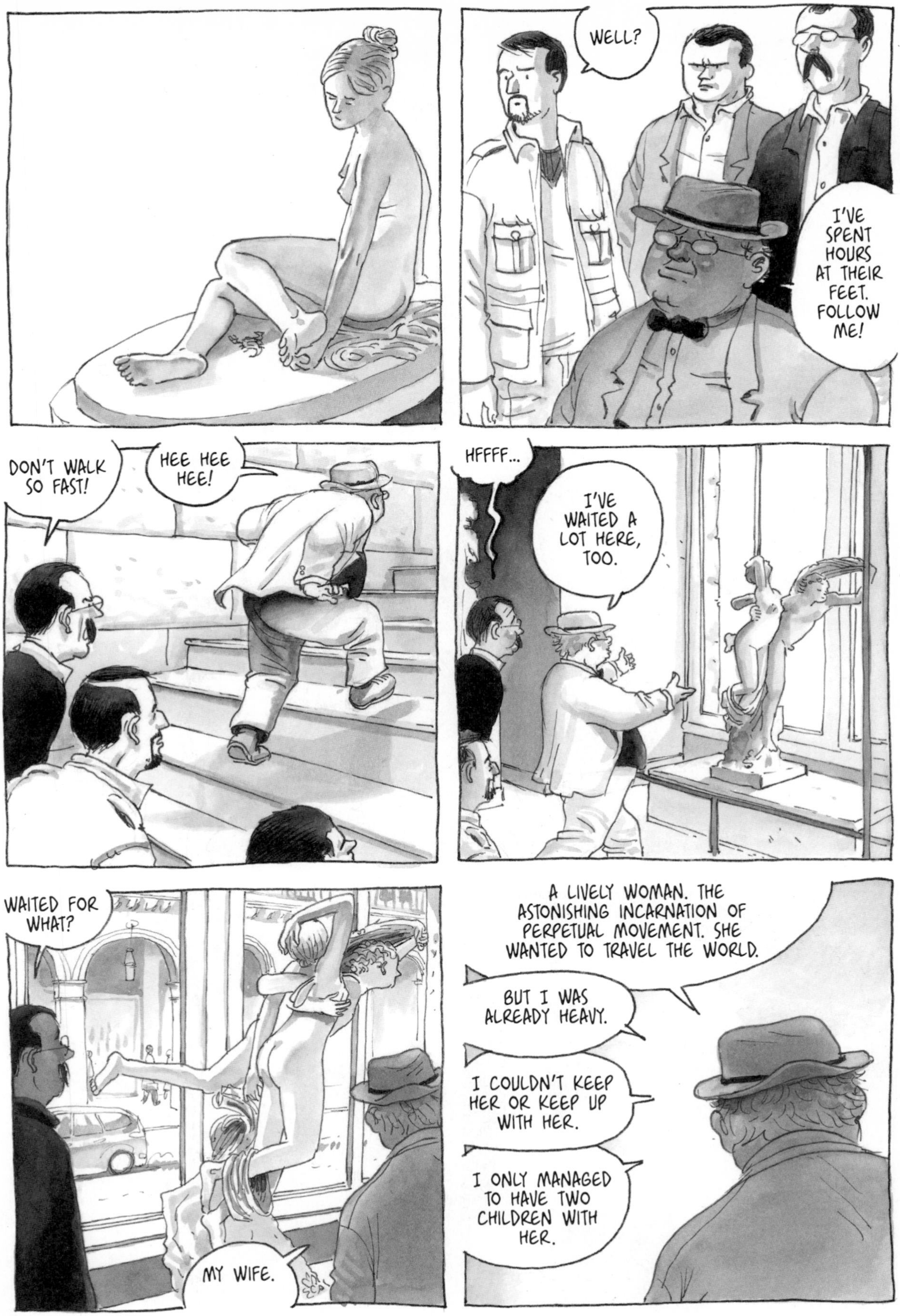
WELL?
I'VE SPENT HOURS AT THEIR FEET. FOLLOW ME!
DON'T WALK SO FAST!
HEE HEE HEE!
HFFFF...
I'VE WAITED A LOT HERE, TOO.
WAITED FOR WHAT?
MY WIFE.
A LIVELY WOMAN. THE ASTONISHING INCARNATION OF PERPETUAL MOVEMENT. SHE WANTED TO TRAVEL THE WORLD.
BUT I WAS ALREADY HEAVY.
I COULDN'T KEEP HER OR KEEP UP WITH HER.
I ONLY MANAGED TO HAVE TWO CHILDREN WITH HER.

I LOVED TO BRING HER TO THE LOUVRE,

ONE DAY, WE WERE HERE. SHE TOLD ME...

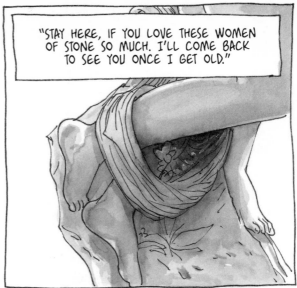

"STAY HERE, IF YOU LOVE THESE WOMEN OF STONE SO MUCH. I'LL COME BACK TO SEE YOU ONCE I GET OLD."

SO THAT'S IT.

I'M WAITING.

BUT...YOU DIDN'T TRY TO FIND HER AGAIN?

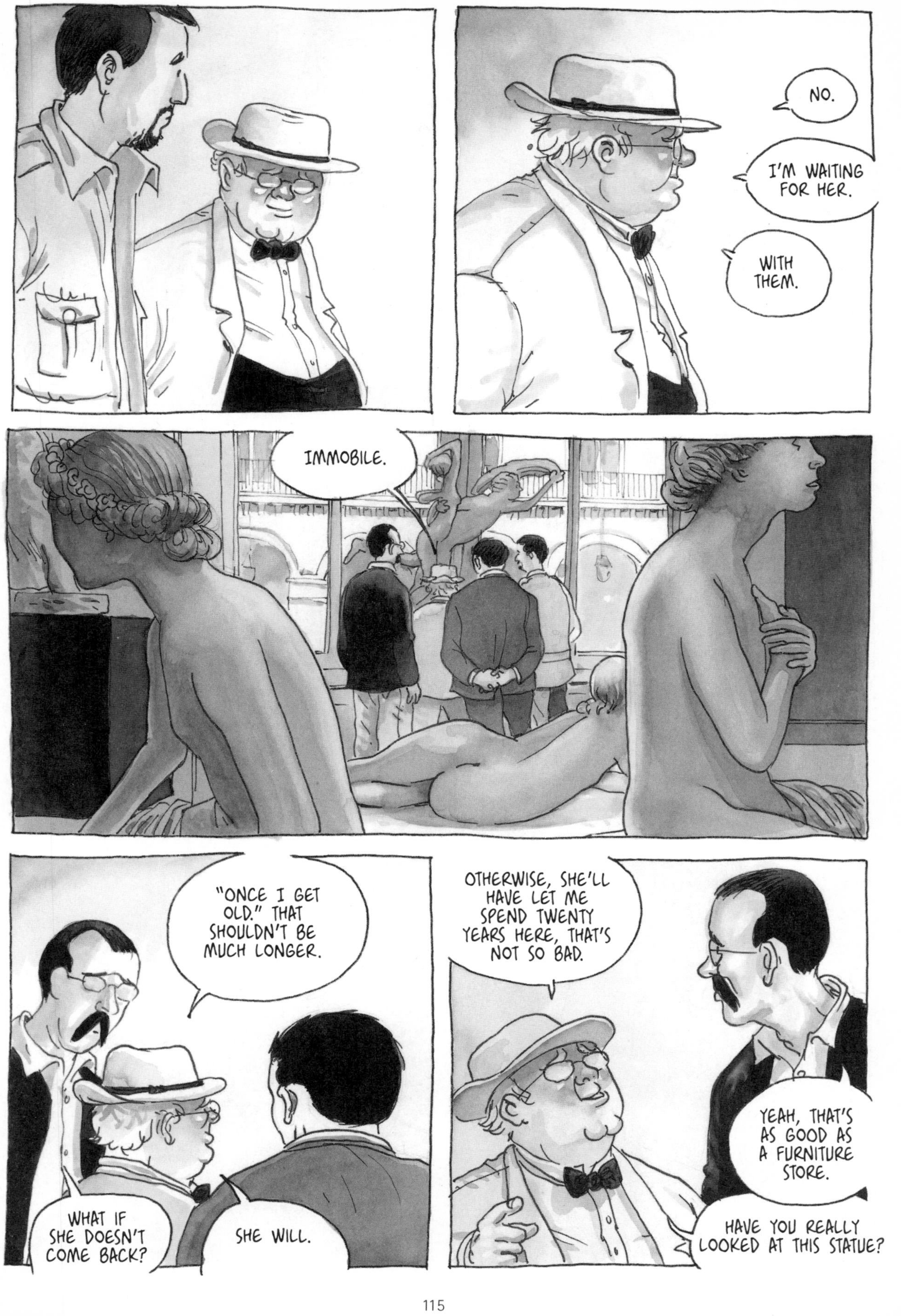
NO.
I'M WAITING FOR HER.
WITH THEM.
IMMOBILE.
"ONCE I GET OLD." THAT SHOULDN'T BE MUCH LONGER.
WHAT IF SHE DOESN'T COME BACK?
SHE WILL.
OTHERWISE, SHE'LL HAVE LET ME SPEND TWENTY YEARS HERE, THAT'S NOT SO BAD.
YEAH, THAT'S AS GOOD AS A FURNITURE STORE.
HAVE YOU REALLY LOOKED AT THIS STATUE?

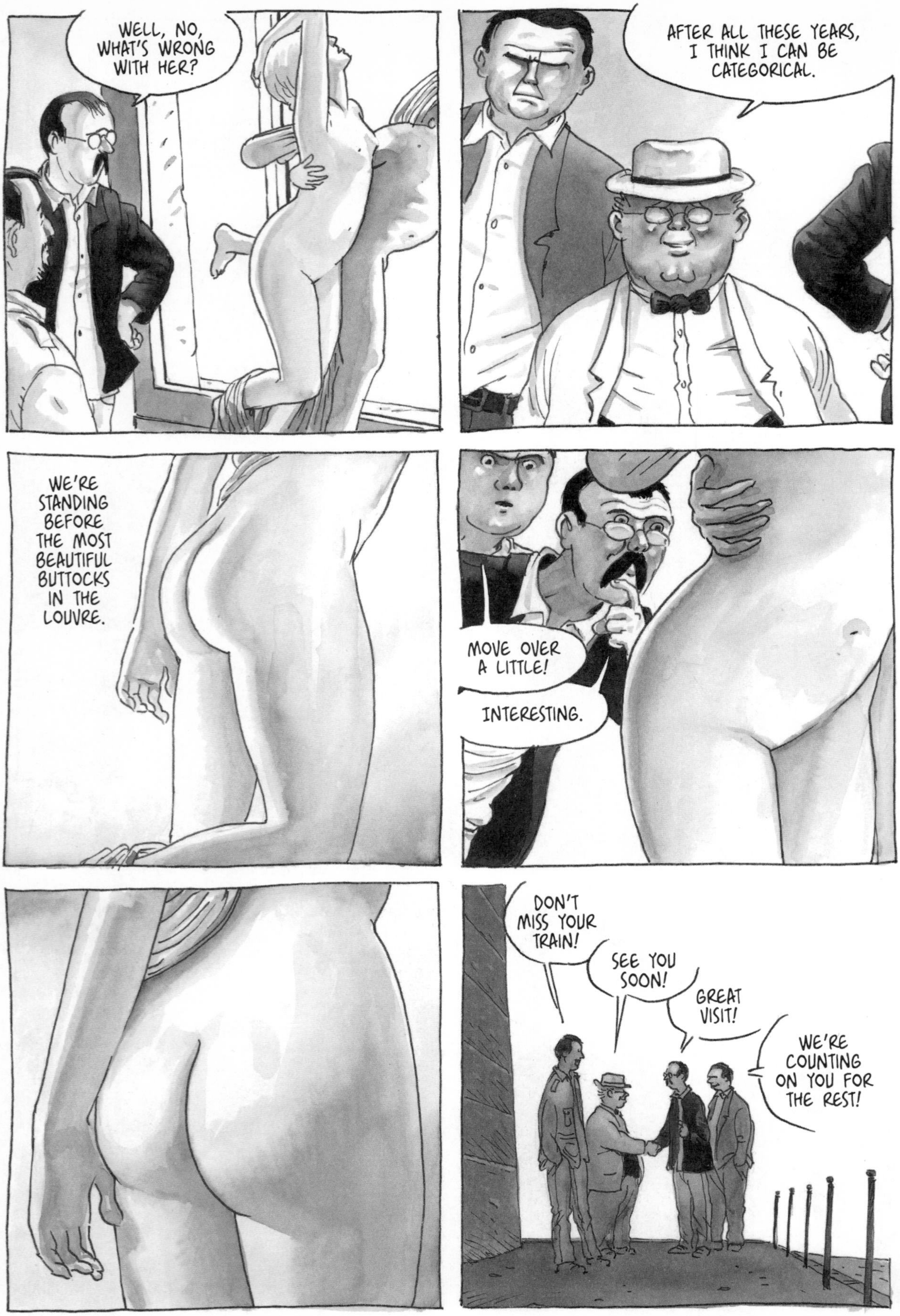
WELL, NO, WHAT'S WRONG WITH HER?
AFTER ALL THESE YEARS, I THINK I CAN BE CATEGORICAL.
WE'RE STANDING BEFORE THE MOST BEAUTIFUL BUTTOCKS IN THE LOUVRE.
MOVE OVER A LITTLE!
INTERESTING.
DON'T MISS YOUR TRAIN!
SEE YOU SOON!
GREAT VISIT!
WE'RE COUNTING ON YOU FOR THE REST!

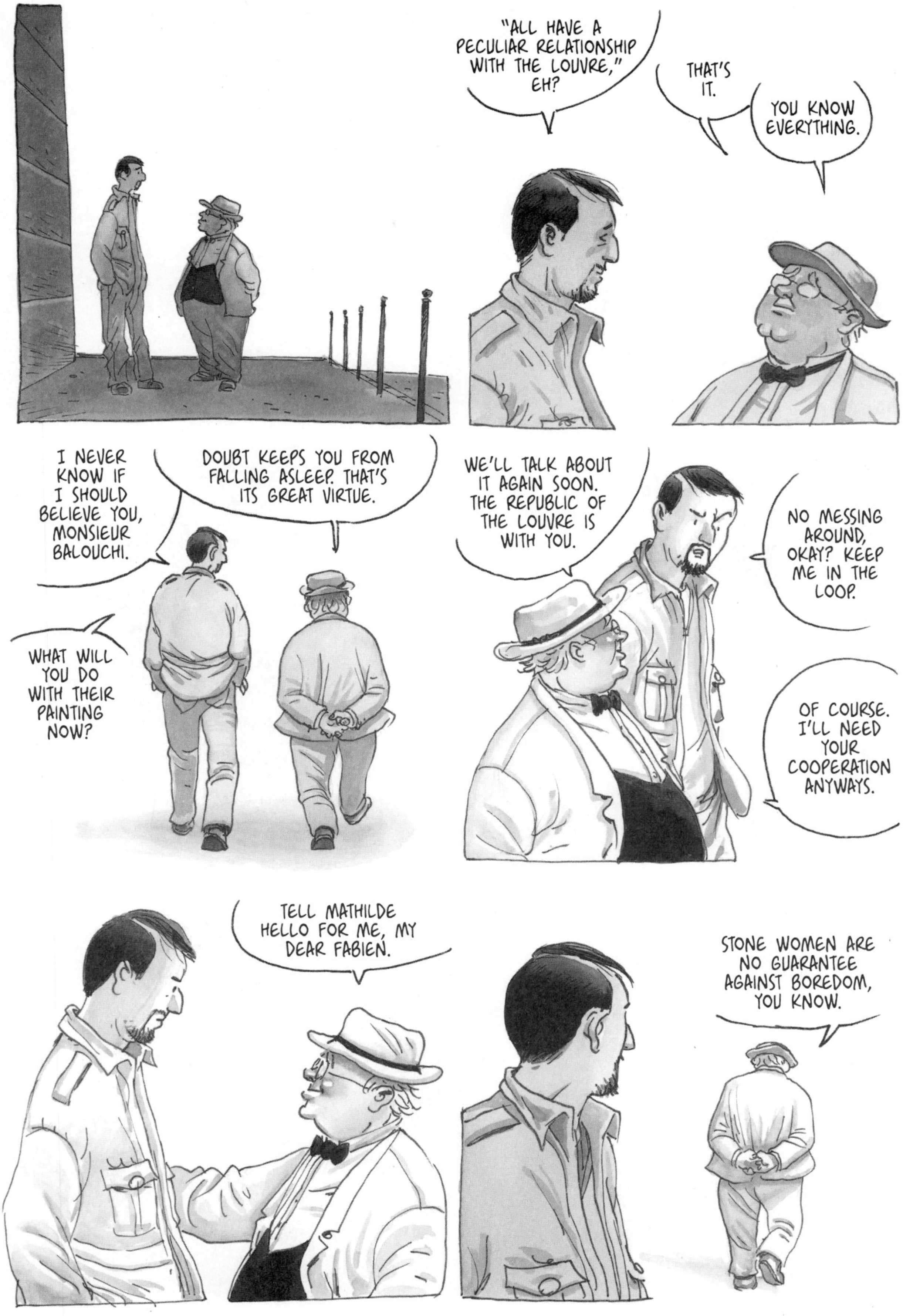
"ALL HAVE A PECULIAR RELATIONSHIP WITH THE LOUVRE," EH?
THAT'S IT.
YOU KNOW EVERYTHING.
I NEVER KNOW IF I SHOULD BELIEVE YOU, MONSIEUR BALOUCHI.
DOUBT KEEPS YOU FROM FALLING ASLEEP. THAT'S ITS GREAT VIRTUE.
WHAT WILL YOU DO WITH THEIR PAINTING NOW?
WE'LL TALK ABOUT IT AGAIN SOON. THE REPUBLIC OF THE LOUVRE IS WITH YOU.
NO MESSING AROUND, OKAY? KEEP ME IN THE LOOP.
OF COURSE. I'LL NEED YOUR COOPERATION ANYWAYS.
TELL MATHILDE HELLO FOR ME, MY DEAR FABIEN.
STONE WOMEN ARE NO GUARANTEE AGAINST BOREDOM, YOU KNOW.

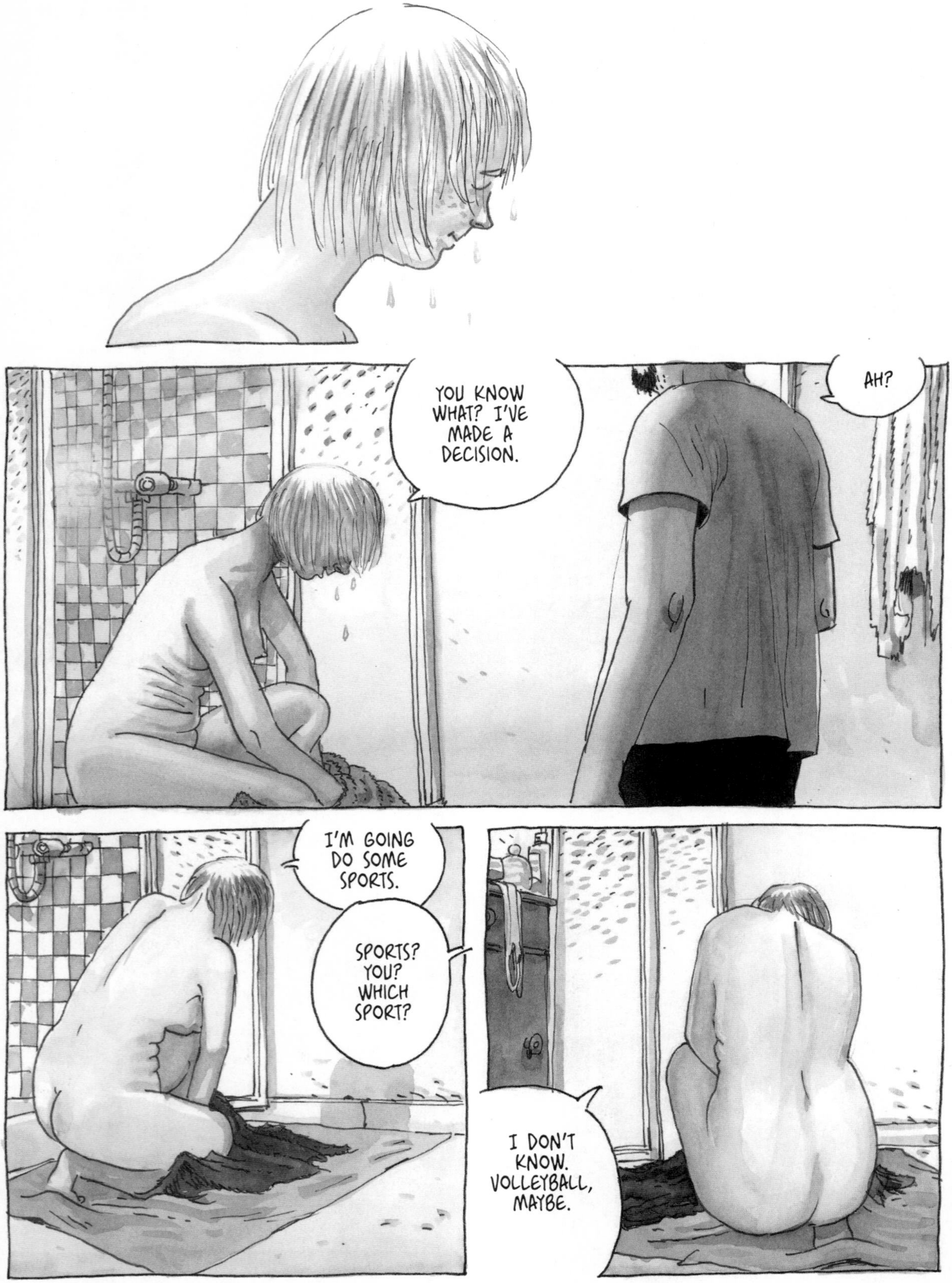
YOU KNOW WHAT? I'VE MADE A DECISION.
AH?
I'M GOING DO SOME SPORTS.
SPORTS? YOU? WHICH SPORT?
I DON'T KNOW. VOLLEYBALL, MAYBE.

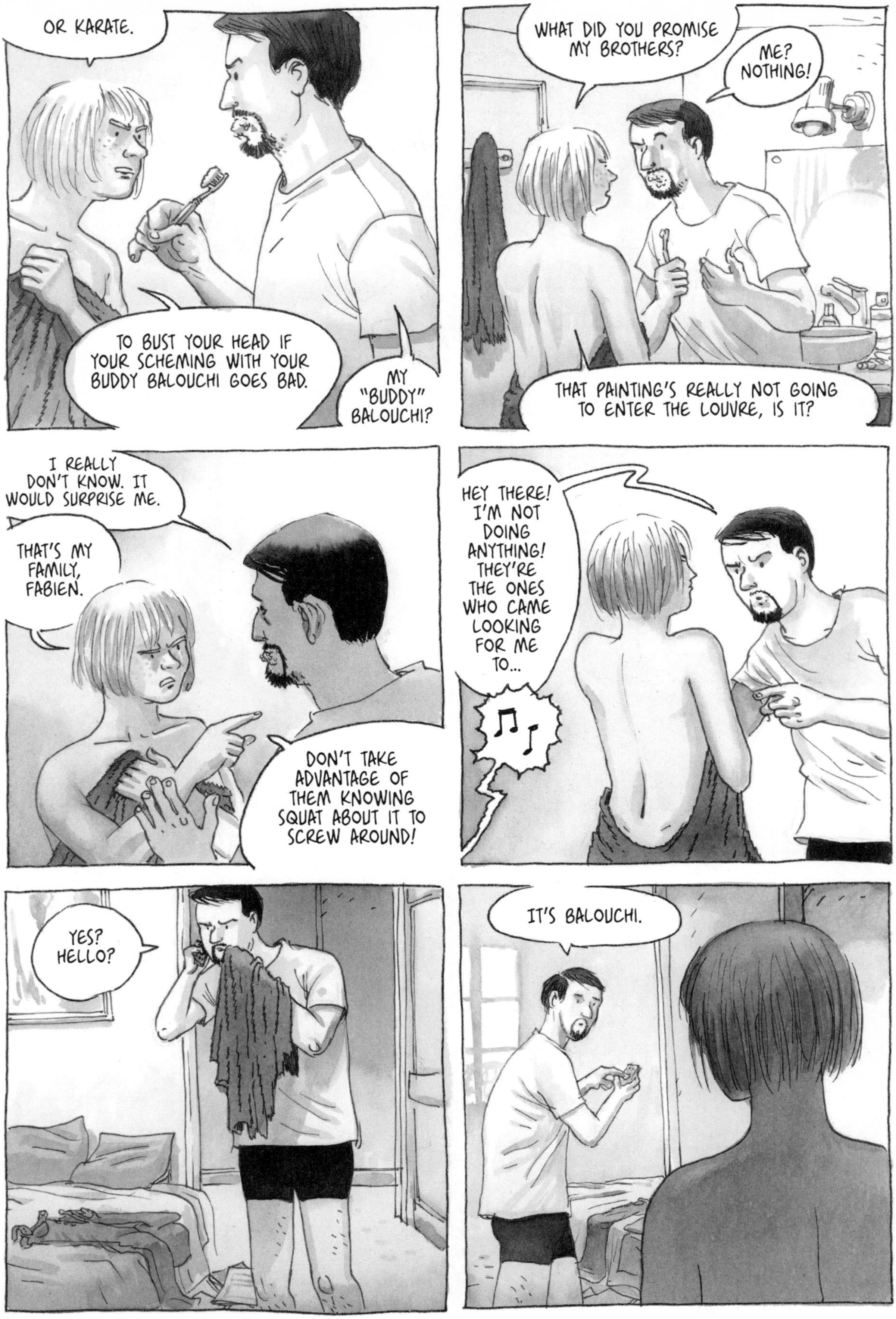
OR KARATE.
TO BUST YOUR HEAD IF YOUR SCHEMING WITH YOUR BUDDY BALOUCHI GOES BAD.
MY "BUDDY" BALOUCHI?
WHAT DID YOU PROMISE MY BROTHERS?
ME? NOTHING!
THAT PAINTING'S REALLY NOT GOING TO ENTER THE LOUVRE, IS IT?
I REALLY DON'T KNOW. IT WOULD SURPRISE ME.
THAT'S MY FAMILY, FABIEN.
DON'T TAKE ADVANTAGE OF THEM KNOWING SQUAT ABOUT IT TO SCREW AROUND!
HEY THERE! I'M NOT DOING ANYTHING! THEY'RE THE ONES WHO CAME LOOKING FOR ME TO...
YES? HELLO?
IT'S BALOUCHI.

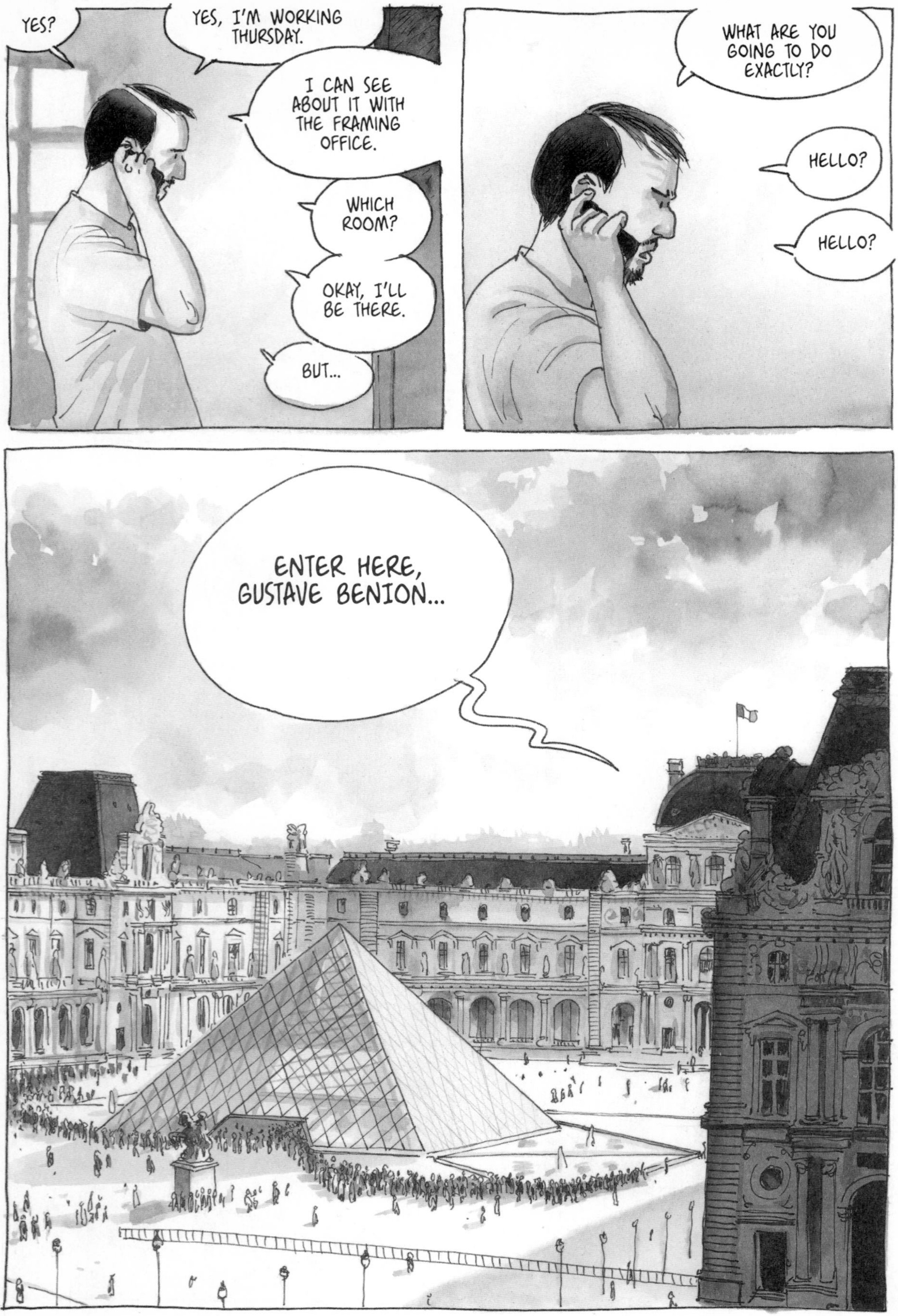
YES?
YES, I'M WORKING THURSDAY.
I CAN SEE ABOUT IT WITH THE FRAMING OFFICE.
WHICH ROOM?
OKAY, I'LL BE THERE.
BUT...
WHAT ARE YOU GOING TO DO EXACTLY?
HELLO?
HELLO?
ENTER HERE, GUSTAVE BENION...

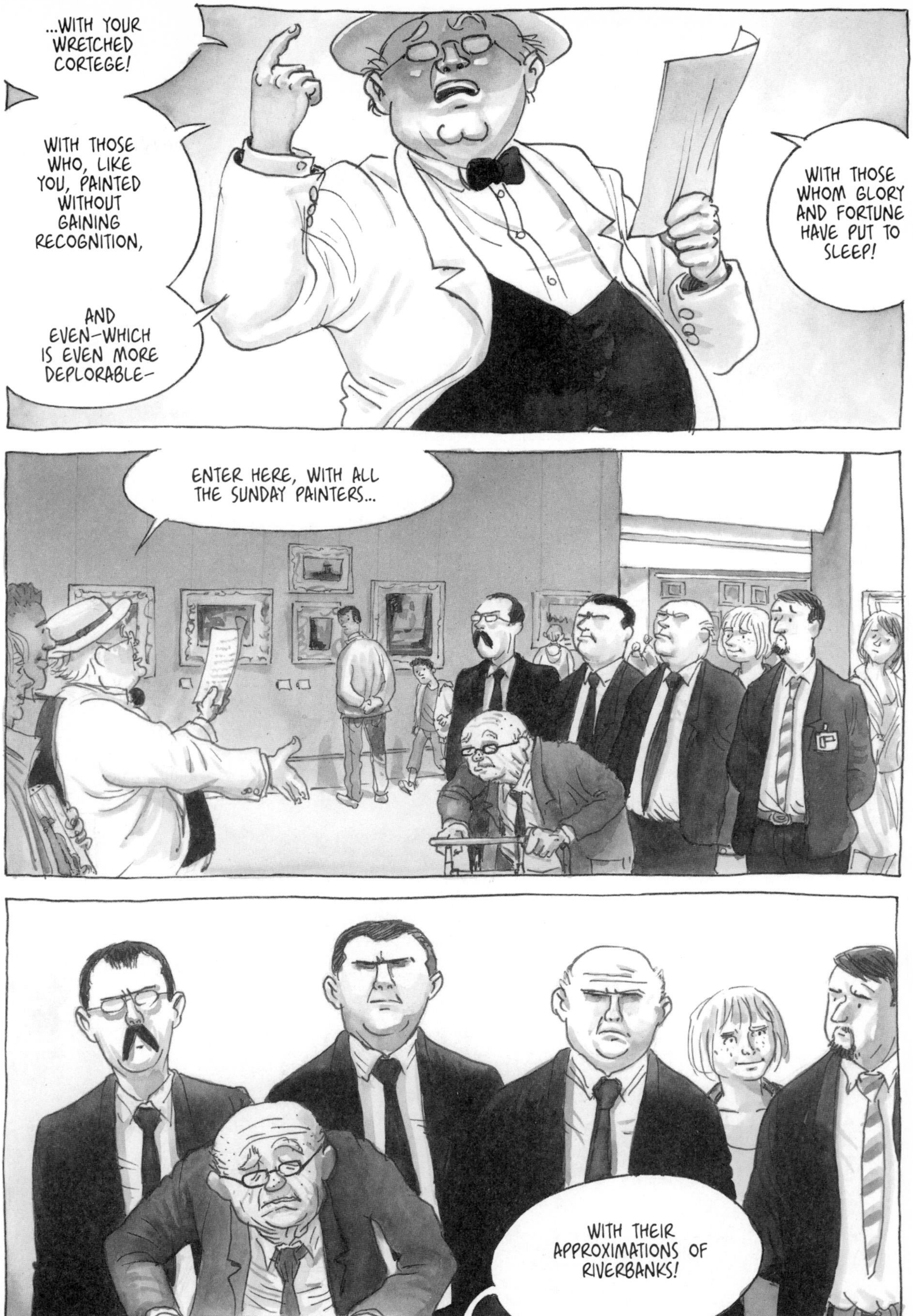
...WITH YOUR WRETCHED CORTEGE!
WITH THOSE WHO, LIKE YOU, PAINTED WITHOUT GAINING RECOGNITION,
AND EVEN-WHICH IS EVEN MORE DEPLORABLE-
WITH THOSE WHOM GLORY AND FORTUNE HAVE PUT TO SLEEP!
ENTER HERE, WITH ALL THE SUNDAY PAINTERS...
WITH THEIR APPROXIMATIONS OF RIVERBANKS!

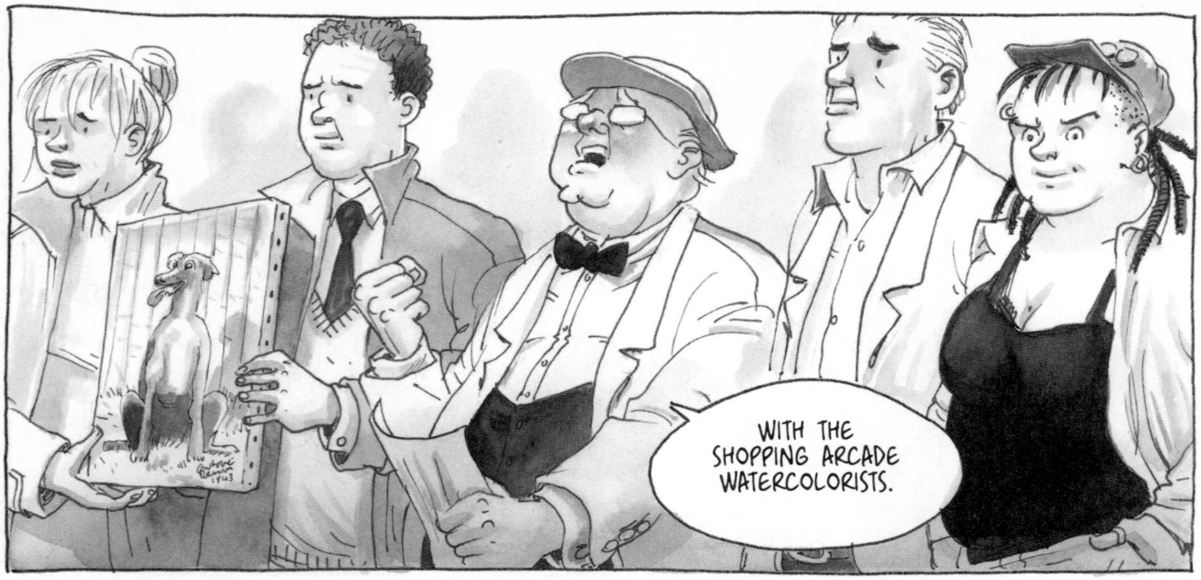
WITH THE SHOPPING ARCADE WATERCOLORISTS.

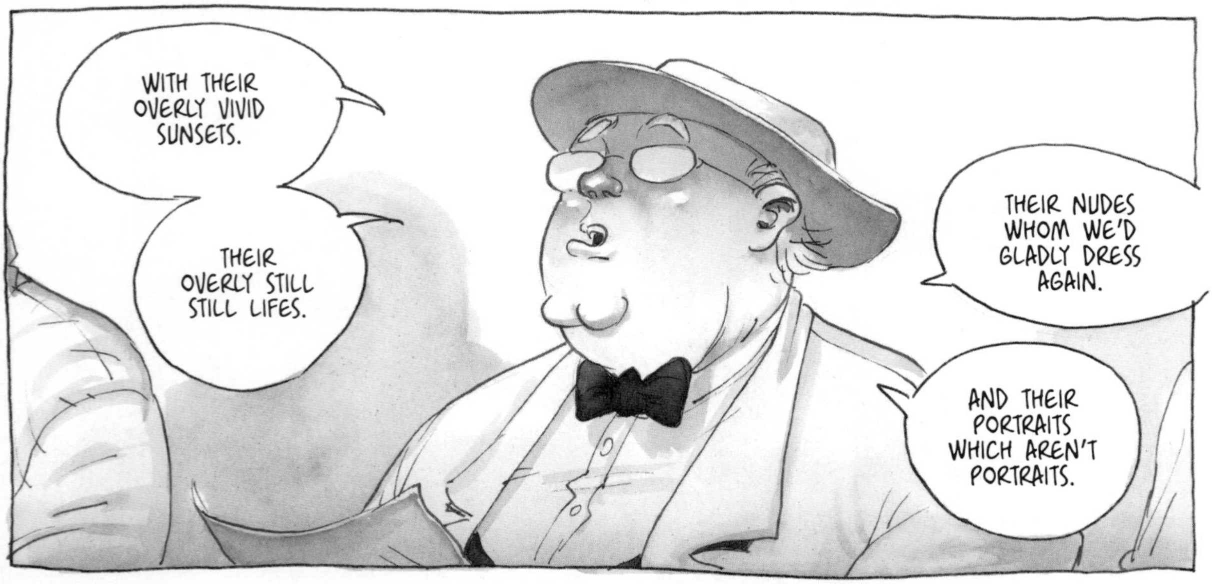
WITH THEIR OVERLY VIVID SUNSETS.
THEIR OVERLY STILL STILL LIFES.
THEIR NUDES WHOM WE'D GLADLY DRESS AGAIN.
AND THEIR PORTRAITS WHICH AREN'T PORTRAITS.

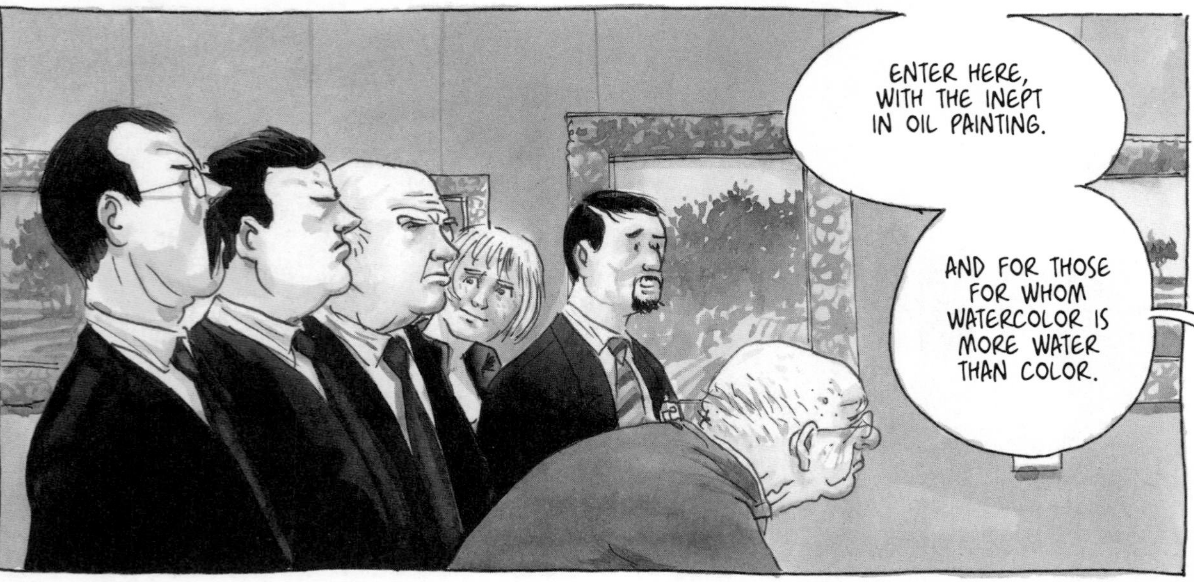
ENTER HERE, WITH THE INEPT IN OIL PAINTING.
AND FOR THOSE FOR WHOM WATERCOLOR IS MORE WATER THAN COLOR.

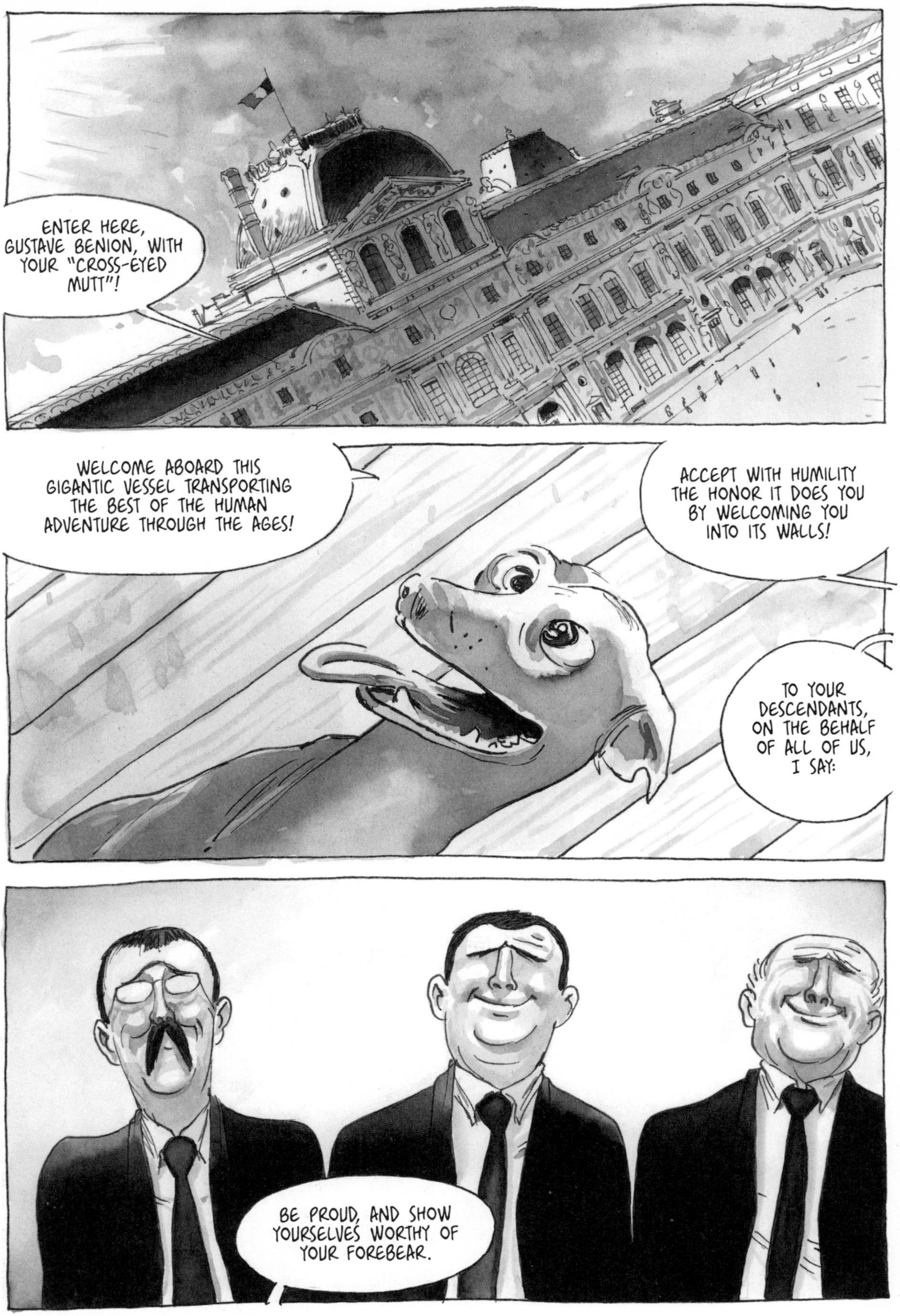
ENTER HERE, GUSTAVE BENION, WITH YOUR "CROSS-EYED MUTT"!
WELCOME ABOARD THIS GIGANTIC VESSEL TRANSPORTING THE BEST OF THE HUMAN ADVENTURE THROUGH THE AGES!
ACCEPT WITH HUMILITY THE HONOR IT DOES YOU BY WELCOMING YOU INTO ITS WALLS!
TO YOUR DESCENDANTS, ON THE BEHALF OF ALL OF US, I SAY:
BE PROUD, AND SHOW YOURSELVES WORTHY OF YOUR FOREBEAR.

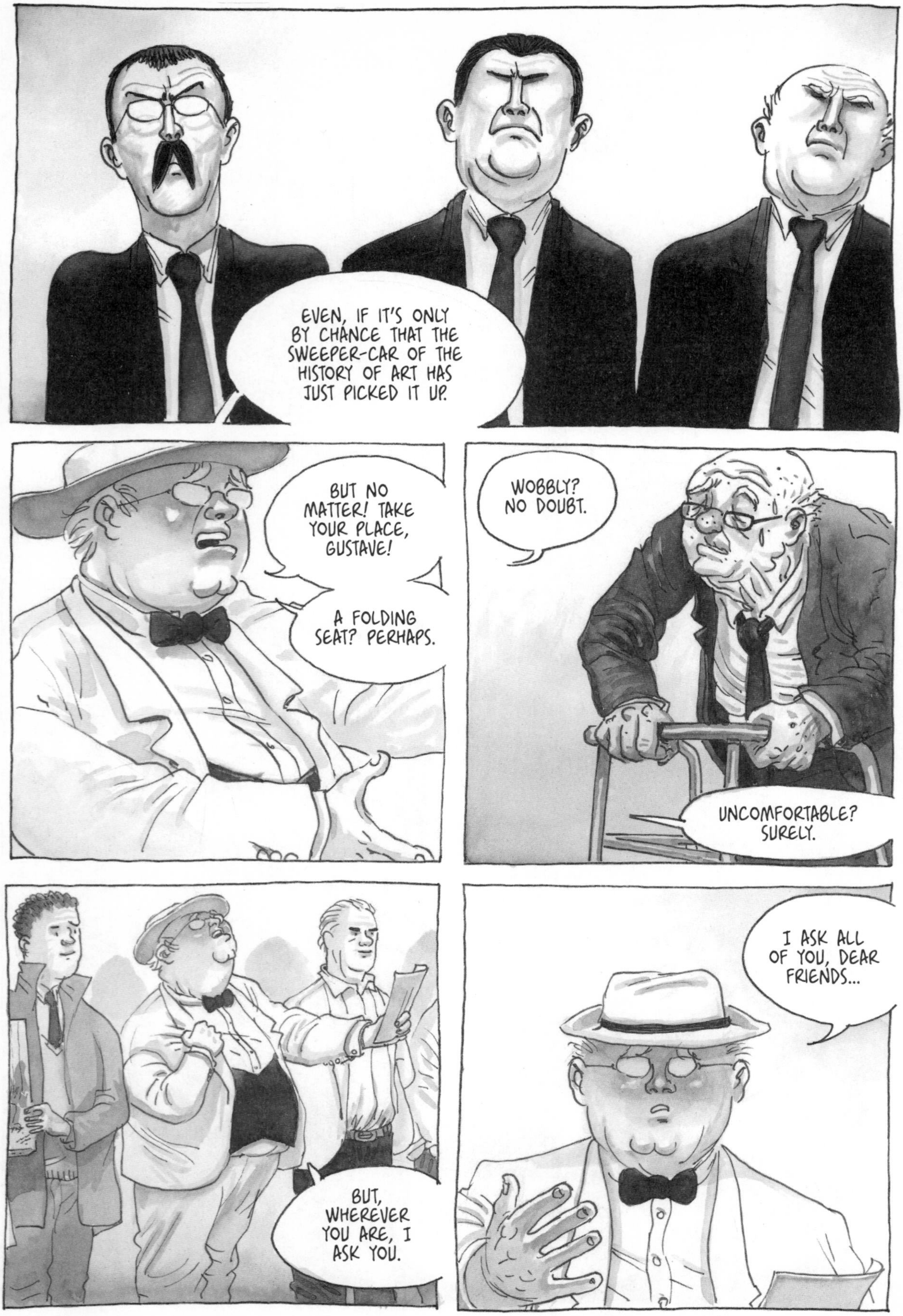
EVEN, IF IT'S ONLY BY CHANCE THAT THE SWEEPER-CAR OF THE HISTORY OF ART HAS JUST PICKED IT UP.
BUT NO MATTER! TAKE YOUR PLACE, GUSTAVE!
A FOLDING SEAT? PERHAPS.
WOBBLY? NO DOUBT.
UNCOMFORTABLE? SURELY.
BUT, WHEREVER YOU ARE, I ASK YOU.
I ASK ALL OF YOU, DEAR FRIENDS...

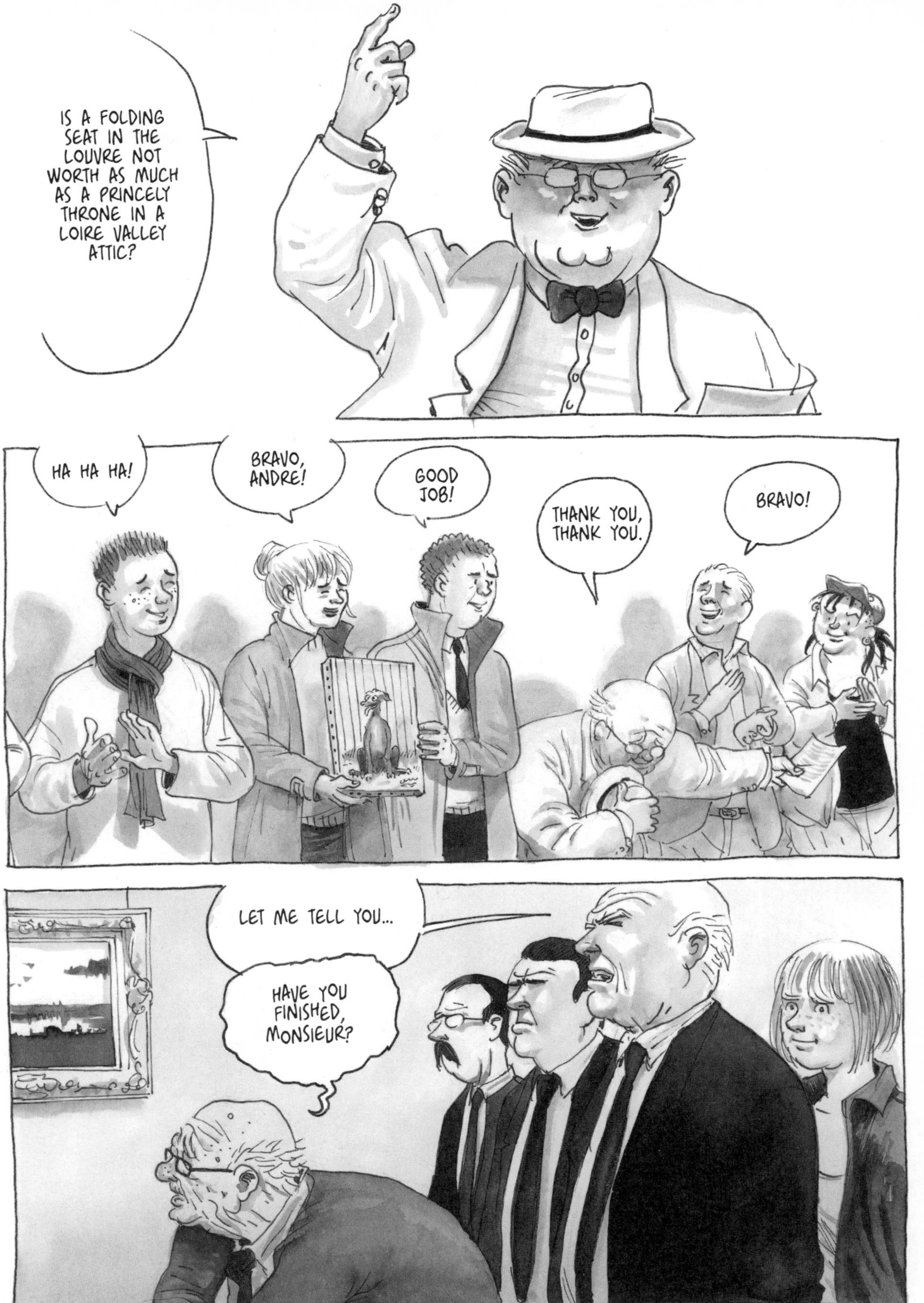
IS A FOLDING SEAT IN THE LOUVRE NOT WORTH AS MUCH AS A PRINCELY THRONE IN A LOIRE VALLEY ATTIC?
HA HA HA!
BRAVO, ANDRE!
GOOD JOB!
THANK YOU, THANK YOU.
BRAVO!
LET ME TELL YOU...
HAVE YOU FINISHED, MONSIEUR?

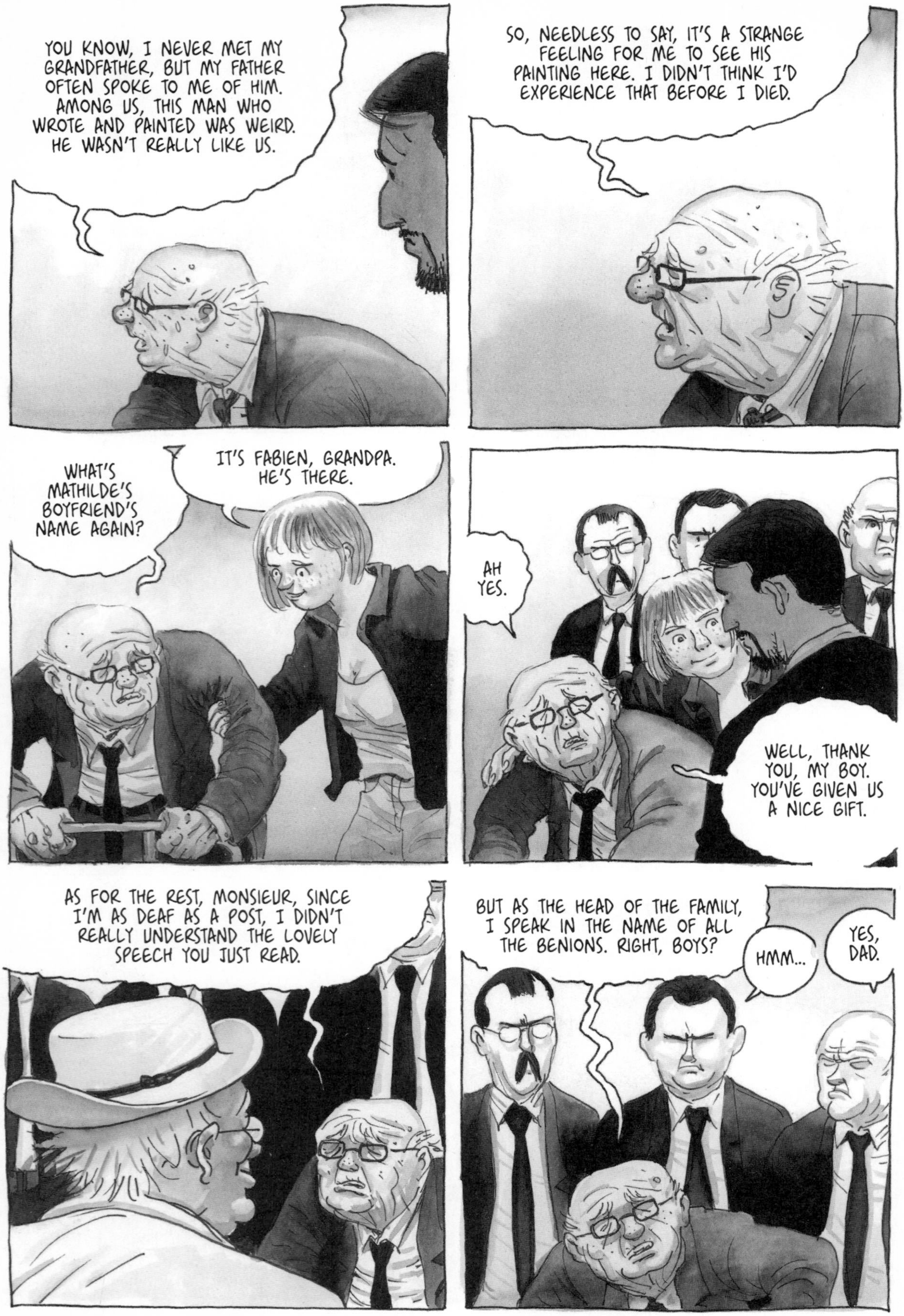
YOU KNOW, I NEVER MET MY GRANDFATHER, BUT MY FATHER OFTEN SPOKE TO ME OF HIM. AMONG US, THIS MAN WHO WROTE AND PAINTED WAS WEIRD. HE WASN'T REALLY LIKE US.
SO, NEEDLESS TO SAY, IT'S A STRANGE FEELING FOR ME TO SEE HIS PAINTING HERE. I DIDN'T THINK I'D EXPERIENCE THAT BEFORE I DIED.
WHAT'S MATHILDE'S BOYFRIEND'S NAME AGAIN?
IT'S FABIEN, GRANDPA. HE'S THERE.
AH YES.
WELL, THANK YOU, MY BOY. YOU'VE GIVEN US A NICE GIFT.
AS FOR THE REST, MONSIEUR, SINCE I'M AS DEAF AS A POST, I DIDN'T REALLY UNDERSTAND THE LOVELY SPEECH YOU JUST READ.
BUT AS THE HEAD OF THE FAMILY, I SPEAK IN THE NAME OF ALL THE BENIONS. RIGHT, BOYS?
HMM...
YES, DAD.

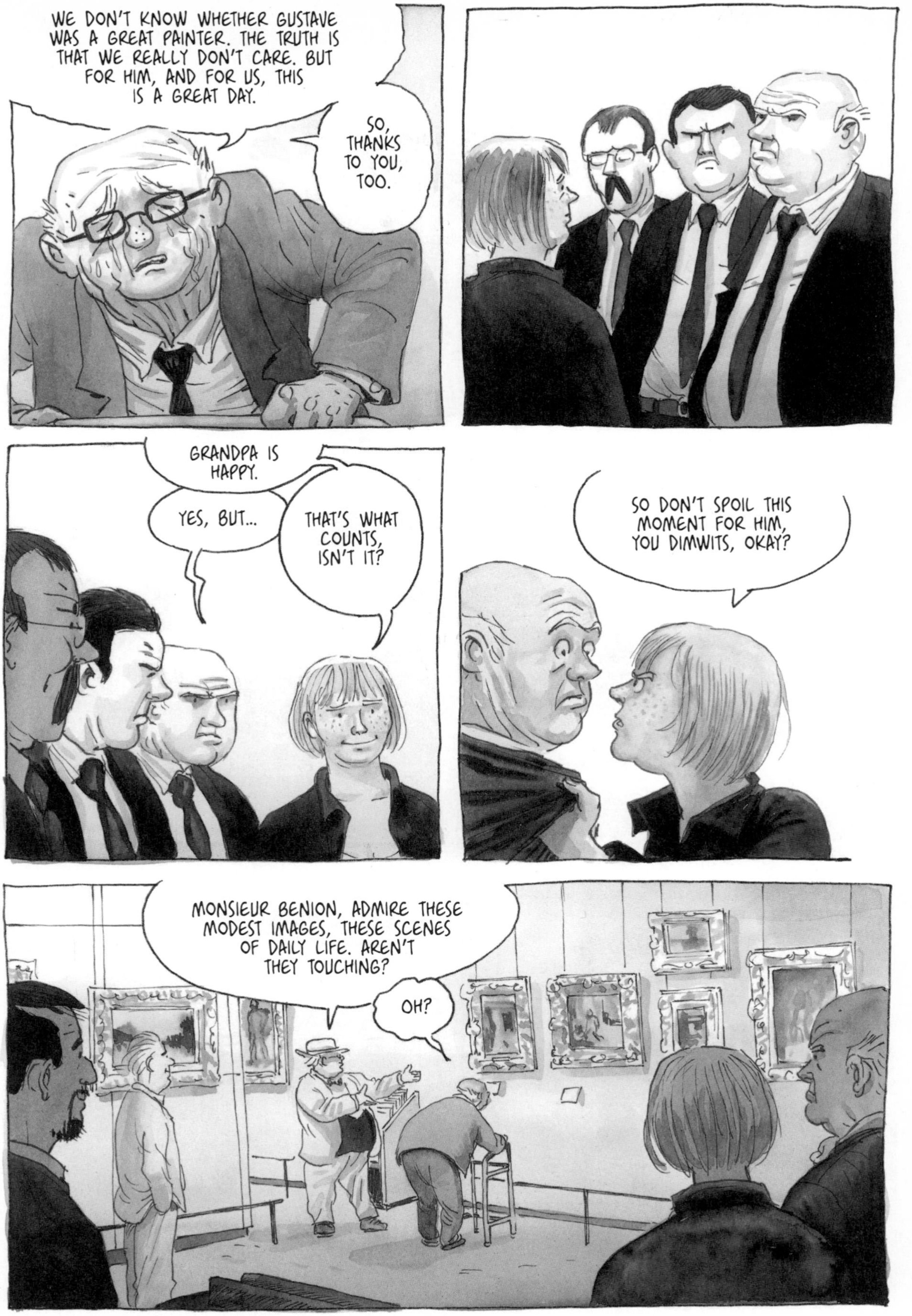
WE DON'T KNOW WHETHER GUSTAVE WAS A GREAT PAINTER. THE TRUTH IS THAT WE REALLY DON'T CARE. BUT FOR HIM, AND FOR US, THIS IS A GREAT DAY.
SO, THANKS TO YOU, TOO.
GRANDPA IS HAPPY.
YES, BUT...
THAT'S WHAT COUNTS, ISN'T IT?
SO DON'T SPOIL THIS MOMENT FOR HIM, YOU DIMWITS, OKAY?
MONSIEUR BENION, ADMIRE THESE MODEST IMAGES, THESE SCENES OF DAILY LIFE. AREN'T THEY TOUCHING?
OH?

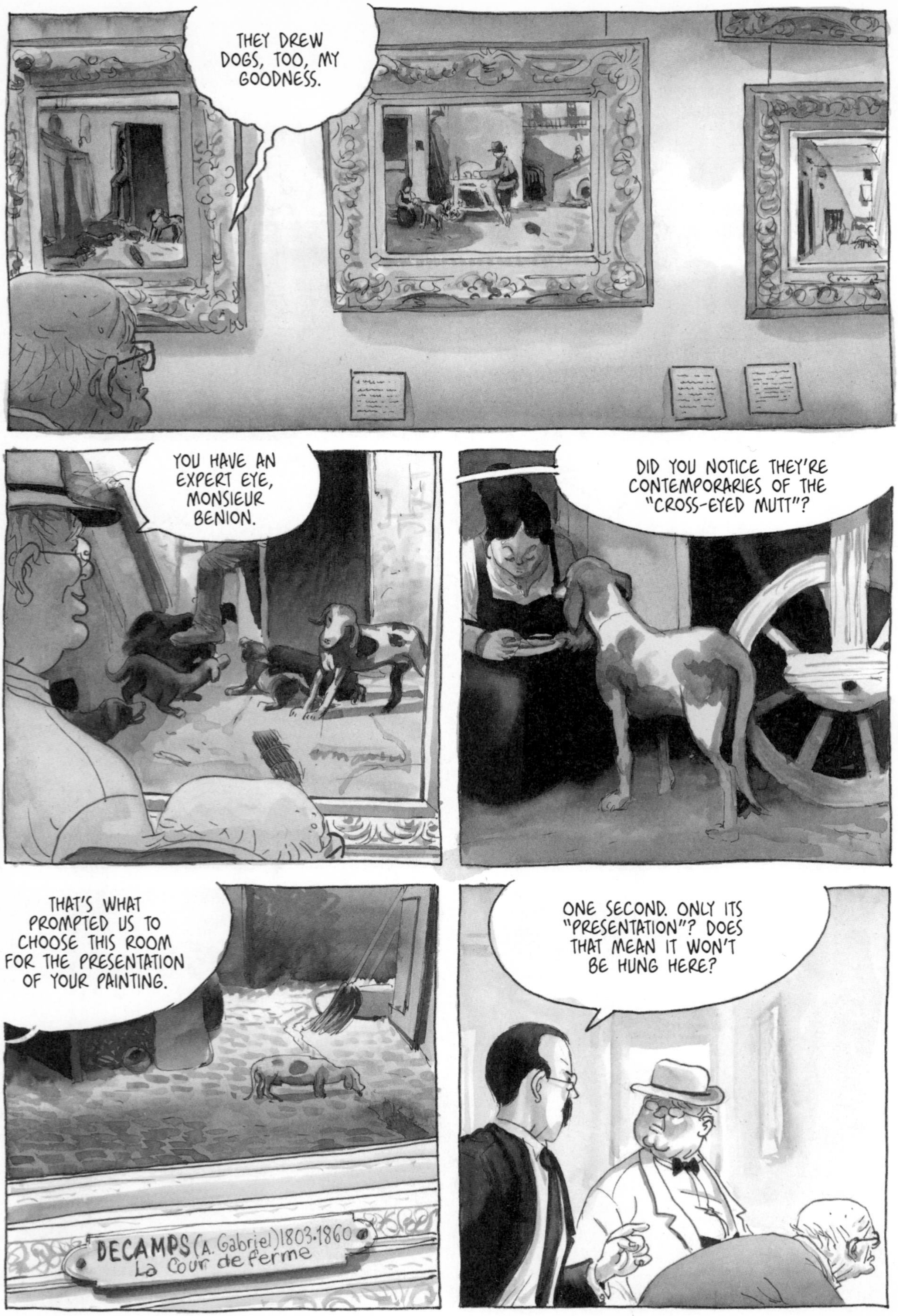
THEY DREW DOGS, TOO, MY GOODNESS.
YOU HAVE AN EXPERT EYE, MONSIEUR BENION.
DID YOU NOTICE THEY'RE CONTEMPORARIES OF THE "CROSS-EYED MUTT"?
THAT'S WHAT PROMPTED US TO CHOOSE THIS ROOM FOR THE PRESENTATION OF YOUR PAINTING.
DECAMPS (A. Gabriel) 1803-1860
La Cour de ferme
ONE SECOND. ONLY ITS "PRESENTATION"? DOES THAT MEAN IT WON'T BE HUNG HERE?

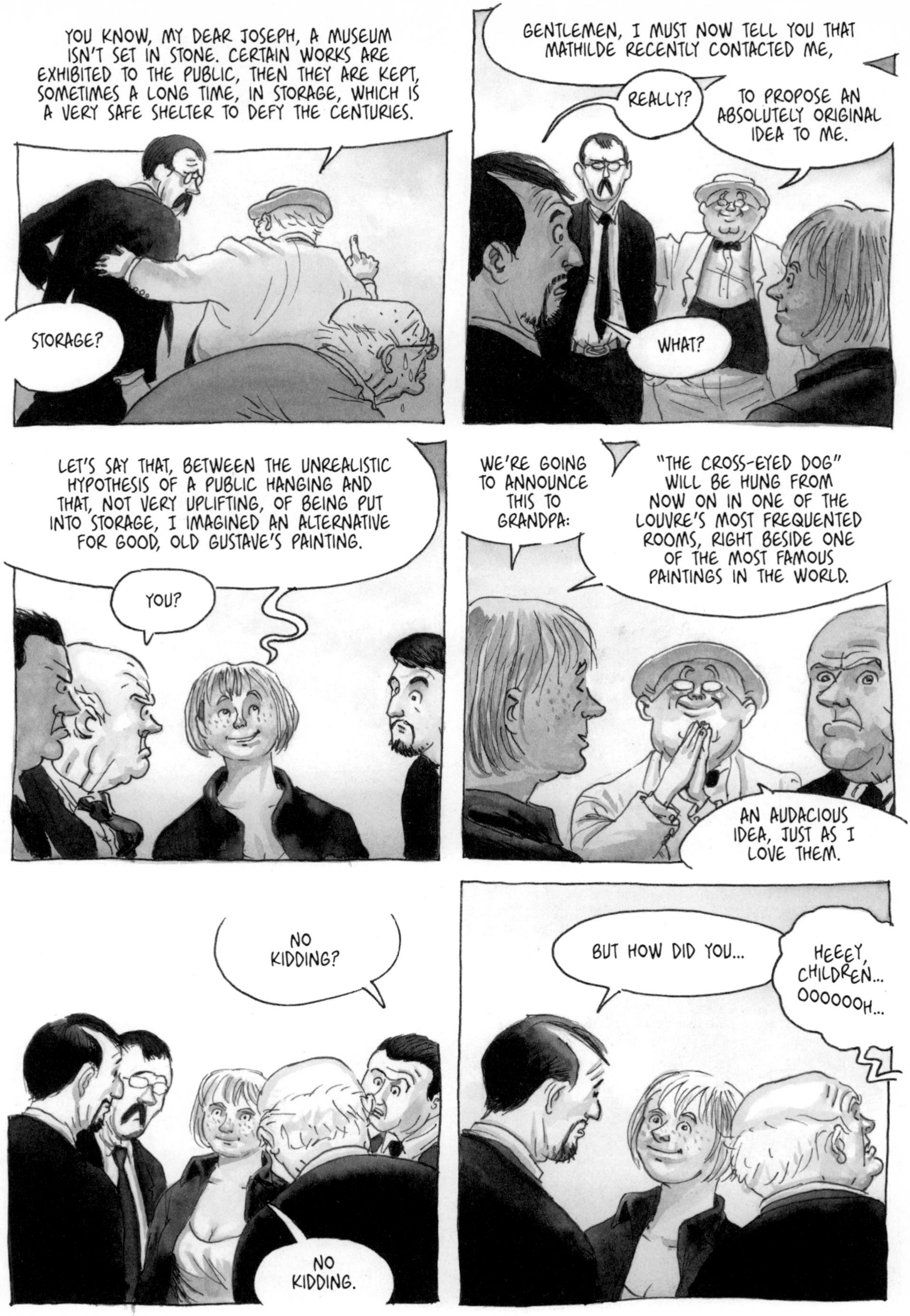
YOU KNOW, MY DEAR JOSEPH, A MUSEUM ISN'T SET IN STONE. CERTAIN WORKS ARE EXHIBITED TO THE PUBLIC, THEN THEY ARE KEPT, SOMETIMES A LONG TIME, IN STORAGE, WHICH IS A VERY SAFE SHELTER TO DEFY THE CENTURIES.
STORAGE?
GENTLEMEN, I MUST NOW TELL YOU THAT MATHILDE RECENTLY CONTACTED ME,
REALLY?
TO PROPOSE AN ABSOLUTELY ORIGINAL IDEA TO ME.
WHAT?
LET'S SAY THAT, BETWEEN THE UNREALISTIC HYPOTHESIS OF A PUBLIC HANGING AND THAT, NOT VERY UPLIFTING, OF BEING PUT INTO STORAGE, I IMAGINED AN ALTERNATIVE FOR GOOD, OLD GUSTAVE'S PAINTING.
YOU?
WE'RE GOING TO ANNOUNCE THIS TO GRANDPA:
"THE CROSS-EYED DOG" WILL BE HUNG FROM NOW ON IN ONE OF THE LOUVRE'S MOST FREQUENTED ROOMS, RIGHT BESIDE ONE OF THE MOST FAMOUS PAINTINGS IN THE WORLD.
AN AUDACIOUS IDEA, JUST AS I LOVE THEM.
NO KIDDING?
NO KIDDING.
BUT HOW DID YOU...
HEEEY, CHILDREN... OOOOOOH...

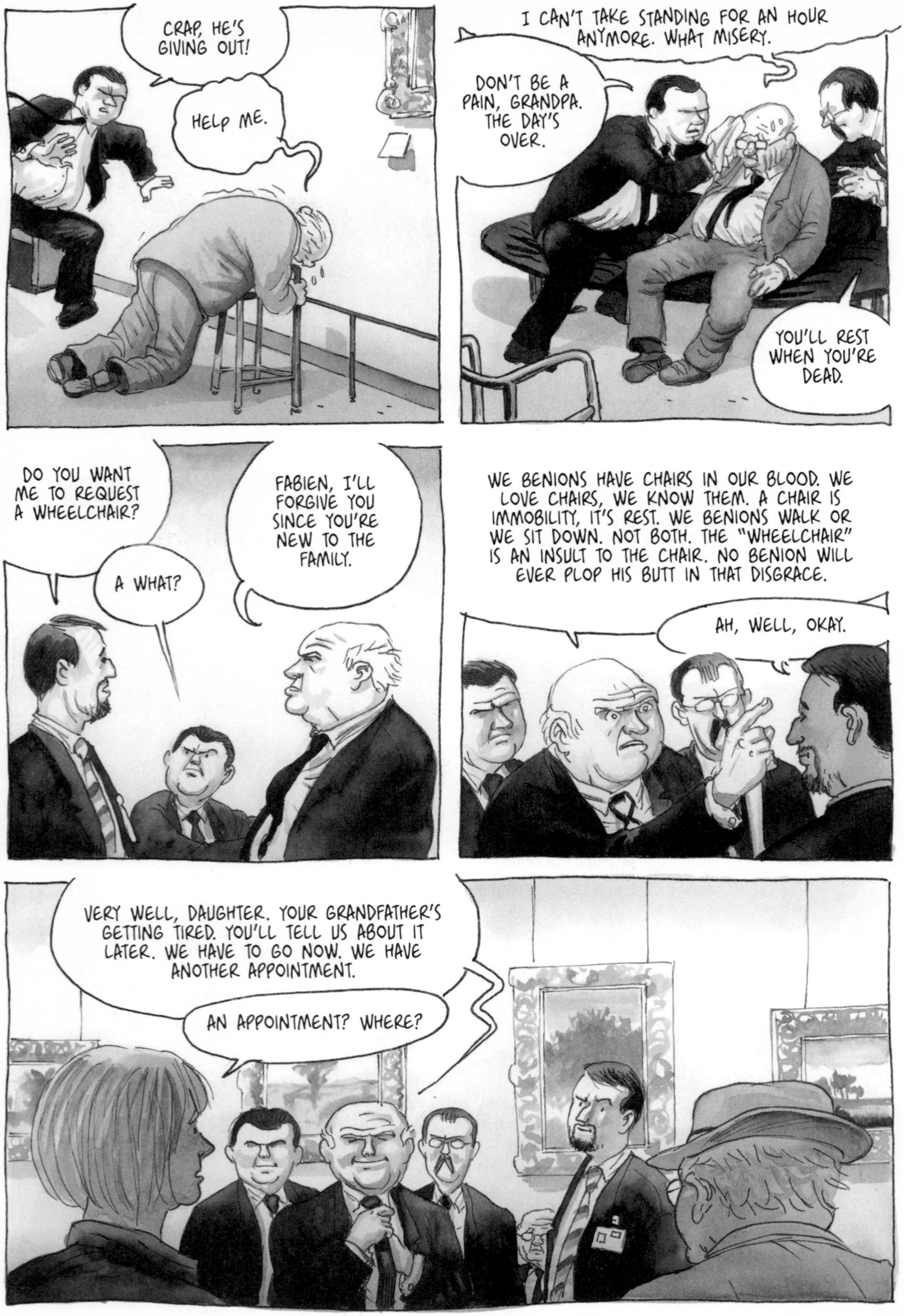
CRAP, HE'S GIVING OUT!
HELP ME.
I CAN'T TAKE STANDING FOR AN HOUR ANYMORE. WHAT MISERY.
DON'T BE A PAIN, GRANDPA. THE DAY'S OVER.
YOU'LL REST WHEN YOU'RE DEAD.
DO YOU WANT ME TO REQUEST A WHEELCHAIR?
A WHAT?
FABIEN, I'LL FORGIVE YOU SINCE YOU'RE NEW TO THE FAMILY.
WE BENIONS HAVE CHAIRS IN OUR BLOOD. WE LOVE CHAIRS, WE KNOW THEM. A CHAIR IS IMMOBILITY, IT'S REST. WE BENIONS WALK OR WE SIT DOWN. NOT BOTH. THE "WHEELCHAIR" IS AN INSULT TO THE CHAIR. NO BENION WILL EVER PLOP HIS BUTT IN THAT DISGRACE.
AH, WELL, OKAY.
VERY WELL, DAUGHTER. YOUR GRANDFATHER'S GETTING TIRED. YOU'LL TELL US ABOUT IT LATER. WE HAVE TO GO NOW. WE HAVE ANOTHER APPOINTMENT.
AN APPOINTMENT? WHERE?

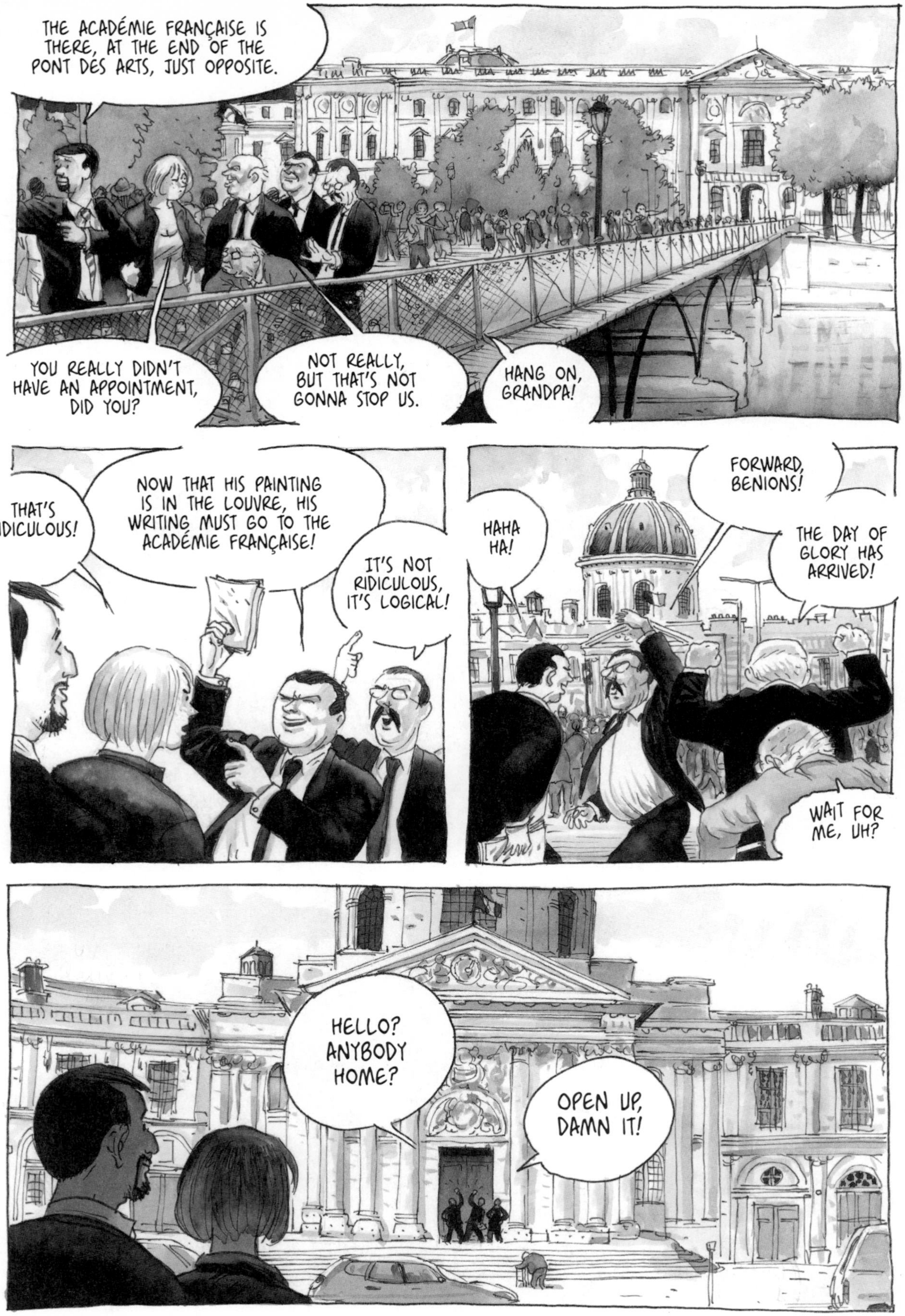
THE ACADÉMIE FRANÇAISE IS THERE, AT THE END OF THE PONT DES ARTS, JUST OPPOSITE.
YOU REALLY DIDN'T HAVE AN APPOINTMENT, DID YOU?
NOT REALLY, BUT THAT'S NOT GONNA STOP US.
HANG ON, GRANDPA!
THAT'S RIDICULOUS!
NOW THAT HIS PAINTING IS IN THE LOUVRE, HIS WRITING MUST GO TO THE ACADÉMIE FRANÇAISE!
IT'S NOT RIDICULOUS, IT'S LOGICAL!
HAHA HA!
FORWARD, BENIONS!
THE DAY OF GLORY HAS ARRIVED!
WAIT FOR ME, UH?
HELLO? ANYBODY HOME?
OPEN UP, DAMN IT!

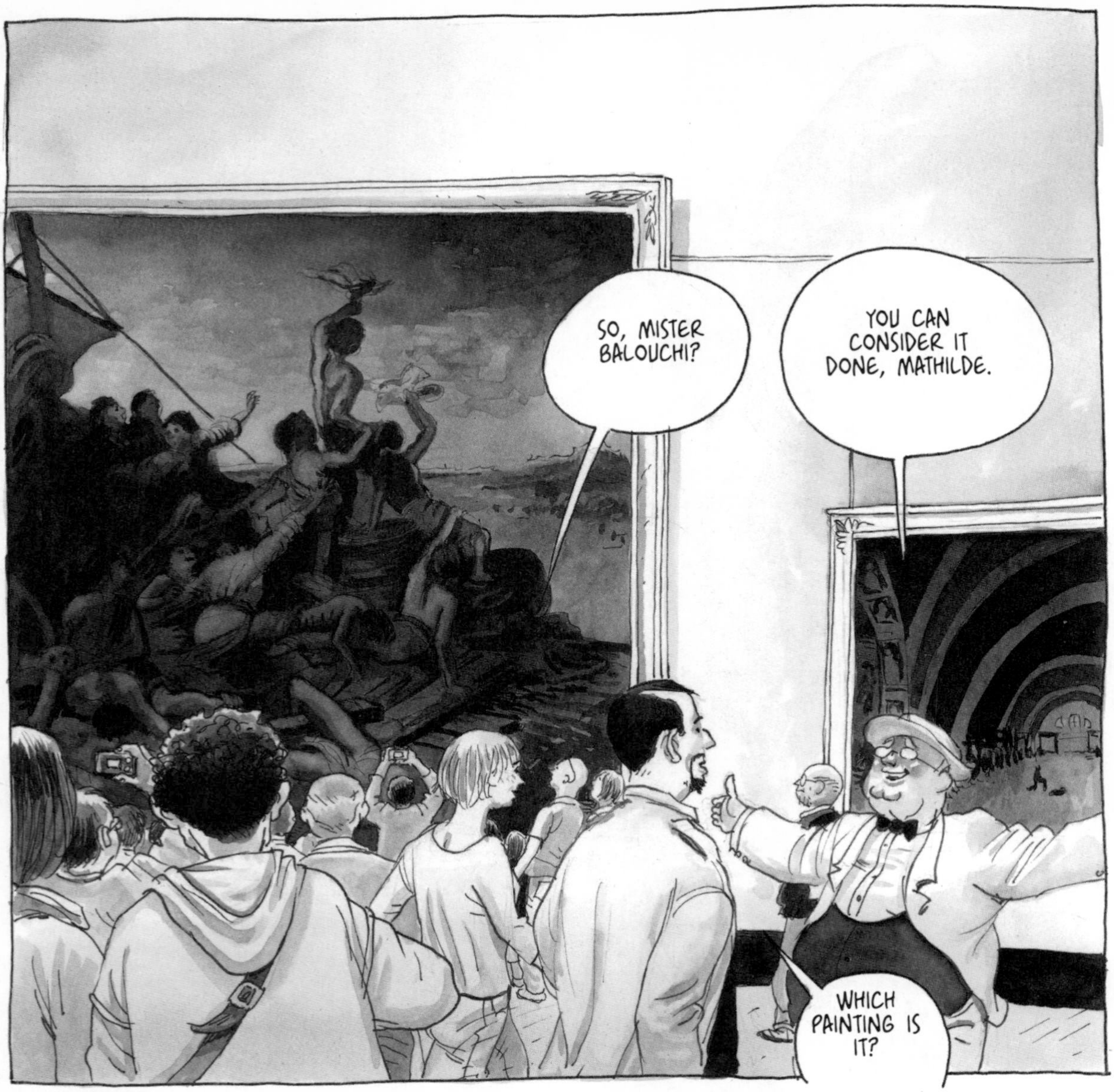
SO, MISTER BALOUCHI?
YOU CAN CONSIDER IT DONE, MATHILDE.
WHICH PAINTING IS IT?

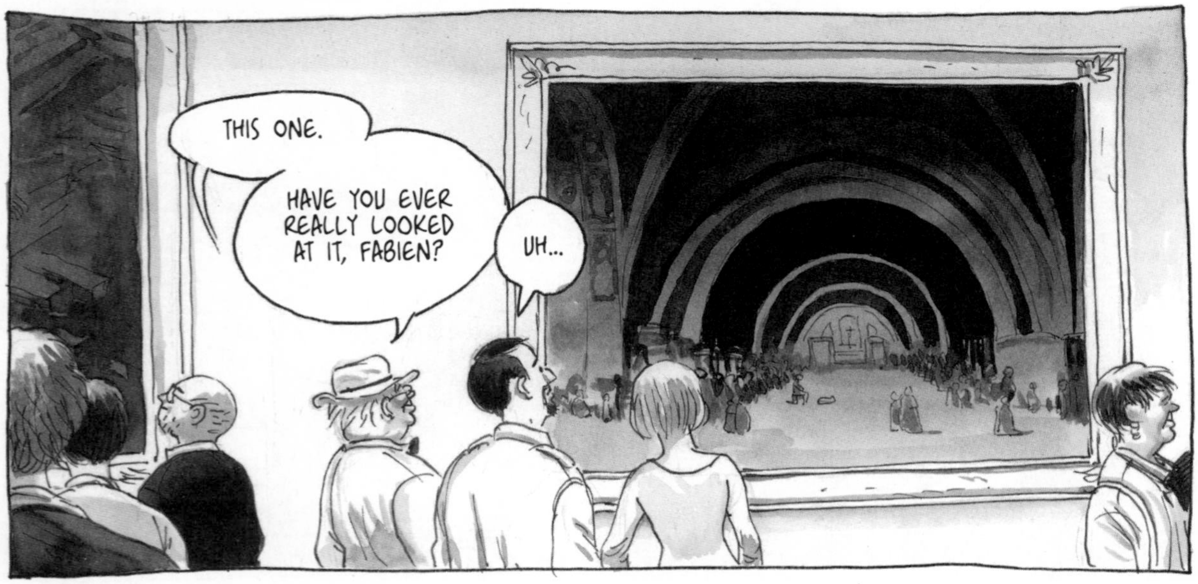
THIS ONE.
HAVE YOU EVER REALLY LOOKED AT IT, FABIEN?
UH...

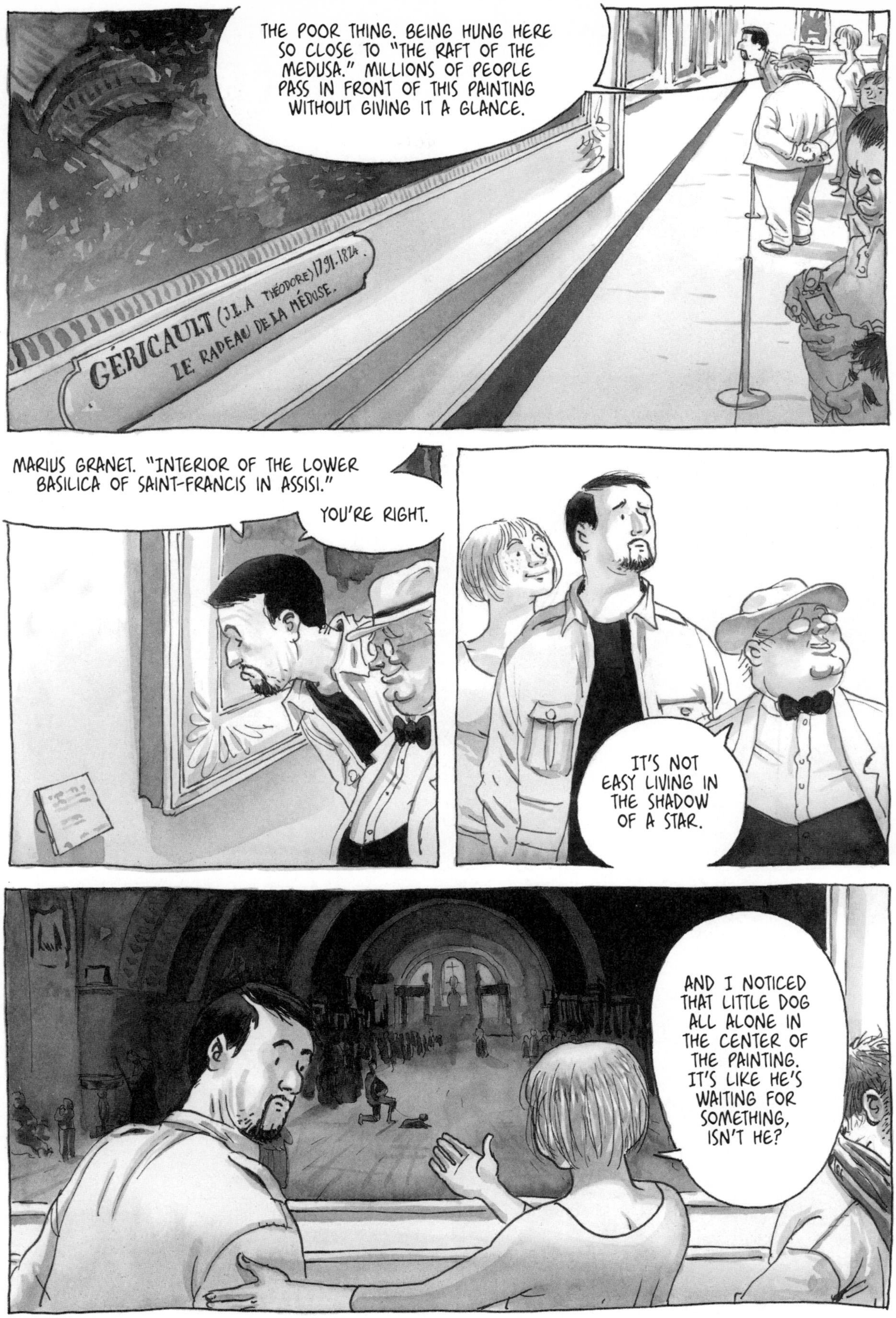
THE POOR THING. BEING HUNG HERE SO CLOSE TO "THE RAFT OF THE MEDUSA." MILLIONS OF PEOPLE PASS IN FRONT OF THIS PAINTING WITHOUT GIVING IT A GLANCE.
GÉRICAULT (J.L.A THÉODORE) 1791-1824
LE RADEAU DE LA MÉDUSE.
MARIUS GRANET. "INTERIOR OF THE LOWER BASILICA OF SAINT-FRANCIS IN ASSISI."
YOU'RE RIGHT.
IT'S NOT EASY LIVING IN THE SHADOW OF A STAR.
AND I NOTICED THAT LITTLE DOG ALL ALONE IN THE CENTER OF THE PAINTING. IT'S LIKE HE'S WAITING FOR SOMETHING, ISN'T HE?

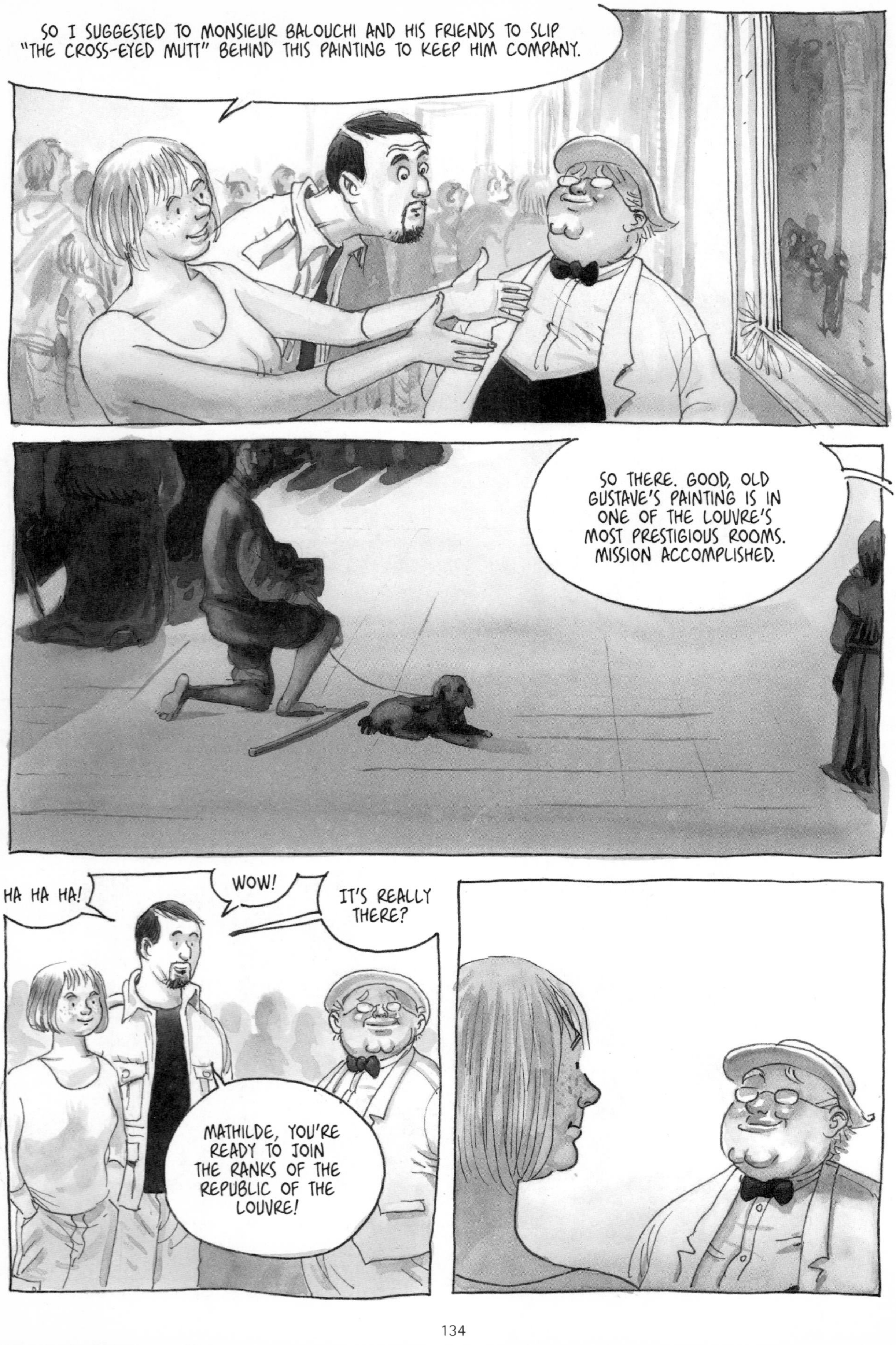
SO I SUGGESTED TO MONSIEUR BALOUCHI AND HIS FRIENDS TO SLIP "THE CROSS-EYED MUTT" BEHIND THIS PAINTING TO KEEP HIM COMPANY.
SO THERE. GOOD, OLD GUSTAVE'S PAINTING IS IN ONE OF THE LOUVRE'S MOST PRESTIGIOUS ROOMS. MISSION ACCOMPLISHED.
HA HA HA!
WOW!
IT'S REALLY THERE?
MATHILDE, YOU'RE READY TO JOIN THE RANKS OF THE REPUBLIC OF THE LOUVRE!

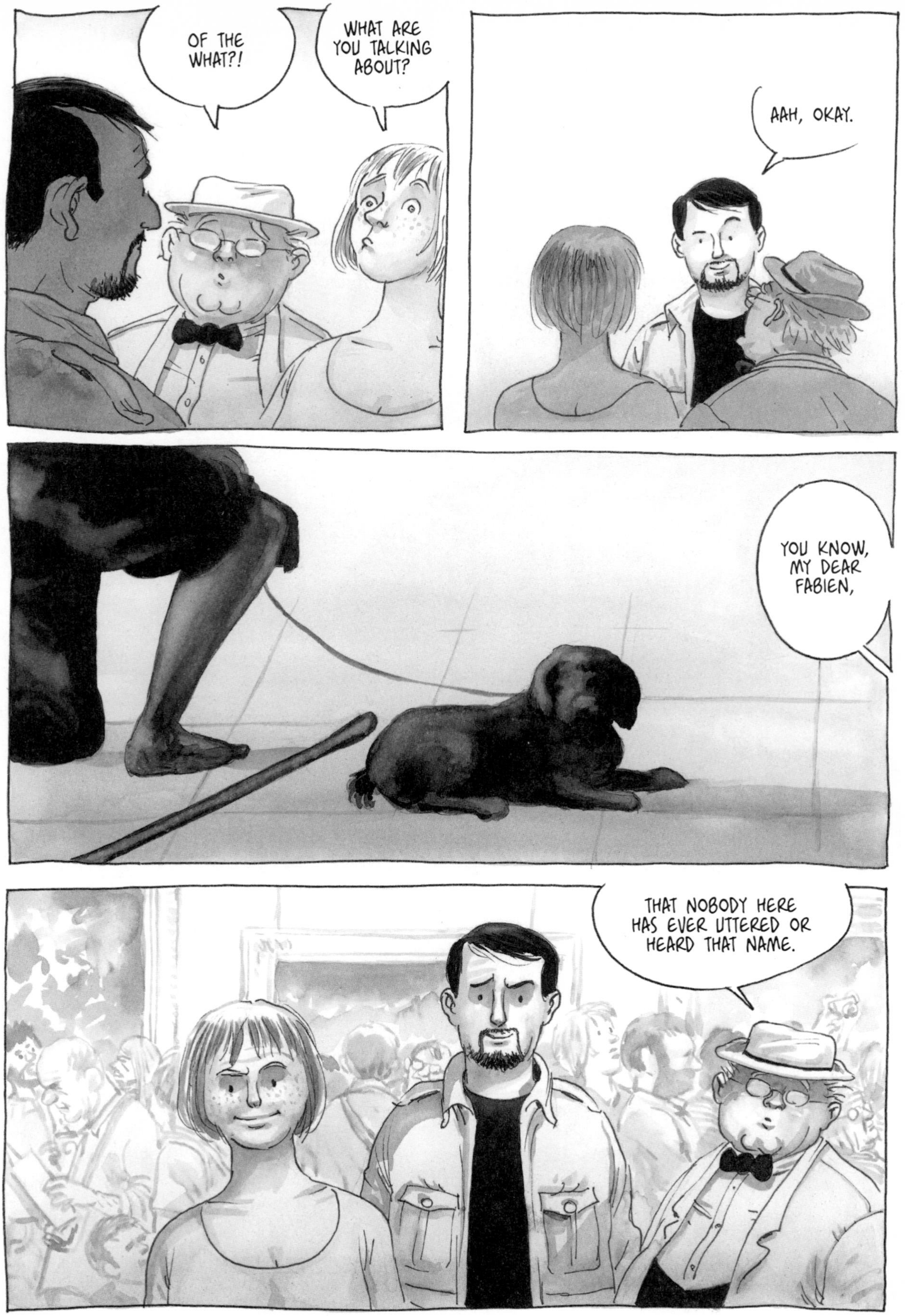
OF THE WHAT?!
WHAT ARE YOU TALKING ABOUT?
AAH, OKAY.
YOU KNOW, MY DEAR FABIEN,
THAT NOBODY HERE HAS EVER UTTERED OR HEARD THAT NAME.

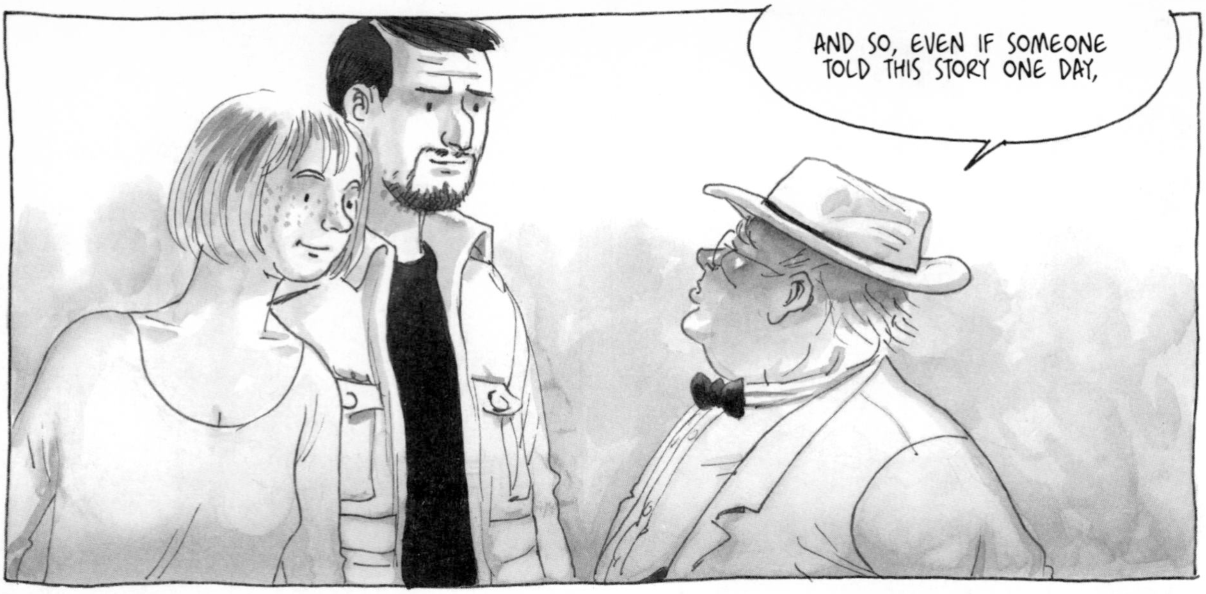
AND SO, EVEN IF SOMEONE TOLD THIS STORY ONE DAY,

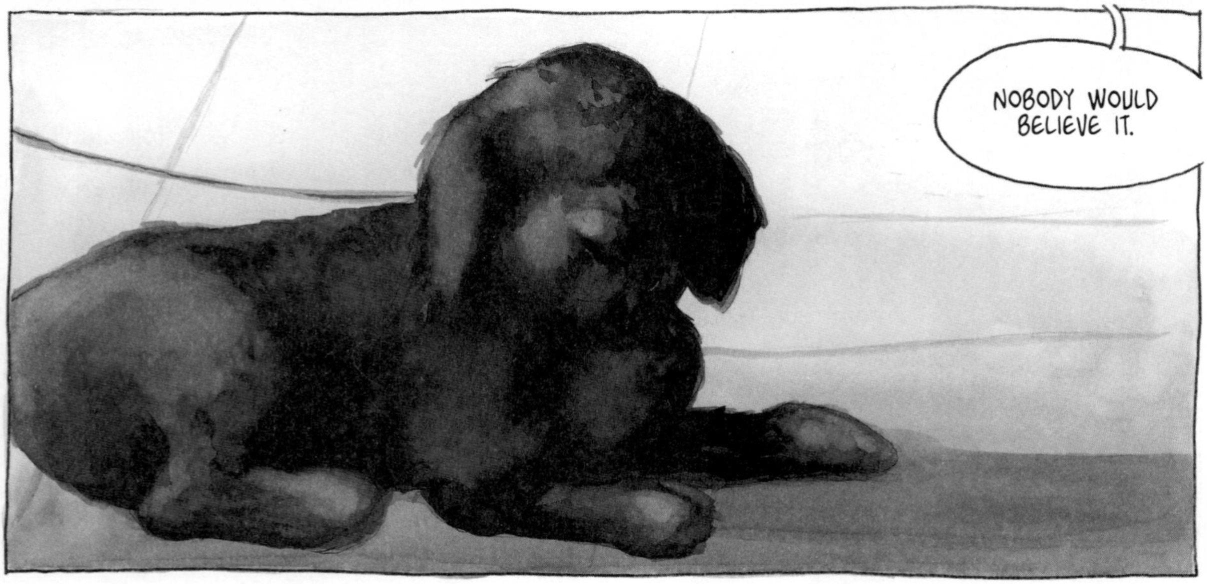
NOBODY WOULD BELIEVE IT.

Etienne DAVODEAU

The Acquisition of works:
Who decides what, and how?

The reader will remember Louis Benion's direct query to Fabien: Would our ancestor's painting have a spot in the Louvre or is it an insignificant piece of crap?"

A simple question, which gets straight to the point, asked forthrightly with no fuss.

Put differently: who can affirm whether a painting deserves to be hung or not, for posterity, on the walls of a museum as prestigious as the Louvre?

How is the choice made of what enters the museum's collections, and who is responsible for that?

Here are some of the answers.

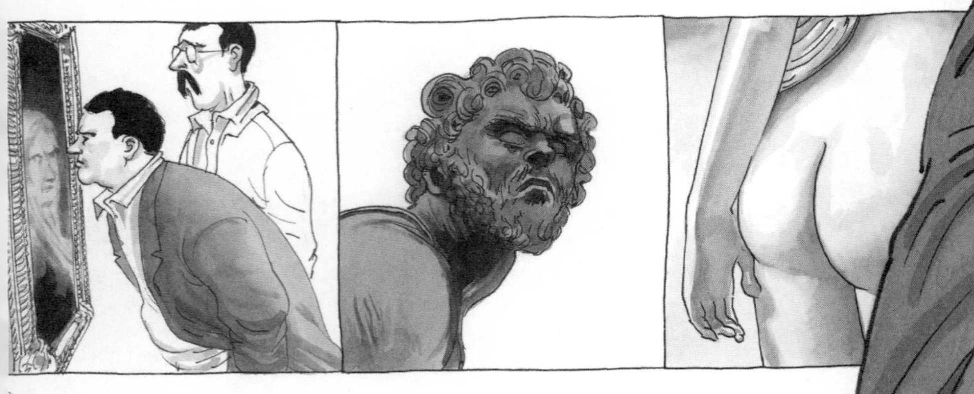

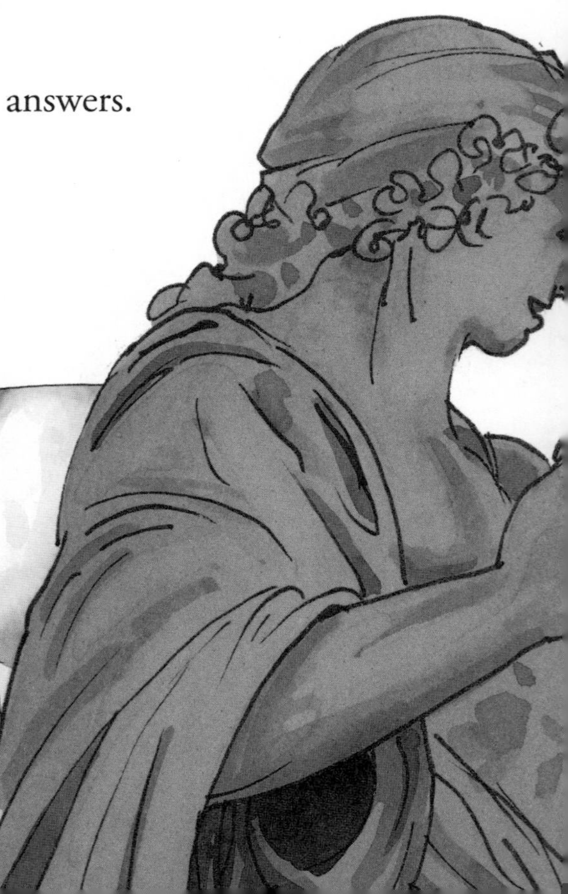

Because of the Louvre's worldwide fame, it's not uncommon for visitors—art lovers, collectors, artists or private owners of works inherited from their ancestors or acquired by themselves—to contact the Louvre to propose to sell, donate, or bequeath to it a painting, a bronze, an engraving, a sculpture, or an ancient relic.

The museum cannot accept all those proposals that do not necessarily correspond to the domains and historical periods covered by its collections, and are not always of sufficient interest to be presented to the public.

Since January 1, 2004, to speak only of how it works today, the Musée du Louvre has expertise with regards to enriching the collections and exercises, in this domain, expansive legal autonomy allowing it to determine and directly finance its acquisitions with its own revenue, without intervention from the government budget.

The museum is charged with contributing to the national collections' enrichment through the acquisition of cultural property, on behalf of the government, for payment or for free. It devotes 20% of the annual box office receipts for these acquisitions to its permanent collections.

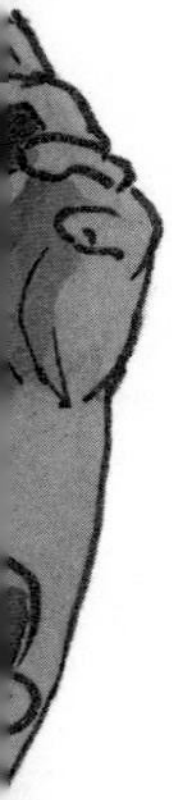

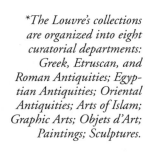

**The Louvre's collections are organized into eight curatorial departments: Greek, Etruscan, and Roman Antiquities; Egyptian Antiquities; Oriental Antiquities; Arts of Islam; Graphic Arts; Objets d'Art; Paintings; Sculptures.*

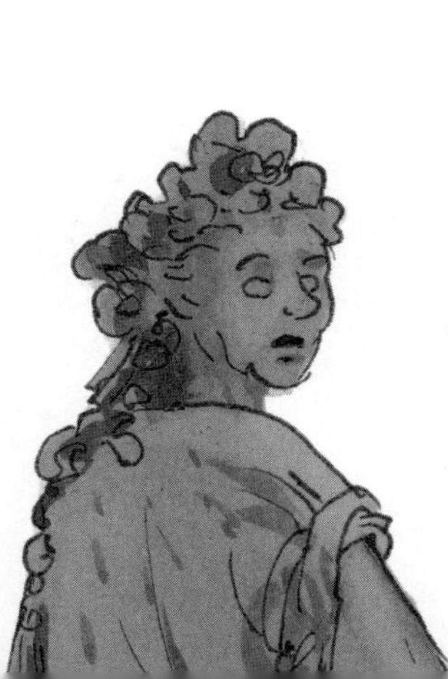

Policy for acquisition of works at the Louvre.

Just as no visitor could simply decide to gift the museum with a work like The Cross-Eyed Mutt, no single curator or even the museum's CEO can decide to purchase or accept the donation of a work on his or her own.

Whatever the price of the work, whether offered for free or sold for several hundreds of millions of dollars, all decisions for strengthening the collections are made as a group, after discussion in one, sometimes two, consultative sessions.

This role has been assigned to a committee specifically responsible for acquisitions, the Acquisition Commission, composed of twenty-two members:

—the CEO of the Musée du Louvre,
—the director of the Musées de France, or his representative,
—the directors of the museum's eight curatorial departments,*
—the president of the Society of Friends of the Louvre, or his representative,
—two members elected for two years from among incumbent curators at the museum,
—the head of a large department of one of the national museums besides the Louvre,
—eight qualified people named for three-year terms by the minister of Culture: collectors, specialists in different domains, donors, and artists.

This Commission decides on the entirety of acquisition plans for the curatorial departments of the Louvre at the end of a preliminary, internal consultation procedure by the curators of each department that permits them to determine the objectives and priorities of the policy for enriching each domain of the collections and closely linking expert personnel with it.

The Commission meets in a plenary session every month (except in July and August) to physically examine the works and to hear the curators present the acquisition plans and to expound on their motivations.

It expresses its opinion by secret ballot, with a two-thirds majority: if a third of the members express a negative opinion, the project is rejected.

The opinion of a second group, the Artistic Council of National Museums, is also sought for projects (for-cost or free) surpassing a certain value determined by the category of the goods: 100,000 € for paintings or sculptures; 50,000 € for relics, drawings, objets d'art, furniture, and transportation vehicles; 15,000 € for photos, engravings, books, archives, and musical instruments.

Also, the Artistic Council gives its advice about seeking pre-emptive rights on public sales.

Beyond these monthly meetings, a permanent delegation can be consulted in emergency cases—notably for public sales between two monthly sessions. It is composed of five members: the CEO of the Louvre, the director of the Musées de France, and three position holders (and three replacements) elected for three years: a director of a department and two qualified people.

In total, there are no fewer than twenty annual meetings devoted to projects for enriching the collections organized at the Louvre.

Preliminary stages for projects

To prepare for the Acquisitions Commission's work and decision-making, the museum has an Acquisitions Department in its administration.

This department sees to the preliminary stages of acquisitions projects before passing them along to the Commission and the feasibility of the projects legally (cultural heritage status, historical status, and origin of the works, etc.), financially (verifying the price levels, negotiating them, and proposing acquisition strategies; finding external means of financing beyond the actual budget for acquisitions) and administratively.

It also organizes the work of the Acquisitions Commission from an equipment standpoint and the whole logistics tied to the organization of the sessions: the transportation of works and their insurance in preparation for their physical presentation to the Commission, the photo sessions, then their delivery to the Artistic Counsel of the national museums as well as their return to departments of conservation (if purchased) or back to the owners (if rejected).

Finally it manages, after the commission and the Artistic Counsel, the administrative and financial matters and all operations through to admission into the collections.

This article was created with the assistance of Anne Vincent, the head of Acquisition Services at the Musée du Louvre.

Musée du Louvre

Jean-Luc Martinez
President and director

Hervé Barbaret
General Administrator

Juliette Armand
Head of Cultural Development

Violaine Bouvet-Lanselle
*Head of the Publishing Service,
Office of Cultural Development*

Publishing

Series Editor
Fabrice Douar
*Publishing Service, Office of
Cultural Development,
Musée du Louvre*

At the Musée du Louvre, thanks to:
*Jean-Luc Martinez, Henri Loyrette, Hervé Barbaret, Claudia Ferrazzi,
Juliette Armand, Serge Leduc, Violaine Bouvet-Lanselle, Pascal Torres, Anne Vincent,
Capitaine Laurent Leclercq, Soraya Karkache, Laurence Petit, Camille Palopoli,
Sabine de La Rochefoucauld, Caroline Damaÿ, Catherine Dupont, Fanny Meurisse,
Diane Vernel, Adrien Goetz, Laurence Castany, Christine Fuzeau, Camille Sourisse,
1ʳᵉ Classe Sébastien Meline, Caporal-chef Mathieu Pochon, Caporal-chef Raphaël Osawa,
Juliette Ballif, Martin Kiefer, Pascal Périnel, Claire Chalvet, Laurence Irollo,
Xavier Guillot, Hervé Jarousseau, Chrystel Martin, Virginie Fabre, Catherine Derosier-
Pouchous, Valérie Coudin, Manon Luquet, Agnès Marconnet, Joelle Cinq-Fraix,
Ariane Rabenou, Christine Finance, Elise Müller, Anne-Sophie Toulza-Colomines,
Jean-Marc Beltran, Esther Goldszmidt, Marine Martineau, Olivier Berrand,
Christine Sastourné, Mireille Manier, Frédéric Biancardini, Julia Rigade, Jacques Font,
Maryvonne Secq, Pascal Wojtal, Maryline Bensérade, Valérie Buraud, Maryline Bobant,
Sophie Toulza-Colomines, Pierre Besnard, Jan Sekal, Moïra Parrucci, Alex Crozilhac,
Denis Toulmé, Yves Maisonneuve, Pascal Marchal, Brigitte van Hecke,
Marie Le Maire-Bodnya, Franck David, Charlie Gaget. Alexandre, Marie-Yolande,
Olivier Beassart, Florence Hellec, Erick Vigouroux, Dominique Wisniewski,
Jean-Louis Bellec, Jean-Pierre Clément, Anne Giroux, Manon Potvin, Bruno Guennou,
Ludovic, Rozak, Marcel Perrin, Carol Manzano, Muriel Suir, Clio Karageorghis,
Niko Melissano, Guillaume Thomas, Xavier Milan, Daniel Soulié, Élisabeth Laurent,
Céline Dauvergne, Coralie James, Max Dujardin, Irène Julietand the drawing montage
studio.*

*To Nathalie Trafford, Denis Curty, Thierry Masbou, Christophe Duteil,
Emmanuel Hoffman, Cécile Bergon, Béatrice Hedde, Annabelle Pegeon,
Carole and Laurence de Vellou for their invaluable support.*